Clare Connelly was raised in small-town Australia among a family of avid readers. She spent much of her childhood up a tree, Mills & Boon book in hand. Clare is married to her own real-life hero, and they live in a bungalow near the sea with their two children. She is frequently found staring into space—a surefire sign that she's in the world of her characters. She has a penchant for French food and ice-cold champagne, and Mills & Boon novels continue to be her favourite ever books. Writing for Modern is a long-held dream. Clare can be contacted via clareconnelly.com or at her Facebook page.

Growing up near the beach, **Annie West** spent lots of time observing tall, burnished lifeguards—early research! Now she spends her days fantasising about gorgeous men and their love-lives. Annie has been a reader all her life. She also loves travel, long walks, good company and great food. You can contact her at annie@annie-west.com or via PO Box 1041, Warners Bay, NSW 2282, Australia.

Discover more at millsandboon.co.uk.

FORBIDDEN NIGHTS IN BARCELONA

CLARE CONNELLY

CLAIMING HIS VIRGIN PRINCESS

ANNIE WEST

MILLS & BOON

First Published in Great Britain 2022
by Mills & Boon, an imprint of HarperCollins*Publishers* Ltd,
1 London Bridge Street, London, SE1 9GF

www.harpercollins.co.uk

HarperCollins*Publishers*
1st Floor, Watermarque Building,
Ringsend Road, Dublin 4, Ireland

Forbidden Nights in Barcelona © 2022 Clare Connelly

Claiming His Virgin Princess © 2022 Annie West

ISBN: 978-0-263-30067-3

01/22

FORBIDDEN NIGHTS IN BARCELONA

CLARE CONNELLY

MILLS & BOON

PROLOGUE

Luca and Olivia's wedding celebration

'ALEJANDRO, I NEED your help.'

Luca beamed like a newly married man despite the fact his actual wedding had taken place months earlier, and this was a 'do over', to celebrate his matrimonial happiness with everyone he'd ever met—by the looks of the humming crowd, at least. And in the midst of all the exquisitely dressed wedding guests, Alejandro stood out like a sore thumb.

Not because he was dressed any differently—like most of the male guests, he wore a tuxedo. No, Alejandro stood out because of who he was, his bearing a testament to the man who'd dragged himself out of extreme poverty by his wits alone, a man who was the definition of having come from the wrong side of the tracks—and wasn't ashamed of that. Rather than hiding his heritage, he wore it like a badge of honour, a flicker of derision shaping his lips when confronted with Europe's elite—old money, who wouldn't have any idea how cruel life could be. They were his antithesis, and he relished that fact, their wealth and privilege something he despised—all the more so for knowing it was a part of *his* heritage too—a heritage—parentage—that had never wanted him, never acknowledged him.

'It's Olivia's sister, Sienna.'

Alejandro narrowed his arctic-blue eyes, following his friend's gaze until it landed on a woman in the distance, standing off to the side, alone, separate from the party swirling around them. She was as different from Olivia as was possible. Where Luca's bride was willow thin with pale blonde hair, Sienna was short, curvaceous, with pale skin and titian-red hair. Alejandro's gaze travelled the length of her body before he realised what he was doing.

'Stop that,' Luca growled. 'Before I change my mind.'

Alejandro shifted his attention back to his friend with surprising reluctance. 'What is it you want from me?'

'Olivia adores Sienna. She's very protective of her.'

Alejandro lifted a brow. 'She seems like a big girl, capable of handling herself.'

'Perhaps.'

'You don't sound convinced.'

'What I'm convinced about is wanting my bride to enjoy her second wedding more than her first. She can't do that when she's worried about Sienna.'

Once again, Alejandro regarded the red-haired woman, something like curiosity sparking inside his chest. He hadn't looked properly before. He'd simply run his eyes over her. But now, he studied her, an alabaster face with eyes that were so green they were like polished emeralds. She smiled, but Luca was right—there was something discordant behind her eyes, sadness and hurt. Alejandro had known enough of both emotions to recognise them instantly.

Alejandro's lips formed a grim line. 'What can I do about it?'

'I'm glad you asked. I want you to entertain Sienna.'

Alejandro turned back to his friend. 'Do you mean…?'

'Absolutely not.' Fierce rejection tightened Luca's eyes. 'What do you take me for? A pimp?' He lifted a hand, palm towards Alejandro. 'In fact, I'm forbidding you from so much as touching her. She's not suitable to be one of your one-night stands, so don't go getting any ideas. She's not your type.'

Alejandro stroked his jaw. 'You're *forbidding* me?' he murmured aloud, fighting an urge to point out that forbidden fruit always tasted so much sweeter.

'Yes. All I'm asking is that you rescue Sienna from their godawful mother.'

Alejandro's smile was cynical. 'And what is so awful about her?' His eyes landed on the woman across the party, stunningly beautiful, far younger in appearance than her age, and utterly aware of that fact.

'That would take far longer than we have.'

'And you're anxious to get back to your bride.'

'My wife,' Luca confirmed with a beaming grin. 'Yes.' He considered his best friend, as though weighing something up delicately, then leaned a little closer, lowering his tone despite the fact they were quite separate from the other guests. 'Angelica, their mother, has spent the day berating Sienna. Olivia has held her tongue, but just barely, and I am truly concerned that if there is one more incident, my lovely, kind wife will turn into a dragon and breathe fire over everyone.'

'Would that be a bad thing?'

'Actually, it would probably be a very good thing: Angelica could do with being put in her place, if you ask me.' He sighed. 'But Olivia is too sweet, and she would hate herself almost immediately. Which is why I need you to stay between Sienna and Angelica so Olivia doesn't have to lose her cool.'

There was no one on earth who meant more to Alejandro than Luca. No one he could rely on, no one he trusted. Those feelings were mutual. Luca was the only person who understood what Alejandro's life had been like *before*. He knew about Alejandro's mother, he knew about her profession, her life, her death, and he knew what home life had been like—why Alejandro was an expert at street fighting, because he'd had to become one, in order to survive. There was no one else on earth Alejandro had allowed to see and understand those parts of him, and Luca had shared the same depth of himself with Alejandro. Theirs was a friendship Alejandro would never jeopardise.

'Fine,' Alejandro agreed, though not without misgivings. He wasn't a babysitter.

'Thank you.' Luca flicked a relieved smile at his friend. 'I think I can remember how to play that part.' After all, it was just one night, just one woman. What could go wrong?

CHAPTER ONE

'YOU LOOK AS though you'd rather be anywhere but here.'

Sienna grimaced even before she turned to address the voice that had spoken, wishing she had been more successful at hiding her feelings and thoughts, wishing she had done a better job of looking as everyone wanted her to.

Naturally, she intended to deny the claim until she was blue in the face, but any idea of speaking flew from her mind the minute her eyes landed on the man who possessed the voice. It wasn't as if he was the first handsome man she'd seen in her life, but, then again, handsome was a manifestly insufficient word to describe him.

Handsome was a word that was safe and ordinary, mild and run-of-the-mill, and none of those adjectives could be safely applied to the man who stood beside her, quirked lips that were moulded with obvious cynicism, eyes the exact colour of the sky at midday, deep blue, flecked with silver and black, so she stared into them and felt as though she were falling through space. His face was perfectly symmetrical, his jaw squared, as though shaped from stone, his brows thick and a dark brown, to match his slightly waved hair. He wore a tuxedo but he didn't really—at least, not in the ordinary sense. The tuxedo was simply a prop, a costume, something donned for the wedding—it couldn't hide his raw strength, his masculine virility, and the way it pulsed from him with an almost magnetic strength.

'Weddings aren't my scene either,' he commented with a twist of his mouth, so her eyes dropped lower without her consent, tracing the outline of his lips until her tummy flipped and flopped and she had to wrench her eyes away or she was honestly terrified she might do something completely crazy and *kiss* him.

Her breath felt hot, trapped in her lungs, and her eyes seemed to dance with stars. She sought refuge in the crowd, scanning the room looking for something, anything, to anchor her to reality, only to clash with her mother's gaze, and the disapproval on her beautiful face as she scrutinised Sienna's appearance for the hundredth time that hour.

Out of the frying pan, into the fire…

'Do you speak English?' He attempted once more, and now, despite the coil that was tightening in the pit of her stomach, she found a small smile, flashing it at him with no idea of how it transformed her face, making her eyes sparkle and pressing a deep dimple into either cheek. Despite many attempts over the years, Sienna had never learned to hide her cheeky, impish nature from her features, and it beamed out of her now.

'I do.' She didn't add that she also spoke several other languages—just managing two words had been an impressive feat.

'Then you're being diplomatic regarding the wedding?'

'Perhaps generally, but not on this occasion. My sister's the bride.' She gestured towards Olivia, who was being held by her husband, dancing softly, slowly, in the middle of the room. 'I'm very happy for her.'

'I can tell.'

Sienna's eyes widened in surprise and then she laughed, a soft, musical sound that had Alejandro standing imperceptibly taller, his eyes narrowing as they raked her face, then briefly dipped to the hint of cleavage exposed by the maid of honour dress.

His inspection was fleeting, but impossible to miss, and heat, a heat she'd never before known, flooded Sienna's body so she had to swallow in an attempt to douse it. But it felt so good! Even as she wrestled for control, she wanted to relish this sensation, to glory in the way her body was stirring in response to his—a total stranger. It felt naughty and nice, all at once.

'Are you always so honest?'

'Yes.'

Her mother would say it wasn't polite to pry, but Sienna was famously bad at following her mother's advice, and found herself asking, 'Why?'

'What is the alternative? To lie?'

'No. To be socially appropriate?'

'Appropriateness is overrated,' he said with a lift of his broad shoulders, so she was torn between a bubble of laughter and a moan of attraction. Thank God, her body settled on the former.

'How do you know the happy couple?' she asked, a hint of worry briefly creasing her eyes as she looked at Olivia and Luca once more.

'Luca is my oldest friend.'

'How come you weren't his best man, then?'

'Now who's being direct?'

'Is it a secret?'

'Not at all.'

'So?'

'Weddings aren't my thing either. It would have been hypocritical for me to stand up there beside him today.'

'Even for thirty minutes?'

'I don't believe in marriage. I don't respect the institution. I don't accept the necessity. Frankly, there couldn't be a worse choice for best man than me. And so I politely declined.'

'But he did ask you?'

The man's dark head dipped forward. 'And with no real expectation of success. Luca knows how I feel about things.'

Heat was a torrent in her veins. 'What did you say your name was?'

'I didn't.'

She poked out her tongue. 'You're very literal as well.'

His grin was slow to spread and delightful to behold. Sparks ignited in her bloodstream. Uh oh. That was probably not a good thing.

'Are you asking my name, *bonita*?'

'I suppose I was,' she responded archly.

'Alejandro.'

The way he pronounced it sent a shiver down her spine, like stepping from the shadows and into sunshine on a cool autumnal afternoon. She stayed right where she was, letting the effect of the word wash over her, the guttural way he'd spoken the middle syllable an aphrodisiac she couldn't ignore.

Aphrodisiac?

Since when?

Aphrodisiacs weren't exactly arrows in Sienna's quiver. It wasn't as if she went around talking to handsome men every night of the week, nor was she remotely familiar with the experiences of what one man's full attention could do to her body. It was as if she were being gradually set alight, blood cell by blood cell, until she could hardly think straight.

'And you are?'

She blinked, blankly. 'I'm...what do you mean?'

Now it was his turn to laugh, a short, hoarse sound that spelled disaster for her already weakened grip on control—and, she feared, reality. Because why in the world would a man like this be talking to her? And even though he was talking, there was no way he was feeling the deluge of fascination and desire that was running rampant through her.

'Your name,' he prompted silkily, holding out his hand to shake. 'What is it?'

'Oh. I'm Sienna,' she mumbled, colour rising in her cheeks. How she hated that! When Olivia blushed, she looked beautiful and coquettish, like some kind of ethereal fairy creature in need of protection. Whereas, when Sienna blushed, with her red hair and freckles, she was more like an homage to a Titian palette after a particularly fruitful afternoon, all blotchy and messed.

'Sienna.' He repeated her name, slowly and tinged with his accent—Spanish?—so a thousand fireworks burst in her belly. His hand moved closer and, of its own volition, hers extended slowly, curiously, as though the simple act of touching hand to hand heralded some kind of unavoidable disaster.

Little could she know.

'Would you like to dance?'

'Dance?' she repeated, staring at the makeshift dance floor—a terrace in Rome strung with fairy lights and surrounded by potted plants filled with night-flowering jasmine that created a heavenly fragrance. A sinking feeling dropped through her stomach. 'Dancing' implied grace and coordination, two things Sienna generally felt she lacked. And yet, it also meant closeness. Touching. A reason to run her hands over this man's muscular torso, to feel—

Oh, for heaven's sake. He's not asking you to take him to bed.

And what would she say if he did? Disastrously, more heat bloomed in her cheeks, so she squeezed her eyes shut, hoping to blot him and the whole world out.

'It is not rocket science,' he said, close enough for the words to brush her ear. 'I can show you.'

He knew. He knew she had no experience. He knew she was nervous. Yeah, well, of course he did! It wasn't as if she could be mistaken for a suave, sophisticated socialite, the kind of woman for whom events like this were run of the mill.

Just be yourself.

Olivia's earlier advice ran through her, but instead of giving her comfort, it brought a smile to Sienna's face. Being herself would have meant wearing jeans and an oversized sweater, and her mutt, Starbuck, firmly planted by her side. She turned to face him, then wished she hadn't when she was assaulted anew by his devastating good looks.

'I don't really dance,' she explained, but despite the demurral her eyes ravaged his face then dropped lower, to the chest she was aching to feel, to understand if it was quite so firm as she imagined.

'You don't like to dance?'

How could she know? Apart from a few school parties, which she'd spent glued to the wall like some kind of Grecian statue, or ferrying drinks for people in the hope no one would notice how awkward and out of place she felt, Sienna couldn't have said.

'I should—' She cast about for an excuse, a reason to leave him, even though her feet wanted to stay firmly planted right where they were. She waved a hand vaguely in the direction of her bestie, Gertie, across the space. Her eyes followed the direction in which her hand pointed, and so the last thing she expected was for him to touch her.

Not just to touch her, but to lace his fingers through hers in an act that was, for Sienna, so intimate her breath hitched in her throat beneath the stars of this ancient city. Everything inside her seemed to shift. She whirled around to face him, lips parted, eyes wide, and a bold sense of daring gripped her, a rush of fearlessness that made her want to tip headlong into whatever madness was whispering on the sultry summer evening's air.

He was watching her through veiled eyes, impossible to see. Unlike Sienna, he was a master at concealing what he was thinking and feeling.

Stop overreacting.

'Come and dance with me, *bonita*. One song.'

His fingers were warm and strong, his hand much larger than hers. She stared down at the contact, her pulse heavy in her throat, so she was conscious of every quiver and rushed beat.

'Okay,' she said after a beat. *Be yourself.* 'But don't blame me when your feet need to be amputated because I've trodden on them so many times.'

His smile set her soul on fire. 'Deal.' And then, because he clearly specialised in Moves That Could Shock Her, Alejandro lifted her hand to his lips and brushed a kiss across it, searing every single cell in her body. How could she feel aflame at the same time a tingly shivery feeling ran along her back? Contradictions flooded her—she was reluctant to dance with him even when it felt like the most important thing to her as well.

She hadn't been exaggerating. Sienna Thornton-Rose was not a natural dancer, and, for some reason he couldn't put his finger on, he found that…intriguing. He found *her* intriguing, in ways he'd probably be better able to analyse if her body weren't so close to his, every little jerk of her legs bringing her voluptuous curves nearer, breasts that were so rounded he found his palms aching to lift up and feel them, to appraise their weight and fullness for himself, to admire them naked, to take one of her nipples in his mouth, to—

She's not suitable to be one of your one-night stands.

Alejandro ground his teeth together, forcing himself to look across the dance floor to where Olivia and Luca were dancing. Luca was completely wrapped up in his bride; he wasn't looking at Alejandro and Sienna.

Because he trusts you.

So? He wasn't planning to do anything to betray that trust. But Luca had asked Alejandro to distract Sienna, to show her a good time, and it was quite clear that she was *not* having a good time. Yet.

Something like adrenaline rushed his body as he put his hands on her hips, those huge green eyes of hers widening like saucers as she stared up at him, her long lashes, painted a dark black, blinking as a frown tilted her full lower lip downwards. She was nothing like the kind of woman he usually dated, but there was something about her that was making Alejandro's breath heavy in his lungs. He was conscious of all of himself and all of her. Did the freckles that leaped opportunistically across the bridge of her nose appear anywhere else on her body? Were her lashes naturally the same colour as her hair, a deep, rich, rusty red? And the hair on her sex?

Hell. Having been told she was off limits was driving him crazy. All Alejandro could think about was a rising tide of desire rampaging his system. But his life was about control and he refused to succumb to the weakness of temptation—not when Luca had been so explicit.

'You have to relax,' he encouraged, even when pressure was building inside him like a coil. 'Feel the rhythm of the music. Let it touch something in your soul.'

'I'd relax a little more if you were a little less like a Spanish-deity-cum-Hollywood-star brought to life,' she snapped, and then flushed, as though she were embarrassed, but her eyes stayed locked to his, something unapologetic and addictive in their depths.

Why did he find her admission so pleasing? After all, Alejandro was well aware of his impact on women. He was a renowned bachelor for a reason, able to take his pick of most women at most events. And yet, her unsophisticated compliment, her irritation at finding him attractive, made him want to tease her.

To tempt her.

Oh, *mierda*. He really needed to think of Luca, but the truth was his best friend was the last thing he wanted in his mind in that moment.

'Is dancing with a deity not on your bucket list?' he prompted, bringing his body closer, even as his brain berated him for such weakness.

He felt the air whoosh out of her lungs, felt it brush his cheek, and immediately he wondered about how she'd sound when she was coming, how her breath would rush over him as she cried his name at the top of her lungs… He held back a curse as he began to stiffen in his pants, the fabric at his crotch a welcome constraint given that he was dancing with his best friend's newly minted sister-in-law.

'Surprisingly not,' she said, stiffly.

'Relax,' he reminded her, and when she didn't, he lifted one hand to her chin, tilting her face to his, holding it there so he could look into her eyes. 'Don't look away,' he commanded, so used to being obeyed in every aspect of his life that it didn't occur to him for one moment she would be any different. He slowly lowered his hand, watching her the whole time, bringing his hand back to her hip, and then moving her in time with the music. Only it wasn't really the music he was synchronising her with, so much as the rhythmic rushing of his blood, the building of awareness deep within him, an ache he would normally know he was within hours of satisfying.

Not tonight, he reminded himself forcibly. *Not with her.*

The maid of honour dress was exceptionally beautiful. He'd noticed that when she'd walked into the church. Unlike other weddings he'd attended, where the bride had sought to outshine all in attendance, Olivia had clearly chosen a dress designed to flatter her sister with every detail. From the deep emerald green that emphasised the mystery of Sienna's eyes, to the floaty material that clung to her full breasts like a second skin then fell loose and flowing to her knees, so Alejandro wanted to bunch the chiffon fabric in his fists and lift it, to slip his hand beneath the hem and feel the curve of her bottom, to—

Cristo. He was losing the plot. Luca would kill him if he continued down this path. Hell, he'd kill himself for betraying his friend.

'You're very good at this.' Her words pulled him back to the present.

'Dancing?'

'Casting women under a spell.'

Her honesty tugged at him. Amused him. But also stirred something he hadn't felt in a long time, a protective instinct that reminded him forcibly of nights worrying for his mother, wishing there were something he could do—

'Is that what I'm doing?'

'Oh, don't ask that. It's even more embarrassing if you're not trying.'

He laughed, aware of the effect the sound had on her, of the way she stopped dancing and simply stared at him. Temptation had never been such a force to be grappled with as it was then. Her lips were so full and sweetly pink, they demanded to be kissed. Not just kissed, but ravished beneath the demands of his own mouth, to be drawn between his teeth, to be dominated completely.

'I'm simply dancing with a beautiful young woman,' he said with a shrug of his shoulders.

It was as if she'd been slapped. Sienna's hands dropped to her sides and she took a step back from him, her face paling so the cheeky little freckles stood out much more.

'I should go and check on my aunts, make sure they have drinks.' Her smile was tight, lacking any of the spontaneity and mirth he'd seen earlier, and it felt as though he'd been cast to the dark side of the moon. He told himself he should be relieved—he needed space to get a grip on the attraction that was humming between them—but he wasn't. 'Excuse me.'

Before he could shake himself back to the here and now and reach out and catch her hand once more, she was gone, slipping through the crowd, spine ramrod-straight, as though she had something to prove—to him and the world. He watched her walk away, a frown on his face and an ache forming, deep, low in his gut.

CHAPTER TWO

BEAUTIFUL? SHE FUMED as she slipped away from the party altogether, towards the edge of the Tiber river, dancing slowly beneath the full moon. Right up until that moment, he'd almost had her. She'd believed his practised seduction. She'd believed that he wanted to dance with her. That he saw her as she was.

Which was *not* beautiful.

She wasn't being down on herself, she was simply being honest. Objectively speaking, it was easy to face that reality when your mother was Angelica Thornton-Rose and your sister was Olivia. It was impossible to have any false hope about your own beauty. She was the thorn amongst two roses, or the fluffy little rust-coloured duck between two elegant, gracious swans, and she'd long ago given up hope of some kind of magical transformation turning her into one of them. She never would be, and she didn't need to be lied to and flattered by some guest at the party. Even one who made her feel as though she wanted to—well, suffice it to say, Sienna was fighting impulses she'd never known before.

She stared out at the river and with each fast, knotty turn of the water she quelled her own blood's rushing, drawing herself back to reality even when the fantasy of what she'd just experienced was so very, very tempting.

* * *

'Have you seen Sisi?' Olivia's beautiful face was placid, but her eyes showed worry.

Alejandro looked at the bride, trying to spot any similarities between the two, and failing. Olivia's face was heart-shaped and symmetrical, her eyes wide-spaced and a deep blue, her hair naturally so fair it was almost white. There were no fascinating freckles on her nose, no flashes of the ocean in her eyes, and her lips were dull and flat when compared to the full, tempting pout of Sienna's.

'My sister,' Olivia clarified, mistaking his lack of response for non-comprehension.

'We thought you were dancing with her.' Luca's voice held a warning, and also a plea.

'Don't worry about it,' Olivia murmured, craning her slender neck as her eyes ran over the guests of the party. 'I'm sure she's here somewhere.'

Alejandro didn't need Luca's pointed stare to offer to go and look for her. Even as he said the words, excitement bubbled up inside his chest. 'I'll find her, if you'd like.'

'No, it's fine. I should go and check on her, make sure she's—'

'Let him do it,' Luca urged. 'You know Sienna hates it when you worry.'

Alejandro suspected, in fact, that Olivia didn't need to worry. Not as much as she did. For all that he'd only known Sienna a matter of minutes—ten at most—he was good at judging people, and he could feel her strength from a mile away. He didn't think Sienna needed to be found to be sure she was all right, but that didn't stop him from wanting to find her. Only his motivations were far from altruistic.

'It is your wedding. It's the least I can do, given I shirked best man duties,' he said with a grim smile, feeling like a wolf in sheep's clothing. Luca's grateful expression made it even worse. What would his friend say if he knew that

Alejandro wanted to seek Sienna out for the pleasure of her proximity alone? That his offer had very little to do with Luca's concerns?

'Ah. So you are still here.'

Just when Sienna was getting herself back into a normal sinus rhythm, Alejandro—or the voice of him—swirled through the balmy Roman air towards her, wrapping around her belly first then spreading and popping through her entire body. She turned slowly, because she needed time to steel herself for this—as hard as it had been to grapple with his ridiculous charisma in the middle of the wedding party, doing so here, alone, in a quiet space away from the restaurant, with only the river and the moon and the ancient ghosts of this spectacular city for company, she feared his god-like abilities would overwhelm her.

Well, duh.

He held a flute of champagne towards her and she reached out, curving her fingers around it instinctively— after all, that was what one did with proffered drinks— only he didn't immediately retract his hand, so their fingers brushed and held and it was as though every star in the heavens had poured its energy into her fingertips. She buzzed all over.

'Thank you.' She jerked the glass back towards herself, lifting it to her lips and drinking, quickly, in a need to extinguish the fires that were ravaging her central nervous system.

He shrugged with indolent relaxation, moving closer, until he was right beside her, just ever so slightly too close, so she was wrapped up in him—his exotic, masculine fragrance, the heat of his body and the sheer magnetic aura of the man, so that she had to fight to stop from sinking into him.

She held the glass with two hands and turned back to

the river, no longer able to pretend her heat rate was anything like calm.

'You ran away from me.'

There was no point in denying it. 'I needed some space.'

'You're not enjoying yourself.'

The problem was, she *had* been enjoying herself, a little too much. 'It's been a long day.' Starting with the horrors of getting ready for the wedding with their mother, hearing her wax lyrical about Olivia's beauty and Sienna's failings—as though Sienna hadn't made her peace with the genetic lottery years earlier!

'Couldn't you have chosen a dress for Sienna that didn't make her look like a chubby leprechaun?'

She was used to her mother's taunts, but she'd been feeling so good about herself in the floaty princess gown, and so the sting had been acute.

'Where are you from?'

She told herself she asked the question to be polite, but the truth was she didn't want him to leave again.

'Barcelona.'

'You speak English very well.'

'I went to school there.'

'Ah. Where exactly?'

He named one of the most prestigious schools in the country, on the outskirts of London. She tilted her head, studying him thoughtfully.

'Yes?' he prompted, his blue eyes stirring plumes of desire—for the feeling was now unmistakable, despite her lack of personal experience.

There was no sense lying to him. She sipped her champagne, needing the rush of flavour, the calming effect of the bubbles. 'You don't seem like a public school snob,' she said and then offered a little grimace of apology.

'Don't I?'

She shook her head, and at the same time a gentle breeze

carried off the Tiber, so her hair brushed her cheek. His hand lifted, catching it and tucking it slowly behind her ear. But even once the hair was restrained, he didn't drop his hand, and she stood perfectly, completely still, not wanting to breathe lest she dislodge the contact.

'Why not?' Had he moved closer? She was sure he had. Or had that been her after all? Their legs were brushing, and if she breathed in or out too quickly the force would jut her breasts forward, to touch his chest. The very idea made her nipples tingle against the soft fabric of her bra and a swirl of temptation moved through her.

'Sienna?' He was asking her to elaborate, and yet it felt as though the question meant something else. As though he were asking—to kiss her?

Breath rushed from between her teeth at the very idea. Her lips parted and she stared up into his eyes, the moonlight hitting them at the perfect angle to cast them not as blue but as silver, and so mysterious she was sure that every fairy tale ever written had somehow had its genesis in their depths. Of its own volition, one of her hands rose and pressed to his chest, so tentative, so uncertain, but the moment her fingers connected with the fabric of his shirt she felt a rush of rightness, that this was just exactly what she'd been wanting to do since he'd first approached her. His body was warm, and his chest, beneath her gently exploring hand, was as hard as a rock, just as she'd speculated it would be. Her touch was light, but its effect was not. His cheeks darkened with a slash of colour and something fired in his expression—hesitation. Doubt. But also, she was sure of it, desire.

And yet his hesitation was obvious and, for Sienna, it was easy to believe that it had been born out of disgust for her. Pity even. How could anyone desire her when there were the Olivias of the world?

'Thank you for the drink,' she mumbled, taking a step

backwards, wondering at the madness that had overtaken her in daring to hope he might be as attracted to her as she was to him. *Fool.* It was the romance of the wedding ceremony. Nothing more.

His brows drew closer together and she held her breath, wondering if she'd got it wrong. Maybe he'd close the gap, lift her hand back to his chest. And maybe merry little pigs would fly right by the nearby Castel Sant'Angelo.

'Luca is one of my oldest friends,' he said quietly, the words flattened of emotion, and in his eyes there was a faraway look, as though he wasn't really talking to her so much as to himself.

'You mentioned that already.' She swallowed past a throat that was suddenly thick.

His eyes pinned hers and then seemed to lance right through her. He didn't speak, nor did she. Not at first. She wasn't capable of it. Her body was vibrating and the longer he stared at her, the more she began to tremble, to feel as though she were both floating and sinking.

'Did you meet him at school?' It was a valiant attempt to grab hold of something normal, to tether herself to a form of reality and normality. 'I know he went to a school in the UK, for a time. Was that where—' She was babbling, and cut herself off short with a slight grimace.

He was staring at her as though he'd never seen a woman before, and maybe he hadn't. Not one like her—wild, untamed, folksy rather than elegant, more at home by the fire with a good book or riding a horse across the countryside than somewhere like this. She lifted her champagne to her lips, took a sip, then clutched the glass in front of her, searching for something to say that would keep him here while simultaneously resigning herself to the likelihood that he would leave again.

'Yes.' A simple statement that confused her completely.

'Yes, what?'

He took a step, closing the distance between them, and Sienna expelled a breath she hadn't realised she'd been holding.

'Yes.' His hands curled around the champagne flute, removing it from her grip. She dropped her gaze, wondering if he was going to put it down. 'That is where I met Luca.' There was only the glow of moonlight, casting his face into angles and planes, but his eyes shone. With determination? He took a sip of her champagne, and the simple act of his having shared her glass was so intimate, she trembled inside.

But it was nothing compared to what came next. A moment after filling his mouth with champagne, he dropped his lips to hers, spilling the liquid into her mouth in an act that was so erotic she moaned, and her knees turned to liquid, so her only options were to melt to the ground or cling on to him for dear life. She chose the latter, wrapping her arms around his neck as she swallowed the champagne and his tongue took its place, plundering her mouth, dancing with her tongue, kissing her in a way she'd never been kissed before. This couldn't possibly compare to the inexperienced fumbles of the various boyfriends she'd had over the years—and they had been boys, not men, not lovers, nothing like this.

Heat stole into her cheeks as the effect of his touch, the dominance of his kiss, the way his huge body made her feel delicate and fragile, made her feel feminine as she'd never felt before, as his kiss changed something essential inside her. She could hardly breathe and she didn't care—other things sustained her now, like the pressing need for *more*, for all of him. She yearned to be closer, to have—to feel—she didn't know what, only his kiss wasn't enough, no matter how sensational it was. Fireworks were dancing all around her, a localised effect, just between him and her, and their private little piece of the banks of the Tiber. His hand caught the back of her head, weaving through her thick hair, holding her head still, deepening the kiss as his body pushed forward, so she moved with him, stepping backwards and backwards again until her back connected with the stone balustrade that guarded the river.

And now she understood the origins of the expression to be caught between a rock and a hard place because she was, quite literally, and it was the most sublime form of pleasure she'd ever known. His hardness pressed to her sex, unmistakable, and she moaned softly beneath him, as his hand reached down, brushing her thigh, lifting her skirt, coming around to cup her bottom and push her forward all at once, holding her tight against him as he kissed her until she saw stars and oblivion.

It wasn't enough to be kissed by him though, it wasn't enough to be touched like this. She needed to touch and feel too. She pushed up, scrambling to sit on the edge of the balustrade, so he could stand between her legs, legs that she wrapped around his waist and hooked at the ankles, and now it was Alejandro that moaned, the sound trapped low in his throat, followed by a coarse Spanish curse, and then he dragged his kiss lower, to her decolletage, working his mouth along her collarbone before flicking the indent at the centre, then roaming lower, to the gentle valley of cleavage hinted at by the beautiful dress Olivia had chosen.

She tilted her head back, staring at the sky, wondering if this was a dream, or a wish come true. Wondering how she, Sienna, had suddenly become the kind of girl that this sort of thing could happen to. Wondering…and enjoying… the perfection of his mouth as he drew it back to hers, kissing her again, pulling her close to him, his hips moving to simulate—she could only guess, but she suspected—sex, and, oh, how she wanted this man to take her here, now, with the river their only witness. The party might as well have been a thousand miles away. It would be her first time, but would that matter? Not to Sienna. She wasn't saving her virginity for anyone. It was an inconvenience, a by-product of her upbringing, little more.

The idea took hold of her, digging into her mind, so her fingers reached for his belt, unfastening it, and she was so sure of what she wanted that her hands didn't even tremble. She had never been surer of anything in her life. Pleasure was the wind at her back, propelling her actions, guiding her, driving any doubt from her mind. How could she doubt when she could feel? His desire, his want, his obvious need? It was a strength and fire she hadn't known was missing until now, but as her hands reached inside his pants and curved around his arousal she felt a burst of triumph, of womanly knowledge, an ancient, feminine understanding of her power, and she smiled like the cat who'd got the cream, pulling away from him, her breath ragged, her eyes holding a challenge and an invitation.

Holy hell.

He stared down at her as though awakening from a dream—the best dream he'd ever had, a dream that had crept up on him out of nowhere, that had dragged him into its centre before he realised what was happening. Or was it a nightmare? A nightmare because this was *exactly* what Luca had told him not to do, exactly what he'd sworn to himself he could control? His best friend deserved more from him, damn it, and Alejandro wasn't the kind of man to ignore his sense of loyalty—no matter the temptation.

'Now who is casting a spell over whom?' he muttered, reaching down and dislodging her grip from his throbbing, painfully tightened cock, staring at her with a sinking feeling that he was putting an end to something that was overwhelming him with the power of his need. But need be damned. He wasn't going to be this man. For Luca to have been so strenuous in warning Alejandro away from Sienna, there must have been good reason. And he could see that clearly for himself: she was *nice*. Too nice for him. Gentle and sweet and kind, exactly the kind of woman he avoided like the plague, because nice women were ripe to being hurt by men like him, and he refused to be an instrument of pain. Luca knew that, and so he'd warned Alejandro. None of which was Sienna's fault.

'I—' Disappointment and surprise crossed her features and then, unmistakably, hurt, so he wanted to undo the last thirty seconds, replace her hand on his arousal, and kiss her again until she was moaning beneath him, those sweet, soft little noises just exactly what he wanted to hear right now.

'I got carried away,' he said, quietly, the understatement shaming him.

'We both did.' She stepped down from the balustrade, ignoring the hand he held out in a gesture of help, fixing him with a cool stare that was only slightly undermined by the shaking of her lower lip.

He watched as she straightened her dress—it didn't even occur to him to turn away until much later—and the way her hands ran over her body, making sure everything was in place, was its own special torment, because while she touched her body all he could think about was his own hands following that exact course. He balled fists at his sides then thrust them into his pockets.

'Listen, Sienna—' But what could he say? How could he explain that he'd made a promise to his friend not to touch her? How could he say that without making her feel like a piece of meat two men had negotiated over? Anger flared in his belly—Luca had asked him for a favour and it hadn't occurred to Alejandro to mind, until he'd met Sienna. Now, the idea of being prohibited from being with her was burning through him like acid.

'Excuse me.' Her tone was like ice, her imminent departure making the decision for him. 'I think I hear my mother calling for me.'

She'd made up the excuse to get away, before she evaporated into a cloud of embarrassment or, worse, begged him to kiss her again, because she liked it so bloody much, but the moment she rejoined the wedding party Angelica wrapped her hand around Sienna's wrist, halting her in her tracks.

'There you are,' Angelica hissed. 'What in the world have you been doing? You look like you've been dragged through the bush backwards.' Disapproval lined Angelica's beautiful, slightly lined face as she reached up and began to neaten Sienna's unruly hair. 'Honestly, the best stylist in Europe worked on you all afternoon and this is what you end up with?'

Sienna felt as though she'd just had a head-on collision with a runaway freight train.

'Leave it, Mother. It's fine.'

'It is *not* fine,' Angelica responded curtly. 'This is your sister's wedding and for whatever reason—charity, I suppose—she's chosen *you* to be her maid of honour. You can't possibly be photographed with her looking like this.'

Sienna ground her teeth together, so used to her mother's harsh put-downs that she barely flinched now. 'I was beyond the terrace. It was breezy.'

'This is useless. We'll have to go and fix it in the ladies' room.'

'Mother?' Sienna reached up and grabbed her mother's wrist, pulling it away from her hair. 'I can do it. This is Olivia's wedding. You shouldn't disappear. Stay with the guests. Mingle.'

It was exactly the right thing to suggest—and not by accident. Sienna knew enough of her mother's vanity and preening instincts to know that what she wanted, most of all, was to be the centre of attention herself—and if she couldn't manage that, to get as close as possible to it. Olivia was where the spotlight shone brightest, not Sienna.

'Fix yourself up,' Angelica insisted, as a parting shot. 'This is not the time to show the world the real you.'

Sienna sighed, so her hair lifted a little at the front, and she turned to do exactly that, but a moment later her wrist was yet again imprisoned by another equally strong grip, and she was being drawn away from the party.

'Hey,' she muttered, but Alejandro didn't let go until they were on the fringes of the guests, and then he drew her even further away, towards the river once more.

'You do *not* look like you've been drawn backwards through a bush,' he said with barely controlled anger. 'Instead, you look like a woman who's been thoroughly ravished and, God help me, I want to finish what we started.'

Sienna's lips fell apart. She gaped at him, in what she was sure was her least Olivia look yet. She scrambled for something to say. 'You stopped what we were doing,' was about as clever as she could manage.

'Yes.' He put his hands on his hips, staring at her, a muscle pulsing in the base of his jaw. 'Does she often speak to you like that?'

Sienna's cheeks paled. 'Forget about it.'

He moved closer and she trembled, her emotions overwrought, her body incapable of doing anything but responding to his nearness.

'But she's right. I should go and make myself presentable.'

'You are *very* presentable.' He took a step closer.

'What are you doing?'

'I don't know.' He stared at her, complex emotions darkening his eyes to a stormy grey.

'A minute ago you didn't want me—'

He pressed a finger to her lips and her eyes shut in instinctive response. The contact felt insanely good...

'You cannot truly believe that?'

'I might not be as experienced as you, Alejandro—' heaven help her, but the taste of his name in her mouth was incredibly erotic; she rolled each syllable over her tongue, delighting in the feel of it '—but that doesn't mean I don't recognise a lack of enthusiasm.'

His laugh was a short, sharp sound, rich with disbelief. 'You recognise nothing.'

She looked away, not in the mood to be lied to, flattered. She'd mistaken what they were doing, what he'd felt. She'd embarrassed herself by basically throwing herself at him...

'My experience is partly why I stopped,' he ground out, dropping his hand from her mouth. But instead of withdrawing it from her completely, he let it fall to her hip, gripping her close.

Sienna was holding on to her pride by a thread. She wanted to understand *why* but didn't dare ask. She didn't want to do anything to reveal how much she cared.

'You are nothing like the women I usually take to bed.'

Her pulse ratcheted up a gear. 'There's no bed here.'

'Fine. Have sex with.'

The raw description of what they'd been doing set her blood well and truly on fire.

'I can imagine the myriad ways in which I'm different.'

He frowned. 'I mean that you are sheltered. Innocent.'

Her mouth formed a circle of surprise.

'You are not experienced, and I refuse to take advantage of you. Not when, for me, it would just be—' He paused, searching for the words.

'Another notch on your bedpost?'

He lifted a darkly sculpted brow, not rejecting the claim. 'More or less.'

Her heart kerthunked against her ribs. So it wouldn't

mean anything to him. He wasn't offering more than this—just one night. A night in Rome, beneath the stars, him, her and sex, finally, so she could at least be assured that she wouldn't end up getting married while she was still a virgin. And she *must* get married, at some point in the next twenty months—the time was drawing closer, and in the back of her mind she had been panicking about the idea of walking down the aisle while still so inexperienced. She didn't mind marrying someone she barely knew and didn't desire, but she resented, a lot, the necessity of doing so without having gained some experience first. Didn't she deserve this?

'So you *did* want to sleep with me?'

'Sleep had absolutely nothing to do with what I wanted,' he responded with a mocking glint in his eyes.

She pushed aside his attempt at humour. There was too much at stake. Suddenly, Sienna was envisaging having her cake and eating it too and she suspected it would be rather delicious.

'What you *wanted*?' She lifted her hand to his chest, her fingers splayed wide as she felt the steady, heavy thundering of his heart beneath her palm. 'Or what you *want*?'

He stared down at her, looking almost as though he were in physical pain. Why was he fighting this? She was torn between her rational, thinking brain and the part of her that had been filled, her entire life, with the worst kind of insults from her mother that made it easy to believe he could never be attracted to her—even when her brain assured her that he was. But she could have sworn he desired her. So why wouldn't he act on it? What was it that was holding him back? It was as if an invisible barrier had formed between them and she wanted, more than anything, to push through it.

'Drop it.' The words were harsh. She blinked in surprise and he winced. 'I'm sorry. But you have to understand—'

Impatience ignited in her gut. 'What? What do I have to understand?' She put her hands on her hips, so frustrated she could barely breathe. She was frustrated by her mother and the cruel taunts she'd lived with for so long, with the limitations that had been put on her life by her father's cruel will, but mostly she was frustrated by the man in front of her, who was saying one thing with his body and another with his words.

'You are a very beautiful woman—'

She made an exasperated sound. 'I don't need to be told I'm beautiful.'

'But this isn't going to happen.'

She narrowed her eyes. 'What if I want to be a notch on your bedpost?'

He stared at her, that same tortured expression on his face. 'You don't.'

'How do you know?'

'Sienna—'

The warning note in his voice tipped her over. Irritated and impatient, she lifted a finger to his lips. 'I'm going to kiss you. If you really don't want this to go any further, walk away right now. Otherwise, stop making excuses and give us what we both want.'

'You want—'

'To be treated like a consenting adult, capable of making up my own mind about what I do and don't want. If *you* don't want *me*, then have the guts to say as much.'

Surprise showed in his face and she waited—somehow—for three seconds, before she reached up and put a hand to the back of his head, drawing him closer. When they kissed, it was like the bursting of a dam wall; passion threatened to drown them both, and relief was a flood inside Sienna's chest. She *knew* she'd been right.

'Come with me.' She laced her fingers through his and pulled before either of them could give this a second thought.

CHAPTER THREE

HE KNEW ENOUGH to know he should put a stop to this, that his friendship with Luca demanded that, so why did he follow her? Why didn't he say something?

'Sienna—'

'No.' She turned to face him, her eyes scanning his face. 'This is happening, Alejandro. I know I'm not as experienced as you, but I know enough to be able to tell when someone's attracted to me.'

'Attracted? Undoubtedly.' She waited, and the word 'but' hovered on his lips, yet he didn't utter it. And suddenly, he was a teenager again, having to make decisions of which he wasn't proud, to go against his own code of morals simply to survive. But having sex with Sienna wasn't a question of survival. So why did it feel as though it were?

Sienna didn't know how she stayed standing upright when every single bone in her body seemed to be trembling. She pushed the door to the room inwards, ignoring the fussy, froufrou décor, ignoring everything but the way his hand felt wrapped around hers, the way her heart was thumping solidly and excitedly for the first time in her life that she was finally taking her destiny into her own hands and claiming what *she* wanted, because *she* wanted it, not for anyone else. She was abandoning her virginity when it suited *her*, not because her father had dictated from beyond the grave that she would need to marry, not because her groom would expect sex to be a component of their marriage. This was her choice, her terms, her life! The rush of power she felt was an added aphrodisiac and she revelled in its delightful possession of her body.

As soon as the door clicked shut he was kissing her again, but without restraint—not that she could have said he was restrained before, but this was different, his mouth taking over her soul completely, the weight of his body pushing her backwards, until they connected with the elegant rococo chaise longue across the room. Neither reached for the lights, so the room was barely illuminated, and Sienna was glad—it heightened her other senses, not being able to see, plus it removed any need for self-consciousness.

She had barely fallen back onto the chaise longue before his hands were pushing at her dress, desperation removing any lingering doubt from her mind that he wanted this as much as she did, that the chemistry she felt wasn't one-sided.

But when his fingers brushed the simple white cotton of her briefs, she froze, embarrassed, even in the midst of passion, at the utilitarian nature of her underwear. She had no doubt what kind of frothy, lacy situation his lovers usually wore.

If he noticed, or cared, he said nothing, simply sliding them down her legs and disposing of them before bringing his mouth back to hers, the weight of his body on her as he kissed her, his tongue flicking her, rolling with hers, and she arched her back in silent, desperate need.

If she'd loved the feel of his name before, she loved it even more now, every time she cried it, passion infusing each syllable, filling her soul with desperate hunger.

'*Cristo,*' he muttered. 'You make me feel as though I am a schoolboy again, making love for the first time.'

His accent was so much thicker, his voice ragged, as he stripped out of his shirt, staring at her with what could have been taken as annoyance. Given his admission just now, she supposed it was, but annoyance with himself? The feeling he'd damaged his pride?

She smiled up at him, the compliment doing something funny to her heart, her chest, her stomach, so she bit down on her lip and he groaned, dropping forward even as his arms still worked to disentangle themselves from the crisp white shirt.

'*La marta...*' he murmured against her lips.

She spoke Spanish fluently—had taught herself as a way to fill in the empty weekends of teenagerdom—so knew that he was calling her a minx. It made her laugh. Where were the nerves she'd expected to feel? Where was the uncertainty?

She felt nothing but a wild, heady rush of gladness and need, and she felt them in a large enough quantity to forget everything else.

'This is heaven.' She pushed his shirt down the rest of the way, lifting her legs up and wrapping them around his waist even as she dropped his shirt to the ground. He rolled his hips and she cried out, because he was *so close*, his arousal pressed right to her most intimate flesh, so it almost felt as though he were already inside her.

'I want to take my time, but I know you have not got long,' he whispered into her ear, but his voice was thick and gravelled when he turned to meet her eyes. 'People will come looking for you.'

No, nobody would look for her. Nobody would care that she was missing. And nobody would expect that she'd be doing this—nor he doing it with her. The deliciousness of that secret bloomed in her chest. She smiled, pushed onto her elbows and kissed him, while at the same time she reached for his pants and unfastened them. This time, he didn't stop her. This time, he let her push them down and moved his legs to finish the job, so seconds later this Spanish deity brought to life was naked on top of her, his bronzed, sculpted body so beautiful to feel; she could only wish it were possible to see all of him too. She wanted to push him to standing and command him to pirouette for her, to allow her time to admire him in the barely there light, but standing would mean distance and she wasn't willing to risk that.

'A moment.' The word was hoarse. Without pulling too far away from her, he reached down, fingers wrapping around his leather wallet, which he dug from the fabric of his pockets, and flicked it open one-handed to remove a condom. Her breath hissed from her lips as she watched him roll it over his length, the darkness meaning she could see only the silhouette of his body, and the length of his arousal froze her to the core. How the hell was that going to fit?

She bit down on her lip, terrified that maybe she couldn't do this after all, but then he was kissing her again. Had he sensed something had shifted? Did he feel her hesitation?

Of course not. He wasn't a bloody mind-reader. He was just a very experienced lover—so experienced he'd somehow intuited that she was 'innocent'. He was giving her time to relax, that was all.

His hands found the top of her dress, pushing it down over her breasts, and Sienna could have sworn she heard the fabric tear slightly, but it barely registered because the moment the dress was down he was feeling her breasts in his hands, the weight of each in his palms, rolling them, his fingers brushing over her nipples. She'd gone out with a guy once who'd touched her breasts. He'd said they were like cantaloupes—he'd meant it as a compliment but ever since then Sienna had been mortified by her huge breasts and done whatever she could to disguise them—and she'd never been able to eat any kind of melon again, which was a shame because until then cantaloupes had been one of her favourite fruits and had the added benefit of being detested by her mother, so Sienna had snacked on them often, if only to annoy Angelica. After Ryan Hawkins, she'd never touched them again.

But Alejandro's touch wasn't like that. He was gentle and possessive at the same time, making her feel as though he had to touch her breasts in order to be able to survive, making her feel as though this were the beginning and end of his world. She arched her back, and then he took one nipple in his mouth—everything evaporated from her mind in a single, shuddering explosion, until a second later his fingers were between her legs, so she had two parts of her body feeling as though they were bursting into literal flame and she simply couldn't cope, even when she also couldn't bear him to stop.

'This is perfect,' she ground out, rolling her hips in an ancient, feminine invitation for more.

He spoke softly in Spanish and, despite her fluency, her brain was too jam-packed with new sensations and feelings, so that she couldn't translate, she couldn't understand, she knew only that his words made her feel good, like pouring warm, melted caramel over her skin.

'Please,' she groaned as his fingers massaged a cluster of nerve endings that had her whimpering hard. She was the only person who'd ever touched herself there, and never like this. Never so skilfully, so masterfully, never with the same mix of pressure then release, so just as she felt she was about to experience relief, he pulled away. Moist heat pooled between her legs; stars jumped behind her eyes, and, out of nowhere, pain.

Stretching, strange, new pain.

Sharp, searing, so she half sat up and cried out, their eyes locking, his showing, at this proximity, obvious shock, hers confusion, until she realised he'd removed his hand

and simply thrust into her, his whole length, all of him, at
once, and she hadn't been prepared, even though she had,
really, been very skilfully prepared, at the same time.

'What the…?' He swallowed a rough Catalan curse at
the end of the sentence—a language in which Sienna knew
only the basics. His face showed torment, shock. Anger.

'What—'

'Tell me you were not a virgin.'

Confusion swamped her, and also something else. Something warm and pleasurable, something that was making
her blood boil again. Pain was receding, and now pleasure
was picking up right where it had left off, so she shook her
head, her nails digging into his shoulder as she dragged him
downwards. 'Later. We'll talk. But now, please.'

He swore again, this time in Spanish, so she understood
it fully, and even if she hadn't the tone of his voice left her
in little doubt that he hadn't been expecting this. Except
he *had* been. He'd said as much outside.

'Sienna—' The word was a warning, and it was also a
plea. For what? Reassurance? She caught his face on either
side, holding him still.

'I came in here because I wanted this. Please don't stop.
And please don't make me beg. Make love to me, Alejandro.'

'But your first time—' He swore again. 'It shouldn't be
with someone like me.' The words were urgent. 'It shouldn't
be like this.'

She moved her finger to his lips, pressing it there first,
before sliding it into his mouth, removing it, then sliding it
into her own mouth. 'I wanted this. I chose you.'

His eyes closed as he emitted a low, throaty groan. 'Oh,
for God's sake,' he muttered, pulling out a little, so she held
her breath, before he pushed back in, deeper, gently, but
also in a way that reminded her he was in charge—as she
suspected Alejandro always would be.

Every movement was like the tightening of a coil, the winding of it around and around, so she could barely think, barely breathe, but when he brought his mouth to her breasts once more and suckled on one nipple first, then the next, she was barely able to hold on to sense, and life. She dug her nails into his shoulders hard, then dragged them down his back, so hard she wondered, in the very back of her mind, if she might have drawn blood, before digging them into his buttocks, clinging on as pleasure exploded through her, tipping her over the edge of sanity and self, so all she could do was cry his name, so loudly that he had no option but to kiss her, hard, to swallow the syllables into his mouth as his own climax tormented his body, racking it in waves, until, like a ship wrecked to shore, he collapsed on top of her. He was no longer sure of a damned thing, knowing only that he'd been wrong: regret would not wait until morning.

'Wow. Just…wow.'

Alejandro was still riding the wave, his breath burning inside his chest, his whole body feeling as though it had been zapped by an electrical current, every cell reverberating with completion and contentment, so that he would have liked to lie there for a moment, relishing every last sensation, before rousing them both back to fever pitch again, and again. Despite the force of his orgasm, his body wasn't anywhere near satisfied. He wanted more. He wanted to explore her, to experience her in every way.

Which was a goddamned warning he heeded.

Pulling away from her, he stared down at her innocently flushed face for just long enough to confirm that she was experiencing a sexual awakening, just long enough for guilt and self-recriminations to overtake everything else, so he pushed up completely to standing and turned his back, wishing there were some way to undo what had just happened.

But even as he thought that, he knew himself well enough to doubt—would he really take it back? Chemistry had overwhelmed them both and it had been a long time since Alejandro had been with a woman in such an organic, essential way. Since he'd felt as though he might die if he didn't sleep with someone. He ground his teeth together as he disposed of the condom and reached for his pants, all without looking at her. He couldn't. He was furious—with himself mainly, but also with her, and he knew enough to know it would be reprehensible to castigate her right after taking her virginity. He snapped on the light with force, anger reverberating through him, an anger he knew he shouldn't—couldn't—express to her.

But damn it, she should have told him. He wasn't the kind of man who would take advantage of a woman like this. He wasn't the kind of man to get involved with virgins. All his life, he'd known the importance of proving to himself, with every decision he made, that he was nothing like his father. Nothing like the man who'd seduced an inexperienced, trusting virgin, made her fall in love, then disappeared into thin air when she'd revealed that she'd fallen pregnant. He had never slept with a virgin. Not even close. Until this night, and it was something he would never have chosen for himself. He didn't have a 'type', in terms of looks. Tall, short, brunette, blonde, curvaceous or trim, Alejandro couldn't explain what features he was attracted to, but he knew, beyond a shadow of a doubt, that sexual experience was a prerequisite. He ordinarily slept with women who were as uninterested in relationships as he was. Women who understood the way he worked. Anxiety tightened in his gut, because even without the proof of her virginity he'd known she wasn't like that. Sienna was gentle and sweet, and definitely not used to mixing in the kinds of social circles he did.

Even without this discovery, he'd known this was wrong. Luca. Oh, *mierda*. Luca. Defying Luca had been bad enough when he'd thought Sienna experienced, but knowing what he did now, he understood why Luca had warned Alejandro away. She wasn't suitable to be one of his one-night stands. Luca had been one hundred per cent right.

He groaned softly, then forced himself to face her, anger and disbelief pummelling his body from the inside out. She was still lying there, wonder on her face, cheeks pink, eyes sparkling, her magnificent breasts round and full, revealed to the full hunger of his gaze, dress ruched around her midsection—*Cristo*, he hadn't even taken the time to undress her properly, so great had his hunger been. He'd treated her like any of his usual conquests, like a woman *au fait* with life and sex. He'd treated her like his equal in this regard, and even after knowing her a short time, he recognised that she'd deserved better.

His lips assumed a grim line. 'That is *not* what your first time should have been.'

She tilted her face to the side, eyeing him thoughtfully. 'Do I look as though I'm complaining?'

Despite his regret, pride swelled in his chest. Childish, arrogant pride. He quelled it. He didn't deserve any hint of pride, not after what he'd done. Heat flushed his skin as he felt the full weight of his betrayal. Less than an hour after assuring Luca he'd care for Sienna, he'd taken her virginity in the powder room of a restaurant. Self-directed anger made his voice harsher than he intended. 'You should have told me.'

It seemed to dawn on Sienna that something was wrong. She sat up a little, reaching for the floaty straps of her dress and bending her face forward as she focussed on securing them in place, so his fingertips tingled with a desire to reach out and stop her. He wanted her to stay like this for ever—no, not for ever, he didn't believe in such a concept, but for a little while longer, until he'd committed her spectacular curves to his permanent memory.

She frowned. 'You called me innocent outside. I thought you knew.'

He stared at her, perplexed, before recalling that, yes, he had referred to her in this way. He brushed a hand through the air. 'I meant that you are innocent relative to me, not completely inexperienced. Tell me you do have *some* experience with men?'

She nodded, just once, her lips pressed together so their outline was a soft white.

'You are too old to have been a virgin.' Too old, too beautiful, too sensual, too hypnotic. How was it possible?

Her eyes lifted to his and she stood, uneasily, unsteadily, so he reached out a hand to offer stability but she flinched away, the features of her beautiful face stiff.

'The facts would beg to differ.'

'Fine, you were a virgin, but *how*?'

'Isn't that obvious? I've simply never had sex before.'

Sex wasn't supposed to be special and intimate. It wasn't supposed to be memorable. It was a transaction, brief and satisfying but of the moment. And now, more importantly, he didn't want to remember that for the first time in his life he'd betrayed a man he thought of more as family than a friend.

Heat exploded at the crown of his head as he came face to face with the reality of what he'd done. But she looked at him with those enormous green eyes and he felt a thousand other things too, emotions that were at odds with his way of living, emotions he shut down before they could take hold.

'This was a very regrettable mistake, Sienna. I wish it had never happened.'

Sienna wasn't an idiot. She knew it would have been poor form to spring her virginity on some unsuspecting partner, but he'd called her innocent and he'd been so gentle with her, as if preparing her for the first time a man's body possessed hers. She'd simply got caught up in the moment, without feeling a need to spell out the true reasons she had never let things go this far with a man. But what they'd shared would never be categorised as a mistake for her.

'I'm sorry you feel that way. And don't worry, I'm not hoping for a proposal or anything. You might not have known I was a virgin—and I'm sorry for that, I truly believed you had somehow intuited the truth—but *I* knew. I knew, and I chose to do this. You didn't take advantage of me.' She scanned his face. 'And you were very clear about what we were going to share, so my expectations from twenty minutes ago to now haven't changed.'

'I used you for sex, Sienna. Are you really okay with that?'

The directness of his words delighted her. Sienna much preferred that to being called 'beautiful'.

'And *I* used *you* right back! I've got no problems with what we just did. In fact, my only problem is that it's over, because I really enjoyed it.'

He stared at her, completely gobsmacked. 'You're being deliberately facetious.'

'No, I'm just pointing out the ridiculous hypocrisy of your perspective. I was a virgin, fine, but I'm still a woman in my twenties with more than two brain cells to rub together. I knew what you were offering, and I absolutely knew what I was doing when we walked in here together.' She tilted her chin at him, brave, fierce eyes daring him to disagree.

Intrigue flooded his features. 'And that was having sex for the first time in your life, with a man you just met?

'You should have been honest with me,' he continued.

'Would you have slept with me if you'd known?'

'Absolutely not.'

The speed of his response floored her. She stared at him, gasping for air, shocked and confused.

'Virgin or not, it was a mistake, but your innocence complicates it.'

'I'm sorry—'

'Don't apologise.' Now it was Alejandro who grimaced. 'And I am not entirely sure it is you who owes one.' The cryptic response didn't make sense, but before she could question him he continued. 'It shouldn't have happened, but we cannot change the fact it did.'

'No,' she murmured, grateful then that a lifetime of being torn down by her mother had given her a kick-ass ability in hiding her feelings. 'But we can do the next best thing and just pretend it never happened.'

CHAPTER FOUR

BEFORE LUCA HAD drawn his attention to Sienna, Alejandro had barely noticed her. He'd been brooding, wondering what had happened to change Luca from the man he knew—a man he felt an affinity with in so many ways—to a doting, adoring, puppy-dog-esque husband, all of a sudden.

But now, Sienna was all he was aware of. He watched from a distance as she moved through the party. Hell, he could still smell her on him, taste her, if he closed his eyes he could *feel* her muscles tightening around his hardness, so he didn't close his eyes, he didn't allow himself to sink back into that memory. It wasn't how he operated.

He watched her, a beer in one hand, grateful for the shadows that turned his symmetrical face into a chiaroscuro, obscuring him from notice, thankful that Luca was now too absorbed in his bride to notice anyone or anything else, because Alejandro had no idea how he'd ever be able to meet his friend in the eye again.

Besides, Sienna looked happy.

She looked as though he was the furthest thing from her mind. She'd stopped walking and was now talking to an older woman with short silver hair and a dress that was the brightest shade of pink Alejandro had ever seen.

As he watched, Sienna laughed at something her companion said, her head tilted back, her fabulous red hair like a beacon. He wanted to catch it all in his hand and wrap it around his fist, tilting her head back until her eyes stared into his and her mouth was open, waiting, needing…

He swore. It was time to get out of here, before he did something really stupid and suggested they spend the night together.

And yet he didn't move. He stayed where he was, watching, wondering, wanting.

'You know I'm not ready to settle down, Gertie. Not yet.'

'But all these men!' Gertie gestured to the party, shaking her head. 'So many options.'

'Yes, and none of them right for me.' Sienna followed Gertie's gaze, using all of her willpower to avoid so much as glancing within a dozen metres of Alejandro, even though she knew exactly where he was, even though she could feel his eyes on her in a way that was making her pulse flutter unsteadily.

'What about my Andrew? You know he thinks the world of you.'

Sienna rolled her eyes, an indulgent smile softening her lips. 'I *work* for him. Have you heard of a small matter of sexual harassment?'

'It is not harassment if you agree to date, and he would make you happy.'

'Gertie.' Sienna laughed, shaking her head. 'It's never going to happen.'

Gertie tilted her hot-pink lips. 'That's a shame. I should have liked to claim you as my granddaughter-in-law.'

Sienna softened, putting a hand on the older woman's shoulder. 'How about just keeping me as a friend?'

'And a lawn bowls partner?' Gertie grinned, chinking her champagne flute to Sienna's.

Sienna sipped in agreement, her head tilted back, so she missed the moment they were joined by another.

'Ah, speak of the devil.'

'I thought my ears were burning.' Andrew Davison— the Earl of Highbury, and also Sienna's boss—approached, holding two champagne flutes. 'Actually, I thought you could both use a drink, but I see you've got that covered.'

Andrew was one of the few people who understood a little of what Sienna's life was like—courtesy of her close friendship with Gertie, cemented when Sienna was only a teenager, and she had been truly miserable, and now their own friendship. He knew that while Sienna was very happy for her sister's marriage, any family event brought with it a tension for Sienna that was almost off the Richter scale.

'That doesn't mean a second drink wouldn't be welcome.' Sienna smiled through gritted teeth, wishing that her entire body didn't feel *different*. Her nipples were so sensitive that every movement brought the fabric of her dress brushing over them, making goosebumps dance on her pale skin, and between her legs there was a throbbing that made it impossible to forget Alejandro, that made it impossible not to want him again.

But that would never happen.

He'd made it clear that he wished they'd never slept together, and she wasn't going to debase herself by begging.

'No man is ever going to want a fat slob like you, Sienna. What did I do to deserve you as a daughter? Tell me that.'

She finished one glass of champagne, then took the other from Andrew. Kindly concern shaped his eyes so she smiled, a practised smile of reassurance, as she took the glass from him.

Gertie wasn't wrong. Her grandson was gorgeous. Definitely eligible bachelor material—strange that Sienna had never so much as looked at him in that light. Oh, he was perhaps too old for her, in his mid-thirties, but then, how old was Alejandro? What was his last name? She gasped, shocked by how little she knew of a man who knew every detail about her body, covering the surprised reaction by quickly drinking from the champagne. That was what they'd agreed after all. Just sex. No strings. No promises. And she was fine with that. No regrets.

'My driver is out the front. You know you are welcome to use his services to escape at any time,' Andrew said, leaning closer, so only she heard the offer.

He thought she was upset about the wedding, and about her mother. He couldn't know that a whole other incident had usurped everything else in her mind.

'Thank you, but I have to stay until Olivia leaves. It will raise questions if I ghost earlier.'

'Fair enough. But the offer is there.'

'Lord Highbury.' She would know Alejandro's voice anywhere. She stiffened, turning to face him, wondering how long he'd been standing there.

'Alex!' To her surprise, mild-mannered Andrew smiled broadly, reaching out an enthusiastic hand and shaking Alejandro's—Alex's—in it. 'I didn't know you'd be here.'

'Luca and I went to school together.' He flicked his gaze to Sienna and a thousand sparks ignited. There was anger simmering in his gaze. Or was she misreading him? She couldn't say. Her fingers curled more tightly around her champagne.

'Of course, of course. I should have thought. I haven't seen you in almost a year. Are you well?'

How did Andrew know Alejandro? And how well?

'Yes.' He didn't ask the same questions of Andrew. 'I promised Sienna a dance earlier. Excuse me.' He reached for her hand and she was so surprised that she didn't pull away, she didn't say anything, she simply stared up at him, the contact searing her soul.

'And who are you?' Gertie's voice, though made frail

by age, still reached through the tension, drawing Alejandro's impatient gaze.

'Alejandro Corderó.'

Corderó. She tasted the word in her mouth, whispering it to herself, before realising that Gertie was watching her from between shrewd eyes.

Pull it together.

'And how do you know our Sienna?'

The possessive nature of the question was obvious, so too his reaction: his hand tightening around hers.

'Through Luca. Excuse us.'

Belatedly, as they cut through the crowd, Sienna went to pull her hand away but he held it fast, his eyes turning to her, pinning her with a warning.

'What are you doing?' she muttered.

'Dancing.'

'I don't want to dance with you,' she lied, and he knew it was a lie, a look of mockery on his face when he turned to face her. He didn't take her to the middle of the dance floor and she was glad; instead, he found a spot on the edge, where there was less light, more privacy, and pulled her into his arms, holding her against his chest.

Sparks flew. She felt each and every one of them embed in her body, felt their heat and warmth, and knew the answer to that warmth, she knew exactly how to relieve them.

'I am leaving after this dance.'

Emptiness trapped her stomach. She stopped moving, and simply stared up at him. It was a betraying gesture and she hated herself for showing it to him, but it occurred to Sienna that she was never going to see this man again. She hadn't expected she would, and yet the realisation that he was about to walk out of her life just as abruptly as he'd walked into it filled her mouth with sawdust.

'Fine. It's late. I'm sure Luca won't mind. I need to stay until the end, until my sister leaves—'

She was babbling. She clamped her lips together and focussed on a point to the right of his shoulder. He drew her closer, holding her body against his body, so she was aware of every part of him, aware of what he felt like, of what he looked like, aware of how his weight had pressed her to the chair, aware of what it was to want someone with your whole, entire heart. Except her heart wasn't the issue, so much as a suddenly awakened libido.

'Listen to me.'

She swallowed, pressing her lips together, waiting.

'I presumed you were experienced. Not necessarily very experienced, but that you at least had some.'

She glared at him. 'Sorry to disappoint you.'

His eyes flashed to hers. 'I did not say I was disappointed by *anything* we shared, *querida*.'

And despite the grim look on his face, she felt a hum of warmth at the admission—or as close as he was going to get to an actual admission—that he had enjoyed what they'd shared *despite* her inexperience.

'I presume you are not on the pill?'

Her eyes widened. She shook her head slowly, feeling like a complete idiot for not having thought of that.

'I see.'

'But you used protection, so there's nothing to worry about, right?'

'Condoms are not one hundred per cent effective. There is a possibility that you have conceived my child.'

She dropped her hands to her sides, the idea exploding in her mind, so she shook her head without even thinking it through.

'That can't be—'

'Of course it can be.' His voice was without emotion, and yet she felt it emanating off him in waves. 'I would expect you to contact me if there are any consequences from what we just shared.'

'There won't be,' she said, because it had to be true. She had never thought about becoming a parent. It wasn't something she'd ever craved, and it certainly wasn't on her agenda any time soon.

'You will let me know either way.'

She swallowed past a heaviness that had built in her throat. 'I'll let you know if there's anything to know,' she conceded. 'Of course.'

Silence fell. He stared at her as though he were trying to read her mind and a moment later, a grim tone to his voice, he asked, 'Did I hurt you?'

She blinked, not understanding at first. 'When?'

'I was not gentle. Not like I would have been, if I'd known—'

'Oh.' She pulled her lower lip between her teeth. 'No. I'm—fine.'

But she could see guilt about the corners of his eyes and wanted to alleviate it better.

'I don't know if I'm meant to say this, because, you know, I have no experience, obviously, but I actually really liked that you weren't gentle. I liked…' She pulled her lips to the side, wondering if she was admitting too much to him. She shook her head. 'I'm fine.'

He expelled a slow breath, as though he was relaxing, but for Sienna the panic was just setting in. Olivia worried about her so much, if Sienna were to have fallen pregnant poor Olivia would probably insist on moving home to England, just to help. If she thought there was even the slightest chance, Olivia would swing into full-blown protective-older-sister mode.

'Listen to me.' Sienna lifted her hand to his chest, pressing it there with urgency. 'No one can know about what we did.'

His eyes narrowed, darkening. 'I am not in the habit of sharing my exploits with other people, Sienna. My opinion is that private lives should remain exactly that—private. I wasn't intending to discuss what we shared with anyone.' But there was a tone to his voice, as though he was torn about something, as though he was unsure.

'Good.' She was, momentarily, placated. 'As far as I'm concerned, what happened between us was about you and me and nobody else. No one needs to know. Especially not my sister or Luca. They'd completely flip out and they've got enough going on in their own lives without having to worry about mine.'

'I will tell nobody.'

He dropped his arms, taking a step away from her, then reaching into his wallet and removing a black business card. 'But do not forget, Sienna. You'll call me if there is any news to deliver.'

She took the card, stared at the number and, when she looked up, Alejandro had turned his back and was walking away, disappearing into the balmy night air.

Eight dates after leaving Rome, Alejandro had to admit two things to himself: he was bored out of his brain, and he wanted to see Sienna again. To be fair, it hadn't taken him eight dates with eight separate women to realise he was trying to replace rich red wine with tepid water, but he was stubborn, and thinking about Sienna seemed particularly stupid, given that Luca was his best friend and he would definitely *not* approve of the X-rated direction of Alejandro's thoughts. And yet, here he was, disappointing yet another old flame by not inviting her home with him, knowing that bedding another woman wouldn't work.

He didn't want to have sex with just anyone.

He wanted more of Sienna. He wanted to explore her properly. To taste her. To tease her. To watch her in the full light as she came apart at the seams. He wanted to make her explode, one passionate caress after another, until he was the only person who could put her back together again. He wanted to let their chemistry burn hot, until it had finally burned out, and then he wanted to walk away, just as he had this time. But it had been premature. He'd made a mistake.

Was it one he could fix?

He strode into his penthouse, through the large open space with double-height ceilings, his eyes travelling the details of the skyline visible from the floor-to-ceiling windows and wrap-around terrace. The ornate, recognisable roofs of the Passeig de Gràcia stood in the foreground and, beyond them, Barcelona glittered like an overflowing jewellery box. He paused just long enough to grab a beer from the fridge and kick off his shoes, then he swung open the glass doors to the terrace, stepping out with a grim expression on his handsome face.

Eight days.

That was barely any time. A blip. He knew from experience that all things became easier with time's passage. He simply had to go through the motions a little longer, and eventually he'd cease to think of her, eventually he would no longer want her. He had no choice: wanting her was forbidden.

'Here, Starbuck, here.' She rubbed behind her dog's ears, the big, open-mouthed, slobbery smile she got in return making Sienna laugh. She crouched down, pressing her chin to Starbuck's head. 'You really are a one-off, girl.'

She pulled back a little, but Starbuck only plonked her furry body down onto the flagstones, resting her own chin on Sienna's legs.

'I see. Are we taking a nap now?'

Starbuck breathed out heavily in response.

Sienna stroked the hair between Starbuck's ears, distracted, happy to rest a moment, to stare out of the open double doors into the almond grove she could just make out directly ahead of her. How many hours had she and Olivia spent hiding out there, away from their parents, pretending they were pirates on the open seas, far away from Hughenwood House and the horrors of their parents' marriage?

She closed her eyes, pushing away those unpleasant memories, and landing right in far more pleasant ones. His hands on her body. His mouth at her breasts. His fiery Spanish words in her ears, working their way into her heart. She groaned and Starbuck shifted, casting a lazy look up before returning to her resting place.

It had been three weeks since the wedding. Three weeks since she'd met Alejandro Corderó and suffered a temporary bout of insanity that had seen her throw herself at the man, regardless of her lack of experience.

It was tempting—and easy—to blame her mother, who'd spent the entire morning of the wedding nit-picking Sienna until she was ready to blow a gasket—she just hadn't known she wanted to blow that particular one! But Angelica Thornton-Rose had been on Sienna's case her entire life. Why had that day been any different? Why hadn't she been able to fend off her mother's attacks as always, filing them away into the 'bitter, vain, aging widow' category of her mind?

Because it hadn't really been about Angelica. It had been about Alejandro. All about him, and his unique impact on her. She'd wanted him and, as was often the case with Sienna, she'd acted on her impulses. She hadn't stopped to question the wisdom of sleeping with her brother-in-law's best friend. She hadn't stopped to question *anything*. She'd wanted him and so she'd done whatever she could to have him, to hell with the consequences.

And yet, there were none. Three weeks later, she'd had confirmation she wasn't pregnant and, as further evidence of insanity, had actually felt a blip of disappointment and emptiness to realise there was no reason to call him. Imagine that! Tethering herself to a man like him for all eternity simply because he'd made her body feel something she'd never known possible.

No amount of orgasms could make sharing a child with Alejandro worth it. Right?

She bit down on her lip, wishing she were fully convinced of that, and for the hundredth time since the wedding she pulled out her phone and loaded up his number. She'd saved it into the phone that night, discarding his business card. She'd known she'd lose it anyway—Sienna was about as organised as the Mad Hatter after a barrel of wine when it came to paperwork. She stared at the screen, wondering what it would be like to press that little green button. To hear his voice. Just his voice.

She stared at her phone and the impulse to do exactly that was so strong her fingertip actually felt as though it were fizzing. Extricating herself from serving as Starbuck's pillow, she stood up and paced towards the door, her heart racing as hard and fast as if she were back at the wedding, Alejandro right in front of her.

What have you got to lose?

How about your pride? a stubborn voice reminded her.

After all, a lifetime of being told she was no good couldn't help but shape the way in which she viewed herself, even when Olivia had done her level best to push Angelica's cruelty aside as though it meant nothing. And weren't some things worth a gamble? Look at Olivia! She'd risked everything by going to Rome and asking Luca to marry her.

Sienna didn't want to marry Alejandro, but she wasn't sure it was doing any good to continue pretending she didn't want *something* from him. But would he feel the same way?

There was only one way to know for sure.

CHAPTER FIVE

'Sorry to interrupt, Alejandro.'

His assistant Maria's voice was clipped and efficient as always. He paused, midway through changing out of his suit and into running gear, clicking the desk phone into speaker mode.

'Si?'

He unbuttoned his shirt and discarded it over the back of his chair.

'There's a woman here to see you.'

Bored impatience settled in his gut. 'I'm heading out.'

'I'm aware of the time.' Maria's response brought a tight smile to his lips. They'd worked together six years—other than Luca, she was the person who knew him best in the world.

'I don't take unsolicited appointments.'

'Again, I am aware of how you operate.'

'Then why are you putting through this call?'

He heard Maria sigh and let out a silent laugh. They badgered one another like this for sport.

He stepped out of his trousers, casting them over the back of the seat before reaching for his shorts.

'She says it's important.'

He arched a brow. 'Who, exactly?'

'Sienna Thor—'

He reached for the phone, snapping it out of the cradle before his assistant had finished speaking Sienna's full name.

'She's here?'

His gut twisted as his future suddenly changed shape, and he imagined the sole reason she could have for showing up in his office like this.

She was pregnant.

'Shall I ask her to make an appointment?'

Ashen, he stared at the wall. Alejandro had known two things about himself for as long as he could remember. He would never be a man who lied to women, who promised them more than he wanted to give. And he would never be a man who turned his back on responsibilities. Not as his own father had. If Sienna had conceived as a result of their one time together, then there was nothing for it. They would marry. And Luca would never speak to him again. That would be a grave price in his life, but one he would pay in a heartbeat if the alternative was shirking his paternal duty.

'No. Send her in. *Immediatament.*'

He clicked the phone back into place, not taking his eyes off the wall opposite. His office, a space that was familiar to him by virtue of the fact he spent long, long hours here each day, and had done for years, changed into a different and unfamiliar shape. The whole world looked different. Everything seemed to grind to a halt. He turned to face the door, a ringing in his ears, as he prepared for all the ways in which his life was about to change.

Which meant he spent precisely zero time preparing for the fact Sienna—the object of some seriously dirty dreams of Alejandro's—was about to walk into his office.

But when she did, it was like being shocked with high-voltage electricity.

The colours that had seeped away from his walls were suddenly back, brighter almost than he could bear. As she walked, everything seemed to shimmer. What was it about her that radiated warmth? She was her own source of energy. Her red hair had been swept up into a loose, chaotic bun, and despite the untidiness all he really noticed was the way it drew attention to her cheekbones, her freckles, and those enormous green eyes, her pouting lips begging...

But, no.

That wasn't why she was here, and it sure as hell wasn't a thought process he could engage in, for a thousand reasons.

'Sienna.' He tried to keep his voice businesslike, and he maintained distance between them, because he needed that.

Only, it didn't help. Not when her eyes ravished his face before sinking to his chest, staring at him as though she'd never seen a naked man before. And hell, perhaps she hadn't. Alejandro hadn't got as far as removing his shirt the night they'd made love. A perverse fascination made him want to stay like this, to welcome her inspection, but an awareness of how badly he'd stuffed up at Luca's wedding had dogged him ever since.

Having sinfully wicked dreams about her was one thing, but inviting her to stare at him, wishing she'd touch him, quite another.

And if she was pregnant? And she must be—why else would she be here?

'Please, take a seat.' He gestured to the white leather armchairs arranged by the full floor-to-ceiling windows.

Sienna turned to face the windows, and her distraction allowed him a brief moment of weakness, to allow his own gaze to drift over her body. It was stupid. A foolish move. How could he see her in that summery mini dress and *not* want to rip it off her? She lifted a brown leather backpack from her shoulder, placing it by the door.

He propped his butt on the edge of his desk, a study in nonchalance, as she moved towards the armchairs. She stood behind one, not sitting down, her eyes troubled when they met his.

'Would you like a drink?'

'No, thank you.'

He crossed his arms, watching, waiting, wondering at the hammering of his blood, the throbbing of his central nervous system. He knew the executioner's blade was about to drop, yet even that couldn't stop him from looking at her and wanting a rehash of the last time they'd been alone in the same room together...

But there were bigger, more important issues at play now. He pushed aside his libido with difficulty. 'So I take it we're having a baby together?'

She looked at him as though he'd started speaking Cantonese, and then her cheeks flushed as pink as her beautiful full lips. 'Oh, no.' She shook her head and a clip of her hair dislodged, dropping down beside her cheek. 'I'm not—that's—not why I'm here.'

He didn't visibly react but, inside, emotions were pulling at him, confusing him.

'You said you'd contact me if we had conceived a baby.'

'But we didn't, so I didn't.'

'To be clear, you are not pregnant?'

'No. Definitely not.'

'That's not why you are here?'

'No.'

Relief was a drug. He closed his eyes, pinching the bridge of his nose, as he allowed himself to walk back from the ledge, to return to the vision of his life as he currently knew it. 'Thank *Cristo*.'

When he opened his eyes, it was to find her staring at him, and he realised he still hadn't pulled on a shirt. 'Then what are you doing here?' Dangerous, full-blown temptation simmered in his blood.

Think of Luca.

He'd made the man a promise, and he'd already broken it once. That had been a truly unforgivable mistake, albeit spontaneous. Twice would be a willing, premeditated betrayal.

'Maybe I will take a drink after all.'

'What would you like?'

'Scotch?' she said with a half-smile.

He strode to his liquor cabinet, concealed behind a darkly wooded pantry, and removed a bottle of aged whisky, pouring a measure into a crystal glass, which he carried across the carpeted floor to her.

He could have handed it to her from a safe distance away, but a compulsion he didn't know how to ignore was flooding him. He came around the chair, so they were almost touching, and held it at her chest level. Her fingers reached out to take the glass, wrapping around his, and a thousand electric shocks danced beneath his skin at the simple contact. He dropped his hand away but stayed right where he was.

She let the drink touch her lips at first, and then threw it back in one measure, screwing up her face as the taste assaulted her body. 'That's better.' She coughed a little.

'Water?'

'No, I'm okay.' She kept the glass cradled between both hands, holding it in front of her, so if he leaned forward his chest would brush her hands. 'I just feel a bit ridiculous, being way out on this ledge over here.'

'You're on a ledge?'

'Oh, yeah. A big one.'

'And you wish you weren't?'

'On the contrary, I'm kind of excited.'

'Are you?'

She nodded. He watched, fascinated, as her hair shifted, then dropped his gaze to her breasts. They were truly stunning. His pants strained.

'Yeah. I think so.'

Sensual heat was throbbing through him but there was amusement too. She was unlike any woman he'd ever known, so artless, but charming, and incredibly likeable. Alarm bells sounded in the back of his brain, and he heeded them. He didn't do 'likeable'. It was the nice girls who would get hurt the worst by men like him. He wasn't going to risk it. Not with Sienna, and not because Luca had warned him off, but because he'd seen what had happened to his mother, how she'd been the quintessential nice girl, too trusting, too innocent, and she'd been completely destroyed by his father.

'Why don't you tell me why you came here?'

She lifted one hand from the glass, tucking that stray clump of hair behind her ear. The action was enough to release a hit of her fragrance—hair conditioner, perfume, hormones—reminding him, powerfully, of the night they'd shared. He was conscious of his body tightening, his arousal starting to strain against the flimsy material of his sports shorts.

'Why aren't you wearing a shirt?'

He'd forgotten about that. 'I was getting ready to go for a run.'

'Oh.' She nodded, but there was a distracted expression on her face. 'Firstly, I've been thinking. And I guess I owe you an explanation after all.'

He stared at her blankly.

'You didn't know I was a virgin.' She darted her tongue out, licking her lower lip. Was she trying to give him a stroke? 'And I didn't know who you were that night, besides being a friend of Luca's—'

Luca. Cristo. Your best friend.

'But I do now. I looked you up online. I get what you were saying to me. That whole "notch on the bedpost" thing is no joke with you.'

Why did he wish, more than anything, that he could deny it? Why did he want to tell her that, in fact, he hadn't slept with anyone since her—his longest bout of celibacy since he'd first discovered the wonders of sex.

'Sex seems to be a bit like a sport with you.'

He couldn't help it. He laughed, but at her look of pique he silenced himself, nodding encouragingly. 'Go on.'

'Sex is meaningless for you. That's why you reacted so badly when you realised I was a virgin, because you thought losing my virginity to you would equate to the sex meaning more to me than you wanted it to. Right?'

He didn't deny it. After all, that had been part of it, but what he couldn't confess to her was that Luca had forbidden him from pursuing Sienna, a detail that had weighed on his mind equally.

'But it didn't,' she rushed to reassure him. 'I liked having sex with you, but that's all it was for me as well. The dreams I've been having about you are not about your mind, believe me.'

Another laugh, short and sharp. He resisted asking what the dreams entailed—but only just.

'The thing is, I want to have sex again. With you.'

It was the *last* thing he'd been expecting, and the response was immediate. His body jerked to attention, his mouth went dry, his heart began to thump hard against his ribs, and he had to count to ten just to stop himself from pulling her to the floor here and now.

'Actually, I think I kind of *need* to have sex with you, so that I can stop thinking about it and get on with my life,' she said with a hint of resentment.

It was a living nightmare. A cruel and unusual punishment. That this woman would step into his office and offer herself to him on a platter, when he had sworn to his friend that nothing would happen between them. He couldn't do this. But hell, how he wanted to.

'It's not possible.'

Her eyes dropped to the floor, shielding her emotions from him.

Tell her. Tell her you made a promise to Luca. Tell her you want to screw her more than life itself, but honour and loyalty prevent that from being possible. Tell her this isn't about her, that it's you.

'I see. I thought that might be the case. I mean, you have sex all the time, you probably barely even remember me, but for me, you're just—I mean—I guess I have no clue about it. Is it always like that?'

This was going from bad to worse. If the conversation devolved into talking about the finer points of that night he would forget his own name, let alone Luca's.

'There are other men, more suitable men, to gain experience with.'

She narrowed her eyes suspiciously. 'More suitable how?'

'More inclined to relationships, for one.'

'But that's just it.' Her eyes flashed to his. 'I don't want a relationship. That's not what I'm suggesting.'

His gut tightened. 'You make no sense.'

'Why? You think it's so impossible that a woman should want to live like you do? Okay, not quite like you do, but to have a physical relationship without making a commitment?'

'No. But I don't think that's who *you* are.'

She didn't fight him on that point. 'You don't get it. For reasons that are too complex to go into, I have to get married before I turn twenty-five, which is in a little over a year.'

She was so young. Even without all the other issues, her age was something he should have paid more attention to. The women he usually went for were closer in age to him— thirty, at least. Uneasiness spread through him.

'You know my feelings on marriage?'

'Yes. I'm not suggesting *we* get married.' She paled visibly, the idea clearly appalling to her. He wondered at that, almost wanted to fight against it on principle—ego, he presumed. 'I need to marry someone, and it would be better if it's not someone I fancy. That would complicate things. I want a husband I can be friends with, but nothing more.'

He stared at her as though she'd sprouted a second head, and then a third.

'As I said, it's complicated.' She waved a hand through the air. 'But before I get married, I want to…' She paused, looking away from him for a moment, then forcing her eyes back to his defiantly. 'I want to know everything I can about sex. To experience it fully.'

'Absolutely not.' He issued the denial swiftly, before he could forget common sense, his obligations to Luca, and every damned reason he had to resist this, and pull her into his arms.

She opened her mouth to protest and then closed it again. Her eyes held his, but there was the smallest slump in her shoulders that made his chest feel hollowed out. A protective instinct he hadn't known in a long time, but that he now realised Sienna invoked, oh, so easily whipped through him. 'Okay, fair enough. I guess it was worth a shot.' She forced a small smile to her face and then skirted around him—far around him—before placing her empty glass on the corner of his desk. She stared at it for several seconds, then slowly pirouetted back towards him. 'Please keep my request between us. I still haven't mentioned anything to Olivia—I don't want her to know any of this.'

He watched her walk towards his door, her back straight, her shoulders squared, and he counted each of her steps, aware that within seconds she'd be gone, out of his life, that the risk would be over. He should have been relieved. He needed this temptation like a hole in the head. But as she approached the door, he felt a surge of adrenaline, a rush of panic, and he knew, even then, that he was losing this fight, and that scared the hell out of him.

'Sienna, wait. Let me explain.' His voice was low and kind, so her heart splintered into a thousand and one pieces. What a fool she'd been! As if he could *ever* feel the same way about her as she did him! Sexual infatuation had gripped her for a long month, tormenting her, but Alejandro Corderó was no stranger to that unique pleasure. He'd had a lot of lovers, if the internet was to be believed. He was hardly pining away for her, wondering about her, waiting for her to swing by his office and ask him to make love to her. How utterly excruciating.

It is a good thing you are smart, Sienna. Your looks are certainly not going to be your success.

'There's no need.' She was as grateful as anything when she reached the door, curving her fingers around the handle. 'I understand.'

'No, you don't.'

'You regretted sleeping with me. Despite my inexperience, that much was obvious.'

His eyes flashed with hers, anger obvious, sparks flecking from him to her and then he was cutting across the office, making short work of the distance, his broad frame right in front of hers so she felt waves of desire and heat buffet her from all sides.

'This is not a question of whether or not I want to sleep with you again. I do.'

She rolled her eyes. 'Please. Don't feel the need to let me down gently. I would always prefer honesty.'

'As would I.' He caught her chin and tilted her face up, so her body jolted with the sheer pressure of awareness. 'So I am being honest with you. This is complicated, not least because of our connection through Luca and Olivia.'

'What difference does that make?'

He stared down at her, his eyes probing hers, reading her, his lips parted, his body tense, and she moaned softly, because this was impossible.

'Look, Alejandro, just forget I came here. You're right. There are other guys I can approach, other men who'll—'

It was as if something snapped inside him. His nostrils flared and then a second later he was right in front of her, temper barely contained. 'Other men? You dare come in here and talk to me about other men—'

'You're the one who said there'd be someone more suitable—'

'I was wrong.' And then he was kissing her, but not as she'd ever been kissed before.

This was a kiss of white-hot possession, a kiss designed to mark her, to change her, and ultimately to claim her. She shivered into his embrace, into the hoarse, Catalan words he groaned into her mouth and she surrendered to him even as she felt a thrill of pleasure, because beyond surrender was the thrill of victory and she let it claim her soul, piece by delicious piece.

CHAPTER SIX

ALEJANDRO EXERCISED CONTROL in all aspects of his life but there was no room for control here, no room for anything but instinct. He'd told her she should find someone else to further her sexual education with and he'd known it was the last thing he wanted, but when she'd thrown that back at him, he'd had to act. Because regardless of what he'd promised Luca, regardless of the limitations of what he could offer Sienna, he wasn't about to let her walk out of his office and into another man's bed.

He couldn't.

Impulses ruled him, just as they had that first night. Impulses that drove thought, reason, obligation and loyalty to Luca from his mind completely, so all he could think about was Sienna and this, and how badly he needed her. He lifted her dress from her head with urgency, dropping it to the floor beside them, not willing to make the same mistake he had last time, leaving her dressed, so that he was unable to appreciate her body properly. It had been dark then too, whereas now the afternoon sun flooded through the mirrored high-rise windows of his office. He wanted to look but that would mean stepping back, so instead he compromised—feeling his way over her body, feeling every curve and undulation, familiarising himself with her sweet spots, those parts of her that trembled when he touched them, kissing her as his hands stroked and pulled and pleasured, until she was a quivering mess against the door. He wanted her. He ached for her.

He lifted her as though she weighed nothing, wrapping her legs around his waist as he strode to his desk and cleared it with one arm, papers landing all over the floor; he didn't care. He placed her butt on the edge of his desk and stood between her legs, kissing her more slowly now as he tried to calm his flaming erection, to tell himself there was time—or risk coming as soon as he drove into her.

'Stay here,' he commanded against her mouth, pushing a desk drawer open to reveal a string of condoms. He lifted one and opened it, rolling it over his length before meeting her eyes and finding a question there.

'You do this a lot.'

He frowned.

'In your office, I mean.'

'No,' he growled, wondering why it felt important to clarify that. 'Never.'

He didn't wait to see her response. He'd given her a straight answer, and now, sheathed and protected from unwanted consequences, he wanted her more than he could express.

'Tell me if I hurt you,' he said into her ear.

'You won't.'

'I wasn't gentle enough with you last time. If I had known—'

'I don't want gentle.' She pressed a hand to his naked chest, her fingertips just touching one of his scars, which ran from one nipple and diagonally downwards. 'I want real.'

'Real? Real I can do.'

And instincts and impulses took over again, so he drew her right to the edge of the desk and drove into her, hard, his first thrust a stake of ownership, a claim on her body that neither had expected, and his next, cementing it. She tilted her head back and his left hand drove through her hair, liberating it from the elastic so it spilled down her back, over her shoulders, her creamy, generous breasts shifting with each movement, her hair brushing them. Desire spiralled into something dangerous, a tornado, as he picked up speed, his fingers moving to her butt, digging into the flesh there as he kept her pushed right to the edge of the desk.

She arched her back instinctively, welcoming him deeper, and he pushed in, her muscles contracting ferociously around his length, until he was simply light and heat, lost to her, this, everything, just as he had been that night.

Pleasure built, a tidal wave that rocked them together, in unison, their breath and cries in perfect sync, so the moment her muscles began to spasm with uncontrollable pleasure, he exploded, burying himself in her with a guttural cry, kissing her hard, silencing her even as he devoured her voice, her impatience, her frantic need.

Like any natural disaster, there was the aftermath to contend with, and for Alejandro it was every bit as dangerous as the first time they'd slept together. He had crossed a line. Not once, but twice, and it was a line he'd thought he'd always, always respect: his friendship with Luca. He'd betrayed that friendship, and the knowledge sat like a stone in his gut because, even while being aware of it, he couldn't summon the remorse he deserved to feel.

He could no longer put an obligation to Luca above the wishes Sienna had clearly expressed. She was a grown woman, who had every right to explore her sexuality, to choose who she slept with and when. And she'd chosen him. He knew Luca's request came from a place of concern, but he also understood that Luca wasn't seeing Sienna as she really was. The picture he'd painted of a woman in need of protection was a far cry from the strong, independent woman who'd come to Alejandro's office and asked him to make love to her again. Admiration shifted through him as he contemplated what that must have taken.

'That was…'

She searched for a word, her eyes twinkling so he found himself smiling—and amusement was not a reaction he usually associated with sex but one he felt now, nonetheless.

'Yes.' Because there was no one single adjective that could do justice to what they'd shared. It was better to simply acknowledge they'd both been rocked by it.

It wasn't that Alejandro had grown bored of sex, so much as of his usual partners, who were so practised in seduction, so predictable. Or perhaps *he'd* grown predictable. He couldn't remember the last time he'd let passion move him to the point he took a woman on a desk. Or a sofa in a restaurant powder room, for that matter.

'How long are you in Barcelona for?'

'I'm booked to fly out later tonight, actually.' He braced his palms on the desk, on either side of her, keeping the irritation blocked from his face.

'So that is all you wanted from me?'

She laughed softly. 'Oh, don't be hurt.' She lifted a finger and absent-mindedly traced one of his scars—gained when he was only thirteen years old, with the craggy edge of a broken bottle. 'I can change my flight.'

'I was not hurt,' he felt compelled to clarify. 'Simply surprised.'

'I didn't know if you'd agree.' She shrugged those creamy, delightful shoulders and her breasts harumphed in unison. He lifted his hands, cupping them, just as he'd wanted to from almost the first moment he'd met her. Her eyes flecked with a whirlwind of need. 'And if you did agree, well, suffice it to say, the logistics all seemed a little up in the air.'

'And now?'

'I suppose they still are.'

'Why?'

'Well, I have to get back to work at some point. I actually didn't think this through too well.' She expelled a breath so her hair lifted, brushing her forehead gently. 'Impulsiveness is my biggest downfall.'

'From where I'm standing, it's a virtue.' She laughed softly and before he knew it, he was grinning like a fool. 'Stay for the rest of the week.' The words were out before he could stop them and panic tightened in his chest. But he quelled it quickly. After all, that was only a few days, and it didn't mean they'd be spending every minute together. 'I will still have to work, but your nights will be mine…'

She hesitated. Having already crossed to the dark side by betraying his best friend, he felt only a hint of compunction in going all the way—he squeezed her nipples, watching unashamedly as pleasure darkened her cheeks.

He sucked her lower lip between his teeth, wobbled it there then dropped his head to one of her breasts, taking a nipple in his mouth and rolling it with his tongue. 'This is not negotiable. If we're going to do this, we're going to do it right, and that will take the week.'

The rest of the week! She felt giddy. She felt…a thousand and one things, actually. Relief, euphoria, delight, joy, satisfaction and hunger, all rolled into one. 'It's good to know the first time wasn't a fluke, though.'

Mock outrage shifted his features. 'You seriously thought it might have been?'

'Sorry to offend your sexual prowess.' She grinned, so he moved his attention back to her mouth, kissing her there, taking her breath away with each flick of his tongue until she saw stars.

'Believe me, I relish the opportunity to continue prov-ing you wrong.'

'Or right. I'm not sure I actually thought it was a fluke, so much as I hoped that the repeat performance, if there even *was* a repeat performance, would live up to the ex-perience.'

He laughed, a low, soft sound. 'You really are quite unique.'

'Why can't you be more like your sister? More like other girls?'

She sobered a moment, sitting a little straighter, pressing a hand to his chest. The ridges of his scar edged beneath her fingertip. 'What happened here?'

He didn't answer and when she looked up at him, his face had changed. A small smile tilted his lips but it didn't reach his eyes; it was an imitation, almost chilling. 'A child-hood misadventure.'

'That you don't want to talk about,' she surmised. 'I understand.' She leaned forward and pressed a kiss to the edges. She understood all about scars—but hers were the kind you couldn't see. Nonetheless, they were scraped right across her heart and soul, and always would be. She didn't particularly want to talk about those either.

'It's not that I don't want to talk about it. It's no big deal. I got in a fight.'

'A fight you lost?'

'A fight I won, though my opponent saw fit to arm him-self with a broken beer bottle.' He ran his own finger across the scar, a distracted look on his face, then lifted his fin-ger to his neck, pointing to another scar, about an inch below his ear.

'My God, it's lucky he didn't get a major vein or artery.'

He lifted his shoulders. 'He didn't. I survived.'

A shiver ran down her spine. 'How old were you?'

'Thirteen.'

Concern shifted through her. 'Who was he?' She could only think of her own father in that moment, and how often she'd been afraid as a child. Not that she'd ever seen him hit her mother, but the way he'd yelled and loomed over her—over them all—had filled the same space in her brain. She'd hatched a thousand and one plans of how she'd defend them if and when he turned violent. She'd lived with that fear until the day her father died.

'Just some drunk.'

Sienna couldn't help herself. She kissed the edge of his scar again, imagining being thirteen years old and attacked by a rambling, violent alcoholic. How was it possible? Where were his parents?

He took a step back, separating them, his face a mask of professional cool. 'My driver is downstairs. He'll let you into my place.' Then, the cool gave way to fire, at least in his eyes, as he leaned forward, almost against his will, and kissed her. 'I'll be as quick as I can be.'

Sienna hadn't thought far enough ahead to know how she'd handle things *if* he accepted her offer. She supposed she'd imagined getting a hotel room, but from the moment he'd suggested she go back to his place curiosity had overwhelmed her, and temptation too, so she'd simply nodded, even when alarm sirens had been sounding through her brain.

Her mother had always acquiesced to their father and Sienna had sworn she'd never be like that. But this wasn't a big deal. Alejandro wasn't a man she intended to date. He certainly wasn't the man she would end up marrying, and, furthermore, his suggestion made sense. She could stay at his place for tonight at least, and then come up with a firmer plan the next day.

His driver was a handsome man named Raul, who looked as if he practised hardcore wrestling in his spare time. His arms were wider than her head's circumference. When he spoke, his voice was gentle, though, and he opened the door for her with a kindly smile, which made her wonder how often Raul was asked to escort women home. She pushed the question aside. She already had the answer to that. Alejandro was a prolific bachelor. That was part of why she'd hatched this plan. She *liked* that she was just another notch on the bedpost to him. She liked that she could share this experience with someone who would likely forget all about her, leaving her free to focus on finding a suitable groom and planning the wedding, when the time came.

Barcelona was stunning. She focussed on the city as the car cut through traffic, the buildings a charming mix of old and new, the prominent Gaudí architecture eye-catching whenever they rounded a corner and one of his masterpieces sprung almost organically from the pavement. The sun was high in the sky, the heat of the day unrelenting, so she was grateful for the car's powerful air-conditioner and tinted windows. Nonetheless, when they passed an ice-cream cart her mouth went dry from the force of her temptation. She stared at it as they passed, wishing she could trade places, just for a moment, with the children playing around it, their hands outstretched for the delicious treat.

The car drove on, turning into a wide boulevard with verdant trees lining either side, creating a canopy of shade for the generous footpaths. The buildings here were almost all old, stunningly ornate, many with either shops or cafes underneath them, so people spilled out, the sound of their laughter permeating the vehicle when they pulled up at traffic lights. The elegance of their dress made Sienna's heart tremble almost to a stop. She looked down at the summery dress she'd pulled on this morning—one of her favourites—and grimaced.

She was as far removed from Spanish chic as it was possible to get.

Unbidden, the images—hundreds of images—of Alejandro's former lovers flashed into her mind, adding to the pool of unease she always felt about her appearance. Oh, she was self-aware enough to know that her mother bore the blame for that completely. She also knew she wasn't as overweight and unattractive as her mother liked to taunt. But nor was she svelte and glamorous like Olivia and Angelica. She was pale-skinned with freckles and auburn hair, and even though her puppy fat had left her when she'd outgrown adolescence, her breasts and hips hadn't got the memo, remaining steadfastly curvaceous, meaning it was difficult to find dresses that fitted because the waists were invariably far too loose if she bought anything that actually suited her bust line.

Except for dresses like this—loose and floaty and somehow freeing.

But definitely not chic.

Definitely not Alejandro Corderó chic.

The car began to move again, sliding along the street. She caught a sign as they went—Passeig de Gràcia—and vaguely recalled having seen an article about this place in one of her mother's high-end fashion magazines. They passed boutiques now, designer names visible between the trunks of the trees, the clientele obviously sophisticated and monied.

Sienna sat back in her seat, trying to stave off the sense of panic. She felt as though she'd stepped into a completely foreign world, and she had no idea what she was doing here. Despite the temptation to stay, she had a stronger urge, albeit brief, to beg Raul to take her to the airport instead.

But Alejandro…

Her stomach flip-flopped so she gripped the handle in the car door, frowning a little as her eyes continued to run over the streetscape without taking in any of the details now.

It wasn't just Alejandro. It was Sienna too. She'd made this choice; she'd chosen to do this because she deserved it. She had never questioned her fate: marriage, as dictated by her father—only she'd long ago started to see her marriage as a form of revenge. He'd been seeking control, but she was going to take the money and use it in a way that he would *hate*. Her marriage was no longer a source of despair for Sienna, but a prospect she relished, because in making the match she could take back her power, could exercise control over her own life, in a way her dictatorial father would have never envisaged. But this was the ice cream on the cake. Another exercise of control, a way to walk her own path, to live her own life, away from the cloying confines of Hughenwood House.

Raul slowed the car, then turned into a side street, pulling to a stop in a driveway. A man in a suit appeared, a concierge.

'Good afternoon.' He opened the door for her.

'Hello.' She slipped into Spanish effortlessly.

'Would you show Senyor Corderó's guest to his apartment?'

'Of course.' The concierge gestured towards the doors—wide, glass, rimmed with thick gold frames.

'My bag.' She reached into the car but the concierge was faster, lifting it by the strap and holding it, so she couldn't help but notice how tatty her holdall was.

'Thank you.' She turned to Raul and smiled. 'I'll see you later.'

He nodded once. Was that scepticism in his eyes? Fair enough. She supposed the women he drove home didn't generally make repeat appearances.

Falling into step behind the concierge, she couldn't help the little gasp that escaped her lips when they entered the foyer. Polished white tiles covered the entire floor, then gave way to walls that were wallpapered in gold and white stripes, a ceiling that was ornately patterned, and enormous chandeliers that hung in a line across the room. The ceilings themselves were at least treble height, creating an elegant and enormous space.

All for a lobby!

There were vases too, copper, overflowing with flowers—as they passed she breathed in and their fragrance was almost intoxicating. Lilies, bluebells and jasmine were surrounded by glossy green foliage.

'Senyor Corderó's apartment is at the top. Did he provide you with a card?'

She stared at him blankly for a moment before she remembered that, yes, he had pressed something into her hand as she was leaving. She'd just been too flummoxed by the reality of what was happening to take it in.

'Oh, yes,' she agreed, nodding towards the bag. 'In there.'

The concierge passed the backpack over. She unzipped the front pocket and removed the piece of plastic.

'Swipe it here.' He indicated a slot, then stepped out of the lift. A second later, the doors pinged shut. She did as he'd said, then the lift was whooshing upwards. A mirror on the side wall caught her attention before she could realise it was there, and she saw the image she made and could only stare.

She looked…wild. Wanton. Her mother would definitely not approve. The thought brought a smile to her lips, a genuine one, because it was her secret, and yet the fact her mother wouldn't have approved—and wouldn't have believed it—was a definite silver lining. It was Sienna's life, her prerogative, and she loved knowing that she was doing something no one would have thought her capable of.

The doors pinged open, not into a corridor as she'd expected, but into a grandiose entrance foyer that gave way to a room positively bursting with light. The south-facing windows bathed the room in afternoon gold, the floor-to-ceiling glass showcasing a stunning outlook—of a large shrub-lined terrace and, beyond it, the varied roofs of the boulevard. Despite the fact her arrival was unexpected, the place was immaculate. In fact, it looked barely lived in. She grimaced at her rustic backpack once more, placing it by the door and trying not to register how out of place it was, before placing her sandals beside it and padding, barefoot, into the lounge room.

It expanded around her: huge, white, overwhelming, beautiful. Everything was the palest of wood or cream, except for a grand piano towards the left, which was dark and highly polished. She moved towards it and pressed a series of keys, wondering if Alejandro played or if it was purely decorative.

Somehow, she couldn't imagine him doing something so ordinary as playing the piano, and yet just imagining him sitting here, shirtless, bathed in the light of the moon, made her heart skip a beat.

There was nothing to do but explore, and so Sienna wandered from room to room, each decorated like a six-star hotel, with barely a hint of personal effects, so it took guesswork to establish which of the three bedrooms was actually Alejandro's—eventually she picked it because the bed was largest and there was, on closer inspection, a newspaper on the bedside table.

A small hint, but enough. She didn't linger in the room. It felt too invasive, despite what she'd come here for.

There were other rooms, which she supposed might have been bedrooms at one point, but which had been converted into other purposes, more suited to Alejandro. There was a state-of-the-art office, with screens mounted on the wall, a large, dark desk, and a leather armchair. It provided a view of the terrace, including the infinity pool in the corner. She stared at it with a deep yearning—how long had it been since she'd gone swimming? As girls, they'd always swum in the lake at Hughenwood House, but without the gardening staff, it had quickly become overgrown with lily pads and slimy algae, not safe to use any longer, and so the pursuit had been abandoned. The turquoise water of this pool looked irresistible.

She stepped out of his office, passing another room—a gymnasium with a boxing ring in the centre—and moved back into the lounge area, wishing she'd brought bathers with her. But why would she have?

She cast a glance about the penthouse somewhat guiltily and then, with another bright, defiant smile tilting her lips, Sienna disappeared onto the terrace, shedding clothes as she got closer and closer to the infinity pool.

CHAPTER SEVEN

HE'D CONCLUDED THE meeting as swiftly as he could, but that had still meant he was delayed by almost an hour, and it was only as Raul pulled up in front of his apartment building that Alejandro wondered what Sienna had been doing to keep busy. She had her phone, so perhaps she'd spent the time scrolling Instagram or similar, but something about that didn't fit right. For some reason, he couldn't see her as someone who spent a lot of time on social media. Reading a book? Writing emails? He frowned, wondering at how little he knew of her, and why that felt strange. He didn't exactly go around collecting the biographies of the women he slept with, so why should she be any different? Because the few things he *did* know about her had sparked a billion fresh questions, and Alejandro liked having answers to his questions.

He'd grappled with his guilt on the drive to the apartment. It still sat inside him, and he doubted it would ever shift—on some level, he was glad for that. To not feel bad for having betrayed his oldest friend would have spoken volumes about his character. He didn't want to hurt Luca. But this was no longer about his friend. Sienna was her own person, with her own autonomy. Alejandro couldn't refuse her simply because Luca had misread her character and needs.

He pushed into his apartment, looking around, frowning. For a moment, he thought she wasn't here, but her rucksack was by the door, as well as her strappy shoes. His eyes scanned the lounge area, and he moved through it, unbuttoning his shirt at the neck, rolling up the sleeves as he scanned the room for a clue of her whereabouts.

Curiosity growing, he continued to move through the apartment, room by room, until he passed his office and a movement, a splash, caught his eye.

He stopped walking.

And stared.

She was in the pool.

And going by the trail of clothes between him and the pool, she was naked.

Despite the fact they'd made love earlier that afternoon, desire burst through him like volcanic lava. He cut through his office, opening the French doors onto the terrace and startling her, apparently, with his abrupt arrival. Almost as though she hadn't expected him, as though she hadn't been swimming naked with the specific intent of tempting him…

'Alejandro.' She breathed his name, her body instantly heating in response despite the water lapping at her sides. Instinctively, she ducked down, so only her head and neck sat above the water's surface. It was no good, though. His eyes clung to her creamy breasts beneath the rippling water, feasting on their outline, so she expelled a soft breath, her eyes clinging to his.

'Well, this is a nice surprise,' he drawled.

She looked around desperately for her clothes—flung with careless non-concern across the tiles of the deck.

'I wasn't sure what time you'd be here,' she murmured. 'I thought much later, to be honest.'

'I'm disappointed. Are you telling me this display isn't to tempt me?'

Her eyes widened. Tempt him? 'Sorry to disappoint, but that didn't even occur to me.'

His laugh was soft and ran like melted butter across her skin. She shivered despite the heat of the afternoon.

'If you'll pass me a towel, I'll get out.'

'Get out?' He shook his head. 'I don't think so.' And with her eyes feasting on his body, he undressed, slowly, purposefully, as if he knew what torment the gradual reveal of his naked frame was doing to her equilibrium. In reality, it took him less than a minute to strip out of his shirt and trousers, but to her disappointment he left his boxers on, diving into the pool with a power that took her breath away. Seconds later, he was right where she was, lifting up just an inch away, his dark hair slicked back from his brow, his eyes glowing with a thousand shades of blue in the afternoon light.

'Much more fun to stay in together, no?'

There was so much she didn't know about him, but one thing she did was that his accent grew thicker when he was flirting. The words softened and ran over her like velvet, so her nipples tingled, silently begging for his touch.

'Definitely.'

Another laugh. 'I'm glad you agree.'

'This place is something else.'

He looked around the expansive terrace, as if seeing it from her eyes. 'I suppose so.'

'You're just used to it.' She pulled away from him, not because she wanted to, but because her body was heating with a need she couldn't control, and she knew, from recent experience, that physical distance was the only way to contain that. 'But, trust me, it's incredible.'

He was quiet, but she knew he was coming, following her, so that when she braced her elbows on the edge of the pool, looking down at the street below, he was right beside her in an instant. So much for distance. So much for *wanting* distance. Her traitorous body felt as though it were partly on fire, and she ached to reach out and touch him.

'When did you move here?' Talking was good. Talking distracted her. Sort of.

'I bought the place about six years ago, and I spend my time between here and Madrid.'

'You have a place there too?'

He nodded.

'As nice as this?'

A smile made his lips tilt off kilter. 'Different.'

'Ah. A man of mystery.'

'Always.'

'Tell me this, then.' She turned to face him, and he capitalised on her shift, pulling her closer, tucking his hands around her bottom and keeping them there. Her eyes dropped closed for an instant, because the sensation and intimacy of it was almost too much.

'*Si?*'

'Do you actually play the piano, or is it a prop to impress guests?'

He grinned. 'Do you think I'm the kind of man who gives a crap what anyone thinks of me?'

She tilted her head to the side, considering that. 'No.'

'So you already have your answer.'

'When did you learn?'

She was making conversation simply because she was nervous, but at the same time she found she was truly interested in understanding him. It should have been a warning, but Sienna was beyond the point of heeding those. 'At school.'

Another thing she knew about Alejandro—he brushed aside questions he didn't want to answer. He acted as though they didn't matter, yet that was a tip that they really did.

'Do you enjoy it?'

He considered that. 'I suppose so. I never thought about it in those terms. It's simply something I do.'

'I'd like to hear you play.'

'Why?'

'Because I imagined you playing when I walked into your sky palace and saw the piano, and, I have to admit, my imagination found the image kind of sexy.'

He laughed. 'I see.'

'What do you play?' She lifted a hand to his hair when she found she could no longer stop herself from touching him. Her fingers ran through its length, her eyes following the gesture, then her hand fell to his shoulder, warm and smooth, strong and fascinating.

'Classical music.'

'Not rock?'

He shook his head. 'Not often.'

'That's strange. You definitely strike me as more Metallica than Mozart.'

'Perhaps in some ways.'

'A penchant for black leather pants?'

'On some people.'

She looked away, cheeks flaming. He wasn't talking about *her*. Leather pants would make her bottom look the size of Alaska, and then some.

He caught her chin, drawing her face back towards him. 'You don't approve?'

'It's not really my thing.' Oh, dear. Her voice sounded so prim—and she definitely wasn't that. She forced a smile to lessen the impact. 'But I dare say most of the women you, um, bring back here...'

A small line formed between his brows when he frowned, and she stared at it, fascinated. But she didn't want to talk about his ex-lovers, nor to really even think about them. They were irrelevant.

'Actually, I don't bring women to my home.'

She blinked at him, surprised and, she hated to admit it, a little flattered. 'Why not?'

'Because they either have homes of their own, or hotel rooms, or because I'm travelling myself.' He lifted his shoulders. 'These circumstances are quite rare.'

'I can rent a hotel room,' she said immediately, pride firing to life. 'That was always my plan, if you were to agree—'

'It makes no sense.' He waved aside the offer. 'My place is big enough to share.'

Her heart skipped a beat. Share. Why did that word sound so…romantic? She pushed the word aside. Romance had nothing to do with it. This was a week of sexploration and nothing more. To prove her point, she closed the distance between them completely, pressing her naked breasts to his chest, moving her hips slightly beneath the water. His only response was a slight dilation of his pupils, and a hardening of his cock against her belly. She dug her nails into his shoulder a little, need flashing white-hot through her.

'And I won't stay long,' she said quietly, still not ruling out the idea of leaving for a hotel the next day.

He lifted his shoulders. 'I work long hours.' His hands moved from her bottom, one straying to her hip, the other finding the sensitive flesh of her sex and exploring it slowly, before sliding a finger inside her moist core. She moaned softly. 'It is only the nights when we will see one another—and these, I believe we have agreed, we will enjoy spending together.'

'Yes,' she whimpered, not sure what she was responding to, only that the word felt perfectly, perfectly right. He withdrew his finger, his eyes watching her, looking at her, and the power of his gaze was its own aphrodisiac, so pleasure built inside her, warm and irresistible, euphoria-inducing.

'You are beautiful when you're close to coming.'

She shook her head instinctively. She didn't need the

flattery. Beauty wasn't something she'd ever aspired to, and it wasn't an adjective she needed to hear employed. 'Just don't stop,' she ground out, moving her hips down, inviting him, needing him.

He made a throaty sound—a laugh?—and moved faster, so she tilted her head back, riding a wave, as he kissed the sensitive flesh at the base of her neck, sucking her there, marking her, so a thrill of pleasure ran the length of her spine along with the deluge of release that was racking her body. 'I feel as though I've died and gone to heaven,' she said honestly, when she could breathe again, and string at least a few words together.

'Don't die,' he responded with a grin. Her hand moved beneath the water, and the sensation was heightened by nerve endings that were over-stimulated. She brushed her fingertips over his arousal, rock-hard against the wet fabric of his underpants. She was shy, of course, because she had no experience with this, but at the same time she was emboldened by what they'd shared, and by the proof she'd just felt that he was as into her as she was to him. 'I want you.'

His eyes widened. 'I know.'

She should have been embarrassed; she wasn't.

'And? Are you going to do anything about it?'

'Soon.' He leaned forward, kissing her slowly, and she relaxed into the kiss, their bodies melded, his hardness against her belly a reminder that this was just the beginning.

'Now?'

Another laugh. 'Not without protection.'

She pulled back, staring at him, startled that she'd forgotten something so basic. 'I didn't even think—'

His shrug was nonchalant. 'You're not used to having to consider such things.'

'No, but still…'

'It's fine.'

She bit down on her lip. 'I'm on the pill.'

'You told me that. Since when?'

'Um, about a day after we—'

He lifted a brow. 'Because you thought this might happen?'

'Because I thought I should be more prepared.'

'Ah.' His smile sent butterflies rampaging through her stomach.

'I just meant, if you wanted, we could—'

He scanned her face, his eyes moving slowly, and then he shook his head. 'There is still a risk of conceiving, and I am not prepared to take any chances. Double protection is better.'

'You really must not want kids,' she said with a hint of humour, to cover her disappointment. Not about children, of course, but because her desire was so strong she found she didn't much fancy waiting—even a short while.

'I don't want to make a woman pregnant.'

She frowned. 'Isn't that the same thing?'

'No.'

'So you do want children, just not unplanned ones?'

'I wouldn't say that, either.'

She laughed huskily. 'You're not making any sense, but that's okay. I don't really need you to explain it to me.'

He nodded, but there was thoughtfulness in his gaze, and a moment later he continued. 'I don't want children, under any circumstances, because I believe a child should be raised by two parents, wherever possible. And I'm not interested in that kind of relationship. Up until a few months ago, I would have said that outlook was one of the many things Luca and I have in common.'

'Oh?'

But he compressed his lips, turning to face the view rather than expand on that thought. Only Sienna was just as protective of Olivia as Olivia was of Sienna, and she wasn't ready to let the matter drop. 'I know he's dated a heap of women. Actresses, models and the like.'

Alejandro made a grunting noise of agreement.

'So I guess leopards can change their spots after all.'

'Some can, evidently.' He turned to face her, pinning her with eyes that seemed to bore right through her soul. 'But not me.'

Something cool stole through her, replacing the warmth he'd so easily flared in her body. 'Do you think he's really changed?'

Alejandro's eyes narrowed. 'You're worried about your sister?'

'Wouldn't you be?'

'Not for one second.'

'But you just said…'

'Luca isn't the kind of man who would do anything half-heartedly. They're married. It's quite clear he loves her.'

Sienna turned, her eyes landing on the street below, uncertainty a spiral in her belly. 'They do *seem* happy.'

'But you are not convinced.'

She kept her gaze averted, wondering at the way she felt as though she could speak so freely to Alejandro, given that they barely knew one another. Was it his friendship with Luca? Or the fact that they'd agreed this would be over in a few nights?

'Did Luca tell you about the will?'

'What will?'

That, then, was her answer. 'Our father's.'

'I only know your father is not alive because he wasn't at the wedding, and when I mentioned it to Luca he said, very matter-of-factly, that he's dead. In fact, he said "The bastard is dead", so I presume there is bad blood between your sister and father.'

Sienna's smile was like ice. 'You could say that.'

'And this somehow impacts their marriage?'

Her eyes lifted to his and she tried to work out if it was madness to confide in him, but something drew her closer, making it impossible to shut the conversation down. 'Perhaps it's better if I explain how my father's will affects me,' she said thoughtfully. It was the middle ground, allowing her to speak openly, without betraying her sister. 'You can draw your own conclusions as to Luca and Olivia and my…concerns.'

But where to begin? Her father's arcane beliefs were almost impossible to express. They were so divorced from any kind of reality, Sienna felt a familiar flush of shame that she experienced whenever she was forced to admit the implications of the legal arrangements.

'My parents' marriage wasn't what you'd describe as happy. They met when my mother was really young, Dad was almost twenty years older. She was an actress and used to being adored. She was, of course, very beautiful.' Sienna kept any hint of bitterness from her voice—she'd long ago grown accustomed to the genetics lottery and how it had skipped her. 'My father doted on her, I gather, in the early days. But she was young, and she made a mistake.'

'A mistake?'

'An affair,' Sienna filled in the gap. 'It was with some director she'd known before she met Dad. She regretted it.'

'They seem to have told you a lot about their private lives.'

'Screamed it at the top of their lungs, more like, during fights.' She angled a face at him, a soft, sad smile catching on her lips. 'He never forgave her. But not only did he not forgive her, he didn't let her go. He hated her, but he also loved her, in a sick, unhealthy kind of way, so he would criticise her and demean her, controlled all the family's finances so she had no ability to travel or do anything without asking him for money.'

'Why did she stay?'

'Because she "loved" him.' Sienna lifted her fingers to do air quotations, showing her cynicism for the idea of love.

'You think love is a lie?'

'I think it's a flawed concept,' she corrected. 'How can you love someone if you don't also respect them enough to treat them well? How can you love someone if you don't want to make them happy?'

'And she was unhappy?'

'We all were.' Her lips tightened into a grimace. 'They fought often, and when they weren't fighting, he was giving her the silent treatment, so we were all trying our best to walk on eggshells, hoping to avoid sparking the next outburst. And walking on eggshells is not something I'm very good at.' Her brows furrowed. 'I used to try to ease the tension, to get everyone talking, or, better yet, laughing, but it never helped. Olivia was much better at reading the room than me. She knew when to keep her head down, when to make herself scarce.'

'And you didn't?'

'I *did* run away a lot.'

'Seriously?'

'Well, no.' Now a genuine smile softened her features. 'I ran, but only to Gertie's house.'

'Gertie?'

'The woman who's looking after my dog. You met her at the wedding. She's Andrew's grandmother, and she lives just over a field from Hughenwood House—our family property. I used to go to her house when things got bad, and she'd make me scones and biscuits and cake and tea with three lumps of sugar, all of the treats Mum had banned from the house in an effort to stay looking perennially young.' She rolled her eyes. 'Gertie would let me hide out for a while, talk it out, then send me home with a piece of cake wrapped in a napkin. She was my saviour as a kid.'

'And you're still close?'

'Very.' Sienna tilted her head back, wetting her hair, then pulled it over her shoulder. For a moment, she'd forgotten she was stark naked, but the moment her hair collided with her breast she startled, fighting a ridiculous urge to cover herself. 'I wanted to go to uni, but it wasn't possible. Gertie introduced Andrew and me and he created a spot in his charities team. It's been an amazing experience.'

'I can imagine.' Was that cynicism in his voice? Of course not. She ignored the doubt, running a finger over the pool's coping.

'Anyway. My father passed away when I was eleven. It was completely unexpected—a heart attack. And Mum, rather than being able to start living her life again, was restricted because of his bloody will. I actually don't even know how the bloody thing is legal, but Andrew's looked into it for me, and apparently it's airtight.'

His features gave nothing away. 'Tell me about it.'

She sucked in a deep breath. 'Well, basically, Mum didn't inherit anything from Dad. He was such a bastard to her, right to the very end. His estate pays a small stipend, and she's entitled to live in Hughenwood House until we turn twenty-five or get married. Once we get married, so long as we do so before we turn twenty-five, the house passes to us, as well as a financial settlement.'

His features tightened into a mask of steel. 'Let me repeat that, to be sure I've understood. You are saying that your father died when you were just a girl, but somehow he saw fit to make sure you would be denied any inheritance unless you were married?'

She nodded once.

'What if you have no interest in marrying?'

'Which, given what I grew up experiencing, I don't, particularly.'

'Right. And so?'

'But in order to inherit, I must.'

He compressed his lips. 'Then screw it. Walk away from the money.'

'I can't do that.'

'Why not? You'd rather take the money even when it means allowing your father to dictate this to you from beyond the grave?'

'I'd rather take the money than let him win.'

'Isn't marrying for the sake of the will handing him that victory?'

Her eyes sparked with his. 'No.'

'Why not?'

'Because of what I intend to do with the money.'

'Which is? Burn him in effigy a thousand times over?'

'Something much more satisfying,' she promised. 'I'm going to donate the money—all of it—to a charity that works with domestic violence survivors, enabling them to start over.'

He considered that for several beats. 'As revenge on your father?'

'When I'm feeling mature, I think of it as simply doing the right thing.'

Alejandro's eyes scanned hers, probing her, reading her, and she thought, for a moment, that he was going to say something, but he held himself back, lifting a finger to her cheek instead, the contact sending a thousand shock waves through her body. 'And you believe this is why my friend married your sister?'

'Oh, I know it's why they married. The question is, is it why they're *still* married?'

'I do not believe so.'

'No?'

'Luca told me he loves her. He told me he would die for her. In fact, he told me that it is only since meeting your sister he has realised that he was never really living at all. I believe him fully capable of marrying a woman to help her escape poverty and oppression, but not to gilding the lily to that extent. He loves her, *querida*. He would not lie to me about this, or anything.' And for a moment, the light went out in Alejandro's blue eyes, so they looked almost grey, and tension flooded his body.

Sienna didn't take too much notice. She expelled a soft breath, relief wrapping around her. 'I hope you're right.'

'I am.' And after a small pause, a brief hesitation, he kissed her, gently, the warmth from the sun and the water and his lips pushing all unpleasant thoughts from her mind, leaving only, for a little while, happiness.

CHAPTER EIGHT

'CORDERÓ.' HE ANSWERED the call without checking who was ringing, not wanting to risk the buzzing of his phone waking Sienna, who'd only fallen asleep a while earlier. He cast her a glance as he slipped from the room, her red hair spread like flames across his crisp white pillows, her body naked, half concealed by the sheet, one leg sticking out tempting him to go back to bed, to begin kissing her on her toes and working his way up...

But it was late, and she must be exhausted, given how they'd spent the last few hours.

He pulled the door closed softly behind him, moving into the corridor and towards the kitchen, as the voice on the other end of the line spoke.

'Alex, how are you?'

He stopped walking, closing his eyes on a wave of guilt.

'Luca. Fine. You?'

'Yeah, all good. I haven't had a chance to check in with you since the wedding. We've been busy.'

'You're on your honeymoon, I hope I'm the last thing on your mind.'

'Right.' Luca's laugh was natural and relaxed, so even if Sienna's revelations the afternoon before had given Alejandro a moment's worry, the sound of his friend's voice alleviated it completely.

'I wanted you to be one of the first to know: Olivia's pregnant.'

Alejandro reached for the coffee grinds and scooped some into his pot, adding water then placing it on top of the stove, the words dropping through him like stones. Marriage. And now children? 'Who are you and what have you done with Luca?'

'What do you mean?'

'You sound happy.'

'I am.'

Alejandro braced his palms on the counter, his gaze lazily tracing another scar, which ran from his thumb across the back of his hand down to his wrist. That one had been from a flick knife. 'Then so am I.'

'I'll take that as congratulations.'

'As it was intended.'

'I also wanted to thank you.'

'What for?' Alejandro reached for a small cup, moving towards the stove and watching as flames licked the sides of the coffeepot.

'For taking care of Sienna at the wedding. Olivia's very protective of her, which means I am too, and their mother is such a bitch. She's a beautiful girl. I hated seeing her so tense at the wedding.'

Alejandro closed his eyes on another roll of guilt. Tell him the truth. Tell him it was your pleasure. That, actually, it went beyond just looking after her. Tell him Sienna isn't his responsibility, that she can make her own decisions in life, that what they were doing was none of Luca's business.

'Sure.'

'Don't sound so happy about it.'

Alejandro frowned, not liking the implication of that, but not knowing how to defend himself—and Sienna—without being frank about exactly how happy he'd been. 'It was no problem,' he tried again. 'I enjoyed meeting her.'

'Good. You'll probably see a bit more of her, given that you're both going to be godparents to our first child.'

'What?'

'You can skip being my best man, but not my child's godfather. Sorry, it is not negotiable.'

Guilt was now a full-blown explosion at the base of his chest. He'd known Sienna would be someone he'd see, from time to time, in some capacity, given her connection to Luca, but sharing godparent duties?

He flicked off the flames abruptly, reaching for the pot and filling his cup with the dark, fragranced liquid. 'I'm not religious.'

'You are a good man. The best man I know. There is no one I would rather have guiding my child in times of darkness. You know that.'

Guilt clawed through him. 'Have you told Sienna yet?'

'No. Why? Do you want to do it?' Luca laughed, apparently oblivious to the slip Alejandro had just made—a question that had made it seem he, Alejandro, was in ongoing contact with Sienna.

'I was just curious.' Lying was not something Alejandro did well. It was not something he had done in a very long time, since he'd been forced into stealing food to survive. He hated this, and he particularly hated lying to Luca. But the situation was too messy to see a way out of. Besides, Sienna had sworn him to secrecy. Even if he wanted to tell Luca what was going on, he couldn't without betraying her trust. And so what was his option? To betray Luca's trust instead?

'Olivia's going to wait until they catch up next month. She wants to do it in person.'

'Got it.'

'So if you should happen to run into her, mum's the word.'

'Why is Olivia so protective of Sienna?'

The question was out before he could stop it. He winced, wishing he hadn't asked it, but at the same time he stood very still, awaiting the response.

'Typical older sister stuff.' There was a note of restraint in Luca's voice and Alejandro understood. There was more his friend wasn't saying, secrets he considered private, shared between a wife and her husband. In some ways, it alleviated Alejandro's guilt a little, because if Luca could have secrets, so could Alejandro. Except Luca was simply protecting his wife's privacy, whereas Alejandro was indulging his ravenous libido because opportunity had come knocking. Because no woman since Sienna had been able to inspire his interest, and he'd been at risk of turning into stone until she came into his office with her very attractive proposition.

So what? That justified this?

But when he remembered the way she'd looked at him, the hope shimmering in her eyes, the uncertainty and raw, unshaped desire, he knew he'd make the same decision every single time. It might be wrong, it might be a betrayal of Luca, but it was, in so many other ways, completely right.

'Anyway, I just wanted to let you know. Our family's growing.'

Our family. That was what they were—like brothers. 'Congratulations, Luc. I'm truly thrilled for you.'

He disconnected the call and dropped the phone onto the benchtop as though it were a venomous snake primed to bite him. He carried his coffee onto the terrace, gravitating towards the swimming pool, remembering how she'd looked in the water, and as he'd lifted her out of it, her creamy skin glossed by moisture, little droplets running over her that he chased with his tongue as he carried her to one of the sun loungers, placing her down on it and kissing her until she was a pool of desire beneath him. Her responsiveness was the hottest thing he'd ever known. She melted when he touched her, and he sparked into flame and fire.

So how did he stop what they were doing from destroying his relationship from Luca?

It didn't matter that Luca would never know. Alejandro had to draw up his own boundaries, to make sure he was able to defend his actions, if the time ever came. So how did he do that?

By making sure he was looking after Sienna. Treating her well. And being completely honest with her, which he had been, right from the start. This was no prelude to love. There was no relationship in the offing, for either of them. Neither wanted that. But he had to make sure she didn't forget. He had to make sure the lines stayed in place, and that they both respected them. And when the week was over, he would move on, once and for all. No more fantasising about her. No more wanting her. And definitely no contacting her. Hers was one number that wouldn't be making it into Alejandro's little black book.

Light streamed into the palatial bedroom, waking Sienna some time before seven. She stretched in bed, languid and relaxed, her hands reaching out on autopilot for Alejandro, wanting him in a way that made her blush, particularly given how they'd spent most of the night before. How was it possible she craved him again already? Her hand ran over her nipples and she breathed out heavily, desire snaking through her. Where was he? She sat up, holding the sheet above her breasts, scanning the room. It was clear he wasn't there; the attached bathroom was silent. Frowning, she pushed her feet out of bed, standing, wrapping the sheet around her as an afterthought as she moved through the bedroom and into the corridor, ears straining for some sight or sound of him.

He was in the kitchen, eating a piece of toast. She

paused, watching him for a moment before he became aware of her and looked up, his eyes roaming her with undisguised hunger.

'Good morning.'

'Bon dia.'

'You speak Catalan instead of Spanish?'

'I speak both.' His eyes narrowed. 'You're familiar with the languages?'

'Spanish,' she murmured, her stomach flipping and flopping as she drew closer. She'd studied languages voraciously as a teen—Spanish, French, Italian and German, anything to blot out the silence and tension of her home life. 'Not Catalan. Want to teach me?'

'In a few days? Perhaps a few phrases.'

She ignored the odd lurching feeling at his reference to a few days. It was what they'd agreed. 'I'm an excellent student.'

'And yet, there are other things I'd prefer to help you learn.'

Heat flushed through her. 'Ah.'

'You are also an excellent student of those.' He reached out, dislodging the sheet, his eyes lightly mocking as the fabric rustled to the floor. 'Better.' His approval sent a tingle of warmth through her body.

'I didn't know where you were. Or if there'd be staff around.'

'No staff. I like my privacy.'

She expelled a sigh. 'So who keeps the place this clean?'

'I live by myself, and work long enough hours to mean I'm rarely here. It's not hard.'

There were so many questions she wanted to ask him. Out of nowhere, Sienna wondered what it would have been like if they'd met differently. If he weren't Luca's friend, and if she hadn't resolved, a long time ago, that her husband would be someone gentle and soft, someone completely non-threatening—the exact opposite to her father. But even if that were the case, she wasn't the kind of woman he usually went out with. He'd have bored of her way, way too soon, and she'd likely have been left broken-hearted, if she were ever stupid enough to give him her heart. This was definitely for the best.

'You're wearing a suit.'

He glanced down at his arms then returned his blue-grey eyes to her face. 'You're observant.'

She rolled her eyes. 'Don't tease.'

'But it's so fun.' He snaked out a hand and caught her at the waist, pulling her towards him. 'Will you still be naked tonight?'

'Waiting for you in the pool, you mean?'

'Excellent.' He nodded.

She laughed softly. 'That was not intended as a confirmation.'

He tilted her face up. 'That won't stop me imagining. Dreaming.'

'Hoping?'

'I never hope on other people's actions.'

'Too much room for disappointment?'

'Something like that.'

'You're a cynic.'

'Yes.'

Her breath was growing thick, hard to control, and her lungs hurt from the effort, as though she'd run a marathon.

'Raul's number is on the fridge.' His hand rose to her breast, stroking it possessively. 'Call him if you'd like to go anywhere in particular.'

She blinked, the desire he was invoking so easily at war with the words he was speaking. 'You're leaving?' It was the only conclusion.

'Yes.'

'So early?'

'This isn't early for me. It's when I always leave.'

And he wasn't about to change his plans for her. Message received. 'Got it.' She smiled, even when a strange lurching feeling gripped her stomach.

But he didn't leave. He stood there, touching her, looking at her, and she knew he was as tempted as she was. At least, she guessed he was, but after a moment he broke away, turning back to the kitchen and retrieving his jacket. He shrugged into it with all the panache of a male model.

'Text if you need anything.'

'I won't.'

He frowned. 'Good.' He hesitated again. Why? She wished she understood him better. 'I'll see you tonight.'

Not 'this afternoon'. Not even 'later'. Tonight. As in, after dark. For sex.

Just as they'd agreed.

She smiled brightly. 'Sounds good to me. See you later!'

There were approximately four million things Sienna would prefer to do than shop, particularly in a high-end place like the Passeig de Gràcia, but the simple fact was she was in need of clothes. She'd brought only enough for one night's stay, and though she could—and would—avail herself of the laundry facilities in Alejandro's apartment, there was also a feminine instinct flaring to life inside her, a desire to look her best, to absolutely wow him.

She strolled the street in the early afternoon sun, succumbing to an ice-cream vendor halfway down, choosing a small cone and eating it as she walked, the warmth of the day wrapping around her as the ice cream sought to bring cool and refreshment. She smiled, for no reason except that, in that moment, she felt abuzz with contentment. How could she not? Alejandro had set parts of her soul on fire that she hadn't even known existed, so for a moment she was able to push aside the worries that usu-

ally dogged her—worries that now included Olivia and
her marriage. While their financial situation was considerably improved—Olivia had ploughed money into
a bank account for Sienna and given her a credit card
linked to it, telling her it was hers to do with what she
wanted—Sienna still couldn't help but wonder if Olivia's
marriage had come at too high a price.

Only Alejandro's voice was there, soothing those worries away, reminding her of what Luca had said, of his
claim to love Olivia. And Sienna smiled, because it was
impossible not to believe Alejandro, and if he was right,
then it meant Olivia had got everything she wanted and
deserved in life.

And Sienna?

Her marriage wouldn't be about love. She didn't want
to run the risk of that. Oh, she was happy for Olivia, but
falling in love—real, genuine, everlasting love—was like
betting on a lightning strike landing at your feet. She
wasn't going to risk her future happiness to something
so unpredictable.

And sex?

Her heart skipped a beat, because a month ago the idea
of a sexless, loveless marriage had seemed reassuringly
practical. But now that Alejandro was bringing her to life,
waking her up, she wondered if she could go back. Would
she be satisfied without making love to her husband?

And what if her husband didn't invoke these same feelings in her? What if this was exceptionally good sex? She
had no point of reference, but it was very easy to believe
that Alejandro was a master at all that he did.

The thought stirred colour in her cheeks and she
ducked between the doors of a department store with
her head lowered, losing herself in the racks of nonde-
script clothes for the afternoon and trying not to think

about Alejandro's mastery over her body—and how any other man might pale in comparison, even her husband...

'I thought we agreed you'd be naked.' His voice caught her completely off guard, but not her body. It flooded with hormones as though it had been waiting for him and was finally at ease.

She spun slowly, turning away from the glass windows that framed a view of the dusk-hued sky, her pulse throbbing when she saw him, so handsome in his suit, the way he looked at her sending a thousand sparks through her body.

'I've been out all afternoon. It didn't feel appropriate.'

He smiled appreciatively. 'Perhaps not. Though Barcelona is a very free society. Expression of self is encouraged.' His gaze raked her figure. 'However, I do like being the only man who's seen you naked.'

Heat at the possessive intent of his words spun through her like mini tornados.

'Even if that does puzzle me.' He was walking towards her, eyes hooked to hers, the look of intent only intensifying as he drew closer.

Her breath snagged in her throat, but she didn't take the easy path and look away; she couldn't. She was mesmerised by him.

'What does?'

'You're a very sexy, beautiful woman.' His fingers threaded beneath the straps of her dress, sending goosebumps running across her flesh. 'Surely there must have been times when you wanted to understand your body better.'

Her cheeks glowed. His fingers slid the dress down further. She shivered at the touch, so light, but somehow with the strength of a thousand thunderclaps.

'When I was a teenager, I had a few boyfriends, if you could call them that. Mum watched Olivia like a hawk—

she was the beautiful one, the one Mum worried would be getting all the attention. Apparently, she didn't think there was much risk of that with me.'

His fingers crept to her back, unlatching her bra, so she forgot what she was saying. Even the feeling of it dropping away from her skin sent shock waves through her. Her nipples, so sensitive from last night's attention, tingled without having been so much as touched.

'So you were able to sneak around a little?' he prompted.

'A very little.' She bit down on her lip, memories of that time in her life unpleasant and troubling. 'It's really not worth discussing.'

But Alejandro wasn't someone to be easily put off the scent. 'Humour me.'

'What do you want to know?' She sighed dramatically. 'My first kiss? A truly disastrous experience that was more like eating eel than anything romantic. So much tongue and wetness.' She shuddered for effect. 'My second kiss was not much better. I felt as though he was trying to eat my face off.'

Alejandro's amusement was in the depths of his eyes, but there was also a tightness there. 'And your third and fourth kisses? Tell me you did not stop at two, *querida*?'

'Third was marginally better.' Hence, she'd allowed things to progress to the point he'd observed her cantaloupe-sized breasts and all the criticism her mother had poured into her teenage brain had flared to life, too big to ignore.

'And?'

'And what?'

'It was a better kiss, but it stopped there?'

She hadn't expected such a direct question. She opened her mouth then closed it, shaking her head. 'Does it matter?'

'You're humouring me, remember?'

'No, you're interrogating me.'

'Yes. But I promise I'll make it worth your while, later.'

Later. 'No, now,' she demanded, surprising him, so he laughed, a low, husky sound, before dropping his lips, kissing her with the kind of mastery she could never have known existed until a month ago. She trembled against him, wanting him with all of herself, needing him in a way that she was smart enough to know was terrifying, because this was temporary and the need couldn't be allowed to take hold of her.

He pulled away, leaving her head spinning, and her heart thumping, his hands curving around her buttocks, holding her close to him, so she could feel the strength of his arousal. 'I have wanted you all day. I have been hard for you, waiting for this moment. But all day, there has been a question too, getting louder and louder, and I would like to know the answer.'

'But why?'

'So I can understand you.'

'Do you need to understand me? That sounds like boyfriend talk and that's definitely not what this is.'

A frown flickered across his handsome face. 'No, it's not.' Her heart twisted at his quick admission. 'But it's who I am. I need to know things, to get how they work.'

'I'm a thing now?' She joked to cover the strange blade of hurt pressing against her side.

'You're a person, but your issues are a thing.'

'How do you know this is an "issue"?'

'Because you're incredibly sensual. I cannot comprehend how you've denied this part of yourself for so long.'

Her stomach was in knots, desire at war with shame—yes, she felt shame, despite the fact she was now a grown woman who understood that her mother had bullied her all her life. Academic understanding of a situation didn't erase its impact—if only that were so!

'Of course, you don't understand. Look at you, Alejandro! Then look at me. There's no big mystery here.'

To his credit, he appeared to be genuinely lost. 'I don't understand.'

'You probably never went through an awkward teenage phase. I did. When Olivia hit adolescence, she went up. I went out. I put on weight, and got these huge breasts, and my mum—' But how to describe Angelica's particular brand of parenting? 'Let's just say, she didn't foster a healthy body image in anyone.'

Alejandro was still looking as though it didn't make any sense to him. 'But you were a teenager.'

'So?'

'So…' He shrugged in a way she found beyond sexy. 'Hormones, development, bodies change.'

'It's not just about my body. It's everything. My hair, my freckles, I'm the antithesis of my mother. Olivia was cast in her image and I'm some kind of throwback to my father's Irish grandmother.'

'Your hair is like flame.'

'It's okay. I've made my peace with my appearance.'

'What is there to make peace with?'

She stared at him, bemused. It was almost as though he genuinely didn't see how unglamorous she was. 'I looked you up online. I've seen the kind of women you usually date. I'm nothing like them. Please, don't treat me like an idiot and act as though you haven't noticed.'

'And do you think I'm not attracted to you?' He pushed his body forward, reminding her of the physical evidence of his desire.

'I don't know what I'm saying,' she said honestly, after a beat. 'But you asked and it's not an easy question to answer without unravelling all sorts of things I prefer not to think about.'

'Your mother criticised your appearance so often and

so easily that you began to believe it. You still believe it. It robbed you of confidence, so you didn't want to share yourself with a partner.'

Her lips parted at the accuracy of his assessment, and she heard herself admit something she'd wanted to keep private. 'There was one time.' She swallowed past a lump of bitter hurt. 'The third kiss. I liked him. But he—'

Alejandro tensed—as though bracing for her to confess something terrible, so she shook her head, quickly reassuring him.

'It wasn't serious. It's just, he—' She forced herself to be honest, and even to smile, because the passage of time helped her see the inept words in a different light. 'He compared my breasts to melons and I never quite got over that imagery.'

'Melons?' Alejandro stared at her.

'I know it sounds stupid.'

He frowned, his eyes probing hers.

Heat flooded her face. 'Cantaloupes, okay. He grabbed them in his hands and said, "These are the most terrific things, like ripe, juicy cantaloupes," and all I could think of was how huge and…fruit-like… I was like a big, chubby berry. Needless to say, it killed my buzz.' She bit down on her lip. 'If it had just been his comment, I might have ignored it, but for years I'd had my mother in my ear, pointing out my many flaws at every opportunity, so whatever confidence I had was shattered into a million tiny pieces.'

He was quiet for so long that she found her eyes lifting to his face. He was very still, his features locked in a mask that she couldn't interpret. 'And you were how old?'

She lifted her shoulders, imitating nonchalance, as though she couldn't remember precisely. 'Seventeen, I think.'

'And he was…?'

'Nineteen.'

Alejandro swore. 'Your breasts are beautiful.' He cupped them gently, reverently, holding them as his eyes drilled into her soul. '*You* are beautiful.' He leaned forward, kissing the tip of her nose, then drifting to her mouth. 'Your hair, your freckles, your eyes, every Irish throwback part of you—whatever cruel lies your mother has fed you over the years, you must know the truth by now.' He teased the side of her lips, then moved his mouth to her shoulder.

'It's just something I accept,' she said after a beat. 'I can't change who I am, so why get upset about it?'

'Are you trying to tell me that you remained a virgin because you didn't feel attractive enough to believe anyone would want you?'

She heard the question, the way he'd distilled her worst fears into a neat little box and placed it between them—a box that was morphing into a bomb, silently ticking, growing closer to detonating.

Oh, great.

Tears sparkled on her lashes. 'You could never understand.'

'That's true. I can't understand. All teenagers go through an awkward phase, but it's fleeting.'

'Are you saying even you were hit by hormones and puberty?'

He dipped his head once in agreement. 'But your mother should have supported you through that, encouraged you.'

'That's not really my mother's style.'

'Olivia?'

'Olivia is a wonderful, supportive older sister.' Her smile, though, was tight. She wanted to break off the conversation, but at the same time her body refused to move. She stayed where she was, feet planted by his, feeling his warmth and nearness and taking comfort from it. 'She has always wanted to fight my battles for me, but we're so different. She loves me but I often think she doesn't understand me.'

'No?'

'She is so poised, so completely in control of her thoughts and feelings—'

'Whereas you say exactly what you think.'

She bit down on her lower lip. 'It's a bad habit of mine.'

'It's one of the things I found irresistible about you, the night we met. You have no artifice, no pretence. You're completely authentic.'

'I think that's called unsophisticated,' she responded with a humorous lilt to her voice.

He caught her chin, lifting her face, surprising her with the dark emotion written across his features. 'Whenever I compliment you, you turn it into a negative. *That* is the only bad habit of yours I am aware of.'

She didn't deny it, nor did she apologise for it. 'It's hard to tune out the internal monologue seeded by my mother. I'm a work in progress.'

Sympathy spiralled through him. 'But she did not attack Olivia?'

'Olivia's life has been far from a walk in the park. Our mother hated her for different reasons.'

'Hate?'

She nodded slowly. 'Olivia is strikingly beautiful in the same way our mother is—and was. It's been hard for Mum to see Olivia blossoming, to realise that her own beauty is fading with age, while Olivia's is at its zenith.'

But apparently, he wasn't interested in Olivia. 'And you, she treated like an ugly duckling?'

Sienna winced because it was so completely accurate. How could he have understood so perfectly? She nodded once.

'What a fool.'

She lifted her shoulders. 'She has a narrow definition of beauty. I'm nowhere near it.'

'As I said, she is a fool.'

Her lips parted on a rush of hot breath, surprise and something else—it felt as if a part of her was waking, stirring to life. Before she could analyse it further, he was lifting her, carrying her cradled against his chest, down the corridor.

'What are you doing?'

'Isn't it obvious?'

She shook her head, though she had a pretty fair idea.

He shouldered in the bedroom door then placed her down at the edge of the bed. 'You are beautiful. Funny. Smart. Interesting.' He ticked each adjective off on a different finger, enumerating the list in a businesslike way. Nonetheless, each word struck her heart like an arrow, making her stronger, not weakening her. A smile played about her lips and then he was nudging her back onto the bed, his body following hers with the ferocity of a wild animal. His weight pressed to her, his hands pinned hers above her head.

'You deserve to be worshipped so often you never again doubt the veracity of what I've said. You deserve to be worshipped until you feel like a goddess.'

A shiver ran the length of her body and goosebumps chased after it. But she couldn't respond—there was no time to reply. He kissed her, hard, until her senses were on overload and surrender was the only option. Their coming together was a victory, a victory she felt in every cell of her body, a victory strong enough to rewrite, she suspected, some of her DNA, so that some of the wounds of her adolescence seemed to tremble, to fall away, leaving her with a sense of levity she hadn't known in a long time—if ever.

The desire to protect her was back. Though, of course, it had never left, only subsided a little, with every display of her strength of character and determination. But hearing her describe the relationship with her mother, the way that had shaped her view of herself, made him want to slap the older woman. Oh, he'd never physically hurt a woman, but the anger was the same. How dared she make Sienna feel like this? Wounds that had been inflicted in adolescence were clearly still a part of how Sienna viewed herself, through the lens of her mother's mistreatment.

Anger fired in his body, and a terrifying need to erase her pain. To make her smile for ever. To make it so that she could never again doubt the power of her appeal... But his own past was right there, hovering on the periphery of his mind, the darkness, the hurt, the pain, his inability to protect his mother; all the emotions were jagged edges threatening to enfold him. He pushed them aside, aware they'd never recede completely, but wanting to keep them at bay, at least for now. In this moment, there was pleasure, and they both deserved that.

CHAPTER NINE

SHE FOUND HIM the next morning, early, in the gymnasium. He stood in the centre of the boxing ring, punching the bag hard, rhythmically. Over and over until it shook uncontrollably. He was naked except for a pair of low-slung shorts, so she stood watching in awe of each rippling muscle beneath his bronzed, sheening skin as he moved swiftly, his feet almost dancing every time he repositioned himself.

He punched the bag as though he hated it. As though it were a vile beast and he the only person who could defend humanity against it. Again and again his fists pounded the black leather, his face a study in concentrated rage, and Sienna's awe, at some point, gave way to concern, so she took a step deeper into the room and cleared her throat. He punched the bag once more then dropped his hand, turning to face her, anger lining his eyes and mouth, so he turned away, reached for a towel and wiped his face, as if he wanted to hide the strength of that emotion from her.

She waited, heart pounding, a cascade of emotions rioting through her—admiration at the beauty of his physicality, the strength of his frame and musculature, but also unease, because she'd sensed something within him, something dark and untamed, that made her pulse run wild.

It wasn't that she was afraid. She was fascinated. The same desire to understand him ran through Sienna as he'd claimed to feel the day before. His body was perfection, and it had spent the night making hers soar, sending her into the heavens again and again, but it was also, undeniably, a weapon, capable of inflicting great harm.

She eyed his scars with renewed interest. A beer bottle had caused the one on his chest. But what about the mark on his hip? And the scar on the back of his hand? There was a chink in his nose too, as though it had been broken, possibly more than once.

'A hobby of yours?' She kept her voice light, somehow understanding he wouldn't tolerate her interrogation as well as she had his.

'Exercise.'

She moved closer, breathing in the masculine fragrance of the gym, her eyes locked to his, not looking away. She wasn't afraid of him. In fact, since meeting Alejandro, Sienna had felt emboldened in a new and exciting way—what else explained her decision to fly here and proposition him as she had? That same spirit of strength moved in her now.

'You seem angry.'

'I'm not.' It was clearly a lie.

She eyed the ring thoughtfully, then pushed apart the two middle ropes, stepping into it with her bare feet. She'd taken a moment to pull on one of his shirts, and she was glad, because she wanted to question him without the distraction of too much skin—his near nudity was distracting enough, but the way he looked at *her* made it impossible to think straight.

'I work out most mornings.'

'That explains this.' She lifted a finger, running it over his chest, feeling the ridges there, a sensual smile on her lips. She drifted her finger sideways then, catching the end of his scar, hovering her finger over it, watching him, so she saw the moment his eyes shuttered to her, pushing her away, blocking her out.

She ignored the uncertainty in her gut.

'You said it was a bottle?'

He made a grunting noise of agreement, but didn't move.

'And a drunk?'

This time he tilted his head in what she took to be a tight nod of agreement.

'And so you got good at fighting.'

His lips shifted as though he was grinding his teeth. 'It was necessary.'

'Why?'

His eyes bore into hers and for a moment she thought he wasn't going to answer. And when he spoke, his voice was completely wiped of emotion. 'Because, Sienna, when you live on the streets, being able to defend yourself is not optional.'

Confusion arrowed through her. 'You—went to school with Luca.'

He nodded. 'So?'

'It's a very exclusive school. That's how you met.'

'Yes.'

'And you also lived on the streets?'

He wiped his shoulders with the towel, stepping backwards and dislodging her contact.

But she was filled with curiosity and, suddenly, it was imperative that she know more. 'How do you go from being a street kid to attending a school like that? And why in England? And how did you end up on the streets? What happened to your parents?'

His smile was tight, and she knew he wasn't going to answer. 'So many questions for this time of the morning.'

She wasn't going to be pushed away, though. Part of his building her up the way he had the night before was renewed confidence, and she felt it in her bones. 'I want to understand you.' She threw his words back at him, making it obvious that she was simply going tit for tat.

'There is not much to understand.'

A half-smile curved her lips. 'You're right. Yours sounds like a perfectly typical childhood.'

He walked towards her with a look on his face that didn't invite further questions. His hand lifted to her—his—shirt, undoing the top button, a challenge in his eyes, a look of mockery playing about his lips, as though daring her to continue her line of questioning while he undressed her.

'Will you stay naked today?'

'Will you stay with me if I do?' She hadn't planned to ask that. It hadn't even occurred to her to ask, but she didn't regret the question. It seemed kind of fair.

'No.' His response was just as automatic. 'I can't.' He softened the rejection with a simmering look, and her heart completed an energetic somersault.

Why did he make her feel like the most beautiful woman in the world? She struggled to think straight when he touched her and, damn it, he knew it. Just the simple act of removing the shirt from her body caused her knees to tremble. Desire stirred in the pit of her stomach. She sank her teeth into her lower lip and when his eyes dropped to the gesture, she knew she was in trouble.

He crooked his finger, pulling her close, and she took the step—just one—with a throbbing, twisting feeling somewhere near her heart.

Their bodies brushed, hers naked, his practically, and she shivered all over now.

'Cold?' But a knowing look glinted in his eyes.

'I—'

Before she could answer, he lifted a hand to her nipple, rolling it between his forefinger and thumb. She felt it harden, felt arrows dart through her, and she tilted her head back, staring at the ceiling as stars flooded her eyes. His touch burned through her, and then his other hand moved between her legs, brushing her sex, so she jerked her face forward, her eyes haunted when they met his.

'You're trying to distract me,' she bit out from beneath clenched teeth, her own hands digging into his shorts, pushing them lower, then removing them until he stood completely naked.

He didn't deny her accusation, simply moved his fingers faster, so she was riding a wave, faster and faster, and she reached for his shoulders, digging her nails into the flesh there, until he brought his head down and kissed her, swallowing her enthusiasm, breathing it in. 'Am I?'

She didn't understand. She was drowning. Pleasure threatened to rip her apart at the seams.

'Alejandro…'

She felt him smile against her mouth, felt his hardness, and sheer longing was a blade in her side. She swore hungrily, pushing at his shoulders, hard, surprising them both, because he stumbled and then she was drawing him to the floor—or perhaps he was leading her, she couldn't tell; Sienna was no longer thinking straight, nor wobbly, she wasn't thinking at all.

He lay on his back and she straddled him, desperate hunger a beast within her.

He went to say something but she kissed him, turning the tables and devouring his words for a change as her body took him deep inside, her muscles tightening around him in eager, grateful welcome. She moved as her instincts dictated, her body's requirements shaping her movements, so she lifted and dropped and groaned as pleasure spun through her, and then Alejandro was moving his body, rolling her onto her back and pulling out of her, so she whimpered at his absence. Then his mouth connected with her sex and all of the pleasure she'd been feeling, all of the build-up, burst in one spectacular hail of stars. She tore her fingers through his hair, lifting her hips as wave after wave of warmth spread through her.

Afterwards, she lay in the centre of the boxing ring, eyes closed, breath rushed, for the several moments it took to pull herself back together, and then to realise that he hadn't experienced the same euphoric release she had. She pushed up onto her elbows, eyes open, one quick glance confirming that he was still rock-hard. She stared at him, confused, and undeniably hurt. It was so easy for her insecurities to creep in, even when he did such an amazing job of making her feel stunning and desirable.

'I— You—'

He moved closer to her, stroking her cheek, his own slashed dark with colour. She stared at him, fascinated, his beauty powerful enough to take her breath away. 'No, I didn't.'

'But—'

She couldn't ask the question that was whispering through her brain. *Didn't you want to?*

She swallowed instead, looked away. Gently, he drew her face back to his.

'I wanted to.' Had he read her mind? How did he know her secret fear? 'But I have never had unprotected sex with a woman, and, no matter how badly I wanted to lose myself in you just now, I will not take that risk.'

She stared at him, not understanding, until the penny finally dropped. She lifted a hand to her mouth, shock making speech, momentarily, impossible.

'I didn't even think—'

'No. You *felt*, and I love how much you feel.' His voice was like a purr, rolling over her skin. 'But I will never lose control in that way, *querida*, no matter how aroused I am.'

'Well, wild horses couldn't have stopped me, so I'm glad you have so much self-control.'

He laughed, unexpectedly. 'That's my job.'

'Why?'

'Because I have more experience with this.'

She considered that. 'So even when I feel as though I'm on the brink of losing my mind, you're still able to function as a rational human?'

His eyes narrowed, and something shifted between them. She couldn't say what, only she sensed a change in him, a tension that made little sense. 'Very slightly rational.'

'That doesn't make me feel any better.'

He kissed her softly. 'It should.' His thumb dragged across her lower lip. 'It just means I respect you enough to take care of you. Neither of us wants an ongoing complication from this.'

He stood up, his body still taut, extending a hand to her, offering her help to stand. She looked up at him, considering that for a moment, but instead she knelt. Her heart was thumping against her ribs so hard she was sure he must be able to hear it, or see it, but his eyes were on her face as she moved closer, her intention obvious to both of them. But would she have the courage to go through with it?

'I've never done this before, so pointers are welcome.' She defused the tension she felt with a joke, then dropped her eyes to his arousal, regarding it for the briefest second before she moved her tongue over his tip, slowly at first, then down his entire length, tasting him before she took him deep in her mouth, relishing the feeling of him there, and even more so when he let out a loud, primal groan that seemed to reverberate against the gym's walls. His body trembled as she moved her mouth, and his hands on her shoulders were gentle, as if he needed her support.

Fierce heat travelled her body, the strength of his desire was an aphrodisiac she hadn't expected, so she found she never wanted this to end, she never wanted to stop. Power exploded through her, and when he lost himself, she felt a part of herself go right along with him, as though they were bound together in an inexplicable, undeniable way.

Was it any wonder Alejandro couldn't concentrate? Whenever he got five minutes to himself, he found his mind replaying, over and over, their morning, and a flood of desire ravaged his body, making it impossible to think, to work, to do anything but pace, his blood as hot as lava.

He'd woken so angry! Furious, in fact. The dark emotions had pounded through him in a way he hadn't experienced since childhood. As a little boy, he'd always felt that anger, his impotence, his inability to fix his mother's life. He'd felt defensive and protective, and yet there'd been nothing he could do for her, nothing he could do to save her. Every time a strange man had come to their tiny apartment and she'd taken him into her room, Alejandro had worried. He'd seen her hurt enough times, seen her with black eyes and bloody noses, and he'd been terrified that she would die. Then one day she did, and instead of feeling guilty he'd felt numb, because he'd always known her life would end that way.

Why, after so many years of detachment, had those protective instincts kicked in all over again, and for Sienna Thornton-Rose?

Because of her eyes.

He closed his own, pressing his hands to his hips as his body faced towards the windows of his office.

Her eyes told him so much, and when she'd spoken of her adolescence, casually referring to the way her mother had treated her, insulted and belittled her, and her unpleasant experiences with flirtation and sex in the past, he'd seen the pain in her features, he'd seen the insecurities that still dogged her, and he'd wanted to stop the world from spinning and fundamentally reshape it. How a vibrant, funny, beautiful young woman like Sienna could ever think she wasn't enough of anything was practically a criminal offence.

It wasn't just the things she'd said, though. He'd felt the same kick of protectiveness when he'd seen her at the wedding in Rome, when he'd heard the way her mother had spoken to her about her hair, when he'd seen her look of compliance and acceptance, he'd felt a powerful rush of anger, a need to replace all that hurt with something else, something warm and pleasurable. He'd wanted her, but he'd also wanted to fix things for her.

He'd woken angry this morning, and sought refuge in his gym, with a workout that had been so intense he could feel each and every muscle screaming now, but he barely even noticed that. He could think only of Sienna as she'd been in the gym, how she'd looked at him, how she'd taken control and ridden him as though her life depended on it. But most of all, he thought about how goddamned hard he'd found it to stop what they were doing, how tempted he'd been to lose himself in her regardless of the consequences. It was a temptation he'd *never* known before, not with any other woman. 'Control' might as well have been his middle name. He didn't lose his head, he didn't lose his mind, and he never lost sight of his rules. But with Sienna, everything had an urgency that was new. He'd wanted her to the point that he could hardly even care what would happen if she fell pregnant.

And that had scared the living hell out of him.

It still did, if he was honest.

What he needed was to change gears, just until he could rediscover his equilibrium with her, to regain control. In his home, all he could think of was stripping her naked and exploring her body, and for the first time in his life he could appreciate the difficulty separating sex from emotions. He didn't *feel*, because he had trained himself not to, but with

Sienna, he saw risk—not only for himself, but for her too, and he intended to avoid those risks at all costs.

The problem was, everything with her was *different*. The way they'd met: she was the first woman he'd ever been asked to spend time with. The first woman he'd ever been prohibited from sleeping with. The first virgin he'd had sex with. She was also the first woman who'd propositioned him in such a cavalier manner, and the first woman he'd invited into his home. What he needed was to make things between them more normal. To make her like any of the women he usually slept with, to make their relationship more familiar, and less unique. Familiar equated to forgettable and at the end of all this, he needed to be able to forget Sienna. He suspected a lot in his life depended on that—including his friendship with Luca and, likely, his equilibrium.

Let's eat out tonight.

Sienna couldn't believe that even a simple four-word text message from Alejandro could stir her blood to fever pitch, but the sight of his name on her screen sparked an instant reaction within her.

She let herself imagine what that would be like, but reality was right there, wrapping around her, even if he'd momentarily forgotten a major part of their agreement.

Tempting, but not possible.

Why not?

Because this is supposed to be our little secret, and you're Alejandro Corderó. You get noticed wherever you go.

Not everywhere.

Curiosity sparked in her blood.

No?

No.

Her heart sped up, but still doubts plagued her.

I don't want Olivia and Luca to find out about this.

Three dots appeared to show that he was typing, then they disappeared, only to reappear a moment later.

Trust me.

Her heart skipped a couple of beats. She looked towards the pool, shimmering in the early evening light. *Trust me. Trust me.* Did she trust him? And if so, why? Trust wasn't something she handed out to just anyone, but the more she thought about it, the more she relaxed, the more she smiled.

Will I need a disguise?

Like a secret agent?

She grinned.

Exactly.

The idea of you wearing a trench coat with nothing underneath holds definite appeal.

She was too turned on to reply. She put her phone down and strolled inside his beautiful home, a smile beaming from her face. Retrieving a drink from the kitchen, she moved back to the deck, and saw he'd sent one last text.

I'll pick you up at eight.

Her heart fluttered with anticipation.

It's a date.

Except, she reminded herself, it wasn't. Not in the ordinary sense. This was...well, she didn't know exactly, but not that. And it didn't matter.

She was enjoying herself. She was learning about men and sex and how great it could feel. She was doing something purely for herself, and she wasn't going to overthink it. She was just going to let go and enjoy the ride, in the full knowledge that soon it would be over, and normal programming would resume.

CHAPTER TEN

JUST BEFORE FIVE o'clock that evening, there was a buzzing sound, and she moved towards it with a perplexed expression.

'Delivery.'

She pulled open the door, bemused to find the concierge there, holding a bag towards her.

She took it, closing the door with a thundering heart, peering inside only once she was deep into the lounge room again.

And a smile lifted her lips, at the same time uncertainty dipped her heart.

'Leather pants?' She squeaked, pulling them so a piece of paper dropped to the floor. She scooped it up, saw his handwriting confident and bold.

Trust me. A

She put the paper down and turned her attention back to the pants, remembering their earlier conversation when he'd joked about wanting to see her in a pair. But it was madness. Sienna had never worn anything so figure-hugging. She *couldn't.*

So why did her fingers curl around the supple material

and lift it higher, towards her chest? Why did she clutch them as she moved into the bathroom?

They fitted like a glove, and when she spun around and peered over her shoulder, into the mirror, she wasn't completely disgusted by what she saw.

She couldn't have said what she expected for their not-really-a-date, but when she stepped into the luxury foyer a few hours later, it was to find Alejandro already there, his eyes pinned to the elevator with an intensity that stole her breath. It was as though he'd been waiting for her all his life, not simply for a few minutes. She tried to modulate her breathing, but it was rushing out of her in fits and spurts, and the closer she got, the worse it felt.

He moved his finger in a semi-circle pattern. 'Let me see.'

Her heart leaped to her throat as she did as he said, and began to twirl, slowly.

The low, guttural noise of appreciation was a salve she hadn't known she needed.

'Almost perfect.'

'Almost?'

He reached into his pocket, removing a small black velvet pouch. She took it without thinking, expecting it to contain something irrelevant, something small and trivial, so she flicked it open and upended it over her palm, only to find a stunning green gem on a fine rose-gold chain. The emerald was raw, not super polished, making it look almost as if it were alive—patches of pale green, vivid green and black swirled together beneath a slightly porous exterior. She stared at it, the beauty unmistakable, a lump in her throat making speech difficult.

'It's lovely.' What an insipid word. 'What's it for?'

'It is for you.' A simple answer that told her nothing.

'Why?'

'Why not?'

Her heart stammered. Was this what he did on dates? How he made his lovers feel special?

Everything slowed down as sense gradually replaced wonderment. Of course it was. This was an act. He did this all the time. It was only her inexperience that made it all seem so special. He was treating her as he would any of his other lovers. It wasn't special. It wasn't unique. It didn't mean anything.

'You don't need to buy me gifts,' she blurted out, the gesture strangely tainted by her knowledge that this was him going through the motions.

'I know that.' He took it from her and reached behind her neck, clasping the necklace in place, then leaning back just far enough to admire it. He shifted his head in a small nod of approval.

'Are you ready?'

Could she ever be? 'Where are we going?'

'You'll see.'

As they approached the doors of the foyer the concierge swished them open and they stepped into the balmy night air, the smell of the sea wrapping around them, so she inhaled deeply, without thinking, the romance of that aroma sweeping her away. She was too distracted to notice the bike at first, too overwhelmed by the way he looked in a navy-blue suit, but when he began to unpin her hair, pulling to loosen it, she gasped at the intimacy and how, on some level, she'd simply known he would do that.

'You don't like it in a bun?'

'I like it fine.' His voice was low and gravelled. 'But this wouldn't fit.'

And he reached behind them, grabbing a shining black helmet off a motorbike, and easing it over her head, so the world faded, like a tinted version of itself.

'A disguise?'

'Safety,' he responded, but with a curl of his lips that showed appreciation for her joke.

He reached for her hand, guiding her towards the bike. 'Have you ever ridden before?'

She shook her head. 'Never.'

'We seem to enjoy sharing your firsts together.'

Heat flushed her body. 'You ride?' She took a moment to appraise the bike, moving around it, admiring the shape of it, the size, thinking that it reminded her of a crouched bull, with barely contained strength indicated by the sculpted metal.

'My first car was a bike.' He cast one powerful leg over the frame, then shot her a look—a dare. 'Hop on.'

A frisson of anticipation warmed her as she did exactly that, taking up the space behind him, her legs hugging his frame. When he started the bike, she leaned forward, wrapping her arms around him, and pressure built behind her ribs, like the gathering of an electrical storm. She felt its charge and its strength and relished the possession of both.

The bike throbbed beneath them, and the storm grew in intensity, so her hands were no longer content to stay as they were, neatly folded over his chest. They explored, stroking his body, his ribs, his muscles, feeling him as the bike seemed to take on the personality of an animal, tearing them through Barcelona. She was aware of the city as he drove, of the changing landscape, from the cultured, exquisite frontages of the Passeig de Gràcia to the slightly grittier feel of the next neighbourhood, with art almost everywhere she looked—on the sides of buildings, billboards, even the street had been painted at the edges, passing her by in a blur until Alejandro stopped at the lights.

Idling, the bike's rhythm stirred her to fever pitch, so she shifted closer on the seat, pressing her legs into him more tightly, until his hand reached down and stroked her thigh, and pleasure burst through her.

He navigated the streets expertly, as though he were wired for them, turning the bike away from a busy road down a side street and then another, with little restaurants dotted between shops and galleries, until finally he drew to a stop right out at the front of a string of three restaurants. It had taken less than ten minutes in all—not long enough. She wanted more. The thrill of being behind him as he expertly drove them through Barcelona had been immense.

'Enjoy yourself?' he asked as she stepped off the bike.

Sienna struggled to catch her breath. 'Yes.' What was the point in lying? She unhooked the helmet—heavier than she'd expected—and held it out to him. 'I liked it a lot.'

His grin showed that he knew, or perhaps that he'd expected. 'I thought you might.' He leaned closer. 'Daredevil.'

She blinked up at him, the moniker not one that had ever been used to describe her, and yet she liked it, and she couldn't entirely argue with it. Since meeting Alejandro, she felt as though all she'd done was take risks—and they'd paid off, big time.

'Where are we?'

'El Born.' He secured the helmets on the handlebar, then took her hand automatically—strange how comfortable that felt—as he strode towards a bright red door with ornate lampposts on either side. Sienna looked up and down the street, noting the small details now—the cobbled road that weaved between the buildings, the terracotta finish of the walls, the church at the end that seemed to have all rounded walls, and then the noise of the restaurants, the chatter and song that overflowed with happiness.

'This is a medieval part of town,' he explained, opening the door for her. The noise grew instantly louder. He stepped in behind her, shutting the door, so they were alone on a small landing. He gestured towards the stairs—too narrow for them to walk side by side. In fact, as she made her way down the stairs, Sienna had to dip her head a little, owing to the low roof.

It opened up once she reached the bottom. The room seemed to grow out of nowhere, stone walls covered in shelves and bottles, plants with long tendrils scrambling wildly across the space, the room dark except for the occasional lamp casting a golden glow, so there was privacy and anonymity in every direction. Towards the back of the restaurant, couples were dancing, their movements unmistakably traditional Spanish, mysterious and beautiful, and so elegant Sienna ached to be able to move just like them.

A waitress greeted them above the noise, and Alejandro switched to Catalan, so Sienna didn't catch what he asked, only a moment later they were shown to a table near the front of the restaurant, a jug of sangria brought almost immediately.

'It's tradition.' He grinned, gesturing to the jug.

She eyed it thoughtfully. 'Another first for me.'

'You cannot be serious?'

'Tell me when in my life you think I might have had the opportunity to drink sangria,' she prompted, pouring two glasses and looking at it curiously.

'You've never been to Spain?'

'I've barely been anywhere,' she corrected. 'In fact, until Olivia's vows in Rome, my passport had been lapsed for about a decade.'

He leaned closer. 'Because money was so tight?'

'Yes. Travelling was the last thing on any of our minds.' She sipped the drink, relishing the flavours. 'It tastes like summer.'

'As it's supposed to.'

'I was thinking, the other day, how money can open the world up to you. I would never have been able to come to Barcelona to see you, before…'

'Olivia's marriage to Luca,' he prompted.

'Right. It's only that some of my father's inheritance has been freed up that we have that liberty now.'

'What about your job? It doesn't involve travel?'

'No. In fact, I work from home. It's the only way.'

'Why?'

She traced her finger around the rim of the glass. 'My mother didn't want Olivia or me to leave,' she admitted. 'And we didn't feel that we could. She might seem like an awful person, and in so many ways she is, but at the same time she's my mother, and I do love her, Alejandro. More than that, I pity her. She's a product of my father's monstrous behaviour. I've got enough perspective to see that she's spent my entire life projecting her own insecurities onto me.'

He was watching her through hooded eyes, seeing too much and revealing nothing.

'Anyway…' She sucked in a breath, eager to move the conversation on. 'Travel wasn't really a big priority. Until it was.'

He leaned closer, and beneath the table their knees brushed, reminding her of the leather trousers she wore, the trousers he'd bought for her.

'These are the perfect size, by the way.'

He didn't miss a beat. 'It's almost like I remember every delectable inch of your body.'

Her stomach flipped.

'Well enough to describe it to a sales assistant.'

'I hope not.' She looked away, heat flaming her face.

He laughed softly.

'So is this all part of your usual modus operandi?' She took a larger gulp of her drink.

'What, in particular?'

'Buying women clothes, jewels, making them feel as though they are the only woman on earth for a night.'

He straightened. 'Is that what I've done?'

Her heart seemed to tighten. He was surprised. No, he was scared, as though she'd suggested he might be about to propose marriage. Damn her straight talking! Damn her inability to think anything through.

'I'm only joking,' she lied, rolling her eyes for good measure. 'I'm just asking what the norm is for you. When you date women.'

'I don't date, remember?'

Something jolted in her chest. 'You know what I mean. I've seen photos of you with women, at events.'

'Sure. As a prelude to sex, nothing more.'

Her stomach turned. She felt hot and cold, and not in a good way. Panic set in, so she reached for her drink once more, sipping it slowly, to buy time, hoping she looked more relaxed than she felt. Why did such a cold assessment of his nocturnal activities make something in her belly spin out of control?

The waitress reappeared to take their order, and Sienna sat back while Alejandro spoke, listing a selection of dishes that she could partially understand.

When they were alone again, she felt a little more clear-headed; her heart—so used to being battered—had recovered as it always did.

'Why don't you date?' she asked directly, curiosity sparking too large to ignore now.

'What's the point?'

She flexed one brow, waiting for him to elaborate.

'Isn't dating the route you take to marriage? Why bother, given that I don't intend to get married?'

'I think you're being too binary in your thinking,' she said after a moment. 'After all, I intend to get married, but not to fall in love. I intend to date to find a suitable husband, not to fall in love.'

'And will you tell your husband how limited you want your marriage to be?'

A cheeky smile flickered on her lips. 'Do you think me capable of lying?'

'Not for one moment.'

She sighed with assumed melodrama. 'Then what choice do I have?'

If he was amused by her comment, he didn't show it. 'And what sort of man do you think you'll find, who's willing to marry you in name only?'

'Oh, I don't mean for the marriage to be in name only, necessarily.'

'What does that mean?'

She lifted her shoulders. 'I'm not getting married with the intention of getting divorced again right away.'

'But to satisfy your father's will, you need only to marry, correct?'

'Yes. But the idea of doing it *just* to meet his dictatorial requirements doesn't sit right with me. I'd prefer to find someone I actually like, someone I can be friends with, and forge a relationship with them.'

'And will sex form a part of this relationship?'

Something like nausea wretched through her. The idea of another man touching her, kissing her, making love to her, was like swallowing acid. 'Undoubtedly,' she said, reaching for her drink only to realise it was empty. Alejandro didn't take his eyes off her face as he lifted the jug, refilling her glass.

'Be careful, *querida*. It tastes sweet but it packs a punch.'

She sipped it defiantly. 'I don't want to live a sexless life, if that's what you're asking. Nor do I want to cheat on my husband. So I suppose I'll have to find someone I find sexually attractive as well.'

But the idea made her head swim, because that had never been part of her plan. Alejandro had set the cat amongst the pigeons, showing her body what it could feel, making her crave him around the clock, so she couldn't imagine going on with her life without that kind of satisfaction.

'Perhaps Tinder?'

Was she imagining the dark edge to his words? Probably. Wishful thinking. Why would he care what she planned to do with her life?

Tapas began to appear at their table, a selection of crumbed olives, anchovies on toast, saffron-flavoured rice balls, and vegetables in olive oil. Sienna ate, grateful Alejandro moved the conversation on to something more general, entertaining her with the history of this area of Barcelona, while Sienna went through the motions, eating though she was no longer hungry, praising the food though she could barely taste it.

She was surprised to realise, when all the plates were cleared, that almost two hours had passed, and the sangria jug was almost empty. She hadn't seen him take more than a couple of sips from his glass, so she suspected she'd had rather too much to drink. Whoops.

When they stood, she did indeed feel a little woozy, but the hand he put in the small of her back anchored her back to this room, this restaurant, to him, so she moved her body close to his, closing her eyes as she inhaled his intoxicating, masculine fragrance.

'Would you like to dance, *querida*?'

'Don't you remember? I have two left feet.'

'It doesn't matter. You'll feel the music.' He stroked her arm. 'Trust me.'

Something stirred low in her abdomen, spreading through her whole body, and when she looked up into his eyes, she was lost. *Trust me.* Why did that sound like both a spell and a curse at the same time?

CHAPTER ELEVEN

THE NEXT TIME he stopped the motorbike it was not at the base of his penthouse, but in a small, crowded area with buildings so close they were like teeth in an overcrowded mouth. Alejandro cut the engine but didn't speak for a moment, so she looked around, watching as a guy slowly approached the window of an idling car.

Two women dressed in revealing outfits watched from across the narrow street.

'Where are we?'

Her question seemed to rouse him. 'My past.'

Curiosity sparked. 'Oh?'

'Let me show you something.'

Anything. She caught the word just in time, proud of herself for finally not saying the first thing that popped into her head. He secured the helmets then laced his fingers through hers, pulling her close to his side. She loved the way it felt there. Just right. They fitted together as though they'd been designed—somehow, she caught the thought before it could go any further, terminating it and turning to him with a bright smile. 'I can smell the sea.'

'It's not far from here.'

'Did you go swimming much as a child? Play pirates at the seashore?'

Her tone was light, but when she glanced up at his face,

she stopped walking. There was a tension there that broke her heart. 'Alejandro? What is it?'

He seemed to rouse himself, turning to face her. 'I haven't been back here in a long time.'

Her brows drew together. 'Then why—?'

'You said you want to understand me.'

She nodded slowly, a tic in her heart making her aware that it was moving too fast. 'But not if it's hurting you to show me.'

Surprise flashed in his eyes. He looked away. A cat scampered across the footpath in front of them, jet black, barely discernible for how dark the street was. Alejandro wrapped his arm around her shoulders, holding her closer, leading her further up the street. It was quiet—no signs of nightlife, but they weren't alone. There were more scantily clad women lined up against the walls, and the men she saw looked as though they were out of it. A sense of danger prickled along her skin, but when she was with Alejandro, she felt safe. Completely and utterly.

'This is where I spent the first twelve years of my life. In this tenement, two small rooms—a kitchen and sofa in one, a bedroom in the other. I slept on the sofa. There was a shared bathroom, used by everyone on our floor.'

Sympathy filled Sienna's eyes. She wrapped her arm around his waist, running her fingers over his side, and she waited. He'd brought her here after all. It wasn't to block her questions.

'The area has been cleaned up considerably since then, believe it or not.' They looked in unison towards a car that was drawing to a stop near the women. One approached the window, spoke for a moment, then came around to the front passenger side. She stepped in, and the car drove down the street.

'If this is "cleaned up", what was it like when you were a boy?'

'Gangs ran everything. The streets were filled with drugs and prostitutes, brothels in every building.' He started to walk, drawing her with him. 'My mother fought so hard, she wanted to get away from it all. She got a job working as a waitress, but once she had me, with no support, her options dried up—she turned to prostitution because she could not see another choice. Her life had not been easy—she'd grown up rough, so coming back here, falling in with the gangs, it must have seemed like her only option. She worked out of our apartment.'

Sienna gasped. She had gathered that he was 'self-made' from the research she'd done, but she hadn't imagined his start in life to be quite so tough as this.

'The gang she worked for controlled her life. Who she saw, what she did. She was only sixteen when I was born.'

Sienna gasped again. 'Oh, Alejandro.' It was no longer enough to stand with her arm around his waist. She moved to the front of him, wrapping both arms behind his back, lifting up onto the tips of her toes and kissing the base of his throat. 'I'm so sorry.'

'It's a long time ago now.'

'You said you lived here until you were twelve,' she said quietly after a moment, trying not to cry, but her mouth was filling with the sting of tears and her eyes hurt like hell. 'What happened? Where did you go after that?'

His lips curled in a derisive half-smile, and then it fell, leaving his expression empty, blanked, a mask of determination that couldn't quite hide all his pain. 'The streets. My mother died. If I wanted to continue living in the apartment—paid for by the gang who'd used her—I had to agree to work for them. If there was one thing I'd learned growing up and seeing the way my mother was treated, it was that nobody was going to have that kind of control over my life. I would not work for anyone. I would not live in fear of anyone.'

Sienna couldn't stop a tear from rolling down her cheek, but she angled her face away, knowing he wouldn't want her sympathy even as it was pouring out of her.

'I moved to the city centre. I stole food. I lived rough. I learned to fight. I grew up damned fast.' His laugh was hoarse, as though his throat were lined with acid. Sienna closed her eyes, shivering to imagine a young boy, only twelve, living that kind of life. Now he turned to face her, looking into her eyes, and what she saw in his expression made her heart thump to a stop. He was still that twelve-year-old boy—fully grown now, but his experiences haunted him, dogged him, and turned him into the man he was today. Uber-successful, determined, but alone. No emotional commitments, he wasn't close to anyone. Except Luca.

And now she was making him lie to his best friend. A hint of guilt stole through her, because she was a grown woman and shouldn't have felt the need to hide the truth from her brother-in-law, but, damn it, she wanted this experience to be hers, just hers. Nobody else needed to know. It wasn't as if he had any reason to share the details of this relationship, anyway. He wasn't the kind of man who'd fill anyone in—even Luca—on the intricacies of his personal life.

'Why the city?'

'Better protection, fewer gangs.'

'You must have been terrified.'

He fixed her with a steely gaze, but she felt everything he was trying to conceal behind a mask of strength. 'It wasn't as though life with my mother was a peach.'

'No?' she whispered, but she didn't need him to elaborate. She could imagine.

'She was treated like dirt. I saw. I heard. I knew.'

His hand had formed a fist at his side; she reached down,

curving hers over it, wishing there were some way she could erase that trauma for him. 'You must have hated it.'

He didn't respond. She ached for him, and for his mother. 'Is that how she died?'

His lips tightened. 'Occupational hazard,' he said after a beat. 'I couldn't save her. I tried.'

Pain ripped through Sienna. She lifted her other hand to his chest, placing it over his heart. She heard his guilt, the failure, the regret. She wanted to obliterate those emotions and memories from his mind. 'I am so sorry you had to live through that.'

He shrugged with assumed nonchalance. 'Others had it worse.'

Perhaps, but not by much.

He caught her hand again, guiding her through the ancient laneways. She shivered involuntarily. What had, at first, seemed like a rabbit warren of streets—ancient and fascinating, albeit rundown—was now subsumed by darkness for Sienna. She could feel only his pain, imagine him as an adolescent, alone and terrified, and she wanted to hug him close and reassure him that he'd never know that pain again.

A chasm seemed to form in her chest, a hole right near her heart. She squeezed his hand, struggling to find any words. They walked past the bike, a little further down the street, to a small green park with a statue of Mary and Jesus in the centre. 'She used to come and pray here, to ask God to deliver her to a better life. I would hear her words and wonder when He would answer.'

Tears slid down Sienna's cheeks; she angled her face towards the street and wiped them away surreptitiously. 'When I bought my first company, and I had more money than I knew what to do with, I made it my mission to answer my mother's prayers. It was too late for her, but not for all the women out there living as she did, who wanted help, who were brave enough to ask for it.'

Now she looked up at him, uncaring that he would see the moisture in her eyes. 'How?'

'In a very similar way to how you plan to help, actually.'

She didn't immediately understand.

'I own hundreds of apartments across Spain. I work with a charity to rent them to women who are in need. Single mothers, predominantly. The rent is affordable, or free, depending on circumstance. It is a small thing, to help them get on their feet, to escape lives in which they might otherwise be trapped.'

Her throat was too thick to allow speech. Her heart was overflowing. It was such a quiet, pragmatic, unassuming way to help. 'I didn't know.'

'Why would you?'

'I work in the charity sector, and I read a few articles about you before I came here. I'm surprised it's not mentioned.'

'I don't make it publicly known. The ownership of the apartments is at arm's length to me. I don't need to advertise what I'm doing.'

It was, if anything, the icing on the cake. To help for the sake of helping, rather than for plaudits and praise. 'Your mother would be very proud of you.'

'I wish there'd been someone who could have helped her.'

'You wish *you* could have helped her,' she said gently, lifting her hand and cupping his cheek.

'Of course. But I was a child. The one time I tried, it only made it worse.'

Her heart splintered apart for him.

'After that, she begged me not to get involved. She gave me headphones and a Discman, made me sit in the lounge room and listen to music.'

'But you didn't.'

A muscle jerked at the base of his jaw and she knew that she was right.

She leaned forward and pressed a kiss to his chest. She felt him still, and was afraid to look up, afraid to meet his eyes, because something was building inside her, a feeling that was growing and bursting, a feeling that terrified her. A feeling she couldn't understand but that she knew she needed to run from. 'Let's go back now, Alejandro. This isn't your life anymore.'

She was wrong. It would always be his life. He had grown up, but never away, from that life, those nights, those feelings.

He watched her sleeping, fascinated by the gentle undulations of her breasts, the subtle rise and fall of her creamy skin, the fire-engine red of her hair, the parting of her full, lush lips, the fluttering of her eyelids and the shifting of her thick, dark lashes. He watched her sleep but he felt the weight of his past and failure, the heavy ache of his own inability to save his mother, to remove her from that situation, when he'd had the skills all along. True, he'd been younger, but after she'd died, and he'd made his way in the world, he'd been better off than when they'd lived in that apartment. If only he'd made her leave sooner, made her run away from that life, those obligations.

She'd been so young, still a child herself in many ways. She'd had no one to fight for her.

He couldn't help it. Despite the fact Sienna slept so peacefully—that she was exhausted—he reached out and brushed his finger over her cheek, lightly, just because he needed to feel her and to know that she was real, that she was here. Attempting to slot her into the box other women had occupied in his life had failed. She wasn't like them, and nor was this affair.

She anchored him in a way he'd never known before. Having her here changed his apartment in some vital way, as though it had become an actual 'home', and not just a place to sleep, and he couldn't put his finger on how or why she'd done that, but he knew that he liked it.

And that was, in and of itself, a danger.

Because Alejandro didn't want to get used to the comfort she offered. He didn't want to soften the edges his life had carved into hard planes. He didn't want to forget that he was alone, that he couldn't rely on anyone, that he didn't want to carry the burden of someone else's happiness and protection lest he fail all over again. He could never forgive himself for the ways in which he'd let down his mother. The thought of doing so again—and to someone like Sienna—was impossible to contemplate.

He'd taken her to dinner in an attempt to get them out of the bedroom, to stall the emotional intimacy that had been luring them closer, dangerously close, and because he'd wanted to lighten the mood between them, but the ploy had failed. And because of him. *He* was the one who'd taken her to the streets he'd grown up in, given her a necklace and shown her more of his true self than he ever had another soul. He'd aimed to push her away a little and instead he'd shown her a part of him that he usually kept locked away.

And he had no idea why, but he did know he had to get a grip on the situation, before things went any further. He stood abruptly and strode from the room, from Sienna, simply to prove to himself that he still could.

Across the Balearic Sea, in Rome, Luca stared at the photograph with a flush of fever-like heat. Alejandro he'd recognise anywhere, and his face was towards the camera when the picture was snapped. The woman he was dancing with was less discernible, given that her back was turned, her face only very slightly in profile. But her skin was pale and her hair flame red, and there was something in the way she had been photographed moving that drove a stake through his chest, because he knew instantly who it was.

What was less clear was how in the world his wife's sister had been photographed dancing in a tapas bar in Barcelona with Luca's best friend. The picture, poor quality so presumably taken from a cell phone by an opportunistic diner who saw a chance to make a quick buck by on-selling the image to the tabloids, was nothing new—Alejandro was photographed at events often. But with Sienna?

Years of friendship and goodwill lived in Luca, but for a moment there was rage too, because he'd trusted Alejandro, and the idea of Sienna being tossed aside after a brief fling—which was the only way Alejandro knew how to treat women—made Luca's blood boil. He'd asked the man to *protect* her, not to treat her like any of his other lovers. Alejandro was incapable of genuine emotion with women, incapable of commitment—there was no other conclusion but that he was flirting with Sienna for fun. And she stood to get hurt if she believed, for even one second, that Alejandro was boyfriend material. Everything he knew about Sienna had come from Olivia. He knew how sheltered she'd been, how protected, how badly bullied by their mother, how that had impacted her self-esteem. He also knew that she had no experience with men, particularly not a man like Alejandro who saw sex as the scratching of a physical itch and nothing more.

He closed the paper hurriedly as Olivia entered the kitchen.

'Everything okay, *caro*?'

'Hmm? Oh, yes. Of course.'

And it would be—just as soon as he'd seen Alejandro and got an explanation as to what the hell was going on.

CHAPTER TWELVE

SHE WAS CONSCIOUS of the sun streaming through her window, she was conscious of Alejandro dressing, but she didn't move. She lay there, eyes closed, feigning sleep, because she wasn't ready to face him yet.

They had one more night together. It didn't feel like enough, even when it was what they'd agreed.

Which was all the more reason for her to get the heck out of there. Since she'd first learned of her father's will, Sienna had formed a clear plan for her life, and it included a safe, sensible marriage. Definitely not this.

Not sex she craved as though it were an essential part of life, not a heart that was falling head over heels for someone—someone who could hurt her, just as her dad had hurt her mother. She was smarter than that—she'd learned the lessons her mother had refused to heed.

And she was no coward. She blinked her eyes open, sitting up, forcing herself to meet his gaze and smile, even when all her good resolutions felt as though they might evaporate in response to the steam that came off his appraisal.

Belatedly, she realised the sheet was wrapped around her waist and she wore the flimsiest of camisoles, barely covering her breasts. 'Good morning.'

He finished buttoning his shirt then strode towards her. Sienna's body lurched; everything felt off kilter.

'Hi.' He sat on the edge of the bed, one strong arm over her legs, his face closer to hers. 'How did you sleep?'

Tortured by dreams of him.

'Fine.' She cleared her throat. 'You?'

His smile showed so much. That he understood what she hadn't said...that he felt it deep within him as well.

'Barely.' He leaned forward, pressing a kiss against her lips, lingering there, so she shifted slightly, pressing her body forward.

His laugh was a soft caress, then he stood, his absence like ice water, dousing her, outraging her. She said nothing.

'We'll go out again tonight. I'll text you details.'

'It could be more fun to stay in,' she said with the hint of a pout about her lips.

He simply smiled, dismissively, so frustration bubbled through her. But perhaps it *was* smarter to go out. Here there was nothing to do but discover one another, to make love and talk and kiss and learn, and she was afraid walking away without a backwards glance would be a lot harder if they kept going down that road.

'See you later.'

A hint of defiance ran through Sienna as she shopped for something to wear that night. It was their last night together, and though she felt her usual desire to downplay her curves, she ignored it, instead opting to try on dresses that emphasised her figure—a stunning cocktail gown with a low-cut neckline, spaghetti straps and a knee-length skirt clung to her body like a second skin, hiding nothing. She was terrified of that, but she'd also seen the way Alejandro looked at her, she knew that when he looked at her body he didn't see the pinchable sides of her stomach or the roundedness of her butt—at least, he didn't see those things in a negative way. She paid for the dress before she could change her mind, then selected some strappy slingbacks. On a whim, she stopped off at a salon near his apartment, getting her hair trimmed and blown out so it hung in loose, voluminous curls around her face.

Excitement built as the day passed, and finally, just after seven, she showered, careful not to dampen her hair, then dressed, nervousness almost making her change out of the revealing outfit and opt for one of her more conservative dresses.

But time was marching on, and she wanted to be waiting for him when he arrived.

Her heart hammered with anticipation and when her phone began to hum, she lifted it up, a smile on her face.

'I'm downstairs.'

Her breath throbbed. 'Okay. I'll see you soon.'

Her heart was racing, her blood firing through her veins, and now she forced herself to do one last check in the mirror. And swore under her breath. Because smiling back at Sienna was a woman who seemed as though she had the world in the palm of her hand. She looked confident and even a little sophisticated. Except for her hands, which trembled as they reached for her clutch bag. She placed it between her side and her arm and stepped into the lift, adrenaline turning her body in a highly charged electrical current.

The lift sailed downwards, and when the doors pinged open it took precisely two seconds for her to locate Alejandro. He was waiting a short distance away, and when their eyes met, time stood still. He stared at her, and she stared right back, a thousand feelings exploding through her, until the lift doors began to close, and she startled, moving her hand between them so they sprang apart once more. But in that split second of inaction, Alejandro was moving, his whole body sliding between the doors and propelling her backwards, dwarfing her and pinning her at the same time, pressing her to the back of the elevator as his mouth sought hers and his hand moved to the panel, pressing buttons without lifting his face from hers.

She whimpered into the kiss, the ache that had been building inside her all day, needing this and him so badly it hurt, both mollified and intensified by the power of his kiss, and without realising what she was doing she lifted one leg, straining the stretchy material of the dress—but she didn't care. She curved her leg behind him, holding him close, and she kissed him as though her very life depended upon it.

He swore, the kind of curse she loved hearing on his lips because it evoked the sea and salt and flavour of this wild, ancient, primal city; she loved it because it spoke of desperation and need, and a fever coursing through his body the way it was hers. The elevator moved upwards and she pulled away just long enough to say, 'What happened to dinner?'

His answer was to lift her over his shoulder and stride out of the lift the second the doors opened. Once in his apartment, he placed her down in the middle of the room, sliding her body along his, and though she wanted, more than anything, for him to kiss her again, there was something in the way he looked at her that made her blood spark like lava. He took a step back, one hand still latched to hers, his eyes slipping from her eyes to her lips, lower to the swell of generous cleavage revealed by her dress, to her pinched-in waist and then the curve of her hips, her legs, until she could hardly stand it a second longer.

'Dinner?' she prompted with an arched brow.

'Screw dinner.' Then he was moving forward, kissing her all over again, undressing her as he moved them backwards, towards the chaise of the sofa, tumbling them backwards, his hands removing the dress she'd so daringly chosen, his groan cutting through time and space when he realised she wasn't wearing a bra beneath it. His hands fondled her breasts, his body pressed down on hers, as she undressed him with the same desperate hunger as he displayed with her, until they were both naked, writhing, tangled together, a war of passion and possession breaking around them, splintering the world apart, so Sienna was conscious of nothing but Alejandro, and him she was aware of on a cellular level. His breath across her skin, the weight of his body, the warmth of his flesh, the vapour on his skin, the smell of his cologne, the taste of his mouth.

'You are—' but he didn't finish the sentence; he couldn't. Instead, he drove himself into her, pinning her arms above her head, staring right into her eyes as he moved, thrusting deep and fast at first, then slowly, and the look in his eyes, for the briefest moment, drove passion from Sienna's mind, because he was lost, and looking at her as though salvation might be found within her.

She pushed up onto her elbows, dislodging his grip, and she kissed him, soft, slow, somehow sensing he needed that, but a moment later he was Alejandro again, all fire and spirit, and strength and power, in control as ever. And she fell apart, holding on to him with the tips of her fingers, as though that might save her from what she knew was coming—what she'd now accepted as an inevitability of their relationship. She was falling all the way into love with him, and there was no use denying it, to herself at least.

'*Cristo.*' He pulled to stand, staring at her with a look in his eyes she couldn't comprehend—until gradually reality shifted and she understood what he was evidently dealing with.

'We forgot protection.' She winced. 'I didn't think—'

'I didn't give you a chance to think,' he dismissed. 'That was all my fault.'

She sat up, wrestling with a lingering sense of self-consciousness, her huge green eyes finding his. 'You know I'm on the pill.'

He dipped his head. 'It's not—'

'It is. In most cases, it's foolproof. And if anything happens, well, we'll cross that bridge when we get to it.'

He was going to argue with her, so she stood, pressing a hand gently to his chest. 'We can't undo it, so why worry? There's no point.'

He didn't argue with her, but she knew she hadn't completely dispelled his uneasiness. 'Dinner,' he murmured instead, looking around at their clothes—tossed destructively throughout the apartment.

'Right.' Her laugh was a soft sound. 'We were going out.'

'Is that what you want?'

What she wanted was more time with him. More than twelve hours, or whatever they had left. She felt the walls closing in on her and lifted her shoulders. 'Sure.' She couldn't meet his eyes. Emotion clogged in her chest.

Tell him.

'Alejandro—' But when he looked at her, he was so much like the first night they'd met—charming and untouchable—that her confidence faltered. Suddenly, *she* was like the night they'd met as well, nervous and unsure of herself, so she stood jerkily, wishing she weren't fighting a war within herself.

She *couldn't* love him. She never wanted to fall in love. She never wanted to get in a relationship—not like her parents'. Growing up with them had given her a crash course in how wrong things could go if you put all your trust in someone else's hands, and she never intended to be that stupid. Even if that someone was Alejandro Corderó? She tried to imagine him hurting her, tried to imagine him ever acting as her father had towards her mother, and she couldn't. The truth was, he was nothing like her father, so the boogieman fear she'd let dominate her all her life suddenly seemed a little ridiculous. Which meant what, exactly? That she was willing to take a risk?

But for what?

Even if she told him she wanted to see him again, to date him out in the open, in a real way, he'd never agree. He'd been clear about that from the outset. It wasn't what he wanted.

And if that had changed? She squeezed her eyes shut as the dominoes kept falling, because it wasn't possible that he would have changed his mind *enough*. She needed to get married before she turned twenty-five and Alejandro was never going to be the marrying type. He might agree to more of this—no-strings sex—but that would be the extent of it. Which left her where, exactly? Falling more and more in love with a dedicated commitment-phobe while she really should have been looking for a man who would make a suitable husband?

It was all terribly, heart-stoppingly useless.

'I'm starving,' she lied, her voice over-bright.

His eyes narrowed thoughtfully, his eyes sweeping her face, but he didn't respond to the slightly brittle tone in her voice. 'Then I guess we'd better get you dressed once more.'

'Would you really have wanted to marry me, if I'd got pregnant after the wedding?'

After a long dinner in a buzzy restaurant in the fashionable Poblenou district, the question blurted from Sienna's lips before she could stop it.

To his credit, he didn't flinch. 'Yes.'

'Why?'

Her heart rabbited in her chest and she dug her nails into her thigh beneath the table, desperately willing her blood to stop rushing. 'Because I would want to be a part of my child's life.'

'That doesn't require marriage.'

'For me, it does.'

'Why?'

He finished his coffee, placing the small cup in the middle of the table then capturing her hands. 'Because I would want any child of mine to know that I was willing to fight to be a part of their everyday life. Not their weekend life. Not their sometimes life. All their life.'

She considered that, his vehemence a little discordant. 'Tell me about your father.'

As soon as she said it, she knew she'd struck a nerve. He flinched, almost imperceptibly, but her hand was held by his and she felt it, a little shock wave that passed through his body.

'There is nothing to tell. I never knew him.'

She frowned. 'Did your mother know? I mean—'

'Yes, she knew who he was.'

'And did she tell you?'

'Yes.'

'So you knew of him, but simply never met?'

He nodded once, a tight shift of his head that many would have taken as a warning: stop asking questions.

'Did he know about you?'

'Yes.'

'How do you know?'

'Because she told me.' His eyes were hooded, his features locked in a mask of ruthless anger. A shiver ran down her spine. 'And after she died, I found the letters.'

'She wrote to him?'

'A lawyer did. Some hack from the tenement. Still, the letter was sound. My father's legal advice was better—he had a team of barristers at his disposal.'

'He was well off?'

Alejandro lifted a hand in the air, silently signalling to the waiter that he'd like the bill—and, more importantly, signalling to Sienna that he wanted the conversation to be at an end.

'You ask too many questions.'

He had inflected the words with a hint of humour but that didn't matter. They hurt. They cut her to the quick. Criticism was something she'd thought she'd inured herself to—she'd learned to take it from her mother, but from Alejandro it was unbearable.

'That was a joke.' He sighed. 'Not a good one.' He squeezed her hand. 'I'm sorry.'

Apology. Another thing Sienna had never received—not from her mother, her father, and nor had she ever witnessed her father apologise to her mother. Alejandro might be six and a half feet of sheer alpha male, but he was also a decent, kind man, qualities her father lacked altogether.

'Forget about it.'

But neither of them could. She felt the sting of his words and it silenced any more questions. A moment later, the waiter appeared, and Alejandro paid the bill, despite Sienna's offer. 'You came to Barcelona. I can buy the dinner.'

'You're also hosting me,' she pointed out as they stepped out of the restaurant, into the balmy night air.

They walked in silence for several streets, moving towards the sea, the smell of salt growing stronger as they approached the water.

'My father,' he said, after so long a silence Sienna had presumed the conversation to be completely at an end, 'was in his early twenties when he met my mother. She was working as a waitress. He was on vacation. He seduced her. He fed her lies, promised her things he never intended to give. She fell for him, believed him.'

Sienna's eyes stung with indignant tears. 'And she fell pregnant.'

'She was sixteen. She told him she was pregnant, he disappeared. She informed him of my birth—nothing. He gave her not a single cent towards my upbringing, nothing to help support her when I was a child. He refused the request for DNA testing. He abandoned her.'

He stopped walking, lifting a hand to her cheek. 'Do you wonder why I would have insisted on marrying you?'

A tingle ran through her. She swayed slightly—not intentionally, but because her legs seemed to have forgotten how to do their job. 'How could any man behave like that?'

'He was worried about the consequences of claiming me,' Alejandro said with a shrug, an air of assumed nonchalance not fooling Sienna for a minute.

'What consequences?'

'My father is an Italian count. His family fortune is considerable. I suppose he worried he might be disinherited. It is difficult to imagine how anyone could abandon a sixteen-year-old woman, but that's all I know.'

She blinked, anger firing through her. 'That's disgusting.'

Amusement quirked his lips, despite the seriousness of their conversation. 'Yes.'

'And now that you're Alejandro Corderó, world-famous success story, do you ever think about contacting him?'

'To what end?'

'Well, I don't know, but if I were you I'd have fantasised about tipping a drink or three over his head.'

Alejandro laughed, a sound that shook her to the core. 'Satisfying in the moment, but then again, why allow him to think that I care?'

'Don't you?'

His frown was reflexive. 'I care for the pain my mother endured—needlessly. I care for the life she should have lived, the care he could have given. He did not have to marry her, but he could have supported her financially.'

'And he could have known you. Loved you.'

He jerked his gaze away, looking towards the ocean. For a moment, he was a little boy again. She saw it, saw him, all the facets that made him the complex, fascinating man he was today. 'As a child, I wanted that. I needed it. But now, I need nothing from him.'

'Or anyone.' She hadn't meant to speak the words aloud, but somehow, she was glad she'd said them, because she needed the answer.

When he turned to face her, there was relief in his expression, as though she understood him and he was glad. 'Or anyone,' he repeated quietly, squeezing her hand. 'And I never will.'

There was a handful of people who knew how to access his penthouse without contacting him first. The concierge. Alejandro's driver, Raul. And Luca.

When Alejandro heard the door click open, some time before seven, when the smell of coffee had just started to fill the room, he tensed immediately, ready to fight, to defend, to protect Sienna, who was still sleeping down the corridor.

But the moment he saw Luca, different emotions knotted inside him. He remained tense.

'What are you doing here?'

Luca stood just inside the door, his dark eyes sweeping the apartment before landing on Alejandro. 'You have not been answering your phone. I was worried.'

A frown crossed his face. Where even was his phone? Usually, it was within arm's reach at all times, but since the night before he'd ignored it, wanting to blot out the world, the passing of time, everything. More than likely, it was charging in his bedroom.

'I didn't realise you were trying to contact me. Is everything all right?'

Luca prowled into the kitchen quietly, bracing his palms on the counter. His countenance had Alejandro worried. 'Probably.' He shrugged before fishing his own phone from the pocket of his dark jeans. 'Explain this.' He slid the device across the counter, and when Alejandro looked at it, something like lava poured down his throat.

'Where did you get this?'

'It ran in a gossip column a day ago.'

Alejandro couldn't take his eyes off the picture. Sienna had been so reluctant to dance, and yet there she was, in leather trousers, hair flaming down her back, body moving as though the music were running inside her bloodstream. He wanted to keep staring at it, but he was conscious of Luca and the implications of this photograph, and he felt the walls pushing in on him. The simple lie by omission was now an enormous canyon, and he stood right at the edge of it, precariously close to falling.

'It's Sienna, right?'

The idea of denying it didn't enter Alejandro's mind. It was one thing not to mention their relationship but quite another to lie to his best friend's face. Heat flushed his body as the reality of what they'd been doing slammed into him. He felt the sharp edge of the question, and badly wished Luca hadn't come here to ask it. But of course he had. What choice had Alejandro left him? His eyes flickered to the photo once more. Careless. Stupid. He should have taken better care of her. He'd failed Sienna, and Luca, and for the first time in a long time Alejandro grappled with a sense of wrongdoing.

'We connected at your wedding.'

'Connected?' Luca's voice was calm, but Alejandro felt the undercurrent of it. 'Is that all?'

'With all due respect, by what measure is that any of your business?' Only it was Luca's business. Sienna was his sister-in-law, and Luca was the only reason they'd met. More heat flushed through Alejandro now, as he imagined having *not* met Sienna. What if the wedding party had proceeded and he'd never noticed her? Never spoken to her? Never touched her? Ice overtook heat at a reality he refused to contemplate.

He turned away, his emotions firing, so he reached for the coffeepot and poured two dark, strong cups, handing one across to Luca even when he could barely meet the other man's eyes.

'You are aware of what she means to Olivia, and what Olivia means to me. Sienna is therefore very much my business.'

Alejandro's gut twisted. And now, he felt like an outsider to their family, a wolf who'd abducted a feisty little sheep. 'But who she spends her time with is not.'

'You forget, Alex, I *know* how you spend your time. I know what you do to women. Please tell me you have not added her to the collection.'

Alejandro's fists pounded. Anger was a beast now, overtaking his body. 'What do I do to women?' he asked, the words dripping with contempt.

Luca waved a hand through the air. 'Nothing they don't welcome, but nor do you offer a chance for anything more than sex, and Sienna is not that kind of woman. She's been through too much to cope with you. She's not your equal in any way.'

The ground tipped beneath Alejandro's feet. He wanted to deny that, to defend her, but, God help him, Luca was right, and Alejandro had known it all along. Had known it and pursued this because he'd wanted her more than any other woman. Because she'd fascinated him—because of her differences from the women he usually slept with.

'Sienna's life is hers to live.'

Luca cursed, the sound filling the room, a loud, furious epithet. 'You are not denying it.'

'I'm saying it's none of your goddamned business.'

'And I'm saying it is. If you have used her, treated her badly, then you must know our friendship is at an end,

Alex. She is Olivia's sister, which makes her my sister. My family.'

Alejandro drank from his coffee because he needed the rush of adrenaline, but also because he needed to cool his temper. He was firing on all jets, and, despite what Luca had just said, they were close friends, and the friendship deserved to be handled with respect. But it was galling to hear Luca claim ownership over Sienna as though she were an object, instead of a fiercely intelligent woman with her own free will—who'd chosen him, and this.

'You shouldn't have come here.'

'I tried to contact you. When you didn't answer I thought one of two things: either something was wrong, or that you were avoiding me. Both warranted a personal visit.'

Alejandro made a sneering noise. 'I don't need to be mothered.'

'I'm not. If anything, I'm mothering Sienna.'

'She doesn't need it either.'

'How the hell would you know?'

Because I know her. Because I know that at her core there is strength and determination, because I see her like nobody else in the whole goddamned world does.

'Because she's a grown woman, capable of making her own choices.'

'And you are saying one of those choices was you?'

'I'm saying you should back the hell away from this.' Those protective instincts were back, raising Alejandro's hackles, so he wanted to push Luca out of his front door. 'Sienna's fine. I would never do anything to hurt her.'

'*Cristo.* It's true, isn't it? You screwed her?'

The crude expression jolted through Alejandro. 'At any point have I ever discussed the intricacies of my personal life with you?'

'You don't need to. I've seen you in person. Which is

why, when this photo came up on my phone, I knew there was more to it.'

'What the hell are you doing trawling gossip columns anyway? Don't you have more important things to be doing?'

'My assistant scans them each morning, looking for any mention of the pregnancy, or PR issues regarding the business.' He waved a hand through the air, dismissing the line of questioning. 'She sent the image, knowing my connection to you. How I happened to see it does not particularly matter, anyway.'

Alejandro compressed his lips, and for the first time since Luca arrived he was conscious of the fact that Sienna was in the room down the corridor, that if they were not careful she would wake and hear this argument. 'Come onto the terrace.' He gestured towards the space, the offer not exactly brimming with hospitality, but it was a stunning morning, and he hoped—

'I don't want to go onto the damned terrace, Alejandro. You're not listening to me. Sienna is not a plaything. She is not some bored socialite looking for a night of fun. She is a kind, gentle, sweet young woman who's been treated like you wouldn't believe by their mother for her whole life. I asked you to take care of her that night to *protect* her. Not just from her mother, but from any other guy who might make a pass at her. I asked you because I thought I could trust you—with my life.'

Guilt tore through Alejandro, splintering him into a thousand pieces. There was no defending what he'd done. Luca had relied on him and he'd betrayed him from the very first. But what about his obligations to Sienna, and to their chemistry? It had burned brightest of all, demanding attention. He had been split in two from the instant she'd turned towards him and blinked, as though she'd never seen a man before in her life. He'd focussed on their desire to the exclusion of all else, and yet his greatest fear was playing out right before him. He'd tried to make everything so clear, but what if he'd failed? What if he'd been inviting the same kind of mistreatment his father had meted out to his mother? What if he'd misled her into believing he could offer more? His goal in life was to avoid exploiting women, to prove to himself he was nothing like his father, and yet here he was, taking what he wanted from an innocent, inexperienced woman, using her body's desire for his justification. Guilt was a rush of arctic wind down his spine.

'You do not need to worry.' Except Alejandro *was* worried now.

'So this is not my wife's sister dancing with you? Or are you saying it was simply a dance, and nothing more?'

Scepticism laced the words and acid filled Alejandro's gut. 'I am not going to get into the details with you. If that is the only thing you're capable of speaking about, then perhaps it is better for you to leave.'

'Are you throwing me out?'

Alejandro ground his teeth together. Was she still asleep? *Cristo*, he hoped so. But just in case, he switched to his friend's native language. He knew Sienna spoke Spanish, but not Italian. At least if she heard the conversation, she wouldn't understand it. 'I'm not going to talk about Sienna any further.'

'Fine,' Luca responded in his own language seamlessly. 'Then let's talk about you. What in God's name did you think you were doing?'

CHAPTER THIRTEEN

SIENNA, ALREADY AWAKE, had dressed quickly when she'd heard voices, and now, as she padded softly, silently, down the hallway, she recognised Luca's.

'I asked you to look after Sienna. I asked you to flirt with her. To dance with her at the wedding. I specifically told you not to touch her, but you couldn't help yourself, could you? Despite the fact I hinted at her insecurities, her family problems, you just saw a willing woman and took her to bed? Accurate?'

They were speaking Italian, but it was one of the languages Sienna had tucked into her arsenal as a teenager. It was, in fact, her favourite. She heard the words without needing to pause and wonder what they meant, and they slammed into her like lead. Luca had *asked* Alejandro to flirt with her? To dance with her?

Her heart hammered against her ribs. Was that what that first night had been?

She pressed her back against the wall, terrified she might slump to the ground and that they'd find her as a big, blobby mess on the pristine floorboards. She squeezed her eyes shut, listening, concentrating on keeping her breathing quiet.

'And I did look after her.'

'You slept with her.'

Alejandro remained silent.

'Alejandro, I love you like a brother. I know you are a good man. But when it comes to women...'

'What? What do I do to women that is so bad?' She heard the hurt defensiveness in his voice and ached for him, because of how hard he tried to fix the lives of all the women who were like his mother.

'Nothing, when they are your usual type: rich, sophisticated women looking for a quick hit of pleasure and nothing more.'

'Do you know Sienna so well that you can say with certainty that she doesn't have those same feminine impulses and needs?'

Her stomach squirmed. She hated this. She hated being spoken about, she hated that they were fighting over her, but most of all she hated, in a way she doubted she could ever recover from, that Alejandro had been *babysitting* her the night they'd met. He'd walked away when they'd kissed and *she'd* chased *him*. She'd been chasing him all along, and now she'd foisted herself on him, in his own damned apartment. Never mind that he was obviously physically attracted to her: the conversation she was overhearing was evidence that he was physically attracted to any woman with a pulse. She was nothing special. But she'd made it impossible for him to say 'no', and he'd tried, several times.

'So you slept with her?'

'I'm not going to answer that.'

'I will take that as a yes.' Luca's voice was tight with tension. 'My God. Tell me this then—was it more than sex? Is that what's going on? Have you fallen in love with her? This would be the only way I could forgive you, you know. Love is different from sex—I understand its ability to change you, to alter what you want from life. Is that what happened?'

Silence stretched. Sienna's nerves pulled and she wanted,

oh, how she wanted, to hear him admit that it was more than a physical thing. But after the longest pause Sienna had ever known, Alejandro's voice practically growled. 'We both know love isn't in my skill set.'

'So you don't care about her?'

The pause almost killed her. She held her breath, fingernails pressing into the palms of her hands as she waited, tortured, desperate; and then finally, he spoke.

'I care about her.' Her heart stumbled. 'She is, as you say, a beautiful, kind, sweet young woman. Of course I care about her, which is why you should not worry. I can promise you I have not done anything to hurt Sienna.'

But he was wrong. Pain squished her organs into a funny shape. She saw stars and the familiar sting of tears clawed at her throat.

'She has been starved for love by her parents, berated and belittled by her mother, insulted at every turn, so I am afraid she would be vulnerable to the first guy who showed any interest in her. Is that what you've done, Alejandro?'

Her heart dropped to her feet. Was this how Luca saw her? Olivia? How everyone saw her? How utterly pathetic. Was that what Alejandro had thought, when he'd come to speak to her at the wedding? Had he pitied her then? And when she'd approached him in Barcelona, was that why he'd eventually accepted? Because he felt *sorry* for her?

She was so hurt, and so angry, and she wasn't going to stand in the shadows and eavesdrop a second longer. They were wrong about her—all of them. She wasn't an object of pity—in fact, her pride had been hard fought and she would never let anyone take that away from her. 'I've heard enough.' Her voice came into the room with only the slightest wobble; she followed a moment later, glad she'd dragged on a pair of jeans and one of Alejandro's shirts, her hair pulled into a ponytail.

Luca whirled around, his expression unlike she'd ever

seen it. She almost felt sorry for him. The panic in his eyes made her want to placate him, because she was every bit as soft-hearted as he'd accused her of being. But then she remembered how they'd been talking about her—Luca with such insulting, patriarchal pity and Alejandro with…cold detachment. She shivered, barely able to meet his look, though she felt his eyes on her, and couldn't fathom what he was feeling.

'Alejandro's right, Luca. This is none of your business.'

Luca's mouth dropped. 'I didn't know you were here.'

'No, and Alejandro doesn't know I speak Italian, so I can see why you each might have thought your conversation was nice and private.'

The words cut through the air. Luca's cheeks darkened. 'Listen, I'm sorry, I don't know what you heard…'

Now, she forced herself to meet Alejandro's eyes. Lightning sparked between them. 'I heard everything.'

Alejandro stayed right where he was, damn him. Didn't he know how badly she needed him? She wanted his arms to wrap around her, she wanted to feel his strength. But for all that she felt her own life slipping out of shape, she knew what she'd done to his as well. She'd put him in this position. She'd known he was Luca's best friend, and she'd pursued him, not caring how that might affect their relationship.

But he'd lied to her, and that was worse. How come he'd never told her that the only reason they'd met was because Luca had asked him to babysit her? Chagrin burned her cheeks pink. And yet, she wouldn't throw Alejandro to the wolves. His lie didn't change the fact that she'd pursued him. She'd come here asking him to make love to her. If Luca wanted to blame someone for the relationship, she was the rightful person.

'You're not giving your friend enough credit, Luca.' She dug her fingernails into the soft flesh of her palm to stave off tears. 'He tried to walk away from this. I pursued him. I wanted him. He did everything that was right and honourable. At no point has he ever misled me into thinking this is more than sex. Does that reassure you?'

Luca dragged a hand through his hair. 'With respect, Sienna, you are no match for him. If he had truly wanted to walk away, he would have.'

'That is true.' Alejandro's voice reached her, wrapping around her, and she heard the hint of kindness in it. He was trying to make her feel better. To undo the hurt that had been pelting down on her. But it couldn't be undone. She'd lived through enough of that sting to know the way it landed in your soul and never shifted.

'More pity?'

His eyes narrowed; there was danger in their depths, an anger and impatience that spoke of lost control. Not with her, but with Luca. He was furious with his friend for sparking this confrontation.

'Pity is irrelevant.'

'So you don't feel sorry for me?' She looked from one to the other, reality shifting to show her the truth for the first time since meeting Alejandro.

'I hate the way your mother treats you,' he said quietly. 'The way she spoke to you at the wedding...'

Luca looked from one to the other, a frown on his face, then he took a step nearer to Sienna. She ignored him.

'And so you slept with me to, what? Make me feel better?'

Luca swore softly.

Alejandro's only response was a visible one—his chest moved in and out, hard, as though he was struggling to draw breath.

'I don't need your pity.' Heat and hurt pride stung her cheeks. She turned to Luca. 'And I don't need you playing the part of the white knight, coming to save me from the big bad wolf or whatever. I appreciate that you're trying to protect Olivia from the fallout of this, from worrying about me, but I can assure you, there's no risk of that. She never needs to know about any of this.'

'I find it harder to contemplate misleading my wife than you two might.'

Sienna sucked in a jagged breath. 'I asked Alejandro to keep this a secret. Not because I wanted to "lie" to you and Olivia, but because my private life is exactly that—private. Olivia has been watching out for me since the day I was born and while I appreciate her to bits for that, it can be stifling, and I wanted to start living my damned life. Can't you see that this has nothing to do with you?'

'Even when I am the reason you met?'

'Because you asked him to look after me at the wedding?' Bile coated her throat. She didn't look at Alejandro.

Luca barely moved, but there was the slightest shift of his head, a small movement of acknowledgement.

'But everything that came after that was his decision and mine.'

'That's my point. Without me asking him to take care of you, none of this—'

'You don't get a say in what two consenting adults choose to do with their lives.' She dug her hands into her hips, her temperature spiking. 'I know you came here with good intentions, but I really think you should leave now. This is personal, and you don't need to get involved. I'm fine. Alejandro has made sure of that, all the way along.'

And he had. He'd been so careful to be honest with her, to keep her at arm's length during the day, making sure she understood that only the nights were hers, only his body.

But what of their dates? What of the way he'd shown her where he'd grown up? Wasn't that proof that he was sharing more than just his body? That maybe he wanted more from her?

She looked at him and her heart went cold, because she didn't see love in his eyes; she couldn't read anything there. Coldness flooded her soul.

'I'll leave. But I will stay downstairs, Sienna. When you're ready, you can come home with me.'

She had never felt more infantilised in her life. 'That won't be necessary.' He loved her sister so much, and he was doing everything he could to care for Sienna in Olivia's stead. She tried to soften her tone. 'Go home, Luca. I don't need you to protect me.' She moved closer to him, putting her hand on his forearm. 'But I do appreciate the sentiment.'

He grimaced, and she wondered if he was starting to rethink the wisdom of this.

'You, I will speak to later,' he muttered towards Alejandro, before stalking towards the door and leaving, so a crackling silence filled the room. Luca was gone, but his words were still there, ringing through the silence.

Alejandro watched her as though she were an unknown commodity, as though he couldn't predict how she might respond.

'Is that why you came up to me that night?'

The words throbbed with hurt she could no longer hide.

Alejandro's eyes closed for a moment and then he was moving towards her, but she flinched, needing him to stay far enough away so that she could continue to think.

'He asked you to "look out" for me?'

'Yes.'

At least he wasn't making up an excuse. 'And then, when I came to your office, you tried to get rid of me—'

'I did no such thing.'

'You did.' She wasn't interested in empty denials. 'But in the end, you took pity on me, because I was so honest, and you felt sorry for a woman like me, with no experience. You felt *sorry* for me.'

A muscle jerked in his jaw. 'Feeling sorry for you is not why I agreed to this.'

A sob was torn from her chest. 'No? Then why?'

'Because I *wanted* you,' he said firmly. 'Every part of you. I wanted you, despite the fact my best friend had told me I couldn't have you. I knew that being with you would jeopardise my friendship with Luca. Can you not see why I hesitated? He is like a brother to me, *querida*.'

She flinched. 'And can you not see how disgustingly patronising it is that you and he should even have had that conversation? To discuss me like…like…some kind of object that one of you has the right to grant permission to?' Heat stained her cheeks, anger rushing through her—anger was so much better than pain. 'You should have *told* me all of this. You should have told me it was why you stopped kissing me. You should have told me after we slept together. You should have told me when I asked you to keep our arrangement a secret. There were so many times when you could have explained why you'd come up to me that night…'

'But by then I knew you.' His words were spoken with devastating effect. 'I knew how others had treated you, I knew the dark voice of self-doubt that you have to work to combat, and I knew that you would take his remarks out of context.'

'Ah, is that what I'm doing?'

'Yes.'

'Really? So you don't think it matters that my brother-in-law begged you to "take care" of the poor, spinster sister? You can't see how that request reinforces every single rejection I've ever known in my life?'

His Adam's apple moved as he swallowed, and her eyes dropped to the gesture. Panic was gripping her, dragging her downwards. She dug her fingers into her hips to stave off the wave of nausea, fixing him with a frosty stare.

'But what does it matter, anyway? I came here because

I wanted to learn about sex, and, regardless of all that, you've done an excellent job of teaching me what I wanted to know.'

His skin seemed to pale, his eyes probing hers, watching her with an intensity that made her shiver. She blinked, looking away.

'That's all this is, right? Sex? And now, we really don't have to see one another again, except in passing. At which point, you'll be civil, I'll be civil, and we'll pretend this never happened.'

'Sienna—'

'That's our agreement, right?'

'And that's what you want?'

What she wanted? She wanted to scream! What she wanted was the exact opposite of everything she'd just said, but how could she have any hope he would feel the same? Suppressing a curse, she pinned him with her eyes. 'What do *you* want, Alejandro?'

God, his name in her mouth still had the power to make her feel as though she'd ingested stars in their purest form.

'I want—I need—to know that he's wrong.' He came towards her then, each step making it harder for her to breathe. 'I want to know that I haven't hurt you. That this thing we've done hasn't hurt you.'

'Because you see me as he does. Weak. In need of protection. Well, I'm not. You might pity the way I was raised but you should also know this: it made me strong. I learned to cope with just about anything, thanks to my mother, so don't worry about hurting me. You don't have that power.' It was, of course, a lie. No one had quite the same power as Alejandro, but she couldn't reveal that to him. Not without revealing too much of her heart.

'Then why are you crying?'

She lifted her hands to her cheeks, dashing away the treacherous tears. 'Because I'm mad.'

'You should be.'

She crossed her arms over her chest. 'I'm sorry things between us are ending like this.'

'It doesn't have to end this way, though.'

She bit down on her lip, not daring to believe he was offering more. Not daring to believe he was going to suggest she stay.

'Don't think about what Luca said. Don't think about any of that. Remember how it felt in my arms. Remember how it felt to dance together, to walk together, to ride my bike together. This was more than either of us bargained for—that's the truth you should hold on to.'

'Why?'

He stared at her blankly.

'What good will it do to hold on to that truth? At the end of the day, it changes nothing. This was just sex. You don't want more from me than that.'

'Are you saying you want more from me?'

She felt the foolishness of her words—but too late. It had been too easy for him to flip them back around on her. 'I— That's not an option.'

He watched her, waiting for her to continue. But what could she say? She needed to get married, and he'd never agree to that, unless of course she was pregnant, but what kind of marriage would that be? She shook her head slowly, clearing the thought—the hope and dream.

'I need to know I haven't hurt you.'

The words were dredged from the bottom of his soul and, finally, she understood. He lived in fear of becoming his father, of fooling a naïve, innocent woman into a relationship, of offering her more than he ever intended to give. He was terrified that history would repeat itself. It was why he'd worried so much about her potentially falling pregnant, why he'd been so adamant about marriage. And as hurt and angry as she was, she couldn't inflict those same wounds on him. He didn't deserve it. Or perhaps he did, but she loved him too much to be the instrument of pain to him.

'I'm fine, Alejandro. I got what I came here for, and now it's time for me to leave—just as we agreed. You've done an excellent job, everything I asked for, in fact. Please don't worry about me. I can't bear it.'

He frowned, scanning her face. 'And that's it?'

'What more do you want?'

She waited, so foolish to still hold hope in her heart, but wasn't that the power of love? To endlessly hope? It was the first time she'd understood her mother, and why she'd stayed with their father, even when he'd made her life a misery. She'd never lost hope that he would change, that one day he would give her what she needed, that he would love her back.

Sienna couldn't be like her. She wouldn't be. She gave up waiting.

CHAPTER FOURTEEN

SIENNA HAD BEEN wrong about hurt, and she'd been wrong about hope. Nothing in her past had prepared her for *this* kind of hurt, nothing protected her from its sting, and hope, damn it, hope was always there, beating its wings within her chest, so, no matter how she tried to push it aside, she felt it every time her phone buzzed, every time a car pulled up the drive of Hughenwood House, until, a month after leaving Barcelona, it was like embers in the woods rather than a proper flickering flame. Dying, but not dead, there within her, even when she knew it was impossible.

Alejandro Corderó was not the kind of man to pine after a woman. He wasn't sitting at home in Barcelona wishing she were with him. Hell, he wasn't thinking about her, remembering her, wanting her—he probably barely even remembered her name.

She knew that to be true, and she'd known it from the moment they'd got involved, but that didn't stop the pain from seeping into her organs, her cells, her blood until it was a thriving part of her.

'Really, Sienna? Pink and purple? You seem to have forgotten you're not an eight-year-old anymore.'

Sienna looked down at the dress she'd chosen—a summery, cotton shift in big bright splotches, and lifted her shoulders, pretending her mother's words didn't cut deep into her chest.

'And with your hair? Perhaps I should get you checked for colour blindness.'

She ground her teeth together. 'I'm taking Starbuck for a walk.'

'It's going to rain.'

'I don't mind.'

'Suit yourself.'

Sienna snapped her fingers and Starbuck came bounding into the room, a big, happy smile for Sienna and a growl for Angelica Thornton-Rose. Angelica grimaced in the dog's direction then turned, sashaying out of the kitchen as though the tiles were her own personal runway.

Sienna didn't walk far. She couldn't. She was so tired. In the first few days since leaving Spain, she'd been possessed by a form of manic energy, so she'd cleaned the house from top to bottom, pruned the orchard and replanted the vegetable patch, but as the reality of what she'd lost had sunk in she'd felt her energy deplete completely, and every day she woke with the same sense of dread in her belly: how was she going to get through this without him?

Alejandro shrugged off the woman's hand before turning to face her. The bar was dark, the music muted, the crowd thick. It was the perfect place to be alone—which was what he wanted.

'Alex, hi,' she purred, her pink lacquered nails catching the down lights, making them shimmer. She lifted one to her lip, tracing the outline of the lower. 'How've you been?'

He grunted in response, turning back to his drink.

'That good, huh?' She leaned closer, her perfume intoxicating. 'I've got some ideas for how you can feel better.'

He vaguely remembered her. They'd slept together a

couple of years ago, after meeting at the opening of a night-club. Her name escaped him.

'I'm not interested.'

'That's because you haven't heard my ideas yet.' And she kissed him just beneath his earlobe, a possessive hand pressing to his chest, so he stood abruptly, dislodging her completely.

'I'm not interested.'

She stared at him, bemused. And could he blame her? He had earned the reputation he had as a womaniser, a de-voted bachelor. No wonder she thought he was a sure thing.

'Excuse me.'

He threw some money on the bar to cover his tab then stalked out, one hand in his pocket, curled around the em-erald necklace that had, for a brief time, hung so close to her breasts and heart, a necklace he'd found curled care-fully on the bedside table after she'd left.

His head was bent low and his heart raced. Because he hadn't been with anyone since Sienna, and though he'd contemplated it, wondering if it might be what he needed to put her out of his head, he now had his answer: when the other woman had touched him, he'd wanted to hurl. Sex with anyone else wasn't the answer. So what was?

'I'm so happy for you guys.' Sienna hugged Olivia close, her eyes meeting Luca's over her sister's shoulder. He had the decency to look ashamed.

'Thanks. I wanted to wait until I saw you in person to tell you. Can you believe it? A baby!'

'Wonderful news.' Sienna nodded, mustering what she hoped would pass for an enthusiastic smile to her face as Olivia spoke almost nonstop about her pregnancy and ex-citement, about where they planned to live and how she wanted to decorate the nursery, and, in the small part of her mind still capable of functioning, Sienna saw for herself that Olivia and Luca were clearly besotted with one another. There was nothing fake about their relationship. Nothing contractual. They were in love. Genuine, mutual love.

Tears crowded her throat and she smiled, hoping they'd pass for happy tears. 'Congratulations. Have you told Mum?'

'I think I'll save that pleasure for another day.' Olivia looked from Luca to Sienna, as if for courage. 'Actually, speaking of Mum, there's something I wanted to talk to you about.'

'Oh?'

'There's an apartment in Rome. Luca…um…gave it to me, and we're not using it, so I wondered if you'd consider moving in?'

She stared at her sister in confusion. 'But why?'

'Well, because I miss you, for one thing, and because once the baby's born, I'll want you close. But also, because it gets you out of here.'

They both looked around the cavernous lounge room of Hughenwood House.

More pity.

'I'm okay, Libby. I've lived here all my life. I know how to deal with it.'

'But I miss you.'

'I miss you too. I'll come visit, I promise.'

'We would enjoy having you close by.' Luca's deep voice shifted between them. An apology? A hope of smoothing over the past?

She lifted her shoulders. 'I'll think about it.'

And on the one hand, she was tempted. She adored Olivia, and missed her like crazy. The thought of being close to her, particularly with her now being pregnant, was like a talisman that Sienna found it hard to turn away from. But it was also an escape route that only a coward would pursue. She couldn't run away from her life, not really.

Even in Italy, the past would follow, and the ache she felt at missing Alejandro would still be there, right in the middle of her heart.

Five weeks. He stared at the pool, the glistening water, remembering her, seeing her, the visage of Sienna so freaking real in his mind that she might as well have been there right now. He reached out a hand, but there was nothing. No Sienna. No hope. His gut twisted.

This was what they'd agreed to.

So why the hell couldn't he move on?

The way she'd looked on that last morning, when she'd put two and two together and come up with eight—that she could actually believe their relationship had boiled down to pity. That he'd slept with her because he felt sorry for her! He'd wanted her so badly, so much that it had been eating through him, between the wedding party and when she'd arrived at his office in Barcelona. She thought he'd agreed because he'd felt sorry for her? He'd agreed because he'd felt as though his life depended on it.

There was no pity there. Nothing but need.

And suddenly, it was imperative that she comprehend that. He didn't know why, but it was vitally important that Sienna not be existing with the idea in her mind that anything other than desire had motivated him to be with her.

He'd wanted her, and so he'd taken her—with no regard for the consequences. But that didn't mean there weren't any—and how would he know? He hadn't spoken to her since. He had no idea what her life was like, what she felt, if she was okay and, more importantly, he didn't know if their passionate affair had resulted in any complications. He owed it to her to find out.

She stared at her phone, disbelief curling in her gut, and she reached for it quickly, before her mother could see Alejandro's face on the screen and ask a barrage of questions Sienna had no intention of answering.

'Hello?'

'Sienna.'

Her name on his lips was like a whisper. She closed her eyes, moving from the dining room without looking at her mother. Starbuck padded along beside her.

'Is everything okay?' She pressed her back against the timber-panelled walls of the hallway, her eyes fixed on one of the paintings across from her.

'I'm outside. Do you have a moment?'

'What do you mean, outside? Outside, where?'

'Your home.'

She startled, pushing off the wall and moving towards the front door. 'My home in England?'

'Yes.'

'But why?'

'Could you come out? Or let me in?'

Her heart went into overdrive. 'I'll— Just a moment.' She disconnected the call, her pulse firing like crazy, her eyes running over her reflection in the hall mirror before she wrenched the door inwards. He was a little way across the drive, his back to her, the darkness of the night making it difficult to see much more than his frame. His large, strong frame. A body that had possessed her and driven her wild. A body she had foolishly started to think of as 'hers'.

She closed the door behind herself, Starbuck at her heels as she walked towards him on legs that felt made of jelly. Every step was the beating of a drum, slow, over and over, reaching into her soul, until her footsteps alerted him and he turned to face her and her world tilted wildly off its axis. Her heart beat way too fast. She couldn't do this. She was so completely in love with him that seeing him like this just made her want to fall to the ground and weep.

But she had to be strong. Not for ever, just for the next few minutes.

'I had to know.'

She shook her head, frowning. 'What do you need to know?' The words were barely a whisper.

'Are you—' But he didn't speak. He moved closer, their bodies almost touching, his gaze devouring her face in that way he had, so she closed her eyes, their past so perfect that to contemplate it was to experience a deep, sharp sense of pain. He smelled of his cologne, but there was the undertone of liquor, Scotch or vodka, something strong, so she frowned. He'd driven here, so he couldn't be drunk, but she could smell it on his breath...

'Your last night in Barcelona. That dress. When we didn't use—' His face contorted and his pain was like a whip, slicing through her.

'I'm not pregnant.' She blurted out the words, pressing a hand to her flat stomach regardless, ignoring the strange wave of longing that dragged on her. 'So you don't have to worry about that.'

'I see.' But he didn't move. He didn't step back, and his face didn't relax. Every line in his body was taut with tension. She knew she should put space between them but being close to him was hypnotic and necessary, after more than a month apart. She'd missed him so much.

And he'd only come to make sure she wasn't pregnant. He just wanted reassurance that he never needed to see her again, that was all. Fool! She cursed herself for allowing hope to catch hold of her.

'That's good.' But his voice sounded heavy. She didn't understand why he wasn't jumping for joy. He took a step backwards then, lifting a hand to his head, dragging fingers through his hair.

'Is that all you wanted?'

He pinned her with sparkling grey eyes. 'No.'

'Oh.' She braced herself for whatever was to follow. The truth was, she wasn't strong enough for this. She wanted to be. She wanted to feel nothing, but instead she felt too much. A river of emotions was coursing through her body, transforming her, so she found it impossible to fight this.

'That morning, with Luca…'

She swallowed, the words she'd overheard burned into her brain.

'I need to explain.'

'No, you don't,' she cut him off unevenly. Because nothing he said could fix it, and there was no point in trying. 'It doesn't matter.'

'It matters to me,' he growled, so Starbuck trotted over from where she'd been tinkering with a dropped apple. He softened his voice. 'Indulge me, for two minutes.'

Sienna looked towards the house and shivered. Only her lonely life and mother awaited her up there. 'Fine.' She tried to brace her heart for whatever would follow.

'Luca asked me to look after you, and, yes, he prohibited me from touching you. I appreciate how that must make you feel. In hindsight, I should have questioned him on the spot, but I didn't *know* you then. I wanted to help my best friend. Who you were was somewhat irrelevant.'

'Thanks.'

He grimaced. 'Let me finish.' She nodded jerkily, but her pulse was on fire, her throat hurt—everything hurt, in fact. 'From the moment I met you, I was waging a war, between what Luca had asked of me and what I wanted. At first, I thought you were like any other woman, that I wanted you because that's what I *do* when I meet a beautiful woman, but that's not true. You got under my skin, Sienna. Even then, on that first night, you bewitched me, with your two left feet and quick tongue, so I had to know more, to understand you completely. I wanted you—just you—and Luca had nothing to do with that.'

She tilted her chin, refusing to believe him, refusing to allow her heart to be vulnerable to him again. 'That's who you are. You said it yourself, you see a woman and you seduce her.'

'Not you. Not that night.'

'Because I wasn't your "usual" type?'

'Right.'

She sucked in a hurt, sharp breath.

'Because you were better,' he insisted angrily. 'You were so much more than any person I'd ever met. Have you ever had the sense that everyone in the world is like a shadow? I'd been so bored, Sienna, so restless, until I met you and you brought everything into focus for me.'

'You regretted sleeping with me.'

'Do you blame me? I'd wanted you, but I knew what that would mean to Luca, if he ever found out. I couldn't tell him—that would betray you—and so I knew I had to hide the truth, that I would have to live with the guilt of betraying him.'

'My sex life has nothing to do with my brother-in-law,' she shouted, so Starbuck weaved between her legs and made a low, reproachful growling noise towards Alejandro. She patted the dog's head to calm her.

'I know that. The situation was complicated. I resolved to leave you alone, even though I thought of you every night.'

'Oh, come on, Alejandro. I might have been a virgin but I'm not that naïve. I know what you're like. I'm sure you found ways to console yourself after the wedding, other women to distract yourself with.'

'No,' he denied vehemently. 'There has been no one since I met you. I went out with some women, in a stupid, misguided attempt to push you from my mind, but I did not so much as touch my companions. I couldn't. I craved *you*, Sienna, and anyone else would have been a very poor substitute.'

'Am I supposed to be flattered by that?' Her voice shook, because the truth was she didn't know what to make of his confession, but it did succeed in touching something deep inside her.

'I'm just trying to explain why I hesitated. You arrived in my office and I wanted to rip your clothes off your body, but I'd been living with guilt, trying to balance what I'd promised Luca, what I knew about you, with what you and I both wanted. I walked a tightrope the entire time together, but that doesn't change the fact that being with you was the most meaningful thing I've ever done.'

She spun away from him, no longer able to see him, to hear him. It was too much. Tears spilled down her cheeks, thudding against her breasts. She dashed them away but more sprang up, rolling with abandon over her face.

'I wanted you. For you. Nothing else mattered. And yet I'd spent my whole life convinced that I would never fall in love, never get married, never live a normal life. I sure as hell never wanted to be depended on, to let someone love me. Do you think any of that mattered? Intentions don't mean a damn, it turns out, when it comes to love.'

She stopped walking and dropped her head, not trusting her brain to properly decode what he was saying, not trusting herself to hope.

'I tried so hard not to love you, but what hope did I have? From the first moment we met, my heart was yours, and I know it will be always, whether you come home to Spain with me or not.'

She was shivering uncontrollably, his words rolling through her, but there was panic too, and despair, because she'd made herself a promise as a teenager and she couldn't think of abandoning it. 'I can't.' She sobbed.

'Right.' He nodded once, surprise in his eyes, but it was

quickly hidden behind a mask of calm. 'I expected that would be your answer, but I needed to tell you. These last few weeks, it's been building like a weight on top of me, so all I could think of was telling you how I feel. I love you. I need you in my life.'

'And I need to get married, and I know that's not something you'll ever want, and I accept that. I knew it about you from the start, but it's only going to get harder to leave you if we prolong this. You're not the only one who's struggled these last six weeks. I have been devastated. You talk about the world growing bright? All the lights have gone out for me. I've barely been existing. What would that feel like in a month's time? In six months? When you get sick of me and realise that your first impulse was right, that you're not into celibacy and happily ever after? I can't do it. I can't walk away from you again.'

'You misunderstand me. I'm not asking you to walk away. I'm asking you to walk into my arms and stay there for the rest of your life. I'm asking you—no, I'm begging you to marry me, Sienna. Whenever, wherever you would like. I cannot imagine my life without you in it.'

She pressed a hand to her mouth, to stop her sob from ringing out through the orchard.

But could she really hope this was happening? Could she really trust him?

'I thought Luca was crazy. He and I have always hated the idea of marriage, but now I see how stupid I've been. Marriage is irrelevant—it's the person you pledge to spend your life with, and all I can think about is wanting you with me. I want to shower you in love, to dote on you, to sleep with you over and over and over again, to work with you, to see you take my charity and turn it into something that changes the world. I want to *live* with you, to live my life, spend my days, enriched by you and supporting you. Not because I pity you. I never have. But because I need you, and I love you, and, frankly, I worship you.'

How could she answer? How could she find words?

'I thought of you as soon as I saw this.' He reached into his pocket, pulling out the emerald necklace. 'It is just like you—strong, unique, elemental and perfect.' He reached into his other pocket, removing another velvet pouch. 'But then I saw this, and I knew I couldn't come here without bringing it, regardless of your answer.'

He handed it to her and as their fingertips brushed a rush of heat spread through her body, tightening her stomach. She tilted it into her hand without looking, just as she had the first time he'd given her jewellery. But the weight of this demanded her attention, and when she looked down it was to see the most enormous solitaire diamond, surrounded by a circlet of black diamonds.

'My answer? I'm not sure I heard you actually ask a question.'

He lifted a brow, and for the first time since arriving he looked like himself. Almost relaxed, even.

'You're right, of course. How foolish of me.' He dropped to one knee, right in front of her, and Starbuck gave him an affectionate sniff. Alejandro laughed gruffly, patting the dog's head, before lifting a hand to Sienna's and holding it in his. 'I came here to explain, but mainly, I came to tell you that I love you and that all I can think about, all I've wanted for a long time, is for you to become my wife. Sienna Thornton-Rose, would you consider marrying me?'

She was silent, not because she didn't want to speak, but because she struggled to find the words.

'You don't have to answer straight away.' He stood, the relaxation gone, hesitation replacing it, so she ached all over because she loved him so much, and he was still suffering, with no idea how she felt.

'I can't,' she explained in a rush, so he nodded, his shoulders tense as he took a backwards step.

'Right.'

'No.' She laughed unevenly. 'I mean, I can't answer straight away. I don't know how to. That is to say, I don't know—you were so eloquent, and I have no words, I just know that I want—that I—' She shook her head in frustration.

He moved closer, taking the ring from her hand and fixing his eyes to hers. 'Do you love me?'

She nodded slowly. 'With all my heart.'

'I know I'm not the kind of man you intended to marry, but do you think you could—'

'I only want to marry you.' She rushed out the words. 'I can't imagine ever, *ever* being with another man. You're saving me from a life of celibacy,' she said with an upward tilt of her lips.

'I cannot picture you as a nun.'

'But a wife?'

'My wife? Definitely.'

In the end, when she and Alejandro were married, Luca and Olivia by their sides, Sienna's father's will was the furthest thing from her mind. As were her father, her mother and the lifetime of insults she'd been made to bear.

Her heart and soul were full of her husband, their future, their promise to one another, and the certainty that she was exactly where she was meant to be. Life was good, and Sienna had every expectation that it always would be, so long as there was love, and Alejandro.

* * * * *

CLAIMING HIS
VIRGIN PRINCESS

ANNIE WEST

MILLS & BOON

With special thanks to my friend Reeze.

For iced coffees and problem-solving on hot summer days.

For laughs over life's sillinesses.

For braving rapacious kookaburras for the greater good.

And for all the rest…

PROLOGUE

'HE MIGHT BE HANDSOME, but I hate him. How could he hurt our Princess like that? She's so nice and now he's broken her heart and she's miserable—'

'Shh! She'll be here any second,' another girl hissed. 'It's almost time and she's never late.'

Out in the corridor of the children's ward Ilsa felt her heartbeat quicken, though she kept her expression calm and her footsteps even. She'd had a lifetime to grow used to public fixation on her personal life.

To pretend it didn't bother her.

Because if she did, she'd go crazy.

Beside her the matron sent a swift sideways glance, cheeks reddening.

So Ilsa paused to admire a whimsical mural, giving the older woman time to compose herself. 'This is new. It wasn't here a month ago. It really brightens the place.'

'Yes, it does, Your Highness. The patients love it. They listed all the things they wanted included. It's good to see the young ones smile when they come out here.'

Ilsa nodded, taking in the painted scene complete with crystal stream, fairy bower, gnomes and animals ranging from hedgehogs to unicorns. Then she noticed, in the far corner, a perfect replica of the Altbourg royal palace she knew so well. Before it stood a familiar figure wearing a coronet on her golden hair, holding the hand of a dark-haired man in the distinctive green military uniform of neighbouring Vallort.

The likenesses of herself and King Lucien were unmistakable. Despite her tension, Ilsa's lips twitched. Would the artist paint Lucien out now their engagement was over?

Except it wasn't really amusement she felt but something deeper and darker.

Not because she and Lucien had ended the betrothal foisted on them by dynastic matchmakers. But because she was tired of being reminded of it everywhere she went. Tired of being defined by her broken engagement.

Not one broken engagement but two.

One fiancé dead in a freak accident and a second spurning her to claim his waitress lover instead. Everyone saw Ilsa as a figure to be pitied.

A bubble of emotion rose and she had to work to hold it in. She longed for privacy, instead of being continually confronted by the debacle of her failed wedding plans.

Except if she stayed away from public duties people would assume she was pining for her ex-fiancé.

Plus she knew from experience that work was the best antidote to such restlessness.

Besides, the children were waiting for her. Kids whose courage in the face of often severe illness put her petty concerns in the shade. They looked forward to her visits.

She turned to the matron with a smile she knew looked serene, as if she hadn't a care in the world. 'Shall we?'

They entered a room where two teenage girls sat in hospital beds. The younger one, bald from her treatment, swept up a magazine and stuffed it behind her pillow.

She needn't have bothered. The palace media team briefed Ilsa daily. If she remembered right that one led with *Ilsa Heartbroken as Lucien Flaunts New Lover* then went on to describe her as *tragic and lonely*.

Sometimes she wished she didn't have such a retentive memory.

By the time she got home Ilsa ached with tiredness.

Smiling continually and being the perfect, composed royal took a toll when you hadn't had enough sleep.

And when paparazzi kept screaming intrusive questions from beyond the security cordons. Between the solicitous pity of the public and the hectoring barbs of the press, she felt as if she'd managed fourteen public engagements today instead of four.

She thanked the footman who opened the door to the royal family's private wing in the palace. As soon as the door shut behind her she rolled her shoulders, took off her slingback shoes and flexed her stockinged toes.

A long soak in the bath would help unknot the kinks of tension and ease her shredded nerves.

A silent laugh escaped at the idea. Princesses didn't have nerves. That luxury wasn't permitted.

As she headed down the wide corridor towards her apartment, she heard voices through the open door of the King's study. The sound of her name stopped her.

'Do you really think it's a good idea, Peter?' asked her mother. 'Ilsa's twenty-seven, not seventeen. Taking her away then was sensible, but to do it now—'

'Of course it's sensible. That time it was only her fantasies about romantic love at risk. This time the attention she's attracting is hurting Altbourg. Everything's up in the air. The strained relationship with Vallort. The end of the treaty negotiations.'

Ilsa sucked in her breath as shock punched her stomach. Her skin turned clammy.

Her father saw her as a *liability* to Altbourg?

She'd always worked hard to serve her country. She

hadn't cavilled at a dynastic betrothal to Prince Justin or, when he died, to his successor, Lucien. Even though the matter-of-fact negotiations had made her feel like a second-hand car being offered to a bargain-hunter. She'd swallowed her pride, just as she'd once buried her romantic dreams and done what was demanded of her.

As for public speculation, she was doing her best to squash it, going about her royal appointments when she'd rather not see anyone.

'Peter! You can't mean it. Ilsa loves her country. No one works harder for Altbourg. She's always done everything we asked of her.'

Warmth flickered behind Ilsa's breastbone and she found herself pressing her palm there. Her mother, at least, understood.

'Of course she does. She was trained to.' Ilsa swallowed hard, forcing down the knot of bitterness closing her throat. Her dad loved her, she knew he did, but she also knew that tone. He was in royal mode and that trumped family feeling. 'But at the moment she's a liability. Things would be easier without her here for now.'

She drew a shuddering breath that didn't fill her lungs.

So much for loyalty and obedience. For never putting her own wishes first.

At seventeen she'd believed love would transform her life. She'd been wrong, of course, but learned you didn't die of a broken heart. She'd emerged stronger and more determined. She'd found solace in duty, the love of her family and the respect of her people.

Except now her people pitied her, strangers asked the most intrusive, salacious questions and her family…

She blinked. No need to dwell on that.

What mattered, she realised, was that she'd spent her life doing what was expected of her. Doing the right thing.

Reliable Ilsa. The caring Princess who softened the

face of royalty in Altbourg and fed the popular craving for a photogenic face.

But she was more than a face to be photographed for the voracious magazines. More than a hostess or gracious ambassador or even a dynastic pawn.

All her life her future had been mapped out and now, abruptly, that map had disintegrated, leaving her rudderless and, if her father were right, a liability.

How long since she'd been simply Ilsa? Since she'd done something for herself?

Maybe that was why Ilsa had felt restless for so long. No, worse than restless. She felt hollow inside. As if all that existed was a shell with no substance.

Ilsa had been trained to be independent. She knew no one else could make her feel better. It was something she had to do herself.

Suddenly, selfishly, she *wanted* to feel better, wanted to feel something other than responsible and dutiful, if only for a short time.

She wanted a taste of freedom.

She *needed* it.

CHAPTER ONE

NOAH NODDED AS the guy beside him elaborated on his business idea.

It wasn't the right time or place. The glamorous Monaco Yacht Club was crowded, and the band's music carried out to the massive deck through the open doors. But Noah understood the need to grab every chance to interest potential sponsors when you were starting out. Besides, the idea had merit.

Yet his attention kept straying to the dance floor.

It was filled with beautiful people, or people rich enough to pretend they were beautiful. The older ones danced circumspectly; the younger ones were obviously conscious of how they looked. Time and again he caught female eyes on him as dancers checked whether he was checking them out.

Only one stood out.

Like the others she was privileged and easy on the eye. But she seemed totally absorbed in the music, uncaring of who was watching. Her body moved to the beat in a way that dragged his gaze back again and again.

It wasn't just her absorption and apparent disinterest in the A-list crowd that set her apart.

In a short glittery dress of cobalt blue, her lips red and her gilt hair flying loose around her shoulders, she was Temptation incarnate.

Just watching her sinuous movements made his body heavy and tight with hunger.

Noah hadn't been able to get her out of his head since yesterday, when he'd deliberately kept his distance.

Ilsa of Altbourg, the alpine kingdom renowned for its ski fields, banking, robotics and quaint royal traditions.

Princess Ilsa.

Noah often dated rich women. He was a billionaire now and met his fair share. But he had a deep-seated prejudice against snobby ones who believed inherited privilege made them superior. Surely a princess would be one of those.

Yet at the charity lunch yesterday he'd wondered.

She'd been chic, composed and gracious, all the things you expected of a royal. Beautiful too, if you liked blonde snow queens. But something else had snagged his interest. Her aura of calm seemed, somehow, fragile.

Which was nonsense. She was at ease with the entitled crowd, confident and able, graciously agreeing to step in at the last minute to conduct the charity auction when the MC was taken ill.

Yet instinct told him she was more than a gilded royal.

He'd spent the lunch watching her, captivated despite himself.

Interestingly, Princess Ilsa had watched him too, though she tried to hide it. Again and again their gazes had met across the room. Each time he'd felt something ghost down his spine. A primal awareness that dragged at his belly, and lower.

Yet her glances hadn't been flirtatious.

She'd been...controlled. Contained. While those around her had grown louder and more laidback as the champagne circulated, Ilsa of Altbourg was as serenely composed at the end of the afternoon as at the beginning.

Tonight she wasn't composed. Noah watched her long, pale gold hair swish around her shoulders as she moved and felt everything in him tighten. His blood pounded a primitive beat that had nothing to do with the music and everything to do with *her*.

The woman who didn't even notice him.

A woman who should definitely not be his type.

'Mr Carson? If you could spare just half an hour somewhere quiet, I could explain properly. With some start-up funds I could—'

Noah swung round. 'I *am* interested in hearing more.' Just not now. 'Email a full proposal this week and I'll have staff look out for your message.' Then, nodding at the other's effusive thanks, he headed inside.

Noah Carson wasn't a man to ignore gut instinct.

It was time to meet the woman who'd haunted his thoughts for the last day and a half.

He was watching her. She felt it like the track of a laser across her bare arms and legs and even through the fabric of her dress, making her nipples peak and her flesh tingle.

She'd slitted open her eyes a minute ago, registering the strange frisson shivering across her skin, and glimpsed him in the distance. The broad-shouldered man with the enigmatic stare from yesterday.

She'd deliberately not asked her lunch companions about him because she didn't want to know. Yet her eyes had sought his time and again.

The music stopped and Ilsa's hair swirled into stillness around her shoulders as she dragged in deep breaths.

Her brief, precious interlude, losing herself in the mindless throb of music, was over. Time to return to the real world. Even if she *felt* different. Maybe it was just from wearing her hair down and a dress that ended halfway up her thighs. She tried to imagine her father's face if he could see her, then wiped the thought from her mind.

'Dance with me?' The dark voice, low and rich, curled around her like a silken rope, drawing her lungs tight.

Slowly Ilsa turned, knowing who she'd see.

His voice made goose bumps skitter across her skin and heat flare low in her body. Impossibly, that voice sounded familiar, as if she'd heard it before.

In her dreams maybe.

Despite her high heels her eyes were only level with his mouth.

The shock of her up-close view ricocheted through her. A tanned, squared jaw was saved from being too aggressively masculine by the hint of a cleft on his chin. And by his wide sensual mouth, curling at the corners and making her lungs squeeze even harder.

A voice in her head urged her to flee, screaming *Danger!*

But another voice whispered *Yes!*

Ilsa lifted her chin and met the most extraordinary stare she'd ever seen.

Under coal-black brows and long lashes, his eyes were turquoise. Not blue nor green but somewhere between. Clear eyes, bright and assessing.

No wonder the women on the other side of the lunch venue yesterday had preened and tittered, trying to catch his attention. Up close he was gorgeous, not merely charismatic.

'Your Highness?'

Disappointment furred her tongue and she swallowed. For a brief second she'd imagined them yanked together by the implacable force she felt vibrating between them. By a deep, inexplicable compulsion.

Of course it was no such thing. He knew who she was. He wanted to dance with a royal. Maybe make a social or business connection and be able to name-drop later.

Ilsa pulled on a princess smile, cool and charming. 'I'm afraid you're too late. The set has ended and I—'

Music rippled on the night air. Not an upbeat pop tune like the band had just played but something slower, melodic and soulful. The lights dimmed and his straight, inky eyebrows rose just a fraction, the grooves around his mouth carving deeper in a look of complacency.

It hit her like a bolt from the blue. He'd arranged it. The change of music. The lighting.

To dance with her.

Ilsa's eyes widened and she read confirmation in his gaze. Not smugness but a level of calm self-assurance that was powerfully appealing.

She breathed deep, telling herself he was just another man wanting an introduction to royalty. But that slow inhale brought a scent that scattered her thoughts, something rich and earthy that made her nostrils flare and hormones spark.

She could say she was leaving. Or that she'd had enough dancing for one night.

Instead she nodded and was rewarded with a flare of what looked like anticipation in those stunning eyes, even as his mouth firmed into a straight line.

As if he too wasn't sure this was a good idea.

Then he took her hand in his and slid his other arm around her, his palm sitting at her waist, all perfectly respectable.

It didn't feel respectable as he led her into a slow dance. Ilsa's nerves jumped and jangled as if she'd touched an electric wire and her breathing turned shallow.

By contrast, she moved in his arms as if they'd danced together for years. As if their bodies knew each other, anticipating every move, every shift of weight and slight pressure of hands.

Still their eyes held, and it felt impossibly intimate.

Which proved how unexciting her life had been.

Then his attention dropped to her lips and heat seared her. It took a second to realise he was watching her tongue trace her suddenly dry mouth.

Did he think she was trying to entice him? Dismay unfurled and she stiffened.

'Easy, Princess.'

He firmed his hold as she bumped into someone behind her. Now he held her closer, near enough that she felt his body heat radiating into her.

He moved with easy grace and she wondered what he did professionally. Sportsman? He had the power and athleticism and, she felt sure, enough single-minded determination. But his air of authority suggested something else. As did the calculation in his eyes, as if he assessed her just as thoroughly as she assessed him.

She was torn between wanting to know everything about him and knowing that when she did this fantasy of an elemental connection between them would shatter.

Was it crazy to hang onto the illusion a little longer?

'Why did you ask me to dance?' she asked finally.

He didn't answer immediately and when he did she wasn't prepared. 'Because I couldn't not.'

That jolted her right to the marrow of her bones.

There was no humour in his expression, just an intense focus that pierced several defensive layers. In other circumstances she'd expect some facile compliment about her looks. Instead his stare transfixed her. Just as well her body was working on autopilot, swaying to the seductive music in perfect time with his.

They were surrounded by people, hemmed in by dancers, yet everything beyond the pair of them was distant, as if they existed in a bubble, cut off from the world.

Ilsa blinked, realising her hand had crept from his shoulder to his hard chest, planted there as if staking a claim. Heat flushed her cheeks and she started to move her hand back when he shook his head. 'Leave it.'

She didn't take orders from any man, apart from her King, but the gravel note in those terse words made her pause.

'Why?' she asked again. 'Why couldn't you *not* ask me to dance?'

His mouth twisted up in a smile that she felt deep in some vital organ. 'I planned not to. I saw you yesterday and didn't approach you.'

Ilsa nodded. She'd told herself she was glad he hadn't. That he clearly wasn't as interested in her as she was in him. But he'd been on her mind ever since.

That was a first for her. Since her ill-fated teenage romance she hadn't fretted over any man. Yet ever since yesterday's lunch she'd wondered if she'd see him again. Monaco was tiny after all.

'But I couldn't ignore *this*.' He captured her hand, lifted it from his chest and skimmed his lips across her fingers.

The instant jolt of sensation buckled her knees and he tightened his embrace to support her. Ilsa's eyes felt like saucers as she met his knowing stare.

'You feel it too.' Yet he didn't look triumphant. If anything, his features looked stern. As if...

'You don't like me.' The words shot out before she could think about them. But tonight, with him, her usual caution had been stripped away.

'I don't know you.'

Ilsa was used to people eager to meet her and spend time with her. It was strange to feel she had to earn his approval, that he might even be predisposed not to approve.

But she wanted him to.

She turned her hand in his and stroked a finger down his palm, feeling him shudder and watching his eyelids droop in an expression of pure sexual desire.

Low in her pelvis she felt a new sensation. Something that made her shift her weight, trying to ease...not pain, but a sort of throbbing tenderness.

Ilsa snagged a deep breath, abruptly conscious that

they'd stopped moving on the edge of the dance floor, while other couples passed them.

She should step back, put distance between them.

But this feeling, this man, were too extraordinary.

If she turned away she knew she'd regret it. This flash of connection was rare. Would she ever experience it again? Instinct said no. Especially not with some appropriate suitor arranged by her father.

'I don't know you either.'

'That's easily remedied.' He paused. 'Come with me and we'll get to know each other.'

His words hung between them, inviting, tempting. Full of innuendo.

The intensity of his scrutiny stole Ilsa's breath. Or maybe it was the effect of standing so close to him, locked in his embrace.

The idea was outrageous. To go out into the night with a man she didn't know. It went against every rule.

Ilsa had lived her life by the rule book.

In her peripheral vision she saw the curious looks they were attracting. They couldn't stay like this indefinitely. They had to move.

Yet she couldn't bring herself to care. She was tired of worrying about image and public perception.

'Who are you?' Amazing to be considering this yet not know his name.

'Noah. Noah Carson.'

The name was familiar. Anyone who read the international press would recognise it. A self-made multi-billionaire known for innovation, dazzling success and the glamorous women in his life. Now she realised it was a hint of an Australian accent she heard in his deep voice.

He read her expression. 'You know the name?'

'You're notorious.'

His mouth turned down. 'Do you believe everything you read in the press?'

Despite herself, she flinched. It was a sore point given the flights of fancy that had been published about her ever since she hit puberty, and now the pity, scorn and lewd speculation levelled at her and Lucien.

She saw Noah register her reaction. 'Absolutely not. Do you?'

Was that why he gave the impression he responded to her against his better judgement? Maybe he saw her as leeching off her people and giving nothing back.

'No.'

He squeezed her hand and her thoughts scattered as pleasure rippled across her skin and into her bloodstream.

Noah leaned forward, his words a whisper across her temple. 'You're safe with me, Princess. You have my word. Nothing will happen that you don't want to happen.'

Her breath hitched at the thought of what she'd like to happen. It was unprecedented to hunger like this for any man.

Ilsa tried to tell herself she was simply feeling bruised and rejected and Noah's blatant interest was balm to her battered ego. But the real truth swamped that totally.

The truth was she'd never in her life been drawn to anyone like this. Every cell in her body screamed that it would be criminal, impossible even, to turn away.

She moistened her lips and saw his gaze flicker and sizzle. In answer her breasts swelled, her already peaked nipples aching.

'It's Ilsa. Don't call me Princess.'

His sculpted mouth tilted up at the corners and that hint of appreciation undid another knot in the fabric of her defensive caution.

How would his lips feel against hers? Hot and decadent or coolly delicious?

'Shall we go?' His arm slipped from around her back, making her sway as if suddenly unsteady on her feet.

Or as if she didn't know how to hold herself without him touching her.

But he still held her hand and somehow, though his was larger and rougher, their palms and entwined fingers felt like a perfect match.

'Where to?' Ilsa tried to imagine taking him back to her hotel room, walking past the studiously disinterested gazes of the staff. And past the shuttered stare of the bodyguard she'd spotted when she left the hotel today. Not one of her own, for she'd ordered them to remain in Altbourg, but one of her father's staff. An unwanted reminder that, though she wanted a taste of freedom, she couldn't outrun her real life, even if she pretended for a week or two.

'Come back to mine.'

Those amazing turquoise eyes held hers and Ilsa felt a moment's surprise at how inevitable, how right this felt.

'Yes. Please.'

CHAPTER TWO

ILSA WAS CONSCIOUS of the stir they made, leaving the crowded party, and was pleased Noah didn't stop to exchange greetings with the people eager to catch their attention.

She was grateful for the clasp of his hand. His touch reassured as a flurry of nerves hit out of nowhere.

Going back to a man's place, any man's place, to *get to know him better*, was uncharted territory. Yet walking beside him felt nothing but right. She was aware of his easy stride, curtailed, she was sure, to cater for her shorter steps, the brush of his sleeve against her bare arm and the heat of his tall frame.

As they left the building she caught sight of a familiar bull-necked figure and implacable face. The guard her father had sent after her.

No doubt before the night was out her father would hear where she'd gone and with whom.

'Are you okay?' Noah stopped, turning to face her. 'Have you changed your mind?'

The tilt of his head spoke of concern, even if his grasp of her fingers spoke of urgency. Ilsa liked that he'd noticed her momentary distraction and asked that all-important question.

She leaned close, breathing in the deep, aromatic notes of his male scent. 'I'm good. I haven't changed my mind.'

White teeth gleamed against his tan as he grinned and

Ilsa had trouble catching her breath. The man was hot, sexy *and* caring.

'Excellent. It's not far.'

Not far turned out to be at the far end of the marina.

Instead of a towering, ostentatious super cruiser, Noah's was a classic vintage yacht, all beautiful lines in sleek white and teak and large enough to have been used for round-the-world royal cruises.

'Your yacht's beautiful.'

Ilsa paused to take it in. You could tell a lot about a man from how he spent his money. If she read Noah right, he appreciated fine craftsmanship and quality as well as luxury. She knew wealthy men devoted to outdoing their rivals with the biggest, flashiest cruiser, jet or car. Noah clearly didn't feel the need to prove himself that way.

Another knot inside her frayed and disintegrated. Surely a man who took the time to appreciate substance and quality was the sort who'd take time to ensure they both enjoyed tonight to the full? A patient man.

It was the closest she'd come to feeling nervous about what was going to happen between them.

'She's not new. But I'm a firm believer in recycling.'

Was that an edge to his voice? She couldn't read his expression from his profile.

'New isn't always better,' Ilsa replied. 'Besides, she's got character.' Even Ilsa, who was no expert on yachts, saw that.

He swung round, his eyes meeting hers, and Ilsa had the impression she'd surprised him. He lifted their linked hands and brushed a kiss across her knuckles.

Desire hit her like a wave, crashing through her and eddying into every part of her body.

'Shall we?' he murmured.

Her smile threatened to undo him. It was full of delight and anticipation, making his own expectations ratchet up to impossible levels.

Noah told himself he was doomed to disappointment. Reality couldn't live up to the incredible build-up.

Nevertheless, he wanted to rush her aboard. He had to remind himself not to jump her the moment their feet hit the deck. They had all night and he'd take his time. Especially as, despite her smile, those smoky blue eyes held a hint of trepidation.

Could it be that Ilsa, the confident, poised Princess with the world at her feet, was nervous?

'Just a second.'

She slipped her hand from his and immediately he felt the loss, his fingers clenching into a fist.

When was the last time he'd held hands with a woman? With Ilsa it felt as natural as breathing.

She bent to take off her shoes then straightened, dangling the sexy stilettos from her fingers. 'They're not good for the deck, are they?'

Noah captured her hand and led her forward. Right now he didn't give a damn about pockmarks on the wood. But he liked her thoughtfulness.

Once aboard he paused, remembering his resolve to take his time. Maybe he'd imagined her momentary nerves, but a slight delay would only make the final consummation more delicious.

Instead of taking her straight to the master suite he led her to the spacious lounge. A few lamps were on, bathing the room in an intimate golden glow.

'What's your favourite drink?' he asked.

'Cherry juice,' she said instantly, then looked as surprised as he felt. Quickly she turned to survey the room, making him wonder if she was covering embarrassment. 'Altbourg is renowned for its cherries so it's a staple for pies, strudels—'

'And juice.'

She nodded. 'But I know you're unlikely to have it. Apple juice would be good, thanks. Or sparkling water.'

Noah had expected her to ask for champagne or some exotic cocktail. Was he in danger of typecasting? Bitter experience had taught him socialites were predictable.

Reluctantly he released her hand and went to the bar, his body already tight with arousal.

'You're right, no cherry juice. But we've got sparkling water.'

When he'd poured them both glasses he turned to find her standing where he'd left her. The only difference was that her shoes were placed neatly on the floor and she held one hand across her abdomen. It fell to her side as he offered her a glass. Was that another hint of nervousness? Surely that was unlikely.

'Is it too cool for you outside? The view's good.'

Because if they stayed in here he wouldn't be able to resist sitting beside her on the lounge. Within two minutes his hand would be up that short skirt and the other hauling down her zip, even though he'd promised himself he'd give her a little time to adjust.

Hard and urgent would be fantastic, but he wanted a second, third and fourth time with Ilsa. Which meant curbing his lust to give at least the impression that he was a civilised man.

'Outside is fine.' She took a sip from her glass. 'If I get cold I'll let you know.'

Then he could warm her, preferably with full body to body contact. Noah repressed a sigh. *Soon…*

They sat looking across the harbour at the lights of the city. The sound of the yacht club party floated across the water but here in the velvety darkness, sheltered from prying eyes, it felt like they were cocooned in another world. The same feeling had hit him yesterday when their gazes had locked across the room. And again tonight.

He shook off the fantasy and turned to the woman beside him.

'We don't know each other except for this.' Noah

reached out and her soft hand slid unhesitatingly into his. Instantly his body responded, relaxing as if in relief at the same time as his flesh pulled tight in arousal. He swallowed, surprised all over again at the potency of this awareness. 'I suggest we take a little time to…explore each other.'

That didn't come out the way he'd intended, but his brain was being hijacked by a hormonal flood. Thinking of anything but sex took effort. Yet he sensed the need to take time with Ilsa. She was eager yet surprisingly diffident. He was determined not to scare her off.

'You want to know about me?' Was she surprised?

'And vice versa.'

She hesitated. 'How about twenty questions? We each take turns answering.'

Noah stroked his thumb across her wrist and felt her pulse leap. His own hammered like a piston, just from being so close to her. 'Not twenty.' He didn't have that much patience. 'Let's leave some for later.'

Her soft chuckle was a caress, teasing his senses.

Was there anything he didn't like about her?

Despite his caution around women who saw themselves as a cut above the rest of society, Ilsa kept surprising him.

'Okay. Tell me, Noah…' She paused on his name and he wondered if she enjoyed saying it. It was the first time he'd heard it on her lips and he liked her sudden huskiness. 'Something you've done recently that made you happy.'

He took a drink while he considered. Beside him Ilsa put her glass down, shifted in her seat and rested her palm on her stomach.

He thought of the fantastic deal he'd just made with a consortium of French companies. That had made him smile. Then he remembered laughing out loud just two days ago when his brother's family had visited him here.

'Easy. Spending time with my nephew. He's thirteen and full of energy. Let him near a windsurfer or paddleboard, or give him a chance to beat me at his new computer game and he's happy.'

'It sounds like you get on well.'

'We're similar types. Lots of energy and drive.' He paused. 'So, Ilsa, why are you here in Monaco?'

It was hard to tell in the dark but, holding her hand, he sensed her tension.

'The simple answer or the complicated one?' she said eventually.

'Both.'

'That counts as two questions.'

She shifted as if getting more comfortable and he caught a hint of the scent that had tantalised him as they danced. Light and citrusy. His breath quickened.

'So be it.' The sooner they finished the sooner they'd be naked together.

'The simple answer is that paparazzi can't operate in Monaco.'

'Ah.' Maybe he was wrong. Maybe what he'd thought on the dock to be nerves was just the wariness of a woman expecting to be spied on wherever she went. He'd looked her up online yesterday and knew she'd been targeted by the paparazzi recently. He felt sorry for her. And curious about the truth of what had happened between her and her two ex-fiancés.

'And the complicated answer?'

Her fingers twitched in his hold and he was acutely conscious of the slow breath she drew in, her breasts rising tantalisingly in his peripheral vision. Noah stifled the need to turn and survey her. Maybe the darkness and freedom from scrutiny would encourage her to share more.

He guessed she found it challenging, sharing something personal. Noah understood that. He was the same. Yet he felt tonight as if the usual barriers had come down.

'What's said aboard stays aboard, Ilsa. I don't break confidences, just as I don't expect you to break mine. But

I don't want you uncomfortable. If I've asked something too private…' Even if he wanted to know everything about her. 'We can—'

'No, it's fine. I'm just not sure I can put it into words. Though it might be good to talk about it.'

She threaded her fingers through his and Noah basked in her willingness to trust him. It was amazing how important that felt.

'You probably know about my broken engagement.'

He turned his head, catching the glint of her bright eyes in the gloom.

'I heard you'd called off your wedding.'

'Thank you.' She swung round to face him fully and even in the dark he felt a slam of heat as her eyes met his.

'What for?'

'Acknowledging I was involved in the decision. I should be used to the press by now, but I'm sick of being painted as some pathetic victim whom Lucien wronged! It was a joint decision and we were both relieved when it was over.'

Interesting. So she wasn't longing for her ex-fiancé. But what about his cousin, who'd been King before Lucien? Ilsa had been engaged to him until his sudden death in a road accident. Did she carry a torch for him?

Noah frowned, his hold tightening on her hand. She was free now but he didn't like the idea of her yearning for some lost love. He wanted her attention on him!

Ego, Carson. She only met you tonight.

Yet logic didn't come into this. It was amazing how proprietorial he felt about this woman. How inevitable it felt touching her, knowing that soon now they'd be naked together.

Again she shifted in her seat, making him wonder if she were uncomfortable or simply edgy. 'You could say my life, and the plans made for me, have unravelled.'

Plans made *for* her? Not *by* her?

'I thought taking up the reins of my usual life would see me through all the fuss and bother. If I kept busy, did my bit for the country, not just with the public events but my other projects, things would blow over and I'd feel…' She paused, making him forget to ponder what her projects might be and wonder instead about her feelings.

'The fact is…' she said with a brittle laugh that raked his spine like nails down a blackboard. 'The fact is I'm not needed in Altbourg at the moment.' She paused and he heard her swallow. 'And I wasn't settling into my old routine. So I thought a little time away was in order.'

'Some R and R. Well, you've come to the right place.' Noah's confident tone hid his sympathy at her vulnerability. She hadn't given details but her voice…

'That's right. It will be perfect for me.'

She sounded so bright and determined he knew she made an effort to mask her feelings.

He remembered her dancing. She'd been absorbed, lost to the people around her, but she hadn't necessarily looked happy.

Noah stroked his finger across her wrist, feeling her pulse jump and, despite his need to know more, desire jabbed.

Sitting so close, hearing each sigh and shuffle of movement, reading her body's unconscious responses to him and trying not to stare at this woman, grew more taxing by the moment. His trousers were too snug across his groin and he knew going slow when they came together would be almost impossible. Maybe they'd manage it the second time.

'Why are you in Monte Carlo?' She yanked his thoughts back to their Q&A session.

He shrugged, stifling the urge to haul her into his arms and plant his lips on hers. If she needed this time…

'I had a deal to finalise, which I've done, and now I'm having a break. Business has been bedlam the last year or so.' Which was good, because his new initiatives were succeeding. 'I worked through a bad flu and it took me longer than it should to shake it off.' His family had been on his back to take a proper holiday. Had even flown here last week to make sure he did. Even if they'd camouflaged it as a long overdue family holiday. 'So I'm taking a few weeks to cruise the Med.'

Except now the prospect of heading off on a sailing holiday had lost its appeal. He'd rather explore Ilsa than any photogenic port.

Urgency filled him.

He needed to hold her in his arms again, properly this time.

Noah sat straighter. 'One last question each.' He felt her eyes on him as he sought to distil the hundreds of things he wanted to know about her into one that would do for now. 'What do you want from life, Ilsa? What's important to you?'

That would tell him what sort of woman she was.

She went still. To his chagrin she slid her hand free of his, leaning forward in her seat and wrapping her arms around her middle.

Instinct told him he'd just made a huge mistake.

Silently he cursed. Why hadn't he asked her favourite ice cream flavour or whether she liked sport?

'What do I want?' She paused, frowning, and he sensed it was something she hadn't considered before. Finally, after a long pause she spoke. 'I can tell you what's important. My people, my country, my family.' Her voice sounded tight and unfamiliar. 'As for what I want from life…' She shook her head and her lush mouth turned down at the corners. Noah felt a phantom jab of discomfort to his gut, seeing what looked like distress. 'That's just it. I don't know any more.'

She shot to her feet and moved away. Instinctively he

followed but when he reached for her she shook her head. Ilsa stood, arms crossed, before him.

He didn't like even this small distance between them. But it was his fault. He shouldn't have probed so deep when she'd obviously had a difficult time recently. What had he been thinking? This woman clouded his usually clear head.

'How about you, Noah? What do you want?'

That was easy. 'Good health, good friends, enough challenge in business to keep me interested, and time with my family.'

'That sounds…perfect.'

Why did she have to sound so damned wistful? It wasn't just her voice either. Noah sensed a change in her. Something was wrong. He stepped closer.

She spoke quickly. 'Could you direct me to the bathroom, please?'

Noah frowned, loath to let her out of his sight.

Then his pulse quickened as anticipation stirred. Ilsa wanted to freshen up, ready for a night making love.

CHAPTER THREE

ILSA SHOOK HER HEAD, not wanting to believe it was true, but knowing it was.

Of course it was. Her life was a disaster lately. *She* was a disaster, according to her father. She should have expected malicious fate would play another trick on her.

She dragged a comb through her hair, tugging hard, telling herself that was what made her eyes water. Not disappointment and razor-sharp frustration such as she'd never known. And plain old-fashioned pain.

Another cramp twisted through her abdomen and she braced against the bathroom basin, breathing slowly.

Some women had easy periods that turned up as regular as clockwork. Not Ilsa. She, like her mother and her cousin, had endometriosis. In her case it meant irregular cramping periods. Usually the aches started long before the bleeding but not tonight.

Tonight she'd barely had any warning.

She blinked into the mirror, eyes filling and mouth crumpling at the sheer unfairness of it. Why now? Why tonight when she'd just met *him*?

Fate definitely had it in for her.

Noah Carson was the first man she'd been really attracted to since her teens. The first man she'd wanted. And, in tonight's strange, reckless mood, she'd decided to let him be her first.

No, that was too passive. This wasn't about *letting* him be her first real lover, but acting on her bone-deep need for him. An urgent desire such as she'd never known could exist, much less between strangers.

She felt ready to risk anything for a night in his arms.

Everything had seemed so perfect, so inevitable, that any last qualms had withered when he took her hand and those unspoken messages passed between their bodies. As if, instead of being strangers, they already knew each other in the most essential ways.

Ilsa blinked, suppressing the urge to howl in outrage and despair.

She'd never experienced anything like this, and probably never would again.

Next time her father organised her betrothal for dynastic purposes, there'd be no escape. She'd marry some man out of duty. The chance she'd feel anything like what she felt for Noah was non-existent.

For years she'd accepted that as her fate. But now…

She'd changed. She craved more. She wanted…

Jerking up her chin she met over-bright eyes in the mirror.

It doesn't matter what you want. Tonight just won't happen. And Noah Carson isn't going to wait around for a week until you're ready. The fantasy is over. You've missed your chance.

Putting her comb back in her purse, Ilsa fought the urge to rage and scream her disappointment. She pushed back her shoulders and schooled her features into a mask of calm.

When she reached the large sitting room, she found Noah waiting for her instead of on the deck.

Her heart bumped hard against her ribs then took up an unsteady beat.

With his hands in his trouser pockets, his stance accentuated his wide shoulders and lean length. He looked delicious, especially when his searing gaze took hers and his mouth curled up in a smile she felt in every pore and deeper, right at the centre of her being.

Ilsa swallowed. She had no choice but to walk away. Yet it felt like the hardest thing she'd ever done. Far harder than ending her engagement.

'Have I told you how good you look?' His words burred across her skin, drawing it tight with goose bumps. 'Absolutely delectable.'

'I—' She'd been about to respond in kind and say he looked good enough to eat. Her mind snagged on the notion of tasting her way across his body. Then snapped back to the fact that wouldn't be possible. 'I'm so sorry, Noah. But I have to leave.'

His smile disappeared. 'Did you get a message? Something urgent?'

'No.' Maybe she should have lied and said yes, but Ilsa was innately truthful. Besides, whatever it was she and Noah shared felt too visceral, too profound for lies. 'But I'm afraid this isn't going to work.'

The discomfort was worse now, a dull ache circling to her lower back to round off the tight, sharp fist of pain low in her abdomen.

Ilsa sucked in her breath and stood straighter, fighting the urge to hunch over.

'I don't understand.' Something flickered in his eyes that she couldn't read. 'Is it something I said?'

'No, nothing like that.' If anything, she liked him even more following his disclosures. How could she *not* be drawn to a man who got his kicks out of time with his nephew? Whose life goal wasn't making money, but enjoying family and the rewards that came from challenging himself?

He stepped nearer, tugging his hands free, and again the air between them snapped and sizzled with awareness.

Ilsa wanted to snuggle close, ask if he'd stay in port

until she was over this inconvenience. But that was asking too much. Besides, she didn't want to blurt out the humdrum reason she couldn't be his lover. Maybe it was pride or prudishness, but this felt too personal to disclose. She'd rather he remembered her as alluring and mysterious.

'It's your prerogative to change your mind, but at least tell me why.'

His gaze bored into hers and she felt it right down to her bones. He was right. He deserved an explanation.

Ilsa was a naturally private person and her royal training had accentuated that tendency. But she had already shared so much, things she'd never imagined sharing with a stranger.

Besides, Noah didn't feel like a stranger.

She drew a slow breath and shrugged. 'My period has started and I'll be spending the night curled up with a hot-water bottle to battle stomach cramps.'

Noah stared, stunned, into her lovely face. Despite her attempt at a wry smile, he read distress in her too-bright eyes. And—he saw it now—pain in the pinch of her nostrils and the pucker of her forehead.

Then her shoulders hunched on a silent gasp and her hand went to her belly, as it had through their game of question and answer.

'Why didn't you tell me straight away?' Her apparent rejection had made him wonder if he'd misjudged her. If she might be another privileged woman who liked to play games.

She shook her head. 'It's not something I usually discuss.'

He heard it in her voice now too. She was breathing through pain and he hated that.

'What can I do?'

Misty blue eyes met his, startled. 'Nothing. I've taken

something for the pain. I just have to ride it out till the medication starts working.'

Meanwhile she looked in no fit state to return to her hotel. Her brow looked damp and to his dismay he realised she was shivering.

Noah moved swiftly, lifting her into his arms before she had a chance to do more than gasp, then marching to a nearby sofa.

'What are you doing?'

Her shoes thudded to the floor as she grabbed hold of him. Noah sat down, cradling her across his lap, trying not to think about how perfectly she fitted his embrace and how his body clamoured for hers.

He looked at the sexy shoes tumbled on the floor rather than the sexy woman in his arms and worked on stifling his physical response. It was harder than he'd imagined, but nor did he like to imagine watching her walk away from him, especially when she was in pain.

'You're hurting.' He cradled her closer, leaning back so she tipped towards his body. 'And I'm comforting you. I don't know anything about period pain but I remember breaking a bone as a kid and waiting for the painkillers to kick in. My mum held me in her arms and it helped.'

She didn't say anything but after a moment he felt her shudder.

Was she getting worse? He tilted his head to see her face and discovered her crystal-bright eyes welling, her mouth a crooked line.

Something in his chest tumbled hard against his ribs. 'Ilsa? Is the pain worse? Do you need a doctor?'

She shook her head and a strand of light gold hair slipped across her bare shoulder. He watched her slender throat work then she blinked, clearing her eyes and offering a ghost of a smile.

Heat exploded inside him. Strangely he'd swear it had nothing to do with sex or the feel of her soft body against his. But everything to do with her smile and that sense of connection, just like when they'd sat side by side on the darkened deck, sharing confidences.

'You're right,' she said eventually, her suddenly husky voice catching at something inside him. 'Being held helps. I've never…' She paused. 'Thank you, Noah.'

Never what? He didn't push. She had enough going on without his curiosity.

So he shifted his weight to get more comfortable and reassured her when she protested that she was too heavy.

Eventually they lapsed into silence. Noah pondered his unprecedented response to this woman as she nestled against him, her head below his chin. Three hours ago he couldn't have imagined his evening ending like this. But then three hours ago he hadn't done more than lust after Ilsa from a distance.

The real woman, close up, was at once more complex and confusing, and far more appealing than he'd imagined. More appealing than any other he'd known.

The part of him that foresaw problems and worked out ways to avoid them warned that Ilsa could disrupt his life, just when he had things going the way he liked.

But a still deeper part of his psyche wanted her on any terms. She'd attracted him on the dance floor. Intrigued him when she asked for juice instead of champagne. Surprised him when she asked what made him smile and what he wanted from life, then moved him when she grew flustered when she couldn't easily answer that herself.

And through it all desire throbbed hot and strong.

She engaged his mind and his heart as well as his body. It was an intoxicating combination.

'How long is your holiday?' he asked abruptly. 'Days? Weeks?'

She tilted her head back against his shoulder. 'I don't have firm plans. I left on the spur of the moment.'

If her schedule was anything like that of the other royals he'd met, that was some feat. Even the quick research he'd done on her last night revealed a woman with a heavy public and diplomatic schedule, more so even than her brother's, the heir to the throne.

He looked down at her and felt the tightness in his belly ease.

Noah smiled and watched, mesmerised, as her pupils dilated. Whatever this was between them, he wanted it. And so did she. His time was his own for the next several weeks and, by her own admission, Ilsa wasn't in a rush to return home.

An idea had come to him that made his skin tingle, in a good way. As it did when he got his best ideas. It would mean taking a chance, but instinct urged that it was a chance he must take.

His smile widened. 'Why not spend your holiday with me? Let's sail the Mediterranean together.'

Ilsa gaped up into his calm, confident face and told herself she'd misheard.

But how could she have? She was curled against him like a kid needing comfort—something she'd feel embarrassed about in the cold, hard light of day—and watched his mouth form the words. And, despite his smile, she didn't read levity in his expression.

'You're serious.' It didn't seem possible.

'Absolutely.'

If she had more energy, Ilsa would have catapulted out of his hold and found a spot elsewhere in the room, where the cocoon of warmth enfolding her, and the firm cushion of his body, wouldn't distract her.

But there was no way Ilsa would give up his embrace until she had to. She couldn't recall the last time she'd been comforted like this and it really did help. Her mother had cuddled her close when she arrived home after ending her engagement, but that had lasted only a few moments, since Ilsa's father had been there too, waiting impatiently to discuss the political ramifications of the scandal.

Apart from that it had been years since she'd felt the comfort of a physical embrace. She didn't count circling the royal ballroom, held close, but not too close, by various dance partners.

'But you want…' She frowned and shut her mouth before she blurted out the obvious.

'You. Yes, I do.' Was it his deep, firm voice saying he wanted her that shot a bolt of longing through her? Or the way his nostrils flared as if drawing in her scent? He dipped his head, as if needing to get closer, and Ilsa's lips parted in anticipation. But he didn't lean in to press his lips to hers.

Her pulse thundered as she imagined Noah's kiss. Even as they'd sat in the dark, holding hands, talking as freely as only two strangers could, she'd been thinking of his mouth on hers.

'I want you, Ilsa.' His words were so potent they seared into her, making her shiver. Already he had a powerful effect on her, but hearing him say it in that suddenly rough voice was unlike anything she'd ever known. 'But you need time.'

'You'd give me that time?' It didn't seem credible. Everything between them had been so immediate, so blatant and urgent. Surely this was a man used to getting what he wanted instantly. 'I'm not talking about a day or two, you know.'

A glimmer of a smile lit his intent features and Ilsa felt it like the tug of a thread, pulled tight within her. 'I admit I'm no expert on the female cycle, but even I know that.'

Finally Ilsa gathered the energy to move, to sit straight, albeit on his lap, with his arms loose around her. It was appalling how at home she felt there. Even the sharp ache in her abdomen seemed more bearable when she was tucked up against him.

The realisation pleased yet at the same time worried her. As if she'd relinquished something to this man she barely knew.

'Why, Noah? Why me? And why go to such lengths?'

It wasn't distrust she felt, but confusion. She wasn't a woman for whom men made spectacular, dramatic gestures. She'd never been invited to a sybaritic idyll. She *hoped* that was what he had in mind.

'Why you?' He shook his head. 'I don't know. Either it's too complex to explain or so simple it doesn't need explanation. But you feel it too, don't you, Ilsa? This bond, this attraction.'

'I feel...something.' There spoke cautious Ilsa, the woman who'd been trained to guard every word and look.

Suddenly she despised that woman, living her life by the rule book, always concerned for what others thought. For once in her life she wanted to be impulsive and utterly selfish. She wanted to feel all the glorious things Noah stirred in her and much, much more.

'Yes,' she said, her voice louder, decisive. 'I feel like something's got into my bloodstream and when we touch it sizzles. But it makes me feel at peace too.' As if such contrary feelings could coexist!

It felt liberating to admit the truth, no matter how outlandish.

'You *do* feel it.' He met her stare with a smile and her heart lifted.

She wasn't alone then. If this was some strange illusion, at least it was shared. Noah Carson had no reason to lie.

'What if we wake up tomorrow or the next day and it's gone?' she asked. 'No sizzle left?'

His serious look turned into a slow smile that threatened to melt her bones. 'That doesn't mean we can't enjoy each other's company. If you get tired of me we'll put into port and you can fly home.'

Home. The word brought no solace. For the last couple of years she'd assumed her home would be Vallort where she'd be Queen, wife of a man she didn't love but whom she respected. Beyond that, home was Altbourg where she'd been born, but that wasn't the place for her now. She was a liability there.

'Ilsa?' Gently he tilted her head back, brushing her hair from her face. She softened, leaning into his touch.

'It's a mad idea.'

'Not mad at all. Following your instincts is never a mistake.'

He spoke with such certainty she almost believed him. She *did* believe him. Not enough to think there'd be no regrets. But Ilsa was tired of living a half-life, hemmed in by caution and others' expectations. She wanted to follow her passions. To live. To take a chance.

She thought of the reports painting her as a tragic victim and the malicious jibes against Lucien's poor lover.

Swanning around the Mediterranean with Noah would give the press something else to chew on, and maybe take some of the heat off Lucien and Aurélie. Her father would have a fit but right now she couldn't bring herself to care.

If the press got wind of it there would be a new sort of scandal and she wouldn't be viewed as *poor innocent Ilsa* any more. She doubted even her clever father would be able to organise an arranged royal marriage for her then. That alone was a good reason to say *yes*.

But that wasn't why she wanted to agree.

She lifted her hand to Noah's neck, pressed her fingertips lightly to his hot flesh and wondered at how magnificent that felt. He shuddered, his eyelids drooping in a look that spoke a language as ancient as the divide between the sexes.

That stare, that shiver, made her feel powerful and desired. She opened her mouth to say *yes* when realisation hit. Elation turned to dismay.

'I can't.' Disappointment tugged her mouth down at the corners. How could she have forgotten? 'I'm guest of honour later this week at a dinner hosted by the Monegasque royal family. I can't back out. I gave my word.'

'I see.' His hand covered hers and his look turned unreadable.

It was one thing to tell herself she was free to make her own choices now. It was another to insult her hosts so blatantly. She couldn't do it.

But that didn't lessen her disappointment.

'I have an important meeting in Athens soon and can't stay here,' Noah murmured.

So that was it. Ilsa's flutter of excitement became a crumpled feeling of sadness. She sighed, trying not to think about how devastated she felt.

'Well, I'd better—'

'Wait.' His eyes held hers. 'Tell me, if you could choose one place to holiday in the Mediterranean where would it be?'

Ilsa frowned. What was the point of asking when she couldn't go with him?

'Ilsa?'

'Turkey. I've never been to Turkey and it sounds wonderful.'

'Then meet me in Istanbul at the end of the week.'

'I…' She swallowed hard, excitement and something that felt like too much emotion clogging her throat. Noah made it sound so easy, so right that they should be together. Nothing in her life had felt easy or right for a long time.

His eyes held hers so intently she felt like she was falling into an endless warm ocean. 'Don't say no, Ilsa. Say yes, or at least that you'll think about it.'

The whole idea was outrageous. So *not* her.

The press would find out and then there'd be a scandal. But she couldn't seem to care.

'That sounds wonderful.'

CHAPTER FOUR

NEXT MORNING ILSA slept later than she had in years. She woke to familiar pain low in her body but also to a luxurious feeling of having rested well.

And fizzing anticipation.

Or was it disbelief at what she'd agreed to last night?

She lay pondering her decision to embark on an affair with Noah Carson. She'd be breaking with her past and burning her bridges. News of it would undoubtedly reach her family and the press. Given her savagely ticking biological clock and fertility problem she should be looking for a man who wanted to settle down, not a holiday fling.

Yet instead of second thoughts Ilsa felt elation. Every instinct told her she had made the right decision.

That feeling intensified when she turned on her phone and discovered a message from Noah inviting her to breakfast, brunch or lunch, depending on when she woke. Ilsa grinned as she texted back.

Excitement thrilled down her spine. Instead of a morning curled up with a book and a heat pack, she'd see Noah.

The man who would be her first lover.

'You look scrumptious,' Noah bent his head and murmured near her ear as he ushered her across the sumptuous lobby and out into the sunshine.

Ilsa's pulse fluttered wildly and she tried to contain her delight. 'You look pretty good yourself.'

That was a huge understatement. In casual jeans and a pale green shirt Noah looked rangy, sexy and utterly masculine. Her heart somersaulted at the way his eyes crinkled at the corners when he smiled at her.

'How do you feel today?' he murmured.

'Fantastic!'

That made him grin, a flash of white in his tanned face and a look in his eyes that made her knees tremble. If she didn't feel so excited she'd worry about his impact on her, but today that didn't seem to matter.

'Me too. How's the pain?'

She shrugged. 'Bearable.' She'd taken painkillers and she didn't want to talk about such mundanities. 'I thought you were sailing today.'

That surely explained her excitement at receiving his message.

Noah took her hand and turned down the street away from the hotel. Once more Ilsa felt that sense of utter rightness she'd experienced last night. Then he stopped, turning to face her, expression serious and eyes intense. 'I needed to make sure you hadn't changed your mind.' His fingers threaded through hers. 'Are you coming to Istanbul, Ilsa?'

She loved the way he said her name in a velvety rumble that made her twitch with pleasure. More, she loved feeling that he too shared the heady excitement of this moment. That it was profound in some way.

Ilsa stood taller. She'd had time for doubts, but none had outweighed her need for what Noah offered. Escape. Adventure. Sexual pleasure. The chance simply to be herself, not burdened by public perception or royal rules.

'I am.'

For a second longer he looked grave, then his shoulders dropped as he exhaled and she wondered if he'd been holding his breath. A smile uncurled from the corner of his mouth and the sun shone brighter.

'I want to kiss you senseless,' he growled, 'but maybe that's not a good idea. Come on.' He started walking, still holding her hand.

'Where are we going?'

She sounded breathless but with good reason. The thought of Noah kissing her senseless...

'A little place I discovered that I hope you'll like.'

Noah's little place turned out to be just that. Tucked away in a back street, it had a tiny back terrace with a glimpse of the sea and a profusion of pot plants. It was busy but not with tourists or fashionable celebrities. It had the charm and bustle of an unpretentious eatery popular with locals.

'I didn't realise there were places like this still in the city. So down-to-earth,' she said as a waiter left a basket of crusty bread and a bowl of olives.

'You like it? I thought it best to have relative privacy. Give the gossips less to chew on.'

Ilsa nodded and reached for an olive. 'Good idea. And I do like it. The scents are making my mouth water.'

'I'm glad.' His voice dropped to a low, intimate note. 'I want to please you.'

'Because you want me.'

Saying it aloud made Ilsa feel...powerful.

His lazy smile became a hungry grin that made her sit straighter, nipples peaking. 'I do. But there's pleasure to be had in simply seeing you happy.'

In another man she'd label that practised charm, but with Noah it felt real. Another first.

'You really are unique. I've met lots of men but none like you.' Noah lifted his eyebrows. 'You know what you want but you're not selfish about it.'

Last night she'd tried to mask the severity of her cramps, yet Noah had wanted to wake the onboard medic to check her. When she'd refused he'd insisted on sitting with her till the pain lessened before escorting her to her hotel. Ilsa couldn't recall anything like it, except once as a child when she was ill and her mother sat by her bed.

Then there was Noah's decision to visit Turkey because it was where *she* wanted to travel. Nor had he asked for details about the scandal of her recent past. That had earned her gratitude and respect.

She lusted after Noah Carson but *liked* him too. With him Ilsa felt she could unwind and be herself, whoever that was. She'd spent so long playing a role devised for her sometimes she wondered who the real Ilsa was.

'You've known a lot of selfish men?'

She thought of the man who'd professed to adore her. Who'd wanted to make love to her. He'd moved to greener pastures when her mother took her away to the States. Her parents had been right. He'd played on her romantic dreams, hoping to carve a lucrative royal niche for himself at the expense of her heart. But he hadn't had the patience to wait for her.

'I've come across one or two.'

One or two dozen.

Noah's hand tightened around hers. 'If ever you want to talk, Ilsa…'

Her eyebrows shot up in surprise. A man wanting to talk? 'You really aren't what I expected.'

Did he stiffen? His eyes narrowed. 'What did you expect?'

She shrugged. 'After that charity lunch I did a quick internet search.' She'd stopped almost immediately when she saw the parade of lovely women through his life. 'The press paint you as brash, brilliant and with an eye for women.'

'Maybe I am.'

'Maybe.' She tilted her head, surveying him. 'I can see why you keep topping those Sexiest Men lists.' To her astonishment, his tanned cheeks darkened. 'Noah Carson, are you blushing?'

'As if.' He lifted his arm, fisting his hand and curling his biceps in parody of a bodybuilder while he waggled his eyebrows.

Ilsa smiled. He might be hamming it up, but the effect was real. He was strong, attractive and potently masculine. Something deep inside stirred into life and it wasn't another period cramp.

'You're probably brilliant, since I know you made your own fortune. But you're not brash.'

Again he shrugged. 'I've been told I'm rough around the edges.'

'Really?' She scanned his shoulders, his strong arms, then lifted her gaze back to his sculpted jaw and brilliant eyes. 'I like what I see.'

His grin melted her bones and she was glad she was sitting. 'Good.' He paused. 'But do you know my background?'

Ilsa shook her head. 'I already knew your name, and that you're Australian. But I didn't do a comprehensive search.'

She'd intended to last night. It made sense to know about him before she embarked on an affair. But despite her elation she'd been tired and sore and had slept instead.

'I wasn't born rich, so my background is different.'

Noah saw puzzlement in her blue-grey eyes.

He was intrigued by how they changed colour. Last night in that sexy dress they'd looked blue. But when he touched her and sometimes when he caught her looking at him, they blazed silver grey and mysterious. He wanted to explore all her mysteries, find out what turned her on and all her secrets.

It was a far cry from the casual feelings he usually had for lovers.

She's not your lover yet. Maybe she won't be, when she hears who you really are.

Was that why he'd engineered this discussion? To check she wasn't like Poppy?

But Poppy was eager to sleep with you. It was only when you naively wanted more—

'Everyone's background is different in some way,' said the woman born in line to take a throne. 'What?' She'd caught his rueful smile.

Noah shook his head. 'Some differences are more acceptable than others.'

There was no need to pursue this. But now he'd started, he wanted to see her reaction. He needed to be sure she wouldn't get cold feet after he left and change her mind about meeting him in Istanbul.

'Tell me about yours.'

He spread his shoulders in a shrug. 'My family is fantastic, warm and funny. Very encouraging and supportive. I grew up happy.' Long summer holidays playing cricket or going to the beach, until he was old enough to get a job and he'd started saving and planning.

'You're lucky.'

Ilsa smiled yet her tone made him wonder what it had been like growing up royal. Whatever she'd been through, he guessed it had taken a toll, though she was adept at hiding it.

'I know I'm lucky. When you asked last night what I wanted out of life I realised I already have it. A happy life with my family around me.' He was the first in his family to hit his thirties and not marry but his experience with Poppy had soured him on the idea. 'I don't want a wife and kids. Or even a long-term lover.' He caught Ilsa's gaze, making sure she understood the limits to what he offered. 'I've got a large extended family and that's enough.'

'I understand.' Ilsa's tone was grave. 'You're not looking to start a family, just have some fun.' Yet something about her tone scraped his nerves, a note he couldn't identify. Then she continued. 'So, how was your family different?'

'My father and grandfather were garbos.' He saw her confusion and continued. 'That's Australian for garbage collectors. The ones who ride the trucks and empty the bins. Though now, with mechanised lifts on the trucks, those jobs are largely gone and it's mainly just driving.'

'And?'

'And what?'

She tilted her head as if to view him better. 'From your tone I'm waiting for something negative. Crime maybe. Violence?'

Was she serious? 'The Carsons are law-abiding. Hard-working but not in jobs people aspire to. Members of my family don't usually go to university.' He'd thought of it but he'd been too busy working. Once his business had begun expanding and diversifying it had seemed irrelevant.

Still Ilsa only nodded.

'Do you know where I started my business? Not trading shares or buying real estate, but with a clapped-out old truck, contracted to do a rural garbage run. Then another, and another. Clearly your online research wasn't thorough. From time to time the press call me *The King of Trash.*'

Imagine the furore if, instead of sharing a short affair with Ilsa, a man like him wanted something more permanent. All hell would break out, including in her oh-so-royal family. Just as well he wasn't in the market for long-term.

'I read that you'd invested in making road surfaces and other things from old tyres. So you run a waste management business?'

Far from being deterred, Ilsa looked interested. It wasn't what he'd expected.

'Partly, but it's extended far beyond that. It began with collection and disposal but our main focus is reuse and recycling. We've invested in a range of innovations that have done well and there are opportunities everywhere.'

Many projects were on an industrial scale, using the expertise of scientists and engineers, while others were grass roots schemes, some in developing countries. The latter mightn't make big profits but it was amazing how innovations in one area leapfrogged from an initiative somewhere else.

'And this is what makes you *rough around the edges*?'

Noah paused as the waiter served their meals but he didn't make a move to eat. 'Dealing with waste isn't what most people aspire to.'

It certainly wasn't a family business Poppy had wanted to marry into. To her he'd been good enough for sex. He'd been an up-and-coming entrepreneur, different to the men her family approved, who had old money and old school ties helping them up the greasy pole. But when Noah naively believed himself in love and asked her to marry him she'd been aghast. As if a whiff of the garbage heap would mar the nuptials. Not that it had stopped her trying to get money from him to support her start-up business.

Then there was the damage she'd done to his sister.

Ally had been in her teens and slavishly devoted to Poppy, who'd enjoyed her adulation. Ally was the one person in his family Poppy had time for, even inviting her to some events with her fashionable friends.

It was only later, as Ally battled depression and bulimia, that he'd learned how negatively Poppy and her friends had impacted his sister. They were so obsessed with appearances. All those comments about her needing to lose weight and the importance of looking model-thin at all costs had taken their toll. Poppy had dumped his sister cruelly too when she'd rejected Noah, leaving Ally battling the belief she wasn't good enough to be her friend.

Ilsa's sharp retort cut across his thoughts. 'You don't need me to tell you to ignore people who put you down because your family earned honest wages doing hard work.' She paused, her eyes flashing bright blue. 'Or did you expect *me* to think less of you for that?'

It was the first time Noah had seen her angry and he was torn between wanting to placate her and admiring how alluring she looked, her cheeks tinted with warmth and eyes sparkling. His skin tightened in response, as if showered by incendiary sparks.

'Not necessarily.'

He reached out and covered her hand where it rested on the table. A second later she withdrew it, cradling her fingers in her lap. It was a first and he didn't like it.

Her face told him nothing. It was composed and unreadable, except for those brilliant eyes.

'I didn't know,' he finally admitted. 'It matters to some people.'

Not anyone whose opinion was important to him.

Ilsa's opinion mattered, though. It surprised him how much.

'Your work is important. Managing our resources better is vital. As for looking down on you because of the family business...'

'What?' he asked finally when she let the words hang.

'Aren't you guilty of the same? Did you think I'd wrinkle my nose because of what *my* family does? Because I was born royal?'

Noah stared. That was precisely what he'd done, even if with some reason, given his history with Poppy. 'You're right. I did.'

He should have known better.

Still she sat unbending, chin up and shoulders back. Even in a simple summer dress of misty blue and no jewellery other than discreet gold earrings, she looked regal.

He wanted her so badly. He couldn't bear the idea of her pulling away from him now.

'Being royal isn't about wearing ermine and going to balls. My great-grandfather's proudest achievement was having a modern network of sewers built under the capital. And if you talk to my father he'd tell you that managing waste collection in a severe alpine winter is an ongoing challenge. Two of his major priorities are making our nation self-sustainable and reducing its waste footprint.'

'Touché.' Noah laughed, raising his hands in a gesture of surrender. 'I stand corrected.'

'I'm *not* my status, Noah. I might have an aristocratic title but that's not all I am.'

His laughter died. He'd struck a nerve. For the first time since they'd met she looked haughty. Not because he'd forgotten she was a princess, but because he'd remembered!

Noah leaned closer. Was that hurt in her eyes?

'I apologise, Ilsa.' He drew a slow breath. 'Having been the subject of prejudice myself I should have known better.'

He took a sip of water to remove the sour taste in his mouth, then laid his arm across the table, palm up, inviting her touch.

'When I'm with you I don't think of you as Your Royal Highness.' Not since they'd met on the dance floor last night. Noah's voice dropped to a gravel note. 'You're too down-to-earth, too sexy, generous and too much fun to fit my idea of royalty. You fascinate me.'

Her hand, smaller and softer than his, touched his palm. Instantly he folded his fingers around hers, feeling his blood pump faster at the connection.

'I want you for the woman you are behind the title, Ilsa.'

Emotion flared in her eyes and the pulse at her wrist beat hectically. Then the tip of her tongue swiped her pink lips and he almost groaned aloud. She seduced him as no woman ever had. The idea of waiting another week…

'That's the nicest thing anyone's ever said to me.'

She leaned across and brushed her lips across his cheek in a feather-light caress that jolted a few thousand volts through him.

Want. It was an insipid word. He'd known her such a short time and every moment had been torture and delight. Delight because she was everything and more than he'd dared hope and torture because sexual frustration reached its limit.

He didn't merely want Ilsa. He *craved* her.

No woman had affected him the way Princess Ilsa of Altbourg did, or so instantaneously.

His breath rasped in his throat and he jerked back in his chair.

'What's wrong, Noah?'

He made himself release her hand, pretending an interest in his meal. 'Nothing's wrong. But we need to eat before I do something that will totally scandalise the other diners.'

Later that week, Ilsa returned to her hotel from the royal dinner, resplendent in satin and jewels. It had been lovely, more enjoyable than she'd expected, but as she entered her room and stepped out of her high heels her overriding emotion was relief that finally she was free of royal commitments. Soon she'd fly to Istanbul to meet Noah.

Her phone rang and her heart leapt. Noah! She snatched it up.

'Ilsa.'

Her pounding heart stopped for a moment then sank. 'Father.'

Half an hour later she ended the call and stared, unseeing, at the landscape painting on the wall, her brain whirling. The King had supposedly rung to discuss that evening's function and various diplomatic matters that had been raised with her hosts.

There had been more too but, to her surprise, not condemnation about her being seen leaving the yacht club with Noah Carson. For once her father had held back, not lecturing about what she owed her royal dignity.

That had thrown her.

He'd flummoxed her further by saying he understood the last months had been tough, hinting at sympathy that her direction in life was no longer simple. Of course he never referred to the fact she'd spent years training to rule Altbourg but was now no longer his heir. Instead he'd reflected that she was old enough to know what she was doing, only adding that he hoped she didn't do anything she'd regret.

He'd ended by mentioning a recent deal Noah had done with a French consortium, saying he'd like to interest Noah in a similar project for Altbourg. Would she raise that with Noah? Persuade him to visit and discuss a proposal?

Slightly dazed at not being read the riot act by her father, Ilsa had agreed.

She frowned and rubbed her forehead with her fingertips. Could it be that he was finally treating her as an independent adult rather than a royal pawn? As for asking Noah to consider a business opportunity in her homeland, why not? If that was the price of keeping her father sweet she'd happily do it.

Ilsa rolled her shoulders and sank back in her chair, revelling in the sudden feeling of utter freedom. It was wonderful but daunting at the same time.

She no longer had a clear role mapped out for her, either as ruler of her own country or as consort to a royal husband in Vallort.

She'd have to decide what she wanted to do, carve out

a role that satisfied her duty to and love of her country, but pleased her too.

That was for the long term. For now, all she could focus on was seeing Noah again, pursuing the attraction between them and embarking on her first ever love affair.

CHAPTER FIVE

ILSA WAS MET at the airport by a stranger who escorted her to a limousine. He was friendly but it was an effort to respond to his conversation. She'd expected Noah.

Nerves hit and her stomach churned. Had she been right to come?

Maybe he'd changed his mind. Maybe he regretted his invitation.

But Noah would have told her.

Her bemusement grew as they drove away from the city, until the driver explained that she was to join the yacht. When they reached the sea it was almost dark. But there was a speedboat waiting for her and out on the darkening water a familiar graceful yacht.

Ilsa's heart leapt even as her palms grew clammy, doubts surfacing.

But when she finally climbed aboard there was Noah, reaching for her, pulling her close so she felt his heat envelop her. His eyes were so bright and hungry that exultation rushed through her.

'Ilsa, at last.' His fingers meshed with hers. 'I wanted to come to the airport but I didn't want to draw attention to the fact we were together. I thought you'd prefer to keep that quiet as long as possible.'

That banished her flurry of nerves and she smiled.

'Thank you. I hadn't even thought of that.'

Her mind had been fogged thinking about him.

'Come inside.' He led her through into a familiar lounge. 'If you're not tired I thought we could have a drink and watch as we approach the city. It's supposed to be spectacular.'

'I'd like that.'

'Good.' He squeezed her hand then headed to the bar, leaving Ilsa disappointed that he hadn't kissed her hello. She'd dreamed of his kisses and so much more.

'Here you are.'

Noah handed her a tall glass and she laughed. 'Cherry juice!'

'Freshly made. The galley is well stocked with fresh fruit for you.'

She tilted her head to one side, surveying him. He was as vital and gorgeous as she recalled and she found it hard to catch her breath when he was close. But it was the laughter in his eyes and his obvious pleasure at her delight that made her pulse quicken.

'That's very considerate. Thank you.'

'Don't look so surprised.'

She shrugged. 'Maybe I'm more used to people focused on what *they* want.'

He put down his glass and took her hand. 'Believe me, Ilsa, I'm *very* focused on what I want.' His voice dropped to an abrasive note that drew her skin tight in delicious anticipation.

'Yet you haven't even kissed me.'

Ilsa caught her breath. She hadn't planned to say it but the words spilled out. Because she was frustrated by the distance he maintained while she hungered for more.

She could have initiated a kiss, but something prevented her. Lack of expertise. Or a shadow of doubt? The only other man who'd professed to want her had lied. He'd been more concerned with her status than her.

Noah squeezed her fingers then let go, shoving his hands into his pockets, leaving her dismayed.

'Noah?'

Why the withdrawal? He'd looked at her as if he wanted to eat her up and his words had implied just that. But she didn't have the experience or the confidence to be sure.

'What do you want me to say, Ilsa?'

His gaze dropped to her mouth and she felt it like a graze, her lips tingling in response. Heat shuddered through her, that strange hollow feeling low in her body teasing her again.

'The truth. Only ever the truth.' She'd had enough of prevarication and polite lies to last a lifetime.

'You know the truth.' His voice hummed low and soft, the sound of pure seduction. 'I want you. Badly. Of course I want to kiss you. All over.' He watched her eyes widen and his mouth snagged up at one side in a smile that looked like a grimace. 'I want to feast on you slowly, Ilsa. And then I want to…'

He closed his eyes and shook his head. She fought the urge to plant her mouth on his. To grab his shoulders and press herself against him from head to toe.

His eyes snapped open and she saw raw longing there. She recognised it because she saw it daily in the mirror.

Noah swallowed, the movement jerky. Finally she noticed the rigid set of his shoulders and the tight clench of his jaw. She'd been so wrapped up in her response to his words she hadn't read the signs.

'I haven't kissed you because when we do there'll be no stopping. But I need to wait till you're ready.' His voice was rough, almost brutal. Yet Ilsa had never heard anything more wonderful. 'Unless you want to be ravished on the spot, kissing will need to wait until you're ready for more.'

Her chest rose shakily as relief flooded. He'd promised her time. Yet self-doubt and unrequited longing had made her wonder. It still seemed incredible that this stunning man should desire her, a woman no man had ever hungered for before.

'You're right. That will have to wait a little longer. But—' she paused '—I'm looking forward to it.'

Noah's breath hissed and she imagined him scooping her up and stalking off with her, because his patience had reached its limit. Excitement raced through her.

'So am I, Ilsa. You have no idea how much.'

By mutual consent they moved apart, not wanting to test their willpower. Even so the rest of that evening became etched in her memory as one of the best of her life.

The ancient city glittered like a thousand jewels displayed just for them under a black velvet sky. The dark water shimmered with lights from ashore and from other boats.

She and Noah stood on deck as they sailed in. Ilsa caught her breath at the floodlit dome and delicate minarets of the Blue Mosque. Then there was the ancient dome of Hagia Sophia and the clustering compound of buildings that was Topkapi Palace, where generations of Sultans had lived. They passed the Golden Horn and the grand Dolmabahçe Palace spreading along the waterfront. Ilsa was glad her first sight of the city was at night, when its beauty seemed more fairy tale than real.

Finally Noah took her ashore to a magnificent, traditional mansion right on the water. Several storeys high, it had tall windows and beautiful ornamentation, as lovely as anything she'd seen in Venice. The ceilings soared and the spacious rooms were decorated in an elegant style that bordered on the romantic.

He'd rented the house rather than book into a hotel or travel to and from the yacht. Because this would give them privacy.

Ilsa's heart softened again at Noah's thoughtfulness. He made her feel that she truly mattered to him.

It was the most wonderful gift she'd ever received.

That night, as she lay in her vast bed, watching the lights reflected on the dark water, she decided Noah was unlike any man she'd known. He heated her blood with a smile. Made her heart turn over with his thoughtfulness. The more time she spent with him, the more she wanted.

She just hoped she didn't come to want too much.

This could only ever be a holiday fling.

Exploring the city with Ilsa was eye-opening.

She was carefree and alluring. Everywhere she drew attention with her smile. She'd looked a million dollars wearing sequins and come-take-me heels, but casually dressed, her hair in a ponytail, she bowled Noah over. Again.

A discreet security team guaranteed they weren't bothered by paparazzi but didn't interfere as Ilsa smiled and chatted her way through the streets.

She talked to fishermen, leaning out from a bridge with their rods. She paused to admire water-sellers in bright clothes, carrying ornate metal urns on their backs, and others selling snacks like peeled cucumbers dipped in salt or rounds of sesame bread.

People were eager to talk with her. She exuded a warmth that drew them like moths to candlelight.

He'd thought from some things she said that public events were a chore. Now he mused that it wasn't the public she disliked, but something else. Something to do with royal protocols and arrangements, perhaps.

Suddenly he found himself curious again about her failed engagements.

He longed to know more but refused to probe.

Noah had wondered too what she'd want to see in the city. The fabled treasury of the sultans? Instead she'd suggested the covered market. Shopping, of course, he should have guessed. Except, instead of going to the Grand Bazaar, Ilsa opted for the Spice Market.

Just inside the door Ilsa's hand slipped into his. 'Isn't it amazing?'

'It is.' The scents hit him. A thousand flavours mingling and filling the air. Beneath the high, arched roof was a kaleidoscope of colours.

Already Ilsa was browsing a shop display. Cones of brightly coloured spices. Open sacks revealing blends of teas, peppercorns, whole spices and nuts.

'What are you shopping for?'

'I'm just exploring. Though that tea with the dried rosebuds looks intriguing. I know someone who'd love that.'

They investigated every part of the market. Noah wasn't renowned for his patience with shopping, but this was different.

Watching Ilsa's face light on discovering some new delicacy was a treat. Hearing her banter with stallholders, basking in her vibrant warmth as she turned to include him in the conversation was actually…fun.

She had asked him what made him happy and he'd instantly thought of his family. Now, remarkably, Noah realised being with Ilsa came close.

They hadn't even slept together. He was in permanent discomfort, on the edge of arousal. He should be climbing the walls with frustration and resentment, and it was true his nights were a torture of unfulfilled erotic dreams. Surely tomorrow…

'Are you okay, Noah?' She turned to him with a big package of Turkish delight in her hands.

He took the package and tucked it under his arm. 'Why wouldn't I be?'

She frowned at the package as if about to insist she

carry it, then shrugged. 'Because I've kept you here. Are you bored?'

'Surprisingly, no. It's been a revelation.'

Shimmering blue-grey eyes considered him as she smiled. 'It's marvellous, isn't it?'

'Absolutely.' Noah wasn't thinking of the market but her. He slid his hand beneath her elbow. Because he couldn't *not* touch her. 'When are you going to eat all these sweets?'

He'd seen her delight at breakfast when she'd found rose petal jelly and a pitcher of fresh cherry juice along with bread and an array of savoury foods. But, despite her sweet tooth, Ilsa didn't have the body of a woman who overindulged.

She had a slender waist and long, lithe legs, her curves just the right size to tantalise...

'It's not for me. There are people in Altbourg who'll love them.' She paused. 'Now, where would you like to go?'

Noah shook his head. 'It's your first visit. You choose.'

'Really?' She hesitated. 'There's something else I've heard about that I'd like to buy, if you'll brave the Grand Bazaar.'

'As long as you appreciate what a sacrifice more shopping will be.'

She leaned close, her breast pressing his arm and shooting fire to his groin. Her light scent of bergamot and warm feminine skin hit his sense receptors like a promise of endless pleasure. 'I promise to reward you.'

Noah firmed his grip on her arm, wanting so much more.

'I'll hold you to that,' he growled.

She blinked, eyes widening. Was that excitement he saw, or nerves? No, Ilsa wasn't nervous. Her body told its own tale of thwarted longing.

'I'll look forward to it. Meanwhile, lunch is on me.'

Instead of a posh restaurant, they grazed on delicious street food, Ilsa ordering enough for the security professionals he'd thought she hadn't even noticed. But then she'd have had such teams around her from birth. Her world was so different, even with his success and fortune as equalisers.

Their visit to the Grand Bazaar passed quickly, though it was an endless Aladdin's cave. It was crammed with shops boasting everything from leather goods to ceramics, metalwork, carpets, lamps and ornaments.

Soon they were seated, drinking apple tea while Ilsa inspected quaint leather slippers topped with brightly striped satin. Their upturned toes made them look like something from an *Arabian Nights* illustration.

Noah was distracted by a woman two shops away who raised her phone in their direction. He couldn't protect Ilsa from every photographer, though he'd like to. Already there'd been plenty of speculation about them.

'Perfect. I'll take four dozen in the full range of children's sizes.'

'Four dozen?' He swung his head around and leaned closer. 'Plans for a big family?' he murmured.

Ilsa stiffened. Then he decided he'd imagined it as she rolled her eyes at him before giving the vendor a shipping address. The children's ward in an Altbourg hospital.

Noah sat back.

She spent her holiday buying gifts for sick kids.

It was a thoughtful, personal gesture. Ilsa could have asked a staff member to organise presents but she'd done it herself. It wasn't just the buying, it was thinking about those children during a time that was supposed to be just for her.

Noah's chest constricted as if a balloon inflated behind his ribs. It took a moment to recognise the sensation. Pride. For a woman who really cared.

Five minutes later they were outside. Noah braced himself for more shopping. But Ilsa insisted he choose their next destination.

The Yerabatan Cistern was an ancient underground reservoir held up by hundreds of towering marble columns. They strolled in the half-darkness on raised walkways, strategic lighting turning the shallow water below them to shot silk. It was amazing and atmospheric.

'How did you know about this place?' Ilsa murmured, shifting closer as they surveyed an enormous stone Medusa head at the base of a column. The fact that the monumental head, with carved snakes in its hair, was upside down, made the blank eyes strangely disturbing.

Noah gave up resisting temptation. He roped his arm around Ilsa, his hand on her cool arm. Immediately two things happened. His hold tightened instinctively and she leaned in, making his heart thud.

He wanted to wrap both arms around her, pull her between his legs and ease the ache in his groin. He wanted to set his mouth on hers, as he'd been desperate to do from the moment he'd seen her sitting, prim and ridiculously seductive, at that charity lunch.

She turned, her chin lifting, and he sucked in air, ready to kiss her.

'Noah? How did you discover this? It's amazing.'

He fought the urge to kiss her till her blood caught fire like his. Except, once stoked, there'd be only one way to quench that fire. Besides, the gloom might screen other visitors, but didn't guarantee privacy.

Noah usually ignored the press but he knew a public airing of Ilsa's personal life had hurt her before. The press was already breathless with speculation about them. He wouldn't draw further attention.

Noah drew a tight breath and fought for control. 'Would you believe I saw this place in a film?'

Her lips curved up and it hit him, again, that she had a sweet smile. As well as a full, passionate mouth. He wanted those lips on him, all over him. He wanted—

'I can believe it. What a great setting.'

A flash exploded from behind a nearby column. It was probably some amateur photographer trying to catch the grandeur of the place. But it was a timely reminder.

Noah stepped away, ignoring an internal roar of protest. 'It's time we left.' This had to stop. He made a show of looking at his watch. 'I have a video conference.'

One he'd only just decided to accept, to put some distance between them.

Yet, even as he decided to accept the invitation, it felt like a mistake. Not because it was bad business; it sounded like an exciting opportunity. But because he'd rather spend the rest of the day with Ilsa.

'Oh. Of course.'

Was that disappointment? Ilsa's expression gave nothing away. Perversely, that annoyed him.

'Perhaps I'll come too.'

Perhaps? Why had he supposed she'd return with him? It stunned Noah how uncomfortable he felt at the idea of her wandering the city without him. The security staff would protect her but he wanted her near him, even as he tried to stay sane by putting space between them.

What did that say about his state of mind? He wasn't accustomed to such possessiveness.

Noah ran his hand through his hair, ignoring the sudden prickle of dampness at his hairline. It was just sexual frustration, magnifying desire so it felt like something else.

Ilsa put her hand on his arm. 'Since you mention business, there was something I forgot to ask. Might you be interested in a project in Altbourg? My father heard about a project you're planning in France and is very enthusiastic...'

Three hours later he ended the video call and leaned back in the desk chair.

His mouth ticked up at the corner. He might have agreed to the discussion to get some space from temptation, but it had been a good business decision. He shot off a message to his team, arranging follow-up.

Someone knocked. Probably the housekeeper, seeing if he needed refreshments.

'Come.'

The ornate door swung open and Ilsa stepped in.

Noah's gut contracted. His breath, when he finally managed to release it, sighed out between his teeth.

Her hair spilled around her shoulders, golden as a summer sunrise. Her dress, azure blue and lustrous, was moulded to her upper body before flaring out to end high above her knees. Which left those long, slender legs bare.

His gaze tracked down to spindle-heeled sandals that consisted of miniscule straps the same colour as her dress.

He raised his eyes, pausing of necessity at her breasts, their sweet upper swell just revealed by the straight edge of the fabric.

The dress was held up by straps so thin they looked as if they'd tear with one tug of a finger, or his teeth.

'Ilsa.' Her name was gruff in his mouth. He swallowed. He needed to sound amiable, not like a man wanting to eat her up centimetre by slow centimetre. 'You look rested.'

She looked bloody fabulous.

Desirable yet understated.

Except for the sandals. They screamed sex so loud it interfered with his hearing.

'Sorry?' He'd seen her lips move but hadn't heard the words.

'I asked if you'd finished your business.'

'Yes.'

He'd planned to stay here, sending a few emails before torturing himself with her company over dinner. But, faced with the sight of her in the flesh, the silky, alluring flesh, all thought of contracts and due diligence disintegrated.

Ilsa took another step and pushed the door shut behind

her. She paused and he saw her breasts push up against the constraint of the shimmery dress.

His mouth dried again. If he tried to talk he'd sound like a bear woken from hibernation. Or a man losing control of his libido.

She turned the key in the lock.

Noah's heart hammered against his ribs, sending every blood cell to his groin as excitement rose.

'Why are you here, Ilsa?' His voice was so rough he wondered if she'd understand the words.

'I want to kiss you, Noah.' His heart stopped then stuttered back to life. 'I want...everything.'

CHAPTER SIX

ILSA'S HEART DID a crazy slalom in her chest and her knees locked, making her stop, her hand on the door.

She'd deliberately not worn a bra and as she drew a deep breath the graze of fabric against her nipples was disconcerting. And arousing.

Noah stood behind a massive desk, looking potently masculine. Worn jeans clung to powerful thighs and his pale shirt emphasised both the breadth of his straight shoulders and the colour of those remarkable turquoise eyes below straight black brows.

She loved that intense hooded stare of his, the way it made her feel utterly feminine and alluring.

Yet this time she also felt a flutter of anxiety.

Her hand tightened on the key.

It was ridiculous to be nervous. Except this was new territory. Her one previous foray into romance hadn't been consummated.

Yet surely this was the most natural thing in the world. A man and woman drawn to each other.

She'd wanted Noah from the moment she'd seen him.

Her desire had only strengthened as she got to know him. There was so much to admire. He kept his word, he cared about others, not just himself. He noticed, listened, encouraged. He was fun and charming and...

He had the most fantastic body. Those hard, shifting

muscles, powerful limbs and taut backside. The determined chin. That mobile, laughing mouth that promised
all sorts of delight.

She wanted to rip his clothes off and quench the empty
ache deep inside.

'You're ready?'

Noah's voice was hot treacle over gravel, making her
shudder and sending a spike of sensation straight to the
apex of her thighs. She shifted her weight, feeling tell-
tale moisture as her body softened there.

Yet he didn't move. Instead his broad brow knotted.

Was it possible he'd changed his mind? Ilsa had spent
ages bathing and primping. Had she got it wrong?

Suddenly she felt overdressed in silk and heels. She'd
scoured her wardrobe for something sexy. This dress, like
the sequinned one, had been an impulse buy in Monaco.
She'd thought both said fun and carefree. But maybe it
was too plain. She wished she owned a black lace neg-
ligee.

'I'm ready.' She lifted her chin. 'If you are, Noah.'
She stepped forward then stopped, amazed to find her
knees wobbling.

Suddenly Noah was there, right before her.

His hands circled her upper arms supportively. 'Are
you okay?'

Ilsa read concern in his voice. Yet he looked at her with
hot eyes that made her think of summer seas and searing
sex. He *hadn't* changed his mind. He'd simply responded
to her tension.

A slow smile curved her lips and she watched his gaze
drop to her mouth. 'I've never felt better.'

Ilsa was surprised that her legs could feel weak when
the rest of her coursed with energy as if she'd been zapped
by an electric current. She swallowed and circled her dry
mouth with the tip of her tongue.

Something flickered in Noah's eyes that made her heart

leap. He released her arms and instead wrapped his arms around her, pulling her hard against him.

Yes! Glorious sensations bombarded her from breast to knee. She slid her arms over his shoulders, tilting her head to his as she strained closer.

His lips, she discovered, were cool and surprisingly soft, covering her mouth lightly in a caress that didn't feel tentative but tender.

The impression lasted just long enough for her to identify it. Then one large hand rose to the back of her skull, holding her as Noah angled his head for better access and plunged deep into her mouth.

Ilsa gasped and held on tight as gentle and questing became demanding. Her breasts peaked and fire roared in her veins as she pressed against him and devoured him right back.

She hadn't kissed since her teens and eagerness made her clumsy. Plus the fact that the kisses in her past hadn't prepared her for Noah's unbridled passion. The passion they shared. She was on fire and the only way to put it out was incinerating herself in the conflagration he'd ignited inside her.

Ilsa's nose bumped Noah's and she grazed his tongue with her teeth. But, instead of pulling back, he shuddered, his hold tightening as a low growl emanated from his throat.

He liked it. And the sound of his approval ratcheted up her own urgency.

She slid her tongue against his, bolder now, giving herself up to the magic they made. When she used her teeth again he planted both hands on her and lifted her up so she felt his erection right where she needed him.

Ilsa tilted her hips, desperate for more. Hunger was a consuming force, taking over her whole body.

Her fingers speared his soft hair as their kiss accelerated into blazing intensity. Her chest heaved, her heart hammering, but she needed his mouth on hers. She couldn't break away, even to breathe.

Until Noah pulled his head back, surveying her through narrowed, glittering eyes.

The air was thick with the sound of laboured breathing, charged as if from a sparking live wire.

Ilsa slid her hands around to cup his jawline, fingers splaying possessively over taut skin and hard bone, her thumb swiping his reddened bottom lip. She wanted to touch him all over with her hands and her mouth, discover the grain and texture and taste of him.

Noah's lips parted just enough that he could suck her thumb into his mouth, drawing against it as his gaze pinioned hers. She arched, pressing her pelvis and her breasts against him. He sucked hard at her thumb and she shuddered helplessly as traceries of fire ignited in her blood, from her nipples to her womb. Between her legs she felt lush dampness.

Ilsa opened her mouth to say something, she wasn't sure what, when the room wheeled.

Noah shifted his grip, lifting her off her feet and swinging her round. Then she was sitting on the desk, Noah standing between her legs, pushing them wide.

It felt deliciously decadent but it still wasn't enough.

He used his teeth on her thumb, just a tiny nip, but it made her shudder, squirming further forward on the desktop, pressing herself against the bulge in his jeans.

In response he pressed his palm against her lower back, holding her close while his other hand shaped her braless breast through the fabric. Ilsa's eyelids lowered as she pushed into his big hand, her body tightening in delight at the unfamiliar sensation. Had anything ever felt so delicious?

He pressed kisses along her thumb then her palm. 'I'd imagined our first time in a bed with a full box of condoms. But this works.' He moved his hips and the friction of denim on silk made her eyes roll back.

Condoms! Her brain snapped into gear.

How could she not have thought of that? She'd been so busy dressing to seduce and imagining the bliss of Noah's naked body, she'd forgotten the basics. Locking the study door had been an impulse. She'd fully expected them to end up in Noah's bed.

She blinked up at him. 'I'm sorry. I don't have one.' Some seductress she was.

Noah grinned, reaching into his back pocket and drawing out a couple of square packets.

'Ever since you came to Istanbul I've carried protection, just in case.' The look he gave her melted a vital organ or two. 'Now, where were we up to?'

He reached around her and found her zip, lowering it slowly, the slide of his fingers against her flesh incredibly arousing. As was the look in his eyes.

'I like that you don't wear a bra with this.'

He spread his hand across her bare back and lowered his head. Ilsa raised her mouth to his but instead Noah kissed her neck, finding a spot near the curve to her shoulder that made her writhe and grab at him. His mouth skated past her collarbone to the tiny spaghetti strap. A second later he closed his teeth around it and dragged it off her shoulder, making the bodice droop on that side, almost revealing her breast.

Ilsa shifted, her thigh muscles clenching as his knowing gaze met hers. Did he realise she was wet between the legs for him?

He dipped his head and dragged the other strap down too.

'Take your arms out of the dress, Ilsa.'

It was an order, his tone brusque. But, instead of being annoyed, she was excited because she read urgency in his glazed eyes and hard body.

She shrugged the rest of the way free of the straps and heard his breath hiss. For a long moment he didn't touch her, just looked, and she forgot that this was her first time and she needed to warn him, lest he be disappointed. She was too caught up in feeling sexy and wanted.

Gently he lowered her to the desktop, pushing away something that thudded to the floor, then put his mouth on her breast.

Nothing had prepared her for the riot of sensation. For such sharp desire. His mouth, and his hand on her other breast, fogged her brain and turned her into a keening, desperate woman. She heard the wild gasps, knew they came from her mouth, but couldn't stop them.

She held him to her breast with hands that shook. But it wasn't enough. She needed more.

Wriggling for purchase, she lifted one leg around his solid thigh, then the other, trying to get closer to all that lovely heat.

Brilliant eyes met hers as he licked her nipple then lifted his head.

'I like your thinking,' he growled, scrabbling at her skirt.

Finally she felt him, flesh to flesh, his hand between her legs.

Noah's eyes rounded as he realised she wore no underwear. 'I *do* like your thinking! If I'd known from the start you had nothing on under this dress...'

He shook his head as his fingers slid and explored.

Ilsa couldn't stay still. With every caress she *had* to move. Every touch sent her closer and closer to the edge.

Lifting her hips, she arched high, her eyes closing as tremulous shivers of anticipation started inside.

When Noah took his hand away she frowned and snapped her eyes open, in time to see him tug at his own zip as he tore the condom packet with his teeth.

Ilsa had expected this moment would seem weighty

and significant. She'd thought of telling him she was a virgin. But all that mattered was their need for each other.

Excitement and desire melded with something that made her chest feel full as she watched Noah frown in concentration.

She'd heard enough to expect her first time mightn't be perfect but didn't care. Next time would be better. Already he'd made her feel so very, very good. Not just aroused, but admired and appreciated. *Special*.

She wanted Noah with every cell in her yearning body. She refused to break this precious moment with a confession, as if lack of experience needed an apology.

So when he leaned over her, his chest bare now, his breath hot on her face and his shoulders blocking the room, she simply reached up and pulled him close. The weight of his erection teased her slick flesh. She knew a moment's surprise at how large he felt, but it was nothing to the compulsion to give herself and have him finally satisfy her craving.

'Ilsa.' She drowned in those tropical eyes. 'I want you so much I can't promise to last long.'

Then, before she could think of a response, Noah pushed slow and deep.

Ilsa's breath caught. She felt her eyes widen at the unfamiliar sensation, heavy, full and disorientating. She gasped as he paused when discomfort dragged at her. Then, after a second, Noah hitched her leg higher, up around his waist, and everything felt easier. With his help she wrapped her other leg higher, clinging to him as the almost-pain ebbed.

Even then he didn't move. Just leaned above her, chest heaving.

Ilsa slid her hands restlessly across his shoulders, feeling the damp heat of his silky flesh. She shifted, clenching her muscles, and felt him shudder.

He was close to the brink, shaking, she realised, with

the effort of not moving. Because he'd read her body's instinctive shock. But the shock was gone, replaced by a need to move and even more, have Noah lose himself with her.

Tentatively she circled her hips and was rewarded with a smooth thrust that took him deep to her core. So deep it felt as if she'd discovered life's greatest mystery.

Or maybe that was the effect of his silent gaze, locked on hers as if there was nothing in the world but them, together.

Holding on tight, wanting, above everything, to give Noah pleasure, she squeezed every muscle and felt him shudder. He withdrew and thrust again, faster, breath ragged and eyes glazing.

Triumph filled her and something softer, delight at his pleasure.

Abruptly everything changed. Noah leaned closer, his broad chest against her breasts, the friction of his body hair teasing her to full arousal again. Or maybe it was the way he nipped at her earlobe as his hand slid to that nub between her legs where sensation centred.

'Come with me, Ilsa,' he breathed against her ear. 'Come fly with me.'

His voice grated deliciously as he took her again, his fingers pressing hard, his teeth grazing her neck until the climax came out of nowhere. It rushed in, shattering her senses, her body, her ability to do more than gasp and hold tight as Noah bucked one last time then shuddered, pulsing within her.

Her senses overloaded. Pleasure frayed her thoughts, taking her into infinite space where there was nothing but ecstasy, and this man, anchoring her to sanity.

Finally, as she came back to herself, she registered the addictive scent of him filling her nostrils. The taste of him on her tongue. The rasp of their gasping breaths. His weight, hot and heavy but oh-so-perfect, his chest palpitating from effort. The last pulses of his body as he shared his essence with her.

Emotion rose and filled every corner of her being. Elation. Gratitude. Satisfaction. Wonder. Greed. Tenderness.

And something else that she had no name for. Something profound. She knew if she could see herself in the mirror there'd be stars in her eyes. But what she felt in her heart...

No one had warned her that her first experience of sex would make her so emotional. That she'd want to stay in her lover's arms for ever. That for the first time she could remember everything would feel *right*.

Not simply because of the physical pleasure but because with Noah she felt...

Drowsily she opened her eyes and looked straight into his. Her heart leapt.

For a second fear tickled her nape. Not fear of Noah but of how she felt about him. How tremendous the emotions bubbling inside her, when she knew this could only be a short affair.

Then he smiled and she bundled her fear to the back of her mind and told herself everything would be okay.

CHAPTER SEVEN

NOAH TRACED HIS finger from Ilsa's bare shoulder, down her arm. The rest of her body was covered by the sheet she'd tucked beneath her arm.

Her tiny shiver of response was echoed by the look in her drowsy eyes.

Strange that such a sensuous woman, a woman who'd brazenly marched into his office wearing no underwear, should be so modest about covering her beautiful body.

But then she didn't make a habit of parading half-naked for other men. She'd been a virgin.

Questions crammed his brain. And regrets. He'd put her slightly clumsy kisses down to rampant enthusiasm, not inexperience. Should he have realised sooner?

Not when she'd pressed that hot body to his and purred her pleasure in his ear. The sounds she'd made when he took her breasts in his hands and mouth had driven him wild. And the feel of her reaching her pinnacle around him, the sight of her eyes blazing silver with ecstasy, had blasted the last of his control to smithereens.

'What are you thinking?' Noah looked up to find Ilsa's sleepy eyes on him. 'You look serious.'

'Just wondering if I should have taken more time and showed more finesse.'

Her mouth twitched at the corners and heat stirred in his groin. Again. He only had to look at her to want her.

'I thought you showed incredible finesse. We barely slopped any water out of the bath. Even though it's big enough for two we were both rather...enthusiastic.'

The twitch of her lips became a siren's smile and Noah let out a pent-up sigh. He'd spent the last half hour trying not to think about sex with Ilsa and failing miserably. It had been an eventful couple of hours and he should give her time to recuperate. He'd only joined her in the bed because she'd wrapped her arms around him and refused to let him go when he carried her from the bath.

'I was talking about the first time. In the study.'

'You didn't like doing it on the desk?' Her brow furrowed. 'I thought—' She bit off the words and her gaze slid away.

Noah reached out, cupping her cheek and turning her head so she met his eyes. 'Of course I liked it. I can't remember being so turned on in my life.'

'Really?' Her eyes sparkled.

She had no idea. 'You're a very sexy woman, Ilsa.' He remembered her challenging stare as she locked the door and the blast of shock when he discovered she was naked under that flimsy blue dress. His groin grew heavy and tight. 'I wanted you so much I was scared I'd come to grief just putting the condom on.'

Her mouth curved again in a smile that made him think of a cat licking cream. She looked pleased, gloating even.

'I'm glad. I wasn't sure if you'd like it.'

Noah shook his head. 'I like everything you do. But I'd have taken it slower that first time. Been gentler.'

Her smile faded. 'Because I was inexperienced?' She inhaled slowly and he had the impression she was gathering herself. 'Did it make much of a difference? To your pleasure, I mean.'

His pulse tripped as he read doubt in her eyes.

Noah shook his head, sliding his hand into her hair and allowing himself one taste of her warm lips, slow and easy and inevitably arousing. It was an effort to pull back, especially when she kissed him back so sweetly.

'You have to be kidding.' She really *was* an innocent. 'I wasn't worried about my pleasure, but yours. For me it was fantastic. Exciting. Exquisite.'

She was exquisite. The tight, slick heat of her body, that impossibly snug embrace and the wonder in her eyes...

He shuddered, erection stirring.

That had to be why it felt so special. Because Ilsa had been a virgin, allowing Noah to be her first lover. That was sure to fire any man's libido. When coupled with her gorgeous body and her hoarse, sensual cries of delight, was it any wonder the experience felt extraordinary?

'I'm glad. I thought so too.' She lifted her hand to his collarbone, tracing a languid line down his pectoral muscle.

Pleasure jolted through him and he struggled for a distraction, something to stop him using Ilsa's body again so soon when she might need time to recuperate.

'It was an honour, being your first.' It sounded old-fashioned and he'd never thought about that sort of thing. But knowing he was the first man Ilsa had given herself to, the first she'd wanted and trusted with her body... It made him feel remarkable.

'You're wondering why I took so long to have sex.'

He tried to read her expression but couldn't. For the first time since Ilsa had walked into his world Noah felt uncomfortable and unhappy at the sudden distance between them.

It was crazy. He didn't need to know her every thought. Yet with him she wasn't the polite Princess who masked her thoughts. He'd grown accustomed to a bright, sexy woman who was both fun-loving and serious, who didn't feel the need to hide herself.

'I'm curious, but it's no one's business but yours.'

Noah planted his palm across her wandering fingers and held them flat against his pounding chest.

Was she so unaware that she didn't know what she did to him with those beguiling caresses? Being naked in bed with Ilsa was testing enough.

'I like that you're not nosy,' she said suddenly. 'Lots of people think my life and thoughts should be an open book because of who my father is. As if I don't have a right to privacy.'

Noah had grown tired of media speculation about him since he'd become rich and successful. What would it be like, facing the limelight from birth?

'I'm sorry to hear that,' he murmured.

'It's not your fault.' Her eyes held his and he wondered if he saw wistfulness there. 'Staying a virgin wasn't deliberate. It just happened that way.'

Despite his determination not to be curious he couldn't prevent a stare of surprise. 'There must have been plenty of men pursuing you.'

She was warm-hearted as well as attractive, plus her social standing would draw many.

'Fewer than you'd think, especially since I live in the media spotlight. As you know, it's tricky, keeping a relationship private. Plus a lot of people are daunted by the idea of royalty, or can't see past the title.'

It was something she'd said before. That she wasn't just her title.

'How could anyone miss the vivacious woman behind the royal name?'

The flash of warmth in Ilsa's eyes spoke of delight and gratitude. Of a woman unused to personal compliments. How could that be?

'Some men aren't interested in the woman if they think the title can get them what they want.'

No mistaking her bitterness. Noah's jaw clenched as he realised she spoke from personal experience.

'You look so fierce.'

He worked to wipe his face clear of anger. 'Sorry.'

Ilsa inched closer. 'Don't be. I like that you're angry for me.' She paused. 'Even when I can fight my own battles, it's good to feel someone's on my side.'

A giant fist crushed Noah's lungs as he imagined her, alone, pitted against men who wanted her for her status.

'For what it's worth, a man would have to be a moron to value your title instead of you.'

Her arrested look revealed volumes. He wanted to scoop her close and tell her no one would hurt her again. As if he had that power. As if she'd cede that right to him.

'You really are nice, Noah.'

His brows rose at *nice*, but he couldn't cavil when she regarded him so warmly.

'I *did* fall for someone when I was in my teens. He swept me off my feet, or tried to.' Her mouth twisted. 'I was smitten and believed he was the love of my life. My parents weren't convinced and organised a holiday-cum-diplomatic tour with my mother. We were in North America for a month.'

She paused, her lips thinning. 'When we got home he'd gone. He'd tried to pressure me into bed and into an engagement, but he didn't even wait a month. Maybe he knew my parents had his measure.'

'You must have been heartbroken.' Noah's hand curled into a fist. He'd met some miserable excuses for men, but to take advantage of a teenager's romantic dreams...

'I thought I was, but I think I was just caught up in the romance of it.' She shrugged. 'The experience changed me. I wasn't so ready to believe every compliment. I became adept at discovering the reasons behind a man's interest. You'd be surprised how often it wasn't about me but about trying to get status or wealth, or even a bet about getting the goody-two-shoes Princess into bed.'

She nodded at his indrawn breath. 'I became less trusting and less interested.'

There was still the fact that Ilsa had been engaged, twice, but hadn't slept with either fiancé. Even in the rarefied world of royalty that seemed odd, but Noah refused to ask. If she wanted to talk about that she would.

'Yet you trusted me. You let me lead you out from under the noses of all those gossipy socialites, straight to my yacht.' He dragged in a breath that hurt because his lungs had cramped, as he thought of the trust she'd placed in him. 'Everyone understood what it meant when we left together.'

No wonder the media had been rife with stories about them.

The risk she'd taken with him made him feel uncharacteristically humble. After her two failed engagements, the press eagerly extrapolated on the next instalment of what it saw as the ongoing saga of her love life. He'd risked nothing while she—

'It was different with you.' Ilsa slid her hand over his chest, covering the place where his heart thudded. 'I can't explain, but I believed you, and I wanted you, so badly. I'd never felt like that.'

'I know what you mean.' With her, everything felt different and new.

Noah gathered her in, not allowing himself to dwell on the idea that their relationship was unique, even though it felt like it. That had to be an illusion, maybe due to their phenomenal sexual compatibility. Yet he forgot about maintaining distance and revelled in holding her, naked and soft in his arms.

'You can trust me, Ilsa. I won't let you down.'

Ilsa knew better than to expect too much from a relationship founded on sexual attraction, yet Noah's words penetrated deep.

She heard the words and clutched them close, like a miser hoarding treasure. Would it really hurt to pretend, just for a short time, that what they had was real and more than a convenient affair?

No, it was too perilous. Just because she felt so much didn't mean this could last. Noah might be different from other men, he might make her feel special, but their paths lay in different directions. They lived on opposite sides of the world. He didn't want a family and she desperately did, though her chances of having a child were increasingly slim.

An ache started in her chest and she fought to suppress it. All she could do was live in the present. This glorious, amazing present. Later she'd worry about her future.

She snuggled nearer, inhaling the warm, spicy scent that was Noah's alone, determined to make the most of these incredible moments.

He rolled onto his back, pulling her so she lay over him, her head near his collarbone, her leg draped over his hip. It was remarkably comfortable. More than comfortable, she decided as she rubbed her face against him, fascinated by the texture of silky skin and crisp chest hair over hot muscle. He felt wonderful.

Yet Ilsa's thoughts kept straying to the fact that their lives would only intersect for a short time. This time together was precious.

'What are you thinking, Ilsa? It can't be good.'

She lifted her head to meet his questioning gaze. 'What makes you say that?'

'You're not relaxed any more.'

He noticed too much.

But Ilsa liked that. She'd never known a man so focused on her that he noticed minute changes in her mood. She propped herself up and stroked her palm across the plane of his jaw, adoring the hint of raspiness there.

She shook her head. 'Nothing really. Just about the

fact this is an escape from reality. When this is over I'll have to go back to Altbourg.'

And try to carve out a new life for herself.

Noah's arms tightened around her. 'But not too soon.'

Those mesmerising eyes held hers as if willing her to agree. As if Ilsa needed persuading!

'No, not too soon.' She wanted to stay with Noah as long as possible.

'Do you enjoy being royal?'

Ilsa blinked. 'Enjoy it?'

'You look surprised. Hasn't anyone ever asked?'

'Never.'

'And?'

'It's the life I was born into. It's all I know.'

'I understand that.' He brushed her hair off her face as if to see her better then stroked his finger along her forehead, making her aware of her frown. 'But is it what you want to do? Does it make you happy and fulfilled?'

Noah Carson wasn't just sexy and compelling. He was downright dangerous. With a couple of words he'd struck to the heart of Ilsa's problem. Though until now she hadn't allowed herself to think of it as a problem so much as passing restlessness.

'Sorry. I'm prying and I promised myself—'

'It's okay. Really.'

Except it wasn't. Not any more. Ilsa had spent so long telling herself everything would work out for the best because she was doing her duty, yet those words sounded increasingly hollow.

She lowered her head to his chest, listening to the thrum of his heartbeat beneath her ear. It was steady and reassuring, like the man himself. The man, she realised, she trusted. There'd been no vetting done by the palace, no discreet enquiries by her family, just her own instinct, yet Ilsa *knew* she could trust Noah as she did few others.

'No, it's not fulfilling,' she admitted finally. 'Not any more.'

Except for some of her projects, initiatives she'd got involved in by choice rather than because it was expected. Maybe that was where her future lay, pursuing those goals.

'But it was once?'

Noah wrapped his arms loosely around her, cocooning her in luscious warmth that counteracted the nugget of ice deep inside.

'To an extent. When I was young I had real purpose. For the first nine years of my life I was the heir to the throne. For as long as I can remember I was trained to lead the country. My parents and tutors aimed to mould me into a queen who could lead the country through thick and thin.'

'Even when you were a kid?'

Noah sounded shocked. Ilsa heard indignation in his voice and felt...cared for. She let herself wallow in it for a second or two.

'Of course. It's easier to learn responsibility and duty early. There were lots of other things to learn too.'

Everything from languages, history and politics to etiquette and understanding her country and its people.

'But when you were nine that changed because your brother was born?'

'You've done your homework.' Ilsa circled a finger across Noah's ribs. 'As a male, Christoph became the heir.'

'It seems damned sexist that he took precedence, especially after all that time being the heir.'

Ilsa had grown up knowing what would happen if there was a male heir, no matter how unfair. 'Sexist yes, but constitutional change is slow and will probably take a generation to push through parliament.'

She paused, innate caution urging her to stop there.

But she wanted to share with Noah. Besides, what she was about to say wasn't really a state secret.

'But it wasn't that simple. My brother wasn't well as a baby and he had health troubles through childhood. For a long time there was doubt he'd be able to inherit.' More than once they'd feared he'd die.

'He's okay now?'

'Oh, yes.' Ilsa smiled. 'He's grown into a remarkably strong young man.' At eighteen Christoph was full of energy, making up for all those years of ill health. 'But until a few years ago that wasn't the case.'

'All that time you were still being groomed to take over from your father?'

She lifted her head and saw the implications register in Noah's expression. She nodded.

'And now you're suddenly just the spare.'

'Spare and surplus to requirements.' She shook her head as the words emerged. 'That came out wrong. I love Christoph. I'm relieved things have worked out well for him. I have no qualms about not inheriting the throne.' She paused. 'But it's strange not to have a clear direction and purpose any more.'

'So where does that leave you?'

She shrugged. 'Supporting my father and doing good works.'

Ilsa liked helping her people. She got a buzz out of making a difference, especially with social initiatives that the government considered too hard or too risky to invest in. It was the other duties, standing in for her father or brother, that she found increasingly frustrating. Because she wasn't valued for what she could contribute but simply as a royal placeholder.

That had to change. When she returned—

'You'd have been Queen if you'd stayed in Vallort.'

Noah's words jolted her, a reminder of her scandalous broken engagement. But when she looked at Noah he seemed lost in thought.

'Yet you decided against that and gave up another significant role you'd been groomed for.' His bright eyes snared hers. 'For someone trained from birth to lead you must feel like your world has been tipped upside down.'

Relief scudded through her. He *did* understand. It felt like he was the only one who did.

'I'll adapt.' She had no choice.

'I'm sure you will.'

His confidence warmed her.

Yet it was difficult when the life mapped out for her hadn't followed the expected route. She'd been brought up to follow expectations. First there was being removed as royal heir, though she still gave thanks for her brother's recovery. Then the arranged match with Justin, Prince of Vallort. They'd known each other for years, and when he died she'd grieved for him as a friend.

But before she'd had time to adjust to that, the powers that be had demanded the engagement proceed, this time with Justin's heir, Lucien.

Ilsa had thought she could do what was expected. She liked Lucien. But even she, raised to expect an arranged marriage, refused to marry a man clearly in love with someone else.

So here she was, with no true vocation. No sense of purpose.

Something stirred inside, a twisting ache she'd tried to conquer, but it never quite went away. Ilsa might have been raised to rule but the secret she'd never shared with anyone was that she'd only ever had one dream. To be a mother. *That* she felt passionate about.

Her aspiration to have children wasn't something she discussed, especially not with her father. But it was one of the reasons she'd agreed to an arranged marriage, hoping to make a family of her own.

Now that dream was in doubt. She was in her late twenties, with endometriosis and a family history of fertility problems. Her cousin, the same age as Ilsa, with the same condition, had tried unsuccessfully for years to have a baby.

Ilsa's doctor had warned of fertility issues. Her chances of having children grew slimmer with time. So when Lucien's ex-lover had turned up, pregnant with a baby she wasn't sure she could raise, Ilsa had considered adopting the child with Lucien. Until it became clear the pair were head over heels in love.

What would it be like to be loved like that? As if nothing else in the world mattered. She couldn't imagine it.

Noah brushed her hair in a soothing sweep that ended on her bare back. Ilsa arched into his touch, preferring to focus on the skin to skin contact than thoughts of what she didn't have.

She was otherwise healthy. She had her family and friends, a comfortable home and worldly wealth that made it possible to help others. She had much to be grateful for. Maybe that, she decided, would be her future. Putting into practise the social support schemes she hadn't been able to convince the Altbourg authorities to fund.

Talking frankly with Noah helped her see more clearly. It put in perspective what she really wanted.

She lifted her gaze to his, stunned at how good it felt to share with a man who didn't judge her but simply made her feel good.

It was weak and dangerous to wish that this idyll could last. Their lives lay in separate directions. Yet she couldn't help wishing...

Noah watched her raise her eyes to his. She looked troubled. Despite her pragmatic words he'd caught an undercurrent of sadness in her tone.

'What are you thinking, Ilsa?'

He'd read between the lines and guessed at how momentous and unsettling recent events had been for her. He wanted to ask if her family had helped her. Had she had support? Did she discuss this stuff with them? Or was she supposed to suck it up and carry on alone?

Yet, as he watched, her mouth curled up at the corners. 'I was thinking how much I like being with you.'

His hold of her sweet body tightened. 'Good. I feel the same. I vote we stay and explore Istanbul before seeing more of Turkey.'

They hadn't discussed a specific time limit and he wanted to hear Ilsa say she wasn't in a hurry to return to Altbourg.

The need was selfish, because his hunger for her wouldn't be sated quickly. There was another element too. He respected her and wanted to help her, cushion her against the blows fate had dealt.

Had he ever felt that way about a woman? Somehow this didn't feel like a normal short-term affair. Unease flickered but he ignored it.

'You have time to do that? You had to work earlier.'

Noah had taken the video call instead of delegating because he'd needed some space from Ilsa.

'That was a one-off. I'm taking a break, remember?' He kept in touch with key staff, but with each passing day he relished his unaccustomed freedom. And his time with Ilsa. Deliberately he slid his hands across her silky skin. 'And we've got a lot of exploring to do.' He dipped one hand to her buttocks, pulling her against his growing erection.

So much for giving her time to recuperate.

Her breath caught. 'I like the sound of that.'

A tide of heat engulfed Noah as Ilsa wriggled into a more comfortable position over him. More comfortable for her. For him, it was torture of the most exquisite kind and a reminder that, despite her inexperience, they were equals in passion.

Everything about this woman, the shape of her body, the scent of her skin, the caress of her hair, even the way her mind worked, attracted him.

Noah's hands tightened on her hips. 'How tired are you, Ilsa?'

Her smoky gaze caught his. 'Not at all.' For good measure she rubbed herself against him. Slowly. Against his engorged arousal.

Noah shuddered and clamped her to him, lifting his rump off the bed as he slid against the slick folds between her thighs. 'You're a quick learner.'

'Does that mean I get a gold star?' Her cheeky grin faded as he cupped her breast, rubbing his thumb hard over her nipple so she gasped, thrusting towards him.

'You get whatever you like, sweetheart.'

'I want more.' She didn't sound so cocky now. Her voice was gratifyingly breathless.

'And I'm just the man to give you what you want.' If she'd said she was sore or tired he'd have had an ice bath. 'Reach over and get a condom.'

Even that was deliciously arousing as she stretched across him then sat straddling his thighs, a frown of concentration on her face as she tore off the wrapper.

'Can I do it?'

Touch him there? Absolutely!

He nodded then gritted his teeth on a hiss of breath as she fumbled it on.

Noah arched his head back against the pillow and tried to calculate mathematical square roots in his head. He didn't get far. Ilsa turned a necessary task into seduction. By the time she'd finished sweat had popped out across his brow and upper lip and he was rigid with the effort of holding back.

Slim fingers encircled him and slid slowly up.

'Do you like it like that or—?'

'I like it. But not now.' He was too close. Opening his eyes, he caught delight on her face. Time to turn the tables.

Noah removed Ilsa's fingers from around him and caught her other hand in his, then moulded both to her breasts. Surprise flashed in those blue-grey eyes, then understanding as he dipped his hand between her legs, slipping straight to her clitoris. She jerked against his hand and her fingers pressed against her soft breasts, her head arching back.

She was indescribably alluring. So sexy he wasn't sure he could last long enough to ensure her pleasure as he urged her further up his body.

'Lift up on your knees.' Finally she was there, poised above his erection. Ilsa didn't wait for more instructions. She lowered herself and Noah felt the glide of taut, wet flesh surround him.

It was too much. He surged higher, hands anchored to her hips, securing her against him.

She felt so good he never wanted to let her go.

'Touch me, Ilsa.' The sight of her cupping her breasts and moving against him, her eyes a silvery blaze, was incredibly arousing. But Noah needed more of their connection.

She leaned forward, hands to his shoulders, breasts against his chest, and planted her mouth on his. The angle of his penetration changed and they were now body to body. Noah clamped one hand to her buttocks, the other to the back of her head, as he took her body and her mouth with thrust after delicious thrust.

Ilsa's moans were music. The restless circling of her hips the most potent aphrodisiac.

After two stunning climaxes he should be sated and lazy. Instead Noah was as desperate as the first time.

She writhed against him, all slender, sinuous femininity. He felt her quiver, her muscles tugging him, then suddenly there it was, like a freight train slamming over the horizon and straight at him.

Noah nipped at her lip, thrusting high and hard till she shuddered and convulsed around him, the sweetest torture of all. He swallowed her hoarse cry that might have been his name. Then the world smashed apart in a blast of white-hot light and pleasure as he pumped his seed deep and hard.

When his mind worked again, Noah realised sex with Ilsa was the best he'd had. And it got better each time.

Why her? How could *perfect* keep improving?

Ilsa posed so many questions. Each hour with her seemed to increase his curiosity.

Just as well he had weeks to discover some answers. He sensed it would be hard to walk away until he had unravelled all her mysteries.

CHAPTER EIGHT

'THANK YOU, NOAH.'

Ilsa wrapped her arms around him, smiling in a way that made the sun seem to shine brighter. He drew her close in the shade of the trees near the ancient amphitheatre.

'What for?'

'Everything! This has been the most amazing day. The most amazing trip.'

Her eyes blazed bright blue, which he knew was a sure sign of happiness. He found it almost as attractive as the misty silver shine when rapture took her.

A familiar ripple snaked through Noah's belly, heading for his groin. He only had to think about sex with Ilsa to want her again.

Their desire for each other showed no sign of fading as they spent more time together. In fact, it seemed to build as familiarity deepened their connection.

'Amazing because we've seen lots of ruins?'

Today was a case in point. They'd come ashore and headed high up to the ruined city of Priene, perched below soaring cliffs and surrounded by pines that scented the air. The place was deserted and magical, and he was glad to be here with Ilsa.

'You really don't mind, do you?'

For a second Noah managed to keep a poker face,

then he grinned. 'I've enjoyed it all. Who'd have guessed scrambling over blocks of stone would be such fun?'

Seeing the old cities through Ilsa's eyes was a treat as well as an education.

They'd explored the grassy hillock of Troy, dotted with blood-red poppies, and she'd told him stories of the Trojan War and the archaeological discoveries made there. Further south they'd visited Pergamum and Ephesus, where he'd walked streets and visited homes erected thousands of years before.

Inland at Pamukkale they'd swum among fallen marble columns and soaked in warm thermal waters.

In between they'd feasted on wonderful food, met interesting people and spent days doing nothing more onerous than swimming off the yacht and having sex. Lots of sex.

'It's the best holiday I've ever had,' she murmured.

'Me too.'

Not that he'd had many. He'd spent years working every waking hour and though he travelled the globe, it was for business. His sexual liaisons were pleasurable but very short-term. He didn't take vacations with lovers.

Ilsa sighed. 'I could do this for ever.'

She leaned against his chest and he was surprised at his response. As if he too wanted to hold this moment and never let it go.

Noah shook his head at the fancy and stroked her ponytail of silky hair. His desire for Ilsa was as fresh as when they'd met.

Two people from such different backgrounds shouldn't be a good match. Yet their interests and personalities dovetailed beautifully.

She enticed and enthralled him and in many ways they were attuned. He respected her strength and honesty, her positive attitude and the way she treated others. She was genuine in a way so many people he met weren't.

But it surely these feelings couldn't last. Did this time
with Ilsa seem special because it was the first real break
he'd had?

'It's okay, Noah. I know it's not possible.' She drew
back, a rueful smile on her face. 'But some moments are
wonderful, aren't they?'

'I suppose they are. It's good to have a break from
business sometimes.'

It was what his family had been saying for ages but it
was Ilsa who'd made him realise it. Ilsa who'd given him
a new perspective on his work-life balance and on his
goals. He'd begun to consider some changes for the future.

'Business!' She stiffened and frowned, then looked up
at him. 'That reminds me. Have you had time to follow
up that contact in Altbourg I gave you? About a business
opportunity there?'

Noah shook his head. He'd had other things on his
mind. Namely her. And the intriguing new thoughts he
was grappling with about what he wanted in his future.

'My PA sent a reminder. My father's office keeps asking. He's very eager about it.' Ilsa shrugged. 'But if you're
not interested—'

'It's okay. I'll follow it up today.'

Damn her father for interrupting this idyll. Ilsa was so
much more relaxed now than she'd been when they met.
Noah would make the call so they stopped hassling her.

At that moment her phone rang and she frowned. She'd
told him she had a new phone and very few people had
the number. Part of her plan to switch off during this trip.

'Sorry, I need to take this.' She turned away and headed
down the rows of marble benches. 'Hello? Lucien?'

Noah's fingers curled tight as he recognised the name.
King Lucien, the man Ilsa had been going to marry.

He heard warmth in Ilsa's tone, and concern. A sharp,
ice-hot sensation jabbed his chest. He breathed deep but
couldn't dislodge the feeling.

Noah turned away to give her privacy, but an exclamation stopped him. He swung around to where she stood at the front of the amphitheatre.

Her shoulders were hunched and he wanted to take her in his arms. She looked so alone.

Despite their intimacy, there was a lot Ilsa kept to herself, as he did. Yet increasingly Noah found himself wanting to know everything.

Thinking of her with her ex-fiancé sent pain radiating through Noah's clenched jaw and deeper, where a phantom dagger jabbed his gut.

She and Lucien mightn't have been lovers but when Lucien rang Ilsa *had* to answer. Did she love him, despite what she'd said earlier?

Finally she ended the call and took a deep breath, tipping her face towards the sun as if seeking strength from its rays.

Because she pined for Lucien? Did she regret leaving him?

Noah took the steps at speed, his shadow falling across her face and making her open her eyes. The warmth in her gaze eased a tightness in his chest.

His hands closed around her elbows. 'Are you okay?'

'Of course.'

'But there's a problem.'

Her eyebrows arched, whether because he'd guessed or at his implicit question, he didn't know. This time he wasn't going to give her space.

'Things are getting complicated in Vallort and Lucien rang to warn me.'

Noah said nothing, waiting for more details.

He sensed Ilsa hesitate. Despite her forthrightness about many things, there were aspects of her life she guarded closely.

A noise made them look up. A group of tourists chattered and exclaimed as they approached. Noah led Ilsa towards the sheltering trees. When they were out of sight they settled on some marble slabs dusted with pine needles.

'Hear that?' Ilsa asked, looping her hands around her knees. Noah tilted his head, registering the rustle of a breeze through the trees and a warbling bird. 'The peace here is incredible. No crowds, no press, no one expecting anything. Like the freedom of a ski slope at dawn.'

'That's why you've enjoyed this trip so much.' Amazing that he hadn't realised before. 'Apart from us being together. It's not just the historical sites but the chance to escape and be almost anonymous.'

Despite his high profile, he could still often be anonymous. Royalty was different.

Ilsa nodded. 'Yes. Being able to breathe and just be me has been wonderful.' She reached out and touched his hand. 'And being with you. Thank you, Noah.'

He didn't pause to examine that warm feeling inside. 'Something's wrong. Do you regret leaving Lucien?'

Noah felt her jolt of surprise, saw her eyes widen. 'I like Lucien, but it wasn't a good match.'

'And your first engagement? Was that a better match?' Maybe she still carried a torch for the fiancé who'd died.

Ilsa's scrutiny turned sharp and assessing. 'You want to know the truth behind my betrothals? The private story everyone is slavering for?'

Her words jabbed like blades. Damn right he wanted to know. But only because he cared about her. The thought of her pining over a lost love made him queasy.

Noah flexed his fingers, releasing her hand. 'I want to know what's bothering you, that's all. If I were going to sell a story about you I already have plenty of material.'

Her shoulders dropped as she exhaled. 'I apologise. Hiding personal matters has become a habit. I don't really believe you'd do that.'

He shrugged. 'I understand. It can be hard to trust.' He

too had developed a tendency not to admit strangers too far into his life. This connection with Ilsa was unusual.

'I knew Justin most of my life. I liked and respected him and was sorry when he died. Because I grew up knowing the marriage was expected it didn't seem odd. Especially as I no longer trusted my judgement of men or romantic love.'

'That makes sense.'

His doomed love affair had changed his whole outlook on romance, women and the notion of settling down.

Ilsa darted a look his way. 'The engagement to Lucien was another arranged match, to strengthen ties as our countries enter a new phase of economic cooperation and partnership.'

Surely that didn't require marriage? But then Noah didn't understand the workings of royal kingdoms.

'I liked Lucien but that was all.'

Noah felt a surge of lightness in his chest and head. Relief? Surely not. Or maybe just relief for Ilsa's sake.

'So you're not in love with him.'

'Hardly.' Her gaze shifted to the magnificent view just visible through the trees.

'But you're still in contact.'

Why did he push?

'We unleashed a furore when we split. It was a serious diplomatic incident. There was talk of not proceeding with the shared economic zone. On top of that the media was desperate for details, making up stories when they couldn't get the truth.' Her mouth turned down. 'They hounded Aurélie, the woman Lucien loves. The lies they printed about her, saying she deliberately split us up…' Ilsa shook her head. 'The vitriol only eased a little when…'

She turned, her blue-grey gaze snaring his.

'When what?'

'When I let you sweep me off my feet.'

The press had been in a frenzy.

It struck him that Ilsa's decision to leave that party in Monaco and embark on an affair had been very convenient for Lucien. It took the heat off him and his woman since the press had to drop the 'poor Ilsa' theme that had been so popular.

Noah's stare sharpened on Ilsa's face, but as the thought surfaced he knew it was unworthy. She would never give herself to a stranger to make a point for the press.

'So Lucien and Aurélie benefited when you agreed to sail away with me. What's the problem now?'

Ilsa's expression was wary. Had she heard the hint of annoyance in his tone? She mightn't love her ex but that didn't mean Noah had to like him. Ilsa had suffered through this.

'Aurélie's pregnant but there's a complication. She might lose the baby.' Her white face pushed any thought of petty jealousy from Noah's head. He moved closer, wrapping his arm around her, and she leaned in, making the tightness behind his ribs ease. 'She's in hospital so there's no keeping it quiet. Lucien rang to warn me we'd all be front page news again.'

'I see.'

For Noah, press interest had revolved around his success, or silly pieces about the world's sexiest bachelors. Neither bothered him. Ilsa's experience was completely different.

'It's not the press interest distressing you.'

Ilsa had already thumbed her nose at the gossips by taking up with him.

'I'm worried about Aurélie and the baby. She and Lucien have been through so much and this child means the world to them.'

Her mouth crumpled. She was such a warm-hearted, generous woman. Clearly she loved children, to be so worried about this unborn child. He remembered the dozens of cute slippers she'd bought for children in hospital, and the way she stopped to chat with kids wherever they went.

Is that what Ilsa wanted? Children?

Noah stared down into her troubled features and found himself crossing a boundary he hadn't intended to. But the pain he saw there dragged the words out.

'When we met I asked what you wanted from life. You said you didn't know. But you knew exactly what was important to you. Your people, your country and family.'

Her eyes met his, wide and wary. 'So?'

'Maybe it's time to put your people and your country further down your priority list.' He paused, trying to get a handle on his tangled thoughts. 'You want children too, don't you?'

Was that pain he saw in her face? Surely not, for abruptly she nodded and said softly, 'Yes. I'd love that.'

Everything inside him stilled. He felt poised on a knife-edge, watching emotions chase each other across her face.

Noah experienced a surge of unfamiliar feelings that made him hesitate.

He felt more for Ilsa than for any other woman. Even for Poppy, whom he'd once wanted to marry. But he'd changed since those days of naïve romantic dreams.

Noah told himself it was good to be aware of Ilsa's desire for a family. It was a timely reminder that what they shared, though spectacular, wasn't permanent.

Strange, though. That sharp phantom pain in his belly was back.

He raised his palm to her face, feeling tenderness well, understanding what a tough time she'd had.

'I can imagine you as a mother, Ilsa. You'll be wonderful with a family.' He paused and made himself go on. 'I hope you meet the right man for that soon.'

I can imagine you as a mother... I hope you meet the right man soon.

Noah's words echoed as Ilsa paddled her kayak in the

early morning stillness. She heard them as clearly as if he'd spoken them now instead of days ago.

His meaning had been clear. *He* wasn't the man for her, not long-term. His plans for the future didn't include her.

She swallowed hard and dug in her paddle, skimming the surface and powering along the bay. She should be tired from lack of sleep, after another night spent making love with Noah. Yet she was filled with restless energy, her thoughts darting uneasily to subjects she'd tried to avoid. Noah. The future. What she really wanted from life.

Once that had been easy. To serve her country and to have the family she'd always craved.

Now there was no defined role for her in Altbourg. None that would satisfy long-term, at any rate. As for a family, at her last gynaecologist's appointment she'd been told to prepare for the possibility she might not be able to have children. It wasn't certain, but time was against her. She shouldn't leave it much longer to try.

Ilsa breathed deep, acknowledging the inevitable wrench of pain and pushing it aside. But then came thoughts of Noah. Her generous, tender, fun, fascinating lover.

She'd never known a man like him. Had never trusted one so much. Never felt so much. She wanted—

Laughter rang out across the water then a babble of excited voices, including a deep masculine rumble that she recognised instinctively. Noah.

Ilsa was torn between the desire to join him and the need to be alone with her thoughts. Except those thoughts would be about him and she worried about exactly how deep her feelings ran for the deceptively easygoing Australian.

What had begun as an act of rebellion and freedom, a choice to indulge in pleasure, had turned into something that worried her. They shared an amazing affair. Fantastic sex, so fantastic it had opened her eyes to her own sensual nature. Camaraderie. Friendship, or so it felt. Caring too.

The problem was what else she felt for Noah.

So, instead of paddling further on her own, she turned towards the shore and welcome distraction.

The white sand beach glowed in the early light. At this hour, before all the visitors arrived, it was magic. The turquoise water was so clear that when she reached the shallows it looked like she was floating on air, not water.

Shouts rose and she turned to see several bodies hurtling down the beach, fine sand spraying from their feet. Noah's powerful form was surrounded by a gaggle of children. A football shot ahead and a boy yelled in triumph, outstripping the others.

Ilsa watched her lover keep pace with the rest of the group, accelerating enough to make the leader look over his shoulder and put on a burst of speed before aiming the ball between two piles of towels that marked an impromptu goal.

Noah had held back enough to let the boy score a goal, but not too much to be obvious.

She imagined him with his nephew, lolling in the yacht's lounge, engrossed in the computer game Noah had bought for his visit.

Ilsa couldn't imagine her father doing either of those things. When she and Christoph were young there'd been no noisy games in the King's presence. He'd loved and cared for them but in a rather distant way. He was more likely to reinforce a lesson in politics or manners than dirty his clothes with boisterous play.

Her childhood hadn't been unhappy but it hadn't been carefree. What would it be like to bring up a child with someone like Noah? To be part of a family that cared and shared and wasn't focused on royal duty?

Everything she'd discovered about Noah indicated he'd

be a wonderful father and supportive partner, if he ever changed his mind about settling down.

For a split second she let herself imagine it then tore her thoughts away, conscious of the dull metallic taste of disappointment filling her mouth.

'There you are. Just in time. We need another player to even the numbers.'

Strong hands grabbed the prow of the kayak as she reached the shore, dragging it up the sand. Then Noah was there, holding out his hand. Ilsa rose and, before she could step out, he lifted her and swung her high.

Laughter glinted in those sea-bright eyes and an answering smile tugged her mouth. Being with him made her feel good. As for being hugged close to that superb body... Sparks ignited deep inside as she nestled in his arms.

Ilsa couldn't have a future with him, but she could enjoy every precious moment together. The ache around her heart intensified. Last night, when they'd collapsed, sated and gasping on the bed, bodies humming with sensual satisfaction, Ilsa had found herself blinking back tears.

She wanted things she couldn't allow herself to want.

Noah's head lowered and her breath caught, anticipating the touch of his lips. Except the clamour of nearby children interrupted. With a wry smile he put her down on the sand.

'Later,' he promised, his lips softly burring her earlobe, making her shiver. Then he straightened. '*Do* you mind evening up the numbers? If you'd rather not—'

'It looks like fun.'

She needed something to distract her.

They were a mixed bunch of varying ages and abilities. One child was so small that he fought back tears after getting caught in a tumble of legs as the older children vied for the ball. Noah swung him up to sit on his shoulders, from where he crowed his delight.

Ilsa found herself on a team with a number of girls, quick and light on their feet. One passed the ball to her and Ilsa took off, passing it when a teenager tackled her, then sprinting ahead, the wind in her hair and her blood pumping. Her partner passed again and Ilsa took a shot.

'Goal!' Noah's deep voice called out.

Instantly she was surrounded by cheering kids, a couple of girls high-fiving her and others dancing in delight. It was her team's first goal.

After that came several more, with Ilsa passing the ball again and again to beaming youngsters who managed to score. It was so long since she'd played group sport. She loved it.

'You have hidden talents,' Noah said as they stood on the shore, waving while the children headed off.

'Kayaking, you mean?'

His lips twitched and Ilsa felt it like a thread pulling tight inside her. She was so attuned to Noah that it was hard to believe they'd known each other only a matter of weeks.

'I was thinking of your football skills. I thought princesses practised curtseys, not kicking goals.'

'We're more versatile than you think. I mastered curtseys by the age of four. And I loved team sports.'

'You don't play now?'

She shook her head. 'Not since my mid-teens. Getting muddy and windblown wasn't considered a good look for the heir to the throne.'

And just like that the outside world intruded again, despite her attempts to keep it at bay.

Last night she'd had a message from her mother, saying her father deemed it time she return. Press speculation about her and Noah was causing headaches.

Her mouth twisted. They hadn't wanted her in Altbourg when she'd been a dutiful princess, because she'd attracted negative press. But now she'd broken out of the mould and was no longer seen as the goody-two-shoes Princess, they wanted her where they could keep an eye on her and manage the fallout.

She didn't want to go back.

She wanted to stay with Noah.

Ilsa swallowed. The truth sideswiped her.

Because she'd fallen for him.

A silent gasp snatched at her breath.

Ilsa had believed herself cured of romantic fancies in her teens. After that she'd accepted she'd marry for duty and that was fine because she'd lost faith in love. She'd loved once and almost made a disastrous mistake.

How could she think of going there again?

But it hadn't been an active choice. It just happened.

She squeezed her eyes shut, trying to control her whirling thoughts.

'Ilsa, what's up? Are you okay?'

She snapped her eyes open, met his searing turquoise gaze. 'Of course. It's just been a long time since I played football.'

Ilsa looked away down the beach, searching for something, anything to divert his attention. 'You're brilliant with children,' she said, hiding a wince. It was like probing a sore spot.

'That's because I've got a big extended family with lots of cousins. There's always a tribe of kids at any family gathering. At beach barbecues or backyard cricket.'

Before she could stop herself her mind conjured a vision of her and Noah on a vast Australian beach with a gaggle of family around them. She drew a breath and forced the image away.

'That sounds terrific.'

'It is. I'm looking forward to seeing them when I get home.'

Ilsa nodded and turned abruptly towards the kayaks. It felt like each movement was jerky and uncoordinated because of the effort of holding in her emotions.

'I don't know about you but I'm craving coffee. I think I'll head back.'

'Me too. Race you to the yacht?'

She pasted on a tight smile and pushed her kayak into the warm shallows, avoiding his eyes. 'You're on.'

But physical exertion didn't dim her agitation.

What was she going to do?

Noah expected her to stay another week or two, but eventually he'd leave her without a backward glance.

Ilsa couldn't handle that. Already she was wretched, anticipating their separation. Staying would only make things worse.

Already she could barely hide her feelings and she refused to reveal them, only to evoke Noah's pity. Every hour they were together intensified her feelings and made it harder to face life without him. Better to make a clean break now than wait for Noah to tire of her.

She had been rejected first by the man she'd fallen for, because he couldn't be bothered waiting for her. Put aside as the royal heir, despite a lifetime's dedication and hard work. Palmed off to not one but two men who'd agreed to marry her only for the sake of their country, not because they'd wanted *her*.

Ilsa might have instigated the break with Lucien but he'd jumped at the chance to be with the woman he actually loved, the woman who was already carrying his child. That had slashed at Ilsa's ego. She hadn't wanted the marriage either, yet once again she'd felt unwanted, rejected at the most elemental level.

Her sense of worth had taken a hit, as it had when her father decreed she was a liability to her country.

She'd had enough rejection to last a lifetime.

Ilsa wanted Noah more than she'd ever wanted anything. Walking away from him would be appallingly hard. But it had to be done. Better that she walk away now than wait for him to call an end to their affair.

She needed to be alone. To lick her wounds and try to work out what to do with her life.

CHAPTER NINE

NOAH GROANED AND arched his head back under the streaming water. With one hand in Ilsa's wet hair as she knelt before him and the other flat on the wall of the shower, his body trembling on the brink of climax, he was stunned he could still stand. The hungry caress of her mouth drove him to the edge of sanity.

A shudder racked him.

'No!'

Somehow he managed to disengage himself, though the sight of her at his feet, lips parted and eyes hooded with arousal as she looked up at him, nearly sent him over the edge.

But some instinct stopped him. The same instinct that had seen him follow her below decks and barge into the bathroom where she was already showering. That had made him strip off and join her despite her wary expression.

For a second something had passed between them, a jolt of emotion he couldn't identify. Then Ilsa had dropped to her knees and taken him in her mouth and he'd lost the ability to think.

Thinking was beyond him now. But every instinct screamed the need to possess this woman. Claim her as his, so often and so completely that she'd never run from him again.

'No,' he said again, his voice a guttural growl. 'I want *you*, Ilsa.'

There. That flash of silver in her eyes was surely a reflection of his own feelings. Noah let the sight reassure him as he dragged in a breath of sex-scented air and drew her to her feet. She was all gorgeous streamlined dips and hollows and long, lithe limbs. Her blonde hair was dark as a mermaid's tresses, plastered to her shoulders and the upper slope of her breasts.

He planted unsteady hands on her narrow waist then slid them towards her hips, ready to lift her up. But she turned in his hold. For a second he thought she was leaving. Just as he had when he'd entered the shower and caught surprise in her eyes that for an instant had looked like panic.

Instead Ilsa put her hands flat against the tiled wall, shimmying her hips back towards him.

It wasn't what he wanted. He needed to share the ultimate moment with their eyes locked on each other. He wanted that silent but powerful communion with Ilsa.

But then she shuffled closer, her legs splaying on either side of his, and Noah couldn't resist. He bent his knees and positioned himself between her thighs, one hand stroking her cleft and discovering her ready. So ready she tilted eagerly into his touch, her breath audibly catching.

He needed to know she was with him all the way, because he sensed that in the last half hour something had altered. Something bothered her and he intended to find out what it was.

With one smooth, strong thrust he drove home. Right to her core. Right to the place where it felt as if he and Ilsa were one.

Delight was a ripple of excited nerves, a bunching of muscles and a tightening of flesh as she pushed against him, his name a gasp on her lips.

Next time they'd be face to face and he'd watch the flare in her silvery blue gaze as they orgasmed together.

Noah held her hips and thrust again, learning anew the rhythm and angle that ignited her blood, feeling her vibrate with excitement. This was what he needed. Weeks with Ilsa hadn't dimmed his hunger for more. For everything she could give him.

He wanted—

It hit him like a blast of summer lightning. He had an instant to feel Ilsa's muscles clutch him, then the burst of ecstasy as the tight, hard weight in his groin exploded into pulse after pulse of powerful delight.

Noah gritted his teeth and held on tight as he lost himself in rapture. The sound of Ilsa gasping his name. The indescribable perfection of them coming together in bliss. Starbursts behind his eyes. Silk and flame, roaring heat and almost unbearably exquisite sensation. And tenderness—tenderness more powerful than anything he'd known.

Finally, sighing and trembling, he bowed forward, bending over her, his arm around her waist, resting his head against hers, absorbing her heaving breaths into his own straining body.

Noah laved her slick shoulder then grazed the curve of her neck with his teeth and had to scoop her against him when her knees gave way.

Gently he pulled back and reached for the soap. Ilsa was limp, her eyes closed and breathing unsteady as he carefully soaped their bodies, then held her as the shower washed them clean.

Even then she stood silent, her head bowed as if from exhaustion. It was only when he turned off the taps and bent to lift her into his arms that her eyes snapped open, pupils dilated as she met his gaze. She huffed a deep breath and shook her head.

'I can walk.' Yet instead of moving she leaned in and brushed her soft lips against his. 'Thank you, Noah.'

He lifted his hand to cup her cheek but she turned away, stumbling a little as she pushed open the shower door and reached for a towel.

Noah had planned to take Ilsa to bed, to drowse with her in his arms, but she was already tucking the towel around her body and reaching for the hairdryer.

Disappointment stirred but he couldn't be selfish. She'd be more comfortable with dry hair.

He dried off, planted a kiss on her shoulder and another on the sweet curve of her neck, felt her tremble and smiled. He loved her responsiveness.

'I'll see you soon,' he murmured.

Noah left the room and threw himself down on the bed.

He should be exhausted after that stunning orgasm. Yet his brain was racing. What was on Ilsa's mind? Something was bothering her this morning and he intended to get to the bottom of it. Not out of prurient curiosity but so he could help.

Noah cared for her. More, he realised, than he cared for anyone outside his family. So much that in the last few days he'd found himself dissatisfied at the prospect of their relationship ending soon.

Short-term affairs had suited him for years, yet now he found himself wanting more. How that could be achieved when they lived on opposite sides of the world he didn't know.

Of one thing, though, he was sure. He wasn't ready to say goodbye to Ilsa. It was time to think hard about what he really wanted from life, and from his lover. Meanwhile he'd talk to her about extending their cruise.

Every instinct urged him to protect her, especially as it seemed to him that precious few people had ever stood squarely on her side. Her family used her as a dynastic bargaining chip and her ex-fiancés... He gritted his teeth at the thought of them.

Ilsa deserved better than to be used. He knew exactly how that felt. He despised people who saw others as convenient tools to be manipulated for their own ends.

Poppy had used him for sex and the thrill of stepping out of her pampered cocoon to be with a guy from what she saw as the wrong side of the tracks. More, she'd tried to use him financially, wanting his money to finance her new business idea, believing he'd be so besotted he'd back her ill-conceived scheme when others wouldn't. In fact it was possible she'd targeted him originally for his money and the sex had been a bonus.

He'd been so bowled over by her he hadn't seen her for what she was until she spelled it out for him. That he wasn't good enough for her. That she'd happily take his money but not his name. By which time she'd also hooked her claws into his little sister, with devastating effect.

Finally the bathroom door opened and Ilsa stepped in. To Noah's surprise she was wrapped in a robe with her hair not only dry but twisted up into an elegant knot, as if she were dressing for a formal function.

Ilsa hadn't worn her hair like that since that very first lunch when she'd looked like some untouchable ice princess. And, if he wasn't mistaken, she'd put on make-up, something she rarely did on the yacht.

He sat up against the pillows, watching her eyes widen as she took in his nakedness before turning swiftly towards the walk-in wardrobe.

She was getting dressed?

Noah frowned. The way her gaze had slid away from his made a phantom chill tickle his neck.

One of the things they both enjoyed after sex was lying in each other's arms. It had been a first for him. Before Ilsa he hadn't been into cuddles. But now he savoured the feeling of closeness he experienced with her. She'd always enjoyed it too.

Until today. Something *had* changed. He'd sensed it before and now instinct warned him it was more serious than he'd thought.

He paused, considering, then rose and strolled to the door. By the time he got there Ilsa was tugging a dress over her head. Not the floaty thing she sometimes wore over a swimsuit. A tailored dress. It screamed *serious* and *city*, not *vacation* or *relaxation*, much less *sex*.

Something turned hard and heavy in his chest.

A premonition of trouble.

It seemed impossible when fifteen minutes ago he'd been deep inside her, feeling her come around him. When five minutes before that...

Noah's fingers curled tight as he grappled with shock.

Ilsa was going somewhere. Every hair on his body rose as foreboding iced his blood. The urge to rip down the zip on her dress and pull her into his arms was almost overwhelming.

He propped his shoulder against the doorjamb and crossed his arms, aiming to look relaxed despite the tension screaming through taut muscles. 'Talk to me, Ilsa.'

She spun around and Noah saw emotion flare in her eyes. The tip of her tongue swiped her lips and he almost groaned aloud. She seduced him as no woman ever had, even when she didn't plan to.

He wanted to taste her, tease her, pleasure her. She'd enjoy it too, he knew. The awareness between them, the insatiable desire, was as strong as ever.

Noah stepped forward and she retreated.

That stopped him, a horrible sick feeling of shock hitting his belly.

'Ilsa?' His voice was a harsh scrape of sound. 'Are you going to explain what's going on?'

She nodded, her hands fiddling with a belt that accentuated her narrow waist. She drew a breath, lowered her shoulders and lifted her chin. Now she looked calm.

'Yes, of course. I meant to tell you when we got back from kayaking, but we were…distracted.'

She smiled but it was a perfunctory movement of her lips, leaving her eyes blank. As if the earth-shattering sex they'd shared had happened to someone else. As if her throat and cheeks weren't still flushed from her orgasm.

Shock stirred that she should dismiss what they'd shared so easily. For it felt and sounded as if she dismissed much more. The closeness and trust that had developed between them.

He *knew* this woman, more than perhaps she realised. He'd read her responses to him. Heard truths she'd shared with no one else, witnessed the bond strengthen between them, *felt* her tenderness.

Noah stood straighter and watched her gaze skate down his body then back, not quite to his eyes. Was that fear he read there? That was another unwelcome shock. What was happening?

'Ilsa…' He moved but she stopped him with one raised hand.

'I have to go. I'm sorry to give such short notice but it's necessary.'

Another of those smiles that didn't reach her eyes.

'Short notice?' His gaze raked her, the sophisticated dress over bare legs and a body that probably still pulsed with the aftershocks of her climax. 'Don't you mean no notice?'

Stunned, he registered how she still refused to meet his gaze. This wasn't the Ilsa he knew. She couldn't be leaving by choice. 'What's happened?'

'I apologise. It's inconsiderate of me to leave without warning. But it needn't interfere with your plans. Once I'm ashore I'll get a taxi and sort out transport from there.'

'Talk to me, sweetheart. I can help you fix whatever it is.'

It was ludicrous to speak of leaving. Neither of them were ready for that.

She blinked and for a moment he thought he saw tenderness in her eyes. He hauled in a relieved breath until she shook her head.

'There's nothing to fix, but thank you all the same.'

Noah frowned, sensing something wrong. Something she wasn't saying. 'Listen, Ilsa, it needn't be like this. If people are demanding things of you…' He repressed the desire to say her royal parents had pushed her around enough, that they'd forfeited the right to dictate her movements. 'I'll help. You know I'll stand by you.'

Strange how easily the promise emerged. Their holiday fling had already changed into something else. In a few short weeks Ilsa had become important to him. If she were hurting—

'No!' She shook her head. 'I'm not being forced.'

She looked down at her clasped hands then back to him. 'Thank you, though, for the offer. And thank you for the wonderful holiday. It's been fun.'

Ilsa's voice was firm, almost businesslike in its crispness, and Noah felt his skin tighten. Because of her abrupt change of tone. And because Poppy had said exactly that when she'd dumped him. That it had been *fun*, but he wasn't good enough for her.

Noah tried to shove emotion aside and read Ilsa's expression. She didn't look worried or upset. In fact she looked totally composed.

As if leaving him meant nothing to her.

As if what they'd shared, all the things that he'd come to value, meant nothing.

Something plunged hard and fast from his chest to his belly.

He had a horrible creeping feeling of déjà vu but told himself it was impossible. Ilsa wasn't Poppy.

Yet looking into Ilsa's eyes was like looking at a stranger. Gone was all that lovely heat, the understanding and mischief, the sensuality and excitement. Instead there was...nothing.

Noah's brain blanked as he fought to reject what he saw and heard. It wasn't just her decision to leave but the way she did it, with no warning or explanation.

They'd agreed to a time-limited affair, but he'd swear she was nowhere close to being bored. Just as he wasn't ready to give her up.

But maybe, despite what he'd observed in the last weeks, he'd misjudged her. Perhaps, after all, she longed for bright lights and A-list parties with aristocratic friends.

A murky thought invaded his brain. Had he been wrong about Ilsa? Had she, like the woman he'd once planned to marry, been turned on by the novelty of a self-made man, and had that novelty worn off?

Had their desperate loving just now been a final titillating adventure before she moved on?

Every instinct rejected the idea. He *knew* Ilsa. She wasn't like that. He was *sure* she wasn't.

Yet past hurts crowded in, clouding his emotions and making it hard to think clearly. For the first time in weeks Ilsa was hard to read, as if she'd deliberately locked him out. Noah *felt* her rejection like a slap.

And hadn't Poppy fooled him completely? Could it be that his judgement, so competent in business, was fatally flawed when it came to women? That, once more, he'd let his emotions override caution?

'What about *us*?'

He'd asked Poppy the same thing. The day she'd laughed in his face and sashayed out of his life to take up with someone whose background was suitably gilt-edged. It left Noah wide open, but he *had* to know.

Ilsa's expression closed even further, like a door slamming shut. 'There *is* no us.'

Like the thrust of honed steel through gathering ice, Noah felt disappointment and hurt meld into a sharp blade, piercing his chest and ripping down through his gut. He didn't want to believe it but the corrosive words spilled out.

'Because you're a blue-blooded princess and I'm a working-class guy? Because of my family background?'

Even as he said it, he wasn't convinced. There *had* to be some other explanation.

'It's not like that,' she said quickly. 'It's time I went back where I belong. My father wants me home now.'

Noah frowned at the mention of her father. Something niggled at the back of his brain.

The business deal her royal father was so keen on. The one she'd raised with him, then reminded him about when he'd been slow to respond. The one he'd promised to look into because he wanted her father to stop pressuring her.

Noah had been as good as his word, following through, investigating the possibilities and finally, *just yesterday*, after his team had researched it, signing an agreement for a joint project in Altbourg.

His nape prickled and he tasted something rancid on his tongue. It was too much of a coincidence. The morning after they'd got his signature on the agreement, Ilsa decided to leave. Had she been recalled by her father, after a job well done?

'Or is it time to go because you got what you really wanted, my name on the joint venture with Altbourg?'

Every instinct shouted it couldn't be true. Surely, confronted with such an accusation, she'd finally tell him the real reason she was leaving.

But all he got was a glacial stare. 'You *really* believe that?'

He didn't know what to think. That was the problem. The woman he'd grown to care for wouldn't treat him this way, use him to get what she wanted then go.

Ilsa wasn't acting like the woman he knew.

Maybe he didn't know her so well after all.

'I believe there's more to you leaving than you're letting on. Tell me what it is and I'll believe you.'

'Noah,' she said finally, 'I'd hoped we'd part as friends.'

'Friends? Friends trust each other. They support and respect each other. But I *know* you're lying to me.'

He watched her flinch, but still she said nothing. His mouth curled in distaste. Her silence spoke volumes. It didn't seem possible, but he had to face the fact that Ilsa wasn't the woman he'd believed her.

Why else would she refuse to explain? He'd offered to help her and he had the determination and resources to do just that.

'What's happened that you're needed so urgently? Has your father found you another aristocrat to marry?' His voice was harsh with hurt and rising anger. 'Or has your fiancé changed his mind and that marriage is back on?'

Ilsa stiffened, a pulse throbbing at the base of her throat. But still she said nothing.

Until this moment Noah had told himself he was wrong.

But she refused to contradict him.

Could it really be that she planned to leave him to marry a man she didn't love, simply to carry on their oh-so-pure bloodlines?

Or maybe, despite what she'd said, she'd been in love with her ex-fiancé all this time. Was that why she'd fallen like a ripe peach into Noah's hand, on the rebound?

Still he waited for her to say she didn't want to go. He'd

gather her close and decide how to help her. Then they could stay together—

'I'm sorry you're upset, Noah.' She did up her belt in a couple of deft movements. 'I'll be packed and gone in twenty minutes.'

Then she turned and reached for her suitcase.

CHAPTER TEN

THE TAXI TOOK Ilsa to the airport. On the way she used her phone to book a flight out of Turkey. The next available was to London and she took it.

She didn't care where she went. Noah's burning eyes and lashing accusations had stripped her bare.

Ilsa could imagine only too well his reaction if she'd told the truth—shock and dismay. For he'd made it abundantly clear he wasn't looking for permanency.

She was shocked herself. Logic told her it should be impossible to fall in love with a stranger after only a few weeks. Yet it had happened and now she was stuck in this terrible limbo, yearning for a man she couldn't have.

Ilsa had opened herself up to him in ways she never had with anyone. Now she paid the price.

She hadn't thought it possible to hurt more than when she'd said she had to leave. How little she'd known.

When he'd lashed out at her, accusing her first of being a stuck-up socialite who'd dumped him because he wasn't royal, and then of using him to secure a business deal... Ilsa had wanted more than anything to set him straight. To explain that he was the best man she'd ever known.

But then would come the questions, the demands. Noah wasn't the sort to take no for an answer, so she'd let him believe that ugliness rather than allow him to glimpse the truth. Because if he realised how much she wanted him he'd be *kind* to her and then she feared she wouldn't have the strength to walk away, pretending to be heart-whole.

She blinked furiously, fighting the tears glazing her eyes. She couldn't let them fall here in the taxi.

Ilsa shivered, folding her arms around herself and staring blindly at the passing landscape.

When she'd got aboard the yacht mere hours ago she'd dashed into the bathroom, needing time alone to sort out what to do. She'd wanted to face Noah fully clothed, hoping that would provide the armour she needed and help her hide her feelings for him.

When the shower door had opened and he'd stood there, tall, naked and aroused, and so incredibly dear, she'd known she fought a losing battle. She could no more tell him to go than she could fly.

She'd wanted to give him everything. To *show* him how much he meant to her, even if she didn't dare tell him. How his care and tenderness, as much as his eroticism, had changed her, giving her the strength to stand up for herself.

Her mouth had wobbled at the realisation she'd have to use that strength to walk away from him.

So she'd given him pleasure, dropping to her knees and taking him in her mouth till he trembled and his powerful body stiffened on the verge of climax.

Yet he'd insisted they go there together.

That demand had nearly undone her. Which was why she'd turned her back on him, knowing she couldn't look into his eyes as they made love and not reveal her feelings.

Ilsa's body throbbed with the memory of them together, his hands clamped on her, holding her against him as he pumped so hard she felt it in her very marrow. She'd revelled in every thrust, every hoarse breath.

'We're here.'

Ilsa blinked and looked out at the airport. Despair engulfed her. She wanted to say she'd changed her mind and needed to go back. Would the yacht still be there? Would Noah let her aboard?

But it was impossible. Other women might believe in fairy tales about finding Prince Charming, who'd turn their life around. A princess born and bred, Ilsa knew fairy tales weren't real. The only person who could turn her life around was herself. Starting now.

Even if walking into the airport would hurt in every bone and muscle she possessed.

She paid the driver, smiled at his thanks and got out. She couldn't look back. She could only go on, even if she had no idea where she'd go or what she'd do with a life that now seemed grey and empty.

'I wish you'd reconsider, Ilsa. Your father…'

Ilsa didn't want to hear what her father thought. Not yet. Maybe not ever.

Noah had believed she'd been an agent of her father, using sex to persuade him into a deal her father wanted. That she'd dumped him as soon as he'd signed on.

A shudder ran down her spine. She wasn't ready to deal with Altbourg or the King.

'I'll be in London at least another week,' she told her mother as she curled up on a seat looking over one of the city's most exclusive squares. The view of green lawns and trees surrounded by impeccable white mansions was soothing. Ilsa was lucky to have the use of the house while her friend was away, travelling. 'But you can assure him that there'll be no more scandal about me.'

The press had gone wild with speculation, starting with photos taken on private phones in Monaco. Ilsa wasn't sure what had caused more fuss. The fact she was with another man soon after her broken engagement. Or that she, the demure Princess, had been seen with bare thighs, her hair loose and wearing killer heels.

She'd read some of the reports and, despite the puerile speculation, it was rather nice to be described as sexy, vivacious and even, in one case, as every man's secret fantasy.

It was a little balm to her wounded soul.

She didn't feel sexy or desirable.

'It wasn't the photos of you partying that concerned him, darling.'

No, it had been the fact she'd spent weeks with a notoriously sexy billionaire aboard his private yacht. The press had been breathless with wild speculation. Had she gone with Noah in the hope of making Lucien jealous? Would the Altbourg royal family accept an Australian suitor? Her heart had cramped at that one.

The one good piece of news she'd had in the last week was a call from Lucien to say Aurélie and the baby were safe.

'Ilsa, did you hear me?'

'Sorry. I was a bit distracted.' She shifted, feeling that ache low in her back she sometimes got. She'd been tired and listless since arriving in London. Usually she soldiered on, even in pain. It was a luxury to relax.

'By Katrin's news? I'm not surprised. It's shocked us all.'

'You can say that again.'

Ilsa had taken a call from her cousin Katrin that morning, listening, dumbfounded, to the news that she and her husband were divorcing. Ilsa still couldn't take it in. The pair had been so happy. But years of unsuccessful fertility treatment had taken a toll and they'd recently been advised that further treatment was likely to be unsuccessful. Soon after, Katrin's husband had announced he wanted a divorce. He wasn't interested in adoption. He wanted a wife who could bear his biological children.

Horrified, Ilsa had offered to fly home to support her cousin. But Katrin was leaving almost immediately for a research job in the States and they'd agreed to catch up later.

They were close friends as well as cousins. Similar in age, they had shared similar symptoms and been diagnosed with endometriosis at almost the same time.

Ilsa was heartbroken for Katrin. As well, she couldn't help wondering about her own fertility. She'd been putting off her next specialist's appointment. Now she realised she didn't want to hear what the doctor might say.

'I always liked her husband,' Ilsa's mother said. 'I'd never have believed it of him. They were so in love.'

'Love doesn't guarantee happiness,' Ilsa murmured.

It hadn't for her.

She tucked her knees up against her chest. Life was delivering one blow after another.

'True.' Her mother sighed. 'But nor does an arranged marriage.' She paused. 'For what it's worth I thought that engagement to Lucien wasn't a good idea. I let myself be persuaded. That's no excuse, but...'

'What happened wasn't your fault.' Funny, to be the one reassuring her mother.

'Nevertheless, it was one thing, you agreeing to marry Justin when you'd known each other for years. It was another to expect you to marry his heir, no matter how useful it was diplomatically. We should have given you both more time.'

Ilsa's eyebrows lifted in surprise. It was the first time her mother had voiced doubt about something the King had decided.

'We've asked a lot of you over the years, darling. So I understand you needing a break now. I just wish you'd come home.'

A wave of warmth engulfed Ilsa. Her mother was worried, not because of the press or the political fallout from her actions, but because she cared.

'I'll think about it. But you're right. I need a break.

That's easier here where my PA can't schedule every hour of the day for me.'

Her mother chuckled and Ilsa heard amusement as well as concern in her voice. 'Fair enough. I'll talk to your father, try to divert him. But promise me you'll take care of yourself.' She paused. 'I could always fly over and keep you company.'

Like when Ilsa was a teenager and her mother had travelled with her through North America. But this time Ilsa didn't need time or distance to discover she couldn't have the man she wanted. She knew it all too well.

Her mouth crumpled as emotion clogged her throat.

'Thanks,' she murmured. 'But I'm fine. I just need a little more time.'

As she ended the call Ilsa felt the ache inside fill her to the brim. The heartbreak she'd felt as a teenager seemed absurd and insignificant by comparison.

She wished she could spend another day alone but the longer she holed up, the harder it would be, facing the public. She'd forced herself out once or twice this last week, but it had taken such effort.

Besides, she had an appointment she couldn't miss. One thing this time alone had given her was a chance to ponder what she wanted to do with her life.

Be with Noah Carson.

Ilsa winced and ignored the needy voice in her head.

She wanted to love and be loved. She wanted a long-term relationship and she wanted children. Which she wouldn't get hiding away. And if, as she feared, she couldn't have a family of her own, she could do her bit to help children in need. That had crystallised in her mind after talking with Noah. Something positive she could accomplish.

This afternoon's appointment would be a step in that direction.

She lowered her feet to the floor and stood up, stretching.

Her heart might be broken, and she was still tortured by thoughts of the man she loved, but she had to try to get on with her life.

Ilsa stepped out of the conference room in the grand Mayfair hotel. She was glad she'd attended the session. It had been as interesting as she'd hoped and she'd made useful contacts. She'd stayed back talking with a couple of the presenters, one from New York and the other from Australia. Their stories gave her hope that a similar initiative might be feasible in Altbourg.

She smiled and nodded goodbye to the other attendees still milling around the foyer, turning to leave, and blundered into someone.

'Ilsa.' A hand caught her elbow and she froze.

For a second she couldn't look up, just stood, absorbing the feel of that large hand on her arm and the rough velvet brush of his voice trawling through her .

She breathed out slowly, searching for calm as her pulse skittered and her mouth dried.

'Noah.'

Finally she lifted her chin, drawn by a magnetism she couldn't resist.

Those eyes. As gorgeous as ever. That face, all strong lines except for his sensual mouth and the hint of a cleft in his chin that accentuated his masculinity and at the same time made it seem more approachable, less overwhelming.

Except she felt overwhelmed. Totally overwhelmed.

Did he feel the fine tremors running under her skin?

His mouth crimped a little at the corners. An attempt at a smile or a grimace? Surely the last thing he wanted was to run into her.

'This is a surprise,' she managed, suddenly aware of the people around them. She snapped her eyes away from his and noticed several suddenly averted faces, as if they'd been caught staring.

Even here, in this bastion of the well-to-do, there'd be curiosity about their reunion.

Was that what this was? Excitement eddied deep inside before she squashed it. Of course it wasn't a reunion. Noah despised her.

'I thought I might run into you here.' His words yanked Ilsa's attention back to his face. And to the fingers still wrapped around her arm.

Why didn't he let go?

She wanted to think it was because he didn't want to. Because he craved the connection as much as she did, but she couldn't let herself fantasise like that.

'Really? How did you—?' No, she wouldn't go there. 'You're looking well, Noah.' Ilsa forced a smile. It was true. He looked fit, well-rested and heart-whole.

She feared she didn't. Sleep had been difficult this week because she'd grown accustomed to snuggling up against Noah's naked body. On his yacht sheer exhaustion from their lovemaking had ensured she'd slept wonderfully, whereas now she spent every night going over what might have been and what could never be.

'So are you.' Yet as his piercing gaze searched her face tiny vertical lines appeared on his forehead as if something perplexed him.

'Well.' She stepped back and he released her arm. Strange how her skin tingled from his touch. 'It's been good to see you but—'

'I thought you were heading straight back to Altbourg. Wasn't your family expecting you?'

She shrugged, not wanting to admit she still had no definite plan. 'I'll go home soon. There are people I needed to see first in London.'

He nodded. 'Ah, yes. Lord Brokebank. You looked very cosy on your date.'

'Breakhurst.' Ilsa's mouth tightened. There was no

mistaking the steely note in Noah's voice. 'You've become a fan of the gossip columns, then?'

She and Antony had been photographed leaving a restaurant. The fact that the pursuing paparazzi had lost them in a traffic snarl had led to speculation that they'd spent the night together.

'Hardly.' Noah looked grim.

Ilsa tilted her chin. She refused to tell him it hadn't been a date. Antony was a financial guru as well as an old friend. They'd met to discuss her plan to endow an enterprise that, given time, would become financially self-sustaining and provide programmes for social change.

'What are you doing in London, Noah?'

His stare seemed to grow darker, even more intense, and her breath seized. He'd come here to see her and, despite everything, a tendril of excitement budded.

Hectic heat rose in her cheeks as she remembered him taking his pleasure, and ensuring she did too.

'I have some matters to deal with before I head back to Australia.' Was *she* one of those matters? No. Their relationship was over. 'We need to talk in private, Ilsa.'

He kept his voice low, but she heard the steely note of determination.

Ilsa raised her eyebrows. 'Really?'

Injured pride surfaced. It didn't matter that she'd lied by omission, letting Noah think she'd used and discarded him. His accusations had hurt and she still carried the unhealed scars. How could he have been so ready to think her shallow?

But, instead of being deterred, he leaned closer. 'It's important, Ilsa.'

This close to him, she inhaled the spicy scent of his flesh. No other man smelled as good as Noah Carson. Dully she wondered if any man ever would.

Ilsa's heart skittered into an uneven beat, pounding

high in her throat. Because the way Noah looked at her, with that searing intensity, told her she was his sole focus.

She tried and failed to rein in excitement.

What did he want to tell her?

Why the heat in his gaze? Was she imagining it? Attributing desire where there was none? Maybe he was simply about to announce his withdrawal from the business scheme in Altbourg.

But then, why the need for privacy?

'I'm not sure that—'

Someone bumped into her. At the same time she felt liquid splash her jacket.

'Sorry!' said a man's voice.

She looked down to see a massive patch of crimson on the pale raw silk of her jacket, dribbling down onto her skirt. A stranger stood beside her looking sheepish, an empty wine glass in his hand. She recognised him from the conference. Behind him a crowed of attendees were chatting over drinks.

'Here, Ilsa.'

Noah grabbed a napkin from a passing waiter and passed it to her. Their fingers tangled and heat shimmied through her.

He'd barely touched her, yet she felt it like a caress. Was she really so needy?

Despite everything, the answer was *Yes*.

While Ilsa dabbed at the stains, Noah said something to the man whose wine had spilled. The stranger apologised again and turned away. Then Noah moved closer, tall and broad enough to block her from the rest of the room. Sheltering her from curious eyes?

The action didn't fit with the angry man she'd left in Turkey. But today Noah was less like that suspicious man and more like the one she'd fallen in love with.

The realisation made all those emotions she tried to suppress rise to the surface. 'It really is time I left.'

'Please, Ilsa.' His voice, deep and full of sensual allure, stopped her. 'There's something you really need to hear. And you can clean up at the same time.' He paused. 'The paparazzi are outside, covering the hotel entrance. It looked like they were waiting for someone.'

Ilsa sighed. 'Just what I need.'

If they saw her covered with wine stains they'd spin stories about her drinking too much.

Ilsa had promised her mother there'd be no more scandal. She didn't intend to add to her family's concern. Besides, she was planning some important initiatives. It would be easier to get people to buy into them and achieve her goals if her reputation wasn't the stuff of lurid press reports.

Noah held out his arm. It was such a familiar gesture. Ilsa wanted to lean into him and pretend, just for a minute, that they were still together.

No matter how she tried to ignore it, the air between them was thick with awareness. Her pulse thrummed too fast and between her legs moisture bloomed as every feminine part of her body reacted.

Because this was Noah, the man to whom she'd lost part of herself.

Ilsa forced a tight smile. 'Okay. I'll clean this and we can talk.'

That sounded simultaneously exciting and terrifying.

CHAPTER ELEVEN

NOAH LED HER across the foyer, holding her close at his side and masking the stains.

Her breath shuddered out then snatched in so hard it hurt her lungs. Having Noah so near, feeling the heat of his body, the press of those strong limbs against her... She felt as unsteady as if she'd spent the afternoon drinking Schnapps instead of listening to presentations.

A few minutes later they emerged from the lift on a luxurious upper floor. There were just two doors in a corridor decorated with Venetian mirrors, vases of fragrant lilies and antique celadon ceramics.

She'd been so befuddled she hadn't thought this through. Now she turned to him. 'You're staying here?'

What were the chances of such a coincidence? Could he have booked a room because he knew she'd be here?

'Yes, I am.'

He opened a door and gestured for her to enter.

Ilsa hesitated. She wanted, badly, to be alone with Noah. Yet she shouldn't.

She looked up at his still form in the doorway. His expression was in shadow but she read tension in his jaw and shoulders.

A frisson of mingled warning and excitement tingled along her backbone. She could no more resist stepping over his threshold than she could fly to the moon.

Ilsa put her bag on a table inside the door and heard the door click behind her. Before her was a vast sitting room as opulent as a palace. For some reason she hadn't imagined Noah staying somewhere like this. Not because he couldn't afford it, but because she'd imagined him somewhere less traditional.

She was conscious of him just behind her, as if he radiated an energy that she registered like a burst of tiny explosions all across her skin.

'If you'll show me the bathroom...' She didn't turn, too hyper-aware of him just there, and of her craving to touch him.

Noah moved past her, so close she felt the waft of displaced air. Her gaze skimmed from his neatly trimmed dark hair to his shoulders, wider than ever in a jacket of dark blue, down to the swing of his arms and the easy stride of those powerful legs.

He didn't say anything, didn't look at her, and she told herself that was good. They weren't lovers or even friends any more.

So what did he want to discuss?

Ilsa swallowed hard, trying not to dwell on her tangle of disturbing emotions, and followed.

He led her to a magnificent marble bathroom. She blinked, telling herself it was because of the bright light, not because of the feelings bubbling inside. All because Noah was here, so close she could touch him. Making her want things she had no right to want. That old familiar craving was back, her body awakening to his presence.

Resolutely she stepped past him, crossing the space till she reached twin marble basins set in a bench that ran along one wall.

'Thank you, Noah. I appreciate this.'

Instead of meeting his eyes in the mirror before her she slipped off her jacket, studying the stain in the hope of distracting herself from Noah, so close, so tempting.

Finally she put the jacket aside and surveyed her skirt. It would be almost impossible to salvage.

Ilsa thought of her promise not to attract any more scandal and drew a slow breath.

Glancing up, her gaze locked on Noah's in the mirror. She'd known he was still there because behind every scattered thought was a deep humming awareness. He stood in the doorway, one shoulder against the doorjamb, jacket open and hands in his trouser pockets.

The bare skin of her arms prickled as she realised her silk camisole was the same green-blue as Noah's eyes.

Not merely similar but exactly the same.

She'd bought the camisole days after arriving in London, drawn by the colour.

Had she bought it because it reminded her of Noah?

With difficulty Ilsa conjured a smile from tense facial muscles. 'I won't be long.'

Instead of replying, Noah silently straightened and took his hands from his pockets as if preparing to go. Ilsa wanted to say she'd changed her mind. She wanted him to stay. She'd missed him, thought of him every day and dreamed of him each night.

'Ilsa! Don't look at me like that.'

His voice was gruff and low and it made every tiny hair on her body stand erect.

Ilsa's pulse thudded. She planted her hands on the marble counter as her legs trembled. In the mirror he looked tall and daunting, his expression compelling.

'Like what?'

Her own voice was unrecognisable. Husky and breathless. Full of a longing she couldn't hide.

Slowly he walked towards her, stopping so close behind her she felt his body and more too, a tickle of sensation from her shoulders, down her back, buttocks and legs, as if he exuded a force field of energy. Except that tickle of awareness curled further, around her breasts to her peaking nipples and across her hips then arrowing down inside her pelvis.

Her snatched breath was sharp in the thrumming silence. Despite the way they'd parted her senses sang, being close to him.

'Like you want me.' He paused and it almost killed her that he stood so near yet didn't touch her. '*Do* you want me, Ilsa?'

She opened her mouth to deny it but couldn't.

Because it was true. She longed for him, despite all the reasons she shouldn't.

Long fingers skimmed her arms from her bare shoulders to her fingertips. It was like fire igniting and racing along a line of spilled fuel. Where he touched sensation leapt and heat burst.

Ilsa closed her eyes as delight coursed through her. How she'd craved his touch!

When their eyes again locked in the mirror, fear scudded through her.

This was wrong. There was no way forward for them together. It was better if she kept her distance.

She spun around, intending to tell him to move away. Instead her breasts rose on a gasp as she met the full force of Noah's stare. It spoke of desire, hot and enticing, and Ilsa melted.

His fingertips brushed back up her arms, the touch sure yet tender.

The locked-tight cast of his features eased into something softer. Even so…

'Noah. We can't. It wouldn't be right.'

Because she'd left him, and she feared being with him again would undo her completely.

'You think this doesn't feel right?' His voice was all gravel and whisky and enticement.

That fingertip touch dragged across her lace and silk camisole. Ilsa's breath snatched in and her breast lifted to his hand. Her mouth turned arid with anticipation as he skimmed her fullness then circled her aching nipple.

'Noah!' His name ripped from her lips and she didn't have enough pride to worry what that revealed. She arched, pressing closer, but still he refused to cup her fully.

'Say it, Ilsa.' His other hand skated around her other breast and she fought to remember why this wasn't a good idea.

She shook her head and grabbed his hand, telling herself she'd pull it away from her and end this torture.

Instead Noah leaned in, his lips against her ear in a delicious caress. 'You want me to touch you properly, Ilsa?'

His caress turned from feather-light to deliberate and strong. He pushed up, taking her weight in his palm, capturing her nipple through her clothes and pinching gently till a fuse lit between it and her womb and everything ignited in a flash of conflagration.

Ilsa shuddered, the feeling so good she wondered for a second if she'd actually orgasmed just from his words and his hand on her breast.

But the hungry throb deep in her pelvis disproved that.

Holding her gaze, he circled her other nipple with his index finger and sparks swirled through her bloodstream. Any second now she'd combust.

'You want me, don't you?'

'Yes,' she gasped, goaded into abandoning her good intentions. 'Yes, *please*, Noah.'

He grinned then, dropped his hands and stepped back.

For a horrible, heart-stopping moment Ilsa thought he was leaving. That this was some sort of taunt, getting his own back on her for leaving.

Then, to her utter relief, he bent and skimmed the hem of her skirt high. Before her brain kicked into gear deft fingers hooked around her pantyhose and underwear, dragging them down her hips and thighs.

Ilsa clutched the surface behind her as Noah crouched low, his hand circling first one ankle then the other as he pulled her shoes off and the fabric free.

Breathless, she straightened, feeling cool marble beneath her soles. She reached for her waistband, then stopped as Noah lifted her skirt again. He bunched it up over her thighs and further, finally pinning the fabric to the flat of her stomach with his palm.

Eyes the colour of a tropical sea captured hers. Heat engulfed her in a whoosh of flame.

'My turn.' His teeth gleamed white against his tan as he grinned up at her. Then he leaned in, his breath stirring a flurry of sensation at the juncture of her thighs.

Firmly he pushed her legs wide. Then came pressure, delicious pressure from his lips and tongue.

Ilsa's head lolled back, eyes shutting as he pleasured her with such delicacy, such intimate understanding, that she felt the quakes building deep inside.

'Noah, please. I want *you*.' Ilsa ached for him, as she'd ached all the long, lonely nights, the hollow sensation within unbearable.

She looked down to discover her fingers clenched in his hair and those eyes, those paradise eyes, staring up at her between thick black lashes.

Still holding her gaze, he moved his tongue, slowly, deliberately, stroking her very nerve centre, and suddenly Ilsa was flying, the world blurring around her. All but Noah's eyes, watching her, holding her, keeping her safe as everything turned liquid and melting and ecstasy dissolved her bones.

When she came back to herself Noah was standing, pressed against her, holding her upright against something hard. She inhaled the spice and man scent she'd missed since Turkey and her throat closed on a sudden rush of tears.

'Ilsa?' He cupped her throat, his eyes questioning as they held hers.

In that moment she felt absolutely wide open and vulnerable. Every defence she'd ever erected around herself had shattered. Pride, common sense, caution, all gone. There was just her and Noah and the undeniable truth between them.

'I need you, Noah. Now.'

He frowned and she wondered if she hadn't spoken English but her native tongue. Then his hands firmed at her waist and he lifted her up onto the cool counter.

She sighed as he shoved her knees wide and stepped between them.

Ilsa's heart catapulted around her ribcage.

It was bizarre that he was still fully dressed and she was almost so. The slick flesh between her legs, swollen from arousal, was so sensitive even the brush of air as Noah moved felt significant.

But he only moved to reach into a pocket and draw out a square packet.

'You put it on,' he growled, pressing it into her palm so he could deal with his belt and trousers.

Ilsa's fingers trembled as she tore the packet and took out the condom. She was so eager she was clumsy, desperate to have Noah inside her. It took a couple of goes to get it right and unroll the latex around him. Noah didn't help her, but she heard the hiss of his breath as she covered him and guessed he was as desperate as she.

'Noah, I…'

Her words died as he kissed her. Hard and deep, yet at the same time impossibly tender. Everything she was rose to meet him. Her hopes, her fears, her yearning.

Her love.

Ilsa wrapped her arms around him and kissed him back as if this were the last time.

Because she knew now what deprivation felt like. The time since they'd parted had been an emotional wasteland.

Now she came alive again, joy melding with arousal.

He pulled her to the very edge of the counter and the action brought her into contact with his erection. Excitement rippled through her, then, before she had time to do more than register anticipation, Noah was there, joining with her, pushing slow and deep until he sank right to her centre.

The weight of him, the sensation of them melding into one, was indescribably wonderful.

Ilsa blinked back tears and she kissed him with a desperation that bordered on wildness. Noah had touched something innate within her. He'd touched her heart, maybe her soul.

Her teeth grazed his tongue and bottom lip and he growled, his hands tightening satisfyingly on her body.

Finally he moved, taking up that smooth, deep rhythm she remembered from before. But this time it was a little uneven, his breathing ragged and his mouth fiercely possessive as he bowed her back in his embrace as if he wanted to imprint himself on her very being.

Tension rose. Wonderful, exciting tension that made her body clasp his in ripples of delight.

At the last moment Noah lifted his head, eyes fixed on hers as bliss stormed her body. Ilsa clutched him with legs and clawing hands and couldn't hold back.

'Noah!' Her cry went on and on and on as the world turned again into that special place that only they could find together.

She heard him shout as he pulsed within her.

Coming down from ecstasy took a lifetime and Ilsa didn't want it to end. Even in bliss she knew reality would be tough. So she hugged her lover close, knowing that for this moment everything was all right. Explanations and solutions could wait.

Finally Noah stepped back, gently disentangling her and moving her back on the counter so she could slump against the mirror. Ilsa knew she was smiling. There was a gentle throb through her body, and it felt as if she'd run a marathon on legs made of marshmallow, but for the first time in over a week happiness filled her.

'Ilsa.'

She blinked her eyes open to find Noah standing before her. Trousers on and belted. Jacket neat on his shoulders instead of halfway down his arms where she'd pushed it. Only his rumpled hair hinted at what they'd just done.

In contrast, her hair had come down from its knot and lay around her shoulders. Her skirt was rucked up around her hips and her knees were splayed wide.

She shuffled her legs closed, tugging at her skirt to cover herself. Suddenly, without him holding her, she felt sticky and self-conscious. She wanted to slip down off the counter but wasn't sure her legs would support her.

Yet the truth spilled out. 'That was amazing.'

More than amazing. It felt like he'd changed her world.

Which he had. She cared so much for this man that even now Ilsa couldn't regret what had just happened. Even knowing they had no future.

Today had confirmed how deeply in thrall she was to Noah Carson.

Maybe she'd been wrong. Maybe she *could* cope with an affair a bit longer and somehow bury her emotions, working out a way to continue on with her life when they split.

Perhaps it was better to be his lover for a short time than not have him at all.

'It *was* amazing. But we have things to discuss. Important things.'

Ilsa read the decisive lines etched beside his mouth, the frown on his forehead, and foreboding stirred.

CHAPTER TWELVE

NOAH PACED THE suite's sitting room, waiting for Ilsa to appear. Surely, after their explosive union, this would turn out well.

He couldn't repress a smile. Their need for each other was stronger than ever. That *had* to be a positive sign. Today she'd come to him as naturally as breathing. As if she too felt bereft when they were apart.

Noah refused to believe she'd been with another man, despite the press speculation about an aristocratic lover in London. The idea sent an army of ants crawling over him.

Ilsa had been a virgin in his arms. Heat curled in his belly and his groin stirred at the memory of taking her across that barrier into experience for the first time. She'd been exquisite and sensuous, and it had felt like the world's greatest honour to be her first.

She'd lived without a sexual partner until so recently. She wouldn't start bed-hopping now.

No matter what he'd said in Turkey, Noah couldn't think of a woman *less* likely to give herself easily. Heat scored his flesh as he thought of the accusations he'd made, including that she'd used sex to seal a business deal.

Noah forked his hand through his hair, guilt biting at his conscience. He spun on his heel and paced the room again, reliving what he'd said to Ilsa. The memory left him feeling diminished and ashamed.

Long dead echoes of the past had risen, melding with new hurt and he'd lashed out, accusing her of using him, much as his ex had done.

Because Ilsa had taken him by surprise and he'd felt vulnerable and hurt. It was the very intensity of his feelings that had undone him. Because he couldn't understand her urgency to leave. He'd been desperate for her to stay.

Because he wanted Ilsa in his life. Wanted her long-term.

That was the truth he'd been grappling with just before she'd announced she was going. The idea would once have seemed outlandish. Now it made total sense.

Noah was the only one of his family in three generations who hadn't met and married his partner by his early twenties. Because, after his early mistake, he'd believed his judgement was flawed.

The Carsons had a tradition of instant attraction and lifelong devotion. Noah had believed he'd avoided that family trait since with Poppy he'd let lust blind him.

But now he couldn't ignore the signs. That immediate slam of awareness, unlike anything he'd known. His total absorption in Ilsa. The fact he'd upended his plans just to be with her.

He'd been happy for years to indulge in short-term relationships. All fun and no expectations.

That wasn't how he felt now. It hadn't been for some time.

So much hung in the balance. He couldn't recall being so nervous before any business negotiation, but this was more important than any commercial deal.

A sound made him look up and he slammed to a halt, heart hammering, every muscle tensed.

Ilsa crossed the sitting room and sank into an armchair. Avoiding the sofas in case he sat beside her? His jaw tightened in disappointment.

Her posture was perfect, her head high. But her skirt

was crumpled and stained, she'd put up her hair again but feathery tendrils escaped as if her hands hadn't been as deft as usual, and her mouth was swollen from passion.

She was the most beautiful woman he knew.

Noah's breath snagged in his lungs.

He hadn't intended to have sex with her before they spoke, much less do it up against the bathroom vanity. But his need had been urgent and so, he'd been grateful to discover, had hers.

Yes, surely they could sort everything out.

'Ilsa, I need—'

'Noah, let me say something first.'

She looked so serious that, despite the urgency gnawing at him, he nodded and sat back. His apology was overdue but it could wait a few minutes.

'I shouldn't have left you the way I did, with no warning. It was rude and it wasn't surprising you jumped to conclusions. But—' she leaned forward, her expression earnest '—I never used you for gain. I didn't know about progress on that business deal. I didn't know you'd come to an agreement and it had nothing to do with me leaving.'

She looked at her clasped hands. 'I went with you for purely selfish reasons. They had nothing to do with Altbourg or my father or business.'

'I know.'

She looked up, startled. 'You do?'

Noah nodded, tasting self-reproach on his tongue.

'I was in such a lather about you going I couldn't think properly. All I knew was that it felt wrong, you leaving like that. I lashed out with wild accusations and insulted you.'

He paused. 'That's why I needed to see you, to apologise. To tell you I'm sorry.'

'I see. Thank you.'

Yet she didn't look happy. He didn't blame her. She'd

torn their idyll apart with her departure but he'd sullied what they'd shared and soured what had been special.

He still didn't understand why she'd run away, but one thing at a time.

'I appreciate you telling me.' She shifted in her seat as if preparing to leave.

'That's not all. You deserve to know the rest.' He drew a slow breath. 'I made the mistake of letting my emotions cloud my judgement and letting past experience prejudice me too. I'm sorry. I'm not making excuses, but I want you to understand.'

After all, honesty was the basis of a solid relationship and that was what he wanted with Ilsa. He was in for the long haul. As soon as he'd convinced her to take a chance on him.

If he gave her honesty, hopefully she'd reciprocate and share what was behind her leaving. He suspected it was because of demands put on her by her family or royal obligations. He hoped to support to her with those but he had a lot of catching up to do.

Ilsa tilted her head as if trying to read his thoughts. He recognised it as her thinking look and something in his chest tightened at that endearing, familiar expression.

'I told you some people look down on my family because of the work they do.'

'And I told you that doesn't matter to me.'

Noah inclined his head. 'I remember. But the day you walked out was a shock to a man like me, used to being in control.' In business and his personal life things ran the way he wanted. Maybe he was growing spoiled by having his own way so often? 'It also reminded me too much of something that happened in the past. A woman who left me high and dry.'

The astonishment on Ilsa's face would have stoked his ego in other circumstances. It looked as if she had trouble imagining a woman leaving him.

But the joke was on Noah, for twice now it had happened and both times it had shifted his world.

He cleared his throat. 'Her name was Poppy. She was bright, sexy and fun and I thought I loved her, though now I suspect I was in love with the idea of love. I thought I'd found my life partner.' He shrugged ruefully. 'My family has a tradition of falling in love early and for life.'

'I see.' Yet Ilsa frowned.

'I'm sure you don't, but you will.' Noah drew a slow breath. 'Poppy didn't love me. It turned out I was just a bit of fun. A change from her sophisticated friends and privileged lifestyle. I had money and a growing business reputation, so it didn't hurt to be seen with me. But when I asked her to marry me she was scandalised. She'd never lower herself socially to marry someone with a family like mine, despite all the lovely money I could provide.'

'That's truly horrible. I don't understand how you hadn't realised what she was like.'

A terse laugh escaped. 'I was very young and good sex can blind a guy. Besides, she was clever. She didn't make her feelings obvious, especially as she wanted me to fund a start-up enterprise she planned. An online fashion atelier.'

'She wanted you to lend her money?'

'Oh, not a loan.' He grimaced. 'She was insulted when I talked about drawing up a legal agreement. She thought I'd give her anything she wanted. Maybe that's part of the reason she took such delight in rejecting me.'

She hadn't held anything back in her scathing description of Noah and his family and he'd seen red when she'd insulted the people he cared most about in the world.

Ilsa said something under her breath in a language he didn't know. Yet he understood the sentiment and warmed at her outrage on his behalf.

'I'm sorry she hurt you and even sorrier that I reminded you of her. I see how my actions might have felt like an echo of that.'

'Thank you. I should have been able to shrug the experience off, but she hurt my family too. My sister in particular.' He'd never forgive her for the damage she'd done to Ally. 'It's no excuse, but that day in Turkey was too much like déjà vu.'

'I'm so sorry.' It wasn't a platitude. He heard Ilsa's sincerity.

'It's in the past, or it should be.' Thankfully Ally was well and happy now, doing a job she adored. 'In the clear light of day I see that, but when we separated I let myself get swamped by doubt. I couldn't think clearly, even when instinct said you were honest and generous.'

'Our pasts affect us all.'

Ilsa's words made him respect her even more, and feel worse about jumping to conclusions. Ilsa battled to overcome her own rejections.

'You didn't deserve to bear the brunt of my temper.' Noah spread his hands and paused, knowing he needed to share something he'd never spoken about. 'The fact is I blame myself for what happened to my sister. I was the one who brought Poppy into her life. That's part of why I suspected the worst about you, even as I told myself it couldn't be true. It was unfair on you.'

'Thank you, Noah, and thank you for explaining. It makes things…easier.'

Did Ilsa's mouth turn down or did he imagine it? Suddenly, despite the desperate way they'd fallen into each other just now, Noah felt the full weight of trepidation press down on him.

'That's not the only reason I'm here, Ilsa.'

He felt his hands clench on the arms of the chair and relaxed them, trying to ease a little of his tension.

'I've done a lot of thinking. In fact—' he paused '—I've had a revelation.'

Noah studied Ilsa closely. Her body language warned him to tread very carefully. He hated even this small distance between them as they sat facing each other, but better to wait to reveal his feelings for her. Instinct warned him she wasn't ready for an emotional declaration.

This was a woman who'd been brought up to expect an arranged marriage, not a love match. He didn't want to scare her off by asking too much too soon.

She took duty seriously and he guessed she'd left because of pressure from her family. Noah planned to visit Altbourg soon and do everything he could to impress the King and win over Ilsa's family.

If that didn't work, he'd just have to sweep her off her feet and seduce her into staying with him. Because not having her in his life wasn't an option.

'Go on.'

'The fact is I've changed. Short affairs were fine for a while but I'm older now. My experience with Poppy soured my view of relationships for years. But our time together made me begin to rethink. It's stupid to make life decisions based on disappointment.'

He paused, trying to calm his now rackety pulse. 'I've realised I want more in my life. Children of my own and a wife.'

Her eyes snapped wide and he read shock in those bright blue depths. Did she have to look quite so stunned?

'Do you mean—?'

'It's okay, Ilsa, I'm not proposing. Or trying to tie you down.'

Yet.

He could be patient. If that was what it took. He didn't want to frighten her off.

'I'm just saying my priorities have changed. You know I wasn't ready to say goodbye when you left. The fact is—' He shrugged, trying to look insouciant instead of mouth-dryingly nervous. 'The fact is I'm ready to start thinking about longer term and I'd like you to think about it too. I'd like to keep seeing you, find out how our relationship develops.'

She didn't respond, leaving Noah at the mercy of doubt and fear.

Finally Ilsa moved, lifting her hand and planting her palm against her collarbone in a classic, nervous gesture.

Noah breathed deep. Was it from surprise and excitement?

Everything—his future happiness, their future together—was riding on her reaction. He leaned forward.

'I don't know what to say.'

Ilsa pressed her hand to her chest as if she could prevent her heart from leaping free. She trembled with shock and excitement.

How badly she wanted to throw herself into Noah's arms, burrow close and feel once again as if everything were right in the world.

But she held back, trying to make sense of his words.

'Aren't you going back to Australia soon? How would a relationship work with you on one side of the world and me on the other? I have commitments here.'

And she planned on more with these new initiatives in the pipeline.

He smiled and spread his hands and pleasure darted through her. He just had to smile at her...

'Where there's a will there's a way. We can work the details out as we go if it's what we both want. It's what *I* want, Ilsa. That's why I came, to find out if you felt the same.'

She sucked in a desperate breath, searching vainly for calm. But how could she be calm when Noah spoke about long term? A possible future together. And family.

It was what she wanted. A dream come true.

Her blood fizzed with excitement and her heart

swelled. She wanted to fall into Noah's arms, pepper him with kisses and show him how delighted she was at the prospect of staying with him.

Strange that she saw no answering excitement in his features. Instead his face was guarded and disturbingly unreadable. Even those gorgeous turquoise eyes seemed flat.

Ilsa surveyed him sitting there, feet planted on the floor, hands on the arms of his chair, no sign of emotion.

He looked like a man negotiating a business deal, not a lover waiting, breathless, to hear the *yes* he longed for.

Her elation dimmed.

She sifted his words and her heart sank.

Noah hadn't mentioned his feelings for her, just the fact that he had changed his mind about having a family. Come to think of it, he wasn't even saying he expected to be with her permanently, just that they should see how things went.

Like a try before you buy scheme.

Ilsa swallowed, horrified to taste a knot of tears high in her throat.

What had she expected? A declaration of love?

No, don't think about the answer to that!

'You're not saying anything.'

'You've given me a lot to think about.'

Noah wanted marriage and children.

Children.

Ice ran along Ilsa's bones.

'You definitely want a family?'

'Absolutely.' He smiled and *now* she saw emotion flicker in his eyes. At the idea of children.

Something dropped, hard and fast, through her abdomen, making her feel suddenly nauseous. She wanted a baby and the thought of having Noah's child would be a dream come true. But was it possible?

Ilsa had missed a recent gynaecologist's appointment,

partly because she feared the prognosis. Her cousin's situation weighed heavily on her mind, and the fear that she too might also be infertile.

Then how would Noah react? He said he wanted a family and she read that truth in his eager expression. He looked more excited about that than when he'd suggested they stay together.

Through their weeks together Ilsa had seen him with kids often and knew he loved being with them. She suspected he'd make a great dad. When she'd asked what he enjoyed most he'd said being with his nephew.

If Noah wanted a relationship would it survive the possibility that she couldn't have children?

There were no guarantees, but she feared she knew the answer. Ilsa didn't think she had the strength to embark on a future with Noah and risk him rejecting her later for something over which she had no control.

If he told her he loved her then she'd scrape together the courage to tell him of her fears.

If he told her he loved her she'd brave anything.

But this wasn't a declaration of love. It was an invitation to continue their affair.

How would her heart fare if she stayed with him, loving him while he didn't love her? Knowing she might not be able to give him what he wanted?

Her life was already in turmoil. She had felt directionless, her confidence damaged and her sense of self-worth impaired by a series of rejections that weren't about her personally. How much worse would it be if Noah pushed her away?

Ilsa shot to her feet so fast she swayed.

'Ilsa?' Noah was on his feet too, just an arm's length away, his brow furrowed with concern. 'What is it?'

Her heart dived as she took him in. Tall and handsome but far more than that. He was the man who had unlocked her heart. And unwittingly broken it.

He reached for her.

'No! Please, don't touch me.'

Because if he did her willpower would crumple.

He reared back, palm raised, and she read shock flash across his features. It almost looked like hurt but that was her imagination. *She* was the one hurting.

'I'm sorry, Noah, but I can't. It's impossible.'

'Because of your commitments in Altbourg? We can work through that.'

Ilsa shook her head. 'It's not just that. It's everything. The truth is I can't see it working between us. We have different lives and different expectations.'

She wanted love, for a start.

After all she'd been through, all the disappointments, surely she deserved that. To be wanted for herself, just a woman, not a princess or a potential mother.

Even if she could have Noah's children, there was no reason to think she'd ever have his love. And she wanted that, so badly it terrified her.

Pain bloomed low in her body and spread slowly but inexorably until there seemed to be nothing left.

Noah moved closer, invading her space so she had to tilt her chin to meet his eyes. His warm male scent tantalised her, the fact that she could reach out and touch him and he would let her. But it wasn't enough.

'Think about it, Ilsa.' His voice dropped to that low note that always undid her. She had to stiffen her knees. 'We're good together. We can be even better.' He paused, his gaze pinioning her. 'You know we can barely keep our hands off each other.'

'This isn't about sex.'

'I agree. But you can't ignore what we already have.' Then he reached for her.

Stepping back was the hardest thing Ilsa had ever done. Harder than ending her engagement and facing pressure from the press, disappointing her family and her nation.

'Please, Noah. I said no and I meant it!' Her voice rose, strident with distress, making him freeze. 'I don't want you to touch me again.'

Then, with tears blurring her eyes, she spun away, grabbed her bag and stumbled out.

It was only as she reached the ground floor that she realised she'd left her jacket behind and that she probably looked thoroughly debauched, perfect fodder for the paparazzi.

That was the least of her worries.

CHAPTER THIRTEEN

'IF YOU'D LIKE to sit here a little longer—'

'No, thank you,' Ilsa hurried to assure the doctor. 'I'm fine. I'm sure you have other patients.'

She'd probably already used up more than her allotted time. She got to her feet.

'Don't forget, tomorrow at nine. We can do the scan here. It's more convenient and private.'

In other words, the staff were discreet and there was less chance of rumours reaching the press.

Ilsa nodded. 'Tomorrow at nine. Thank you again.'

She emerged into a quiet boulevard with leafy shade trees. She drew a deep breath and walked briskly to her car. Ilsa preferred not to be photographed outside her doctor's office but she hadn't wanted an appointment at the palace, where it was impossible to keep a secret.

Instinctively she headed out of the city, driving on autopilot to a small country road and her favourite thinking spot looking across meadows and woodland to a shimmering lake.

A little while later Ilsa sat in the flower-starred grass and tried to absorb the peace that surrounded her. The bright sunlight warming her. The song of a bird nearby. The sight of a couple of butterflies looping and wheeling across the wildflowers.

Yet her blood effervesced and her heart raced.

She was pregnant.

At first Ilsa had refused to believe it, because what were the chances?

It felt like a miracle.

It was, if not a miracle, an extraordinarily fortuitous event. That was the medical view.

If it hadn't been for that torn condom weeks ago in Turkey…

Ilsa sank back against the meadow grass and closed her eyes. Her breath hitched as tears spilled down her cheeks.

She'd never believed this day would come.

She hadn't dared to hope it would.

Even now she could hardly believe it, despite the doctor's assurance. The chances against it were so high.

Ilsa's hand crept across her flat abdomen and wonder filled her. Her tiny baby rested there. Hers and Noah's.

Behind closed lids she saw turquoise eyes, warm with laughter.

Noah, so caring and considerate, yet with a devil-may-care streak that she found impossibly enticing. They were qualities that would make him a wonderful father. He wouldn't be a stick-in-the-mud, too busy with work to find time for his child.

Noah would be a hands-on father. Ilsa could see him now, cradling a tiny baby against his strong body. Or teaching a toddler how to kick a ball.

Her heart dipped and she shivered despite the balmy sunshine.

But would he want anything to do with her now? She'd left him in Turkey and again in London, rebuffing his offer of a relationship. Ilsa shivered, remembering the pain and anger in his voice as he'd spoken of the woman he'd once loved. Who had spurned him and hurt his family.

Was that how he viewed Ilsa now? A woman who, despite her words, thought he wasn't good enough?

How she wished she'd been truthful and told him her real reason for rejecting him. Except it wouldn't have helped. He wanted a woman to give him children. He'd have politely but firmly rescinded his offer.

A cracked laugh escaped her dry throat. Ironic that she now carried his child.

Besides, that had only been half the problem. The other part was that she loved him and couldn't face a future pining for him to return those feelings.

How could they agree on sharing and supporting their child after what had passed between them? Especially when she wanted too much from him.

Ilsa tried to imagine telling him her news. Would he even see her after she'd walked out on him? Noah had been kind and warm-hearted before. But a self-made billionaire must have a formidable side. No doubt he could be ruthless as well as proud. Would he let her close enough to talk? Or would he reject her unheard?

She cringed, remembering that disastrous day in London. She'd escaped from the hotel's back entrance with the help of the manager who'd seen her emerge, dazed, on the ground floor. He'd bundled her out of sight and ordered a trusted hotel driver to wait at the back entrance for her. They had been discreet, never breathing a word about her dishevelled and unconventional departure.

Since then she'd heard nothing from Noah. All she knew was that he'd returned to Australia and was making a splash escorting a parade of gorgeous women to one high profile event after another.

Yet she had to tell him about their baby.

Ilsa sighed. It would be the most wonderful thing in the world to share news of her pregnancy with the man she loved, if he loved her too.

But this was no time for fantasy. She grimaced. Noah probably never wanted to see her again. Plus— her heart pounded at the thought—she'd just been told her condition had to be closely monitored. Her chances of miscarriage were higher than average.

She lifted her chin and gazed at the pale blue sky.

All that was true. Things wouldn't be easy. But this was her miracle and she intended to embrace it.

'Noah?'

He stopped on his way into the conference room, turning to his PA. 'Yes, Bree?'

She got up from her desk, glancing at the open door. Only when she stood before him did she respond.

'I haven't had a chance to catch you in person. I wanted to double check. That instruction about personal calls still stands, doesn't it?' She leaned closer. 'No unsolicited private calls from women you haven't mentioned to me.'

'Oh, that. Yes, it still stands.'

Noah had learned to screen calls from women claiming to know him. Some were convinced that because he'd smiled at them in passing it was an invitation for an affair. The number who'd spun lies to his staff in the hope of getting access to him never failed to amaze.

His thoughts shot to Ilsa, the one woman he *wanted* to see. To the husky sound of her voice when she said his name. To the lilt of her laughter he'd missed so much. To her blank stare as she'd rejected him.

Pain clawed his belly.

But he'd resolve this soon, because seeing her again was a necessity.

He'd given her time but couldn't wait any longer. He'd engineered an invitation from her father. Did she know about that? It would give him the opportunity to see her in her own setting, get to the bottom of whatever stood between them, and prove to her that she needed him as much as he needed her.

He dragged his mind back to Bree. 'You know I don't have patience for time-wasters.'

'It's just…' Bree paused. 'I've taken some calls and I'm not sure if she counts as a stranger. Princess Ilsa of Altbourg.'

Ilsa? Calling his Sydney headquarters?

Shock slammed into him.

And something else. Excitement.

The woman bamboozled him. Undid him completely. She'd used and discarded him without a second glance. Yet they'd had searing hot sex in a bathroom because she'd wanted him every bit as much as he wanted her. Neither had been able to wait to get horizontal on a bed.

The two actions didn't make sense together.

Nor could he easily lump her in the same category as Poppy. He'd *swear* she was different.

'When?' His voice scraped from a suddenly constricted throat. 'When did she call?'

'This morning. And yesterday.' Bree's wide eyes betrayed that she wasn't used to seeing her boss agitated.

Noah ran a hand through his hair, scraping his fingertips hard across his scalp, trying to get his blood pumping and his mind working. He felt dazed.

Why would Ilsa contact him now?

His heart gave a great leap and he scowled.

Instantly Bree shook her head. 'Okay, boss. I get the message. No calls from the Princess.'

Noah yanked a deep breath into his lungs. 'Did she say anything? What she wanted? Where she was?'

'Just that she wanted to arrange a meeting.'

Noah rocked back on his heels. A meeting? Not just a phone call? She didn't have his private number, as he didn't have hers. There'd been no need. They'd met and been inseparable.

His pulse quickened. If she wanted to meet, was she in Australia, or coming here? But what about those royal commitments that mattered so much?

Excitement scudded down his backbone.

'Don't worry, Noah. I'll fob her off if she calls again.'

'No!' Bree's eyes widened at his tone. 'If she calls put her through. And get her number.'

Ilsa watched the suburban houses blur through the bus window and tried to tell herself she wasn't being foolish hoping her news might change things between them. Would having a child together unlock tender feelings in Noah?

She bit her lip. Of course it was crazy. Even if Noah hadn't found another woman in the time they'd been apart, even if he was happy about the baby, didn't mean his feelings for her would alter.

Just as well an already broken heart couldn't break again.

She firmed her lips and shifted in her seat but that didn't stop her inner voice trumpeting unpalatable truths.

You still love him. And he has no reason to feel kindly towards you.

If she could turn back the clock…

No. She had to concentrate on the future. That was all that mattered.

She pushed down her sunglasses to look at the sign that gave details of the next stop.

Ilsa drew in a choppy breath. Not far now. She pushed her sunglasses into place and looped the strap of her bag over her shoulder.

Sunglasses, casual clothes and a ponytail weren't much of a disguise but so far they'd worked. She'd arrived in the country without fanfare, thanks to a friend who travelled to Sydney via private plane, and so far the paparazzi hadn't got wind that she was in Australia.

Her heartbeat pattered faster as she pressed the button for the stop, holding onto her seat as the bus swayed out of the traffic towards the side of the road.

Could she do this?

It wasn't ideal. Ideal would be her and Noah completely alone, but she'd take what she could get. Repeated rebuffs from his protective secretary meant Ilsa had no choice but to be creative in arranging a meeting.

Would Noah hear her out?

Had he given explicit instructions to bar her calls or hadn't he known she'd called? No point wondering now. She'd *make* him listen because he needed to hear this.

The bus stopped. Thanking the driver, Ilsa stepped out and put on a sunhat. Even with a cool breeze the Australian sunshine was bright.

Before her stretched a large park that fitted the picture Noah had painted when he'd spoken of weekend barbecues in the sun. There was an enormous children's playground plus shaded picnic tables and beyond those a vast parkland.

Fear clutched her heart and she breathed deep, willing herself into calm.

Surely, if the Carson family kept the tradition Noah had described, this was where they would be. The first Sunday of every month, regular as clockwork, he'd said. He'd even named the sprawling park where the clan gathered.

This was her chance to see Noah face to face. She couldn't imagine putting her news in an email.

Yet she couldn't imagine spilling it in front of his family either. Nerves tightened and her step faltered, but she kept going. What choice did she have?

Finally, she spied a group that might fit the bill. Tables were set up under shade trees but out in the sun were a number of tall, dark-haired men in amongst children and some older figures. One man in particular caught her eye. Even from a distance he was familiar. The set of his wide shoulders, the athleticism of that toned body as he loped forward and caught a ball tossed in his direction.

Noah!

Suddenly the absurdity of her plan struck her. Was she going to march up and haul him away from his curious family in the middle of a game?

Maybe she should wait till they took a break. Or was that cowardice?

Either way, she needed a moment to consider. She headed towards the trees when shouts made her turn.

A ball arced high through the air towards her. Instinct, prodded by a cry of, 'Catch it!', made her step to one side and cup her hands as it came straight towards her. Ilsa's hands closed around the ball and she heard applause.

A girl in her early teens ran up. 'Brilliant catch!' She grinned and held out her hand for the ball. 'Now it's my turn to bat.' She paused. 'Do you want to play?'

'I...' Ilsa looked past her to the heads turned her way. One in particular. Even from this distance she felt the heat from eyes that she knew were a stunning turquoise. It was an effort to drag her attention back to the girl.

'Please say yes. We girls are always outnumbered. I'm Jess and it's my birthday.'

'Hi Jess, and Happy Birthday, I'm Ilsa. I'm afraid I'm not up to running at the moment.' She probably could but she'd take no chances with this baby. 'And I don't know the rules.'

'You've never played cricket?' Jess's eyes widened so much Ilsa had to suppress a laugh despite the tension winding through her body.

'I'm not from around here.'

'Now's your chance to learn.' Jess ushered her forward. 'It's simple. If you're in the field the aim is to catch the ball and get the batsman out. If you're batting, hit the ball between the fielders and run. But we'll get someone else to run for you.'

Ilsa let the words slide over her. Her attention was on the man who'd moved towards them then stopped, hands on hips as he watched them approach. Tall, imposing even in faded jeans and a polo shirt, the light breeze riffling his coal-black hair. Her heart squeezed. He was every bit as glorious as she remembered.

He surveyed her through dark glasses that gave nothing away.

'Ilsa.' His voice was deep and it ran like dark treacle across her skin, making her shiver.

'You know each other? Great!' Jess turned to the rest of the group. 'Everyone, this is Ilsa. She's joining us.'

Through the pounding in her ears Ilsa heard welcomes, but she couldn't acknowledge them. She was too busy staring at Noah, trying and failing to read his mood.

She didn't have to wait long.

'Ilsa won't be playing, Jess.'

He stalked closer. What was he going to do? Pick her up and carry her away from his family in case she contaminated them? Her heart dived.

Noah stopped so close Ilsa felt the air sizzle with his tension. His jaw set hard and she *felt* his stare despite his reflective glasses.

'I'm not here to—'

Another voice interrupted. 'Welcome!'

Ilsa saw a middle-aged woman with greying dark hair and a familiar-looking face march towards them.

'Mum.' Noah didn't turn. His voice held a hint of exasperation. 'You don't understand. You don't know who this is. She's not here to play cricket.'

The woman stopped beside him, her gaze penetrating. Ilsa felt as if she saw straight through her efforts to look calm and right down into the morass of nerves and fear.

'Princess Ilsa.' Noah's mother smiled, reminding Ilsa heartbreakingly of Noah as he'd been all those months ago. Before everything went wrong. 'It's a pleasure to meet you. You're even lovelier in person than in the press.'

'Just Ilsa, please.' She felt flustered. Noah's animosity she'd expected. But kindness from his mother left her floundering. If Noah had told her about Ilsa, surely she wouldn't be so welcoming? Or had she only seen the speculation about them in the media?

'And I'm Joanne.' She shot a sideways look at her son and Ilsa saw Noah incline his head the tiniest fraction, as if giving permission. 'Would you like to join us? It's only a friendly game. We'll break soon to have lunch. Then the pair of you can catch up.'

Her simple generosity undid something deep inside Ilsa and her tangled emotions threatened to burst free.

She swallowed hard and didn't dare look at Noah, her feelings too raw. 'Thank you, Joanne. I'd like that very much. If you don't mind a raw beginner joining in.'

What followed was a revelation.

It shouldn't have been. The high-spirited game reminded her of playing football on the beach with Noah and the children they'd met. The game was hotly contested, with a high level of skill, but with camaraderie, jokes and kindness despite the occasional mock outrage and protests.

Ilsa's family loved her but they never shared anything like this. They didn't gather for barbecues or casual ball games at the weekend. The idea of her father taking time out to play sport with her or Christoph was unthinkable.

Yet that wasn't all that made this unique. Joanne had announced that Ilsa was a friend of Noah's, visiting from Europe, and that was all it took to be accepted. His family must be curious but instead of staring they drew her in, as if closing ranks around her. She felt accepted in a way that felt rare and precious.

Whatever happened after she and Noah spoke, Ilsa wouldn't have missed this for the world.

During lunch, Noah was busy at the barbecue, partly, Ilsa was sure, because Joanne kept finding work for him. It might have been entertaining, watching the decisive tycoon at the beck and call of his mother. Instead she found it sweet, because she knew he allowed it because he loved his mum. Seeing him with his family reassured her that he'd treat their child well, no matter how he felt about her.

She sat with Noah's cousin on one side and his sister Ally on the other. Ally was bright and engaging but clearly protective of her big brother, questioning Ilsa closely until Joanne intervened.

Ally apologised for being nosy, saying quietly that Noah had been her rock when she'd gone through tough times years before. Apparently he blamed himself, wrongly, for not protecting Ally better. She was convinced that he needed to concentrate on his own happiness now.

Ilsa ignored Ally's meaningful look but recalled Noah saying his ex had hurt his family and especially his sister. Seeing his close-knit family, she could understand why it was a sore point for Noah. Guilt swirled at how her rejection might have reinforced his negative feelings.

When Noah finally appeared beside her, Ilsa's pulse kicked up and nerves replaced the sense of wellbeing she'd clung to as a distraction from her inner turmoil.

Silently he reached out to help her up from the seat hemmed in against a table.

Ilsa stared at that strong hand, stunned at the friendly gesture, remembering how she'd spurned him in London. Colour flooded her cheeks and, before she could reach out, Noah dropped his hand to his side.

She scrambled to her feet, but he'd already stepped away and she felt a yawning hollow in her chest. It had just been a polite gesture for the benefit of his family.

Noah was already saying goodbye and there was a chorus of good wishes from his family.

'You have a lovely family,' she said when they were out of earshot.

'I know.'

His voice was tight and his face remained unreadable, but he didn't pause, though he shortened his stride to her pace. So she felt more comfortable? Or was it just a courtesy that had been drummed into him from an early age? Ilsa's mouth turned down. Probably the latter.

He gave no indication he was glad to see her.

She'd expected that, yet still she felt bruised.

'Where are we going?'

'Somewhere we can talk. Privately.'

He darted her a sideways look and something about it made her blood quicken. 'Where's your bodyguard?'

Of all the things he might have said, that was the least expected. 'At my hotel. I wanted…needed privacy for this.'

It hadn't been easy but she couldn't face doing this with a bodyguard in tow.

Noah nodded but he didn't look happy. Because he worried about her safety? More likely he was annoyed that she might have brought attention to his family. His next words seemed to confirm it.

'Hopefully you weren't followed.'

He surveyed the park as if looking for security threats or the photographers who followed her in Europe.

The lovely sense of freedom Ilsa had felt earlier dissipated. 'What about you? Don't you have security?' He was a wealthy, powerful man.

That provoked a laugh, warm and genuine, and the sound swirled through her like a warm tide. 'You sat next to my cousin Jake at lunch. He's the head of my local security team.'

Ilsa could imagine it. Jake was big and solidly built but very fit and his gaze had been alert.

Her heart did a strange little tumble in her chest. Had Noah asked his cousin to look after her?

He led her to a car park and a gleaming blue vintage convertible. Ilsa stared, taking in its glorious lines. She knew there hadn't been many of these made and they had a reputation for great handling.

'Is there room for your legs?'

'More than you'd think.' He paused. 'What's wrong? You don't feel safe in a convertible?'

Ilsa met his narrowed eyes and shook her head. 'I was thinking how great it would be to drive the mountain roads at home in a car like this.'

Did she imagine a flare of approval in those sea-bright eyes? No. It was an illusion, gone already. Her mind was playing tricks and she couldn't afford that. Her positive experience with his family had skewed her thoughts.

Fifteen silent minutes later Noah ushered her into the lounge of a large house with a cliff-top view over the Pacific Ocean.

She didn't take the seat offered. She was too wired. Instead she moved to the large windows, trying to calm her breathing.

'So, Ilsa.' His voice, deep and powerful, scraped across her nerves. 'Are you going to explain what this is about?'

CHAPTER FOURTEEN

NOAH FROZE AS Ilsa stepped away from him. Her shoulders were high and she clutched that shoulder bag to her side like a protective shield.

She didn't want to be here.

He'd leapt to the conclusion that she'd come halfway around the world to see him. Now he realised, whatever this was, it wasn't the reunion he'd hoped for.

Bitterness filled his mouth. He should have learned his lesson by now. For all her fine words, Ilsa didn't fancy a future with a self-made Australian.

Yet still he'd hoped. He'd planned to see her in Europe. To persuade her, seduce her if need be, into seeing things his way.

It took everything he had not to reach for her. His palms actually tingled with the need to feel her satin skin.

She looked incredible, if a little pale, utterly gorgeous in casual clothes that took him straight back to the paradise days on his yacht when they'd been inseparable and the world had glowed around them.

But she didn't want him.

He remembered her dismay as he'd reached to help her up from the picnic table. The hectic colour flooding her cheeks. How she'd looked away and kept her distance.

His stomach cramped. No wonder she'd been silent in the car coming here.

But after seeing her with his family it was clear that, she wasno snob. Poppy would have turned her nose up at mingling with them. Ilsa, on the other hand, had been a delight with them all.

This woman did his head in. She made him feel too much. For years Noah had called the shots, both in business and his personal life, but she left him reeling.

'Ilsa. Talk to me.'

Finally she swung around. Her closed expression and tight mouth made his heart hammer painfully.

She regarded him steadily, her gaze troubled. 'I'm sorry.' She swallowed. 'Walking out on you the way I did…' She shook her head. 'It was too much like the way Poppy behaved. I'm not surprised you don't want to see me.'

Ilsa remembered the name of his ex-girlfriend? Noah struggled not to feel it was important that she recalled such a detail.

He frowned. She was broadcasting conflicting messages. Obviously she didn't want to be here, yet she apologised as if sincere.

'You've got it wrong. I wasn't unhappy to see you.'

Ilsa shook her head, hurrying on. 'I'm sorry for intruding on private family time.' She lifted her chin as if in challenge. 'I tried organising an appointment but—'

'You don't need to explain. My PA has instructions about fielding calls from people I don't know. I only found out you'd tried to reach me after she'd fobbed you off.'

'Oh.' Ilsa's tight shoulders eased down.

'I asked her to get your number if you called again.'

'Oh?' No mistaking her surprise. 'But you didn't want me there today.' Her voice was flat. 'You didn't want me to meet your family.'

She was right. Because he needed privacy to deal with Ilsa and resolve their issues. Trying to act nonchalant before his extended family, and his mother's appraising regard, had been almost impossible.

On the other hand, it had been an eye-opener seeing her interact with them. She'd seemed as relaxed and happy with some retired garbage collectors, a mechanic, a kindergarten teacher, a café owner and the rest as if she'd been at a party of sophisticates.

Just like when she'd played football on a beach in Turkey. Or chatted with fishermen or rug-sellers or anyone else she met.

Ilsa was what he'd thought her—genuine. The knowledge created a glowing kernel of warmth low in his body. A warmth he shouldn't feel, because what they'd shared was over.

'You took me by surprise. I thought you were in Europe.' Doing her royal duty.

'It's okay, Noah. You don't have to pretend. I realise—'

'I'm not.' He shook his head. 'It wasn't that I didn't want to see you, but a desire for privacy. If you came all this way to see me, it's not to play cricket with a mob of curious relatives.'

Ilsa's eyes widened and he saw a flash of silver there that catapulted him back to those times when Ilsa had looked at him with wonder and approval. As if his love-making had the power to change her world.

'You weren't trying to shoo me away,' she said softly.

Noah shook his head. 'I wanted to get you alone so we could talk.'

He paused, watching her absorb that and trying not to categorise his feelings. Because even now he felt far, far too much for this woman. Just seeing her, so close yet so untouchable, turned him inside out. He wasn't used to being at the mercy of emotions. He was used to being in control of every situation. Ever since Poppy.

'So, Ilsa. Why are you here?'

She might be good at looking calm and composed for

the public, but Noah could read her better now. The hectic flutter of her pulse at her throat. The swift inhalation that lifted her breasts. The way she pushed her shoulders back as if preparing for something tough.

Noah felt himself stiffen in anticipation of bad news. Was she ill? But why travel to tell him when she'd washed her hands of him?

'Because I'm pregnant.' She paused and Noah heard the drum of his pulse in his ears once, twice, three times. 'We're going to be parents.'

'Parents?' His eyes locked on hers and it was like watching lightning flash down to earth. Ilsa *felt* the judder right to the soles of her feet. 'Us?'

'The baby is yours, Noah.' She grabbed for air then blurted out the truth. 'There's been no one else but you.'

He looked stunned. Who could blame him?

'That's why I'm here. I had to talk with you in person. I didn't want to tell you by phone or email.'

Not just because of her news.

Ilsa had *wanted* to see him. She craved the feel of his arms around her. His solid, reassuring presence. His smile that turned the world into an exciting, spectacular place. He'd accepted her as an equal, just as Ilsa, not because of her royal name or anything else. Had that man totally vanished or was some part of him left?

She waited for his response.

Would it be elation at impending fatherhood?

Wariness because he'd already moved on to a new relationship?

Or suspicion that she tried to pin a pregnancy on him?

She got none of those. Noah stood so still he didn't even seem to breathe. Yet that pulse of energy between them was like a live wire, crackling in the silence.

'Here.' Abruptly he took her arm and led her to a sofa near the window. 'Sit down and tell me everything.'

Ilsa was grateful for the seat. She'd screwed up her courage to come here and she'd ridden a wave of tension for too long. Her knees loosened and she plopped down onto the cushioned seat.

Noah took a chair opposite, leaning forward, his elbows on his knees. He looked intent, absorbed, but that was all. Ilsa had expected…fireworks. Delight or dismay.

Maybe because he didn't yet believe her?

'I suppose you'll want a paternity test.'

His brow furrowed. 'When did you find out? Is the baby okay? Are *you* all right?'

Ilsa put her hand up. 'The baby is fine so far and so am I. There's not even any morning sickness.'

She'd been tired, terribly tired, but she didn't know if that was from the pregnancy or the malaise she felt, nursing a broken heart and trying to find the enthusiasm to plan a future for herself and her baby. No matter how hard she tried, her mind skittered away from any concrete decisions. Maybe now she'd shared this with Noah she'd be able to focus.

He nodded. 'So, you conceived that day in London?'

'Actually, no. It was earlier.'

Ilsa looked down and realised she was threading her fingers together in a repetitive nervous gesture. The sort of gesture she'd been taught to avoid. But a lifetime's training in composure went out the window when she was around Noah. He tied her in knots so that everything inside seemed tangled.

'But the timing…' He shook his head. 'Just how pregnant are you?'

'Twelve weeks.'

'Twelve weeks?'

His gaze dropped and she realised her fingers were laced together, this time over her abdomen in an age-old gesture of protection.

'Why wait to tell me?'

Ilsa wished she could read his voice or his face. Work out what he was thinking. But there was nothing to hint at his emotions, apart from the intensity of his stare and the way he canted towards her as if focused on her every word.

'In London it hadn't even occurred to me that I could be pregnant because we'd used condoms. My cycle is very irregular, so I didn't think it odd that I'd had no period. On top of that…' Ilsa looked past him to the vast ocean beyond the windows. 'I never expected it to be possible. I'd been warned I could find it difficult to have a baby. Plus you took precautions—'

'Except there was that one time when the condom tore.'

She nodded. She'd assumed at the time there was virtually no chance of her falling pregnant.

'That still doesn't explain why you waited to let me know.'

Ilsa couldn't read his tone, though that tall body looked primed and ready for action. But what action?

Nerves fluttered in her stomach. Noah was so *contained*, giving nothing at all away. A reminder that, while he might have been a phenomenal lover, a man who'd broken through her protective shell and made her dream of a fantasy happy ever after, he was a hard-nosed tycoon. He'd built his business from nothing and managed problems all the time.

Did he view their baby as a problem?

Ilsa sank further into the lounge, one hand resting on her abdomen.

She swallowed then moistened her lips with her tongue. Once more she sought comfort in the view of the ocean, rather than face Noah's piercing stare. Ilsa already felt too vulnerable around him.

'I didn't tell *anyone*. I thought it best to reach the twelve-week mark. The chance of miscarriage is greatest before that, so it seemed sensible to wait.'

There was movement in her peripheral vision then warm fingers covered hers.

Ilsa swung round to find Noah on the seat beside her, so close his masculine scent teased her and she felt she could dive into the clear depths of those stunning eyes. He was turned towards her, one long arm on the back of the lounge behind her head, his knee brushing her thigh.

'You were that worried you'd lose the baby?' His deep voice had a husky edge that undid her.

She nodded. 'I didn't dare hope. I've spent so long believing I'd have difficulty becoming a mother...' Her throat closed and just as well, before she blurted out more of what she felt.

'What do the doctors say? Is this dangerous for you? For the baby?'

For a second Ilsa couldn't speak, fighting the lush, warm feeling that filled her when Noah asked about her as well as the baby.

But it shouldn't surprise her. Noah was a decent man. Even if he didn't love her.

'I'm being closely monitored as I have an elevated risk of miscarriage.' She heard him suck in a sharp breath. 'But we're both doing okay and I trust my doctor to look after me.'

His tight grip fastened even harder around her fingers. Then abruptly he sat back, releasing her.

Ilsa felt it like the sudden chill when the sun disappeared behind a cloud on a winter's day.

'So everything's *not* good. But as good as we can hope for.'

Ilsa nodded, repressing a humourless laugh at the buzz of excitement she got, hearing him talk about *we* not *you*.

The trouble was that she still loved this man who, despite his concern, clearly wasn't excited by her arrival. She'd imagined he'd at least be thrilled to discover he was going to be a father. After all, kids were in his new long-term plan.

Had she allowed herself to hope that news of her pregnancy might magically erase the bad stuff between them? That he'd pull her close and whisper all those sweet promises she yearned to hear?

Who was she kidding? She'd dumped him when he'd offered her a future together. She'd kept her distance in case she lost the baby. Had she waited too long?

Ilsa shot to her feet and moved away. She put her palm on the wall of glass separating the luxurious room from the terrace with its infinity pool and sweeping lawn.

Dully she imagined Noah teaching a child to play cricket on that lawn or kick a football.

But she guessed it wouldn't be their child. Noah had shown concern for her health, and the baby's, but that was all. Duty rather than happiness.

Maybe he only had it in him to care for children by a woman he chose as his partner. Maybe he'd already found a new partner, one of those gorgeous women he'd been photographed with recently. Her heart dived.

'I came here to tell you about the baby and begin making arrangements so you can be part of its life.'

Ilsa turned to find him still on the sofa, his expression giving nothing away.

'But it's not as if we're a couple or live near each other.' She paused because she feared her voice revealed that she was crumbling inside. Then she forced herself to go on. 'So I understand if you've moved on and you prefer not to be actively involved.'

CHAPTER FIFTEEN

NOT BE INVOLVED!

She had to be kidding. How could she even think it?

'You couldn't be more wrong, Ilsa.'

Her eyes snapped to his and emotion thumped his chest as he met that silvery gaze.

In the past he'd seen her eyes turn that colour when they made love, or when she was particularly moved. He'd believed it proof that she'd begun to return his feelings.

Now he wondered.

She'd avoided looking at him, preferring the view of the sea, but when she did he felt that familiar pulse of connection. The question was, did she?

Ilsa wasn't as calm as she pretended.

Deliberately Noah got to his feet, blocking the way to the door just in case. She looked so skittish.

'How could you believe that, even for a moment? Far from not wanting to be part of our child's life, I intend to be there every step of the way.'

Starting now. The thought of her miscarrying gutted him. Ilsa and their child needed him and he intended to care for them both through the pregnancy and beyond.

Her eyes grew round. What? She couldn't really have thought he'd walk away from her or his child.

His heart pounded like a jackhammer and his blood fizzed, and it was only partly to do with being near the woman with whom he'd planned to spend his life. The idea of becoming a father was the most exciting thing he'd heard in forever. He wanted to shout in elation. But not yet. First there was unfinished business.

'Why would you think I wouldn't care? That I'd ignore my own flesh and blood?'

She lifted one shoulder in a half shrug. 'Because it's *my* child and I spurned you.'

There was a shuttered look in her eyes that Noah hated. And something else. Pain.

It added to the ache deep inside him. An ache he'd carried since they'd separated. Telling himself she preferred to be with her titled friends and relations hadn't eased it and distance only made it worse.

'You think I hated you so much for leaving that I'd turn my back on my child?' Noah shook his head, holding her gaze. 'I admit it hurt.'

The moment she'd told him not to touch her had been one of the worst of his life. As if he'd been some bully using his superior size to intimidate her. As if she feared him. Everything inside him had shut down in disbelief.

Noah breathed deep, reaching for control, determined not to be railroaded by emotion. 'I knew you must have your reasons, even if I didn't know them.'

Ilsa frowned and Noah shoved his hands in his pockets. The time for prevarication was past. He was a proud man, but he'd learned love was more important than pride. He wanted something better for them, and for their child.

'I checked into that London hotel because I discovered you were to attend a conference there on diversion programmes for young people in trouble with the law.'

Warm colour flooded Ilsa's face. Even her parted lips looked redder, and far too alluring. Noah wanted to grab her, tuck her close against him and not let her go.

But he leashed his inner caveman and focused on patience. Time apart from her had only reinforced his feelings. Life had been empty without Ilsa. He had to get this right.

'Now tell me straight, why did you leave? You never gave me a decent reason. Was it because of your family's expectations?'

Noah's eyes narrowed, his nape tightening and instinct prickling as she looked away.

When she turned back he stared into eyes of polished pewter, bright with troubled emotion. He sensed her turmoil, pain even, and wanted to reach for her, hold her close and support her.

But Noah stood still. He couldn't force this. She had to trust him.

'No, nothing like that.' Ilsa breathed deep and slow. 'I thought I couldn't be the woman you wanted.'

'Sorry?' He couldn't have heard right. 'I've never wanted a woman so much.' His mouth dragged wide in a reluctant smile so tight it hurt. 'With you I'm insatiable.'

He'd always had a healthy sex drive but with Ilsa...

'I don't mean for sex.' But he didn't miss the way her mouth curled at one corner, like a seductress proud of her power. Even that made him hard. Everything about Ilsa aroused him. 'We both knew that it was a holiday fling. A short-term affair.'

'In the beginning, yes.' He frowned. 'But even in Monte Carlo there was no way on earth I could have walked away from that party without you. I've never felt anything like it with anyone but you. It felt like we were destined to be together. I spoke about a short affair because that's all I knew. But the fact is, right from the start, what we shared felt different.'

There, it was out in the open.

Ilsa's breath was an audible hiss. But he didn't read shock in her face.

Perhaps the notion wasn't new to her after all? Noah's pulse quickened.

'Was it like that for you too, Ilsa?' He'd believed so at the time but, if so, why walk out on him?

Slowly she nodded and Noah exhaled a breath he hadn't realised he'd held. His punished lungs eased and the constricting band around his chest vanished.

Noah stared at this complex, alluring, surprising woman and tried to get his brain back into gear. If she wasn't talking about sex, then...

'If you felt that way, why walk out on me in London? And don't say it was because of royal duty alone. I know that's important to you, but I know too that it doesn't completely satisfy you any more. I don't believe you'd turn your back on me only because your father crooked his finger.'

Ilsa squared her shoulders, her chin rising, and he *knew* she was fighting not to appear vulnerable. It made his heart turn over. She might have secrets but in so many ways he knew this woman almost as well as he knew himself.

'When you spoke of long-term you said you wanted to try for a family and I knew how important children would be to you. I've seen you with kids time and again and you're a natural with them. I've heard you speak of your nephew and it's clear you love him. Your voice changes when you speak of him, did you know that?'

Slowly Noah nodded as, finally, some of the puzzle began to make sense.

'And you weren't sure you could have children.'

The realisation was simple but devastating. His gut twisted as he imagined how Ilsa had felt. He remembered how her face had glowed when she told him she wanted children. And today the stark fear mingled with determination on her features when she'd said there was a chance she mightn't be able to carry this baby.

Noah couldn't hold back any longer.

He took the step that brought them together, his arms

wrapping around her, and it felt like coming home, even though she stood straight, not leaning against him. Her light citrus scent tickled his nostrils and he longed for the taste of her. Soon, he vowed. They'd clear everything up here and now. No more hiding or prevarication.

Ilsa was home to him in a way that no mere place could be. Being with her, he felt *right* for the first time in too long.

'You thought I'd reject you because you mightn't be able to have children.'

It was a statement, not a question, and the tremor he felt running through her confirmed it.

Ilsa had pushed him away, but how often had she been rejected? Once in her teens, then passed over for her brother, then recently spurned by a fiancé who'd chosen his lover over her. Of course she was wary.

'Oh, sweetheart, if I'd known.' He cupped her jaw, the better to meet her eyes. 'Yes, I want children. But I want you more.'

It felt good, finally to admit it.

Was that hope shining in her eyes? Or the over-bright glitter of unshed tears?

It made him wish he'd told her last time they were together. But then the realisation had been new to him and he'd still been grappling with the implications. Plus he'd convinced himself Ilsa wasn't ready for such a declaration.

'Noah.' Her voice was a husky whisper. 'I...' She shook her head. 'You don't have to choose now, do you? Now that I'm pregnant.'

The words pummelled him, opening up a yawning ache inside. How wary his lover was. How badly she'd been hurt to think that way. To imagine he'd choose a child over her.

Silently he cursed those in her past who'd made her doubt her intrinsic worth.

It felt like the most difficult thing he'd ever done, re-sisting the need to tug her closer. He settled for standing as he was, because nothing could make him pull back.

'I can understand you thinking that, Ilsa,' he said slowly. 'I can understand it might take months, even years, for you to believe I care for you because you're the one woman in the world I want to be with for ever.'

Noah sucked in a breath and forced himself to face the unthinkable. 'Even if something happened to the child you're carrying—to *our* child—I'll still need you.'

Though he prayed with every fibre of his being that their baby would be safe and healthy.

'Even if you could never carry a baby, I'll need you. There's adoption. There are my siblings' and cousins' children we can spoil and help raise. There are plenty of kids whose lives we can help, even if they're not techni-cally ours.'

He breathed deep, willing her to believe him. 'I can live without children, Ilsa. I can't live without you. These last weeks have been torment. That's why my mother welcomed you with open arms. She knows I'm a mess.'

Noah lifted both hands to Ilsa's still face, gently hold-ing her jaw, brushing her cheeks with his thumbs and feeling the tremulous pulse at her jaw. Did she tilt closer into his hold?

'I love you, Ilsa. I've loved you from the first. Though it took a while to realise I'd joined the family club.'

'Family club?' she whispered.

He nodded, his soul shrinking as he read her doubt, her reluctance to believe him.

'The Carsons fall in love early. All the adults find their life partner by their early twenties. We have a tradition of long, happy marriages.'

'But not you.'

'Not until now. I'd been waiting to meet you.' That was how it felt. 'With you it was like pieces of a puzzle finally falling into place. Even though I didn't want to believe it initially. It was easier to pretend it was just lust, easily satisfied by a short affair.'

Because he'd doubted his own judgement after his mistake with Poppy. Looking back, he suspected he'd fallen in love with Ilsa that very first evening, but the defence mechanisms he'd erected and his own stubbornness had stopped him realising till it was almost too late.

Reluctantly Noah pulled his hands away, knowing he had to give her space. 'But I understand I need to prove how I feel. You'll need time to trust me.'

A ripple of emotion crossed Ilsa's face and her mouth crumpled. 'I want to trust you, Noah.'

'I know, sweetheart. It's okay. I can be patient. I'll do whatever you need. You can stay in Sydney and see what life is like in Australia. There's plenty of space here.' He had a large home, too large for one person. 'Or if you'd rather not, I'll arrange somewhere else private for you. Or I'll come to Europe and find out about your life there.'

He paused, knowing he was in danger of rushing her. 'If you need more proof of my feelings, I'll get my assistant to send you my flight arrangements for the end of this week. I'd planned a visit to Altbourg. Ostensibly it's to scope that joint project. But in reality it was an excuse to see you.'

Her finger on his mouth stopped him. To Noah's horror he saw tears brighten her beautiful eyes.

'There's no need to persuade me.' Her soft words were like a bar clanging down on his hopes. Wouldn't she even give him a chance to prove himself?

Then she smiled. It was strained and a little watery but so beautiful that his heart leapt.

'I want to trust you because I love you too, Noah. I've loved you since Istanbul. No, before then. I've been miserable, thinking of how I treated you and how you must despise me.'

'Oh, my darling.' Noah looped his arms around her and pulled her to him. Feeling her softness against him was like nothing else on earth.

But, before he could kiss her, she spoke again. 'You wanted to know why I left you. My possible infertility was just part of it.' She paused, her eyes dazzling as she met his look head-on. 'The main reason was because I realised in Turkey that I'd fallen for you, hook, line and sinker. I was scared, Noah. Scared that I wanted so much more than you did. I was afraid if I stayed with you—'

This time it was Noah who stopped her words with his hand. He felt her soft lips against his fingers and the sensation sent fire streaking through him.

'If only I'd known.' He shook his head. 'It was in Turkey I'd begun to realise I wouldn't be satisfied with an affair. I was already planning to ask you to stay longer when I found you packing, determined to leave straight away. That's why I was so savage. What I felt for you, what I still feel, is far beyond what I've ever experienced before.'

'Noah, my love. I've been such a coward. I should have told you. You mean so much to me.'

He'd never heard anything so beautiful in his life. Or seen anything more glorious than Ilsa, looking up at him, eyes blazing with love and joy.

Tenderly, careful of this precious woman, Noah gathered her to him and kissed her gently, allowing all his adoration to show.

'I want you more than I'd ever thought it possible to want, Ilsa. I'd give up everything else to be with you.'

Her hands anchored on his shoulders and he felt her rise on tiptoe, kissing him with a sweet insistence that healed the pain of separation.

Finally, when they pulled apart to gulp in oxygen, she spoke. 'You don't have to give up anything, Noah.'

'And nor do you. Whatever it takes to make this work, I'll do it. Maybe relocate to Europe or—'

Her lips on his tasted like paradise and he lost his train of thought. But that didn't matter because Ilsa was here in his arms, and she loved him.

'We've got all the time in the world to make those decisions, Noah.' She paused. 'But I've got one condition I do insist on.'

His head jerked back and he surveyed her through dazzled eyes. 'Name it.'

His groin tightened as she pouted and lifted her hand to the buttons of his shirt. 'I'd like a tour of your home. Specifically, the master bedroom. It's been ages…'

'But in your condition—'

'The doctor didn't put a ban on sex, you know. And I've missed you so very much.'

For answer Noah swept her up into his arms but his laughter faded as he looked down into her dear face.

'I love you, Ilsa. Whatever the future brings, I'll always love you. I'll strive to make you happy.'

'You already do, Noah. So much I feel like my heart might burst.'

'You took the words out of my mouth, sweetheart.' Then he strode to the door and the beginning of their life together.

EPILOGUE

'THE VENUE IS just as spectacular as I remember from last time.'

Ilsa's mother smiled as she stared through the soaring windows of the Sydney Opera House. Beyond, the harbour stretched like midnight silk towards the bridge, proudly illuminated against a dusk sky of neon pink edging to indigo.

Beside her Joanne Carson nodded and sipped her wine. 'The old Coat hanger still looks good, doesn't it? One of my uncles used to be a rigger up there, decades ago.'

'A rigger?'

The pair were soon engrossed in stories about work on the iconic bridge, and Ilsa felt that warm glow she'd experienced the day her mother and Noah's had met and immediately struck up a friendship.

Around them theatregoers were dressed in everything from evening finery to more casual yet dressy outfits. Some had recognised their group, craning to get a better view. A visit to Sydney by the King and Queen of Altbourg was seriously newsworthy. Plus the press never seemed to tire of photos of Noah, Ilsa and their son.

But the intense, almost breathless reporting of their romance had eased since their wedding in Altbourg's main cathedral last year and then little Oliver's birth.

Ilsa glanced at the familiar suited security officer just

beyond her mother and mother-in-law. And then across to Jake, Noah's cousin, on her other side. He nodded and grinned. He'd confessed that the first time he'd attended a ballet in his security role he'd expected to hate it. But now he had a newfound appreciation for the athleticism and artistry involved.

'What are you smiling about, sweetheart?'

Noah's warm voice rippled like molten caramel through her body. She turned and there he was, as breathtaking as ever.

Her husband. Her man. Her other half that made her whole.

Ilsa's heart leapt as she read the smile he reserved just for her.

'Thank you.' She accepted the glass of sparkling wine he held out. 'I was just thinking about how we've changed your cousin's life. He's now a fan of ballet as well as cricket and rugby.'

Because Noah always kept his wife and mother company at the ballet.

'It's good to expand our horizons, like me taking up snowboarding.'

Noah had taken to the slopes in Europe so easily it was hard to believe he hadn't been born to it.

'Or my father learning to change a nappy,' Ilsa added.

She couldn't stifle a giggle at the memory of King Peter's pride when he'd announced that he'd changed little Oliver.

Maybe it was the chance to relax away from the royal court, but she saw her father more and more as a man, and a doting grandfather, than a royal. Tonight he and Noah's father had been eager to pack the rest of them off to the ballet. No doubt they planned to settle in the media room, babysitting Oliver and watching football over a beer. The growing friendship between the two families was more than she'd dared hope for.

Ilsa and Noah spent part of the year in Australia and part in Altbourg and so far it worked well. Noah said the months based in Europe were a bonus to working in the region. Meanwhile, Ilsa pursued her passion for helping vulnerable children in both her home countries and further afield.

But her main passion was her own family.

How blessed she was.

Warmth slid around her waist as Noah pulled her close, his arm coming to rest on her hip. Instantly her pulse thrilled and her mouth dried.

'Have I told you how beautiful you look, my love?'

'You have.' Frequently. 'But don't ever stop.'

'No chance of that.'

His eyes danced as he surveyed her. From the lustrous, large Australian pearls at her ears and throat—a gift from Noah—to the new silk dress in the colour that had become her favourite. A unique blue-green turquoise that matched her beloved husband's eyes.

As she watched he frowned, his mouth tightening, and she felt a shudder rack his tall frame.

'What is it, Noah?' Alarmed, she put down her glass and pressed her hand to his chest. 'Are you unwell?'

His mouth hooked up at one corner in a rueful half smile. He bent so his words feathered her ear. 'Just impatient. I need you alone, naked, in bed, as soon as possible.'

He straightened as her pulse shimmied to a decadent tango beat as she imagined being naked with Noah. Ilsa's eyelids fluttered. 'We could leave. Our mothers would barely notice.'

'Is that the voice of my dutiful Princess?' There was laughter in Noah's voice but love in his eyes. 'Imagine the explanations. No,' he said decisively. 'We'll wait. There's only one act to go. And I'll make the wait worthwhile, Ilsa.'

'You promise?'

'Have I ever let you down?'

She shook her head. From the moment they'd acknowledged their feelings to each other, he'd been everything she could want in a companion, lover, partner.

'Never, darling.'

Ilsa smiled and, ignoring the curious glances, pressed her lips to his, clinging for a few luxurious seconds as he wrapped his arms around her.

The world was already full of photos of them kissing. What was one more?

* * * * *

COMING SOON!

We really hope you enjoyed reading this book.
If you're looking for more romance, be sure to
head to the shops when new books are
available on

Thursday 17th February

To see which titles are coming soon, please visit

millsandboon.co.uk/nextmonth

MILLS & BOON

Coming next month

BOUND BY HER RIVAL'S BABY
Maya Blake

A breeze washed over Amelie and she shivered.

Within one moment and the next, Atu was shrugging off his shirt.

"W-what are you doing?" she blurted as he came towards her.

Another mirthless twist of his lips. "You may deem me an enemy but I don't want you catching cold and falling ill. Or worse."

She aimed a glare his way. "Not until I've signed on whatever dotted line you're determined to foist on me, you mean?"

That look of fury returned. This time accompanied by a flash of disappointment. As if he had the right to such a lofty emotion where she was concerned. She wanted, no *needed* to refuse this small offer of comfort.

Return to her room and come up with a definite plan that removed him from her life for good.

So why was she drawing the flaps of his shirt closer? Her fingers clinging to the warm cotton as if she'd never let it go?

She must have a made a sound at the back of her throat because his head swung to hers, his eyes holding hers for an age before he exhaled harshly.

His lips firmed and for a long stretch he didn't speak. "You need to accept that I'm the best bet you have right now. There's no use fighting. I'm going to win eventually. How soon depends entirely on you."

The implacable conclusion sent icy shivers coursing

through her. In that moment she regretted every moment of weakness. Regretted feeling bad for invoking that hint of disappointment in his eyes.

She had nothing to be ashamed of. Not when vanquishing her and her family was his sole, true purpose.

She snatched his shirt from her shoulders, crushing her body's instant insistence on its warmth as she tossed it back to him. "You should know by now that threats don't faze me. We're still here, still standing after all you and your family have done. So go ahead, do your worst."

Held head high, she whirled away. She only made it three steps before he captured her wrist. She spun around, intent on pushing him away.

But that ruthlessness was coupled with something else. Something hot and blazing and all-consuming in his eyes.

She belatedly read it as lust before he was tugging her closer, wrapping one hand around her waist and the other in her hair. "This stubborn determination is admirable. Hell, I'd go so far as to say it's a turn on because God knows I admire strong, wilful women," he muttered, his lips a hairsbreadth from hers, "but fiery passion will only get you so far."

"And what are you going to do about it?" she taunted a little too breathlessly. Every cell in her body traitorously strained towards him, yearning for things she knew she shouldn't want, but desperately needed anyway.

He froze, then a strangling sound leaving his throat, he slammed his lips on hers.

He kissed her like he was starved for it. *For her.*

Continue reading
BOUND BY HER RIVAL'S BABY
Maya Blake

Available next month
www.millsandboon.co.uk

MILLS & BOON

THE HEART OF ROMANCE

A ROMANCE FOR EVERY READER

MODERN

Prepare to be swept off your feet by sophisticated, sexy and seductive heroes, in some of the world's most glamourous and romanti locations, where power and passion collide.

HISTORICAL

Escape with historical heroes from time gone by. Whether your passion for wicked Regency Rakes, muscled Vikings or rugged Highlanders, aw the romance of the past.

MEDICAL

Set your pulse racing with dedicated, delectable doctors in the high-pres sure world of medicine, where emotions run high and passion, comfort love are the best medicine.

True Love

Celebrate true love with tender stories of heartfelt romance, from the rush of falling in love to the joy a new baby can bring, and a focus on th emotional heart of a relationship.

Desire

Indulge in secrets and scandal, intense drama and plenty of sizzling hot action with powerful and passionate heroes who have it all: wealth, statu good looks…everything but the right woman.

HEROES

Experience all the excitement of a gripping thriller, with an intense ro mance at its heart. Resourceful, true-to-life women and strong, fearless face danger and desire - a killer combination!

To see which titles are coming soon, please visit

millsandboon.co.uk/nextmonth

LET'S TALK
Romance

For exclusive extracts, competitions
and special offers, find us online:

f facebook.com/millsandboon

🐦 @MillsandBoon

📷 @MillsandBoonUK

Get in touch on 01413 063232

For all the latest titles coming soon, visit
millsandboon.co.uk/nextmonth

JOIN US ON SOCIAL MEDIA!

Stay up to date with our latest releases, author news and gossip, special offers and discounts, and all the behind-the-scenes action from Mills & Boon...

 millsandboon

 millsandboonuk

 millsandboon

It might just be true love...

MILLS & BOON

HEROES

At Your Service

Experience all the excitement of a gripping thriller, with an intense romance at its heart. Resourceful, true-to-life women and strong, fearless men face danger and desire - a killer combination!

MILLS & BOON
MEDICAL
Pulse-Racing Passion

Set your pulse racing with dedicated, delectable doctors in the high-pressure world of medicine, where emotions run high and passion, comfort and love are the best medicine.